DAICAN'S HEIR

I0522745

DAICAN'S HEIR

ILYON CHRONICLES – BOOK SIX

JAYE L. KNIGHT

Living Sword Publishing
www.livingswordpublishing.com

Daican's Heir
Ilyon Chronicles – Book 6
Copyright © 2023 by Jaye L. Knight
www.ilyonchronicles.com

Published by Living Sword Publishing

Ilyon Map © 2014 by Jaye L. Knight

Cover Images
© Kjolak - Dreamstime.com
© kjpargeter - Depositphotos.com
© smaglov - Depositphotos.com
© oskarcalero - Depositphotos.com
© Kiselev Andrey Valerevich - Shutterstock.com

All rights reserved. No part of this publication may be reproduced, stored in a retrieval system, or transmitted in any form or by any means—electronic, mechanical, photocopying, recording, or otherwise—without prior written permission of the author. The only exception is brief quotations in written reviews.

Scripture taken from the New King James Version®. Copyright © 1982 by Thomas Nelson. Used by permission. All rights reserved.

For Don "Mother"
You will always be deeply missed.

ILYON
N
W E
S
SAMARA
AMBERIN
STONEHELM
SINNAI MTS.
GRAYLIN VALLEY
ARCACIA
DUNLOW
FORT RHALL
KINNIM
LANDALE
VALCRÉ
SIDIAN OCEAN
ARDALUIN BAY
MERNIN
FORT RIVOR
KEATON
FALSPAR
TROAS
ARDA

GRAER MTS.
ARVAEL
TRAYSE RIVER
BEL-GARD
ANDROS FORD
DORLAND
WILDMOR
KRELL MTS.

JACE DIDN'T LIKE SHIPS.

His stomach had threatened to heave itself up his throat since he'd reboarded the talcrin vessel an hour ago. So far, he'd managed to keep it in place, but Holden wasn't so lucky. He had already lost what remained of his supper over the edge and now leaned heavily on the railing. Clearly, it would take a lot more than the two days they'd previously spent on board, sneaking the Landale Militia into Samara, for their stomachs to get used to the sea.

A low groan rumbled from Holden's hunched form. "Remind me never to set foot on a ship again after this. I'll happily stick to dragons."

Jace had to agree with him there. As much as he hated heights, he'd far rather fly with Gem right now. And it wasn't just his churning gut that bothered him. Despite only small waves rippling the sea, each dip and tilt of the ship robbed him of balance. The lack of solid footing left him feeling vulnerable. Not that he had any threats to worry about just yet. Those awaited him on shore.

Footsteps passed behind him, and he looked over his shoulder. Though pre-dawn darkness cloaked the ship, and they'd forgone any lanterns that could give away their position, General Torva crossed the deck with a confident stride. He made an impressive figure, as most talcrins did. He reminded Jace of Sam, especially in stature, though his hair was long and gathered into small braids, and his eyes flashed a cunning copper.

Their talcrin allies were obviously masters of the sea. Jace hadn't seen any of them on the verge of losing their stomach contents, though maybe that had not been the case when they'd first left Arda a few weeks ago. Somehow, Rayad and Trask didn't seem affected either.

Torva stopped at the railing a couple of yards away, feet planted and fists on his hips as he stared out over the dark sea. His bronze scale-mail glinted faintly like dragon scales. Jace had never seen armor quite like it before meeting the talcrin army.

"We should be nearing the city."

Jace scanned the horizon. He could barely make out the shore from this distance—just a black line against the indigo water and sky. No signs of Amberin, but the talcrins would know better how far they had traveled northward since setting off.

Someone else drew near. Jace shifted, and Rayad put his hand on his shoulder.

"How are you doing?"

Jace wasn't sure if the question was in regards to his queasiness or what lay ahead. He shrugged. He still thought Balen should have chosen someone other than him to lead this mission. Someone with actual leadership skills and experience. But then, he was the one who could see in the dark, and their plan to take back Samara's capital depended on infiltrating the city undetected. Logically, he offered the greatest chance of success.

Rayad gave his shoulder a squeeze. "We'll be right behind you."

A bit of Jace's nerves settled. Rayad, Holden, and Trask were among those who knew him best. This would have been much harder with people he wasn't so comfortable with.

Barely fifteen minutes later, a change in the horizon caught Jace's eye. It seemed to rise slightly and take on a vague shape. Here and there, pinpricks of light winked from the darkness.

"I think I see the city."

General Torva glanced back at him and nodded firmly. In another few minutes, he ordered the ship's captain to reduce speed, and they glided over the gentle waves until they came parallel with Amberin. Here, the captain commanded his men to douse the sails.

Jace craned his head back to peer up at the sailors maneuvering deftly across the rigging to gather up the huge square sails. His stomach flipped and forced him to swallow it back into place. The thought of climbing the masts was almost worse than remembering his time in Arvael last summer. At least crete bridges and porches had handrails. No such safety measures existed here to keep the talcrin sailors from plummeting to their deaths other than their ability to maintain their balance and hang on.

They dropped anchor, the men straining to lower it slowly so it wouldn't cause an echoing splash. Who knew how far sound would carry over the open distance to the city? All around them, the rest of the talcrins' dozen ships dropped anchor as well, their dark masts silhouetted against the sky like a leafless forest. According to General Torva, each ship transported one-hundred fifty or more warriors. Warriors who could make all the difference in this fight to first reclaim King Balen's homeland and then, Elôm willing, Arcacia after that.

Jace and the others kept out of the way while the talcrins worked until General Torva beckoned to them.

"My men are lowering your boat. You've got about two hours until dawn."

Not a lot of time to get into position. They would have to hurry.

Torva rested a hand on one of the longboats waiting to be lowered next. "We'll be at the sea gate to join you as soon as you open it."

Once a smaller, more maneuverable rowboat settled in the water, Jace moved first, climbing over the railing and down the rope ladder. He tried not to look down at the black water below, but his legs still wobbled, his breaths coming short and shallow. The distance seemed greater going down than it had climbing up. When he did step into the boat, it rocked under his weight, and he grabbed the side to stay on his feet.

Rayad and Holden followed, and finally Trask, who took the seat in the center of the boat. "I've got the oars."

They pushed off from the ship, and Trask rowed them toward the city. Jace sat at the front so he could navigate but looked back at Rayad and Holden in the rear. Holden leaned over the edge like he was about to be sick again.

"Will you be all right?"

Holden glanced his way, his face pale against the dark water. "Just get me to shore, and I'll be fine."

It would be hard to recover so quickly after being sick for the past hour, but Jace had no doubt his friend would do what needed to be done. They both would. Everyone was counting on them. If they failed here, they wouldn't get another shot at this—at least not one that would minimize casualties.

Not that the four of them would live to see it if they did fail. Kyrin's face flashed to mind, of saying goodbye on the shore farther south of the city. It was the first time they'd had to part since they were wed four months ago. He'd held her tightly and breathed her in before having to tear himself away from her.

He set his mind on the present. Success in this mission was the only way back to her, and that required all his focus.

It took longer than he wanted to reach the city but, at last, the walls of Amberin loomed above them. Though not nearly as impressive as Samara's border wall, it would repel an army for a time. That is, if there was no one to help breach it from the inside.

Torches glowed at regular intervals, and sentries patrolled between them. Jace's skin prickled at sitting right out in the open like this, but he reminded himself that, against the dark water, they would be invisible to the men. Especially with the thick cloud cover. No chance of Aertus and Vilai giving away their position or that of the talcrin ships.

Jace scanned the base of the wall and spotted a dark opening. He directed Trask toward it, and when they drew near, the boat scraped bottom. They all stepped out and quietly pulled it closer to the drainage culvert Balen had told them about. Inky darkness lay ahead, spewing a putrid, stinging odor of mold and rot. Jace held his breath as he bent to look inside. Though he could make out the opening at the far end, the others would have to go through blind.

He looked over his shoulder. "Ready?"

The three of them nodded.

With one last gulp of semi-fresh air, Jace ducked into the tunnel. He had to stay bent over to avoid scraping his head against the curved ceiling. Stagnant water sloshed around his ankles, and he tried not to think about it seeping into his boots. Just behind him, Holden half choked, half gagged. Good thing he couldn't see the rotted rat carcasses floating past. Jace's own stomach threatened a violent protest, but he held it in place.

About a hundred feet in, they reached the gate at the other side. If their spies within the city hadn't been able to unlock it, the entire plan would fail here and now. Jace paused to peer into the city. Only one lantern burned far down the street, the rest of the area quiet and abandoned. He reached out to test the gate. It swung open with minimal resistance and creaked only faintly. Someone must have had the foresight to oil the hinges.

He released a sigh and slipped out to check the area one more time before motioning the others to follow.

Holden all but scrambled out, murmuring under his breath. "Thank Elôm."

Hopefully, no one would come by and notice the splattered wet footprints they left on the dry cobblestone. That was something they had not considered. Especially now that they'd come to the most dangerous part of their mission. They had to reach the barracks where General Mason and the other leaders of Samara's army had been kept under house arrest for the past two years. That meant navigating within the city and avoiding patrols. Suspicious footprints could lead a snooping guard right to them.

Well, there was nothing they could do about it now except remain close to the wall where the dark shadows would hide the evidence as well as shield them from the sentries above.

A couple of city blocks later, he caught the thump of footsteps on the cobblestones ahead. He skidded to a halt and held up his hand. Torchlight flickered from a nearby side street. Heat flushed his limbs, and he spun around to usher the others back. They rushed into a dark alley. Ducking down, he peered around the corner. At least by now their boots had almost dried.

The torchlight grew closer, and two guards in black and gold appeared. One of them held the torch higher and looked down the street. Jace shrank back and held his breath.

"Probably rats," one muttered. "I'm sick of rats."

They should try wading through them.

Neither moved for a long moment. Jace squeezed the hilt of his sword and prayed they would be on their way. It was far too early for a fight to break out.

With another grumble about rodent-infested streets, the men ambled off in the opposite direction. Jace let the trapped breath in his lungs seep out and peeked around the corner again. The guards continued on, far up the street, and turned a corner toward the center of the city out of sight. Only then did he motion for the others to follow again.

They traveled the next few blocks without incident and arrived at the barracks undetected. Now came the tricky part. Two guards stood at the gate. According to the information they'd received from General Mason, at least eight more patrolled inside. Where they would be at any given moment was anyone's guess.

Jace shed his coat to uncover the Arcacian military uniform underneath. The others did the same. Jace wasn't too confident in his acting skills, but he would leave that part to Trask. They had put him in the captain's uniform after all.

As one, they left their hiding place across the street and marched toward the guards. Jace prayed with every step the men would believe their deception just long enough for them to get close enough. The guards straightened at attention when they spotted them, and Trask took the lead.

"Did you see a group of men pass by here?"

The two guards looked at each other and then back at Trask. Though Trask was unfamiliar to them, his captain's uniform and commanding tone seemed to allay suspicion.

One guard shook his head. "No, sir."

"Are you sure?" Trask pressed, keeping them focused on him as they drew within arm's length.

"Yes, sir."

Trask smiled, the act slipping. "Good." His hand slid into his pocket.

Jace snatched a damp cloth from his own pocket and grabbed the nearest guard, pressing the fabric against his face. The acrid concoction their head physician, Josef, had mixed up permeated the night air with a sharp tang that Jace avoided inhaling as much as possible. The guard struggled against him, but Jace pressed him up against the wall and held him there. Rayad jumped in to help until the man finally went limp and collapsed in a heap next to the other guard.

Sticking the cloth back into his pocket, Jace scanned the street. Still empty. Nothing stirred within the flickering lantern light, the shadowed side streets, or darkened windows of the other buildings. He stepped over the guards to the door and tested the latch. It lifted without resistance, and he pushed the door open a few inches to peek inside. The courtyard was as quiet as the street. He turned back to the others.

"We can't just leave them lying here in the open."

He bent down and grabbed one of the guards by the arms, then dragged him inside the dark courtyard. Holden hauled in the other. They stashed the unconscious bodies behind some barrels and made their way deeper into the barracks. It took careful maneuvering and a couple of close calls, but they managed to neutralize the remaining guards before any of them could raise the alarm.

Confident they were in the clear, they hurried to the sleeping quarters, where a barred door blocked their path. Jace peered in at the rows of bunks containing almost one-hundred fifty men—mostly captains and other military leaders. The room was far too quiet for them to actually be asleep.

"General?"

One of the men in a bunk closest to the door threw back his blanket and pushed to his feet, fully clothed. His short black hair identified him immediately as General Mason. He met Jace at the door, not a sign of sleep in his eager gaze. A cunning smile broke out when he recognized Jace, and he turned toward the other bunks. "It's time to move, men."

Blankets flew off as the other soldiers scrambled from their bunks to gather around the general. Jace unlocked the door with one of the keys they'd taken off the captain of the guard. Mason ushered everyone out, and the men gathered along the hall. When the last man passed through, Jace turned to Mason.

"We need to hurry and open the sea gate and then the main gate." Dawn would soon break and reveal the forces waiting outside. If things were to go as planned, they needed to secure the way for their armies to get inside before that happened.

"We're at your command."

Those words itched under Jace's skin, especially coming from a general like Mason, but he accepted it. The faster they accomplished their goals here, the faster he could transfer leadership back to those who were good at it, like Marcus.

Taking the lead, he guided them to the armory they'd found. Though it wasn't well-stocked, each man grabbed a sword. Now they had to move back out onto the streets. It wouldn't be easy to remain undetected with one-hundred fifty men to account for, yet they moved quickly and stealthily.

Not far from the barracks, they arrived at the sea gate and successfully disabled the guards there. General Torva waited on the other side just as planned. Dozens of longboats filled with talcrin soldiers bobbed in the bay just beyond him. It was the first time Jace was able to see the size of the talcrin army for himself. Just Torva's men alone were enough to secure the city, but Jace knew Balen was anxiously awaiting his chance to free his people.

"We'll continue on to the main gate to open it for the Militia. Once your men are inside, join us there. The Arcacians will no doubt know we're here by then."

Torva nodded, and General Mason instructed a couple of his men to stay behind and guide the talcrins while the rest hurried on toward the city's main gate. When they drew near, they crouched in the shadows, and Jace surveyed the area. Four guards stood at the gate itself, and another four patrolled above.

Too many to approach undetected. It all depended on whether or not they could stop them from raising the alarm, not that it would make much difference now that General Torva's army had access.

Jace motioned for Mason and his men to move in. The guards jumped to attention, reaching for their weapons. The soldiers quickly overpowered them, but not before the ringing of swords pierced the quiet of the early morning. While no alarms were forthcoming, it was only a matter of time. Someone would have heard the noise and grown suspicious. The time for secrecy had passed.

Jace turned to a couple of the men. "Open the gate and raise the portcullis."

They rushed to do his bidding.

Their one goal now was to hold this gate so the Militia could enter undeterred. The gate groaned open behind him, and gears ground together as the portcullis lifted. Above it all, however, an alarm bell rang out just down the wall from them, resonating in Jace's ears. Another bell tolled deeper within the city, and then another, until it was as if they echoed in his bones.

He spun around to look up at Trask, who had helped take out the sentries on the wall. "Give the signal!"

Trask nodded his acknowledgment. A moment later, a torch flared to life and waved in the air. Balen and the others would be waiting for that signal. Behind Jace, slamming footsteps filled the streets, and somewhere far too close by, the roar of a firedrake rumbled across the city. Others answered.

Jace drew his sword and stood to face the oncoming enemy soldiers alongside the other men.

Mason took a stand beside him. "How far out are the Militia and your dragon riders?"

"Not far." He hoped. Balen, Daniel, Marcus, and Captain Darq had been preparing their men to approach the city when

Jace had boarded General Torva's ship. Surely they had arrived by now.

Even so, they would have to hurry, or Jace and the others would quickly become firedrake bait. The gusting air from a beast's wings drew near and buffeted them as it soared over the gate. He watched the beast circle widely. They were not agile creatures, particularly in the dark, but now that its rider knew their exact location, it would surely attack in the next pass.

Movement ahead of Jace showed that scores of Arcacian soldiers were closing in. Yet they hung back. Of course. They wouldn't want to get caught in the fire. They would wait for the firedrake to take them out in one fell swoop.

The beast soared at them again, its giant black wings beating the air. Jace's hands grew slick around his sword. It was getting too close.

"Come on, Kaden," he muttered under his breath. Five more seconds and they would all be nothing more than a scorched heap.

His heart sank toward his stomach for one horrifying second before the echoing roar of a dragon blasted overhead. A dragon rider intercepted the firedrake, completely engulfing it in flames. The beast screeched, and Jace let out a gusting breath, though his attention fell to the Arcacians soldiers. Now that the dragons had arrived to save them, the soldiers charged in. He raised his sword, but before he could even engage, shouts and the rumble of feet thundered from behind him. The Militia poured in through the gate to meet their foes. Heat surged through Jace's body, and he joined the fight to take back Samara.

KYRIN HAD TO hold herself back from rushing ahead of everyone. Amberin lay in the distance, and though she had never seen the city before and was curious what it was like compared to Valcré, her attention focused on the men milling about the main gate. She strained to pick out a familiar face or form, but it just wasn't possible yet at this distance. Her heart raced all the same.

Anne and Jace's sister, Elanor, walked alongside her on their anxious trek across the grassy space between the city and the forest, where they'd hidden during the battle. Now that the fighting had ceased and the city was under their control, it was time to reunite with their men. Kyrin's brother, Liam, and his girlfriend, Cassie, followed just behind them along with Josef. Leetra had flown on ahead with her dragon to begin setting up a triage area for the wounded. Kyrin first prayed Jace had not been injured and then prayed also for Trask, Daniel, and the rest of those closest to them.

Not knowing if Jace was all right put a knot in her stomach and a creeping chill in her veins. She'd hardly slept last night, tormented by the thought of losing him today. Though they'd faced such dangers before, it seemed so much harder to let him go now that they were married. They were one now, sharing their lives and everything in them. To lose him would be to lose a part of herself.

She fought to quell her anxious thoughts. *Elôm, You have protected, rescued, and brought us back together time and again in even worse situations than this. No matter what the future brings, help me to trust You. I know worrying won't change things or bring Jace back to me when we're apart. Only You can. Please, let him be safe, and protect him in whatever lies ahead. And please provide me the strength and peace to trust and accept Your will.*

She had barely finished her prayer before a lone figure caught her eye coming from the city. Though still some ways off, the sight of Jace was unmistakable. A breath slipped joyously from her chest, carrying a quiet laugh, and the tension melted from her body. She could no longer stop herself. Hiking up the panels of her skirt, she rushed to meet him. His own long strides helped eat up the distance between them, and the moment she reached him, she threw her arms around his neck. He wrapped his strong arms around her and lifted her off her feet.

"I'm so glad you're alive," she breathed. *Thank You, Elôm!*

When he set her back down, his arms remained enclosed around her, and he bent his head to capture her in a lingering kiss. Kyrin leaned into it, savoring it, wanting it never to end. However, Jace pulled back a little sooner than she would have liked, his arms loosening. Only then did Kyrin remember the others, who had nearly caught up to them. Lengthy displays of affection in front of an audience did make Jace uncomfortable. Still, the tenderness in his eyes told her how much he wanted to keep kissing her. If only they were alone.

Privacy, however, would have to wait. Jace's arms slipped from her waist as his attention shifted to the rest of the group, though he did take her hand. It wasn't hard to read the anxious questions forming in Anne and Elanor's eyes as they looked to Jace for the answers. He did not keep them waiting.

"Don't worry. Trask and Daniel are safe. I saw them before I left the city. I don't think they were injured."

They reacted much the same way Kyrin had and thanked him for letting them know. Turning toward the city again, they resumed their trek. Kyrin leaned close to Jace and studied the city walls. They didn't quite have the same golden hue as the fortress of Stonehelm or its wall at the border between Samara and Arcacia. The mountains north of here must produce a different type of stone than those farther to the south. Dragons dotted the top of the wall, presumably as lookouts.

Josef drew up alongside Jace and Kyrin. "Has the triage area been set up yet?"

Jace nodded and gestured toward the gate. "Just to the right there. Leetra was directing setup when I walked by."

"Are there many injured?"

"More of Davira's men than ours. As soon as the talcrins joined us, the majority of the Arcacians threw down their weapons in surrender. That ended the fight quickly."

Kyrin squeezed Jace's hand. It was just as they had all hoped when planning the surprise attack.

At the edge of the city, they paused at the triage area. Marcus stood there with Leetra. Members of the Militia, clad in the blue and gold uniforms Kyrin had helped produce, carried the wounded from the city and laid them on blankets in the grass. Thankfully, it was as Jace said. Very few militiamen or talcrins rested among the wounded.

Liam stepped up beside Marcus and shifted the heavy pack he carried from his shoulder. "We're going to need somewhere to put the enemy soldiers once we've patched them up."

Marcus surveyed the area. "I'll mention it to Balen and General Mason. Depending on how many prisoners we have, the barracks would probably be the best place to secure them. Until then, I'll ensure there are plenty of men around if someone decides to cause trouble."

Kyrin darted a glance at Leetra. Though the crete hadn't said anything, she had one hand planted on the dagger at her hip, and the hilts of the two short swords strapped to her back rested within easy reach just over her shoulders. Unlike Liam and Josef, who would far rather heal than fight, Leetra was just as much a warrior as a physician. Kyrin didn't doubt she would bring a swift end to any enemy soldier who dared to turn violent. Still, she couldn't watch everyone, so extra men would be a good idea.

Since things seemed to be well in hand with the wounded, Kyrin continued toward the city gate with Jace, Anne, and Elanor. On the other side, they joined the rest of their group gathering around the leaders. Anne broke away from them first, joining Trask nearby. Jace looked like he was just about to say something to Elanor when she dashed off toward Daniel. His mouth snapped shut, and his brow furrowed.

Kyrin bit back a laugh. "You can't blame her for wanting to make sure he's all right. I was just as anxious to see you."

He grumbled. "There might still be hostile forces around. She should stay close."

"Daniel is quite capable of protecting her, and Aric and Trev take their duties very seriously. They'll protect her same as they will Daniel. And look, Elian is with them too. He'll keep an eye on her."

Jace only grunted in response.

She didn't want to dismiss his fears, but she couldn't help finding a bit of humor in his over-protectiveness of Elanor where Daniel was concerned. Though he'd given them his blessing to court months ago, it seemed fraught with reluctance.

The humor must have crept to her face because Jace raised a brow at her now. "What?"

She shook her head. "Nothing. You're very protective, and it's cute."

He snorted.

She did understand his concern. He'd suffered painful losses, just as she had, and she didn't blame him for his deep-seated desire to protect his family. Even if that meant looking at Daniel, their rightful king, with suspicion when it came to his sister.

Just ahead, General Mason strode through the gathering crowd to reach Balen. He wasn't as fit as Kyrin remembered, but he had been a prisoner for two years. That would take anyone out of prime fighting condition.

"We still have to sweep the city for any pockets of resistance, but a path has been secured to the palace."

"Good. We must find the queen and make sure she is not being held there as a hostage." Balen glanced to where Kyrin could just make out the rusty red, clay-tiled roof of what must be Darham Palace above the surrounding buildings. "Has anyone seen her lately?"

"Not for months."

The grimace on Balen's face spoke of genuine concern for the former queen despite her hand in surrendering Samara to Daican and how she had reportedly treated Balen over the years. Kyrin wasn't sure she would be so caring, but that was what made Balen such a good man and king.

Dividing up his men, General Mason gave orders to secure the barracks and armory to one group, while the rest remained with him to guard Balen and Daniel, along with some of the Militia. Kyrin wasn't sure where she and Jace fit into everything, so they joined Trask and other members of the group to follow behind.

Jace held Kyrin close as they moved toward the palace, scanning the streets and buildings. She also kept a lookout for danger, though she spotted no signs of any Arcacian soldiers. They did see people along the way—citizens of Amberin peeking out from their homes and shops. No doubt the fighting had roused most of them from their beds. At first, they peered at the armed procession with wide eyes and grim expressions, no doubt expecting the worst after two years of enemy occupation. However, as soon as they recognized Balen, exclamations rang out, faces lighting up. Neighbor rushed to tell neighbor. Men, women, and children lined the streets in minutes, welcoming their king back with uproarious enthusiasm. Though Jace eyed the growing size of the crowd with one hand on her waist to hold her close and the other on his sword, Kyrin caught a flash of Balen's brilliant smile as he turned to wave and greet the people. That one glimpse held more contentment than she had seen in the two long years since meeting him.

They reached the palace without incident, and Kyrin took it all in. While still majestic in its own right, it was only half the size of Auréa Palace in Valcré and lacked the decorative architecture commonly seen in Arcacia. But simple and sturdy was the way of life here in Samara, and the palace proudly reflected that.

The soldiers did a quick sweep of the courtyard, and once they declared it safe, they all climbed the front steps of the palace. Mason and a few of his men pulled open the door, cautiously entering first. A couple of minutes later, they gave the all clear, and the rest of the group entered behind Balen.

The grand foyer of Darham was void of life when they stepped inside. Kyrin scanned the entire room and the staircase leading to the second floor. Where Auréa boasted stunning marble pillars and crystal chandeliers, Amberin's palace featured carved wood and burnished bronze. Rich-colored tapestries draped the walls, interspersed by mounted deer antlers. It had a warmth that Kyrin hadn't found in Auréa, though perhaps that had more to do with the inhabitants.

They all paused in the middle of the room. Not a sound came from anywhere in the palace. It seemed the Arcacian occupiers had fled, but where was the palace staff?

Balen turned to some of his men. "Locate the queen and the servants."

They split up to search, and everyone else followed Balen through the halls leading to the throne room. Huge wooden beams supported the vaulted ceiling, and though the hall floors had been wood, here lay rust-colored tiles. A carved wooden throne draped in a black bearskin sat on a raised dais. Everything in the room complimented and worked well together except for the two stark gold and black banners depicting Aertus and Vilai hanging behind the throne.

Balen wasted no time. "Take those down."

General Mason and a few of the other men promptly did so, and the banners came down with a satisfying rip. As they backed away, Balen slowly approached the throne. He ran his hand along one of the smooth armrests but did not take a seat. Had he ever sat in that chair as king? Perhaps at his crowning, but he'd ruled Samara from Westing when they'd met him. Kyrin knew he felt responsible for Arcacia's takeover of Samara, even though it was the queen who had surrendered to Daican, so she could well imagine the significance of this moment.

A couple of minutes later, some of the men returned with a group of servants. Their worn, ragged appearance spoke of much hardship suffered under Richard, who had been Davira's appointed ruler over Samara. However, their expressions and postures lifted the moment they recognized Balen. If nothing else, his return marked the end of their suffering.

A stately, older man stepped forward. The way his clothing hung on him said he was not normally so thin. Based on this and the appearance of the others, Richard had no doubt half-starved them all, especially if the winter had been as harsh here as it had been in Arcacia.

The butler dropped to one knee, bowing his head in reverence. The others followed suit.

"Your Majesty. Praise the King you've returned."

Balen looked decidedly uncomfortable with this. He reached for the man's arm, gently guiding him back to his feet. "Please, rise."

The butler seemed a bit startled and overwhelmed that Balen would go so far as to touch someone of his station. Both were going to have to figure out a happy medium when it came to their roles moving forward. The man's gaze flitted from Balen's hand to his face as if unsure where to land.

"Is there anything I can do for you, my lord?"

"Can you tell me where the queen is?"

At this, the butler's face fell, and Kyrin wasn't the only one to notice it. Balen had been bent slightly toward the man, but he straightened now as if steeling himself.

"I regret to have to be the one to relay such news, but…" The butler grimaced. "The queen is dead."

Balen's jaw tightened, his lips a grim line. Though the queen had never accepted him or treated him with kindness, he would experience deep regret at her passing. That was just the way he was.

"Was it Sir Richard?"

The butler's pointed chin dipped heavily. "She sought mightily to oppose his treatment of the people until three months ago when he executed her here in the hall."

Balen glanced over his shoulder as though he would find the evidence of it. Though the floor was spotless, a shadow seemed to hang in the room. The queen had sold out her country under the foolish belief it would save her people, and she had paid the ultimate price for that decision.

Now that the firedrakes had faded far into the distance and didn't appear to be regrouping for another attack, Kaden swung Exsis back around toward Amberin. A few crete riders turned with him. Most of the riders had stayed behind to guard the city and set up camp.

When he neared Amberin, Kaden landed with Exsis in the lush grass outside the city walls, where his dragon riders set up camp next to the crete army. The dragons seemed to like the area. Those who had already been unsaddled lounged in the sun, some even rolling about in the grass like dogs. Good thing there were no crops in this particular area.

He dismounted. Only now that the adrenaline of battle was wearing off did he start to notice the burning sting creeping across the back of his hand and up around his elbow. He glanced at the reddened skin on his hand and through the blackened fabric of his sleeve. At least the flesh didn't appear blistered. He'd suffered worse burns. His leather bracer had protected most of his arm. He probably should've worn gloves but preferred to go without them.

A moment later, he spotted Talas striding toward him from amidst the tents. As far as he could tell, none of his men had gone down during the brief battle, but he wanted to know for sure. "Any casualties?"

Talas shook his head upon reaching him. "No. And no major injuries."

"Good." The fewer men they lost securing Samara, the more they would have when it came time to take Arcacia. Today had only been the first step in a much grander plan to reclaim control of Ilyon. They would need every able-bodied soldier they could get to accomplish that goal.

Talas appeared to be eyeing Kaden's arm. "Yeah, especially since we cut it a bit close this morning."

Kaden winced. The Arcacians must have had firedrakes already saddled when the alarm sounded. It was the only explanation for how they had been in the air so fast. Had he and the other riders arrived a few seconds later, the consequences would have been devastating.

"Hopefully, Jace won't tell Kyrin just how close." Kaden wouldn't have wanted to have to explain things to his sister had Jace been killed this morning.

Talas agreed but finally gestured to Kaden's arm. "A bit singed?"

"Robbie got into a bit of trouble. I was just close enough to intervene."

Their newest recruit had only been training for a couple of months. This morning had been his first battle.

Talas eyed Kaden up and down, probably looking for more injuries. A bit of a smirk lifted his lips. "Looks like you lost a bit of hair on that one."

Kaden brushed his hand through it. Ashy residue dusted his fingers, and he now caught an acrid whiff of burnt hair along with his singed clothing. At least he didn't find any bald patches, and his scalp didn't feel burned. His hair needed a trim anyway. Maybe Marcus could give him one later. The militiamen were good at keeping up their appearances.

He ran his knuckles over short whiskers along his jaw. None of them seemed to be missing. "At least the beard is still there."

"You humans and your beards."

Kaden snorted. Cretes might not grow facial hair, but they had their own vanities. "Says the one with hair halfway down his back. I bet it takes you longer to wash it than it takes me to keep my beard trimmed."

Talas shrugged. "Maybe."

Kaden clapped him on the shoulder, and they turned to join the rest of their men near the tents, where they met

Robbie. At eighteen, he wasn't much younger than Kaden but was still developing his confidence. He approached a bit reluctantly, eyeing Kaden's arm with a guilty look.

"Sorry about this morning, Captain. I don't know why I didn't see that drake coming."

Kaden waved off the apology. "Your first battle is always the hardest. It takes time to get used to the chaos around you. And we don't typically fight in the dark. Don't worry about it. Go get some rest. You'll be more prepared next time."

A little of the guilt seemed to ease as Robbie nodded. He turned away, and Kaden started taking off his bracers and other armor. Though he wouldn't admit it, his burns had begun to throb. Talas must have noticed the wince that crossed his face because he waved toward the triage area near the gate.

"Are you going to have someone look at your arm?"

Kaden gave his head a decided shake. "No, because your cousin will just put some of that antiseptic on it. Sometimes I think she enjoys causing pain."

Talas chuckled. "Depends on the patient."

Kaden reached into one of his packs and pulled out a small jar of ointment Liam had given him for minor burns. "This will do."

After cleaning his arm and applying the ointment, Talas helped wrap the burns with a light bandage. By tomorrow it would probably be mostly healed anyway. He changed into a fresh shirt and saw Captain Darq and Lieutenant Glynn making their way through the other riders. Actually, Darq was more of a general now since the crete lord Vallan had given him command of all the crete dragon riders. Still, he retained his more humble title.

"King Balen has taken control of the palace," he announced.

Kaden crossed his arms. "How did the queen respond?"

"The queen is dead. Apparently, Richard killed her a couple of months ago for opposing him."

Tragic, but Kaden couldn't say he was surprised. Any of them could have told her Richard was both ruthless and vindictive and surrender was a bad idea. "How's Balen taking it?"

"He has his regrets, I'm sure, but any mourning will have to wait until things are more settled. We need to send out scouts. The surviving firedrakes and the rest of the men who escaped fled southeast toward Stonehelm. We need to know if they'll hole up there with the rest of their army or leave Samara for good. I'm sending Glynn and thought you could send one of your men to join him."

"I'll do that."

If the Arcacians chose to remain at the fortress on the border, that would mean another fight and soon, but this was what they had prepared for.

Darq turned to Glynn, drawing him into the conversation. "Once you have answers at the fort, bring word to Prince Haedrin and Saul of our success here so they can get into position should we need them to help take the fortress."

HAPPY VOICES AND laughter filled the ballroom and adjoining atrium garden inside Darham Palace. Sounds Daniel was sure hadn't been heard here in quite some time. Perhaps even well before Arcacia's takeover. While not an official celebration, the celebratory mood could not be ignored as Samara's once-captive lords and their families mingled with their allies. What would it be like to celebrate this same victory in Valcré? To free Arcacia from Davira's tyranny as they were here? That was the ultimate goal, though they still had a long way to go before it became a reality.

Sipping a cup of spiced Samaran wine, he worked his way through the crowd. Most nobles were eager to meet and speak with him. A few were understandably suspicious, considering what his father and sister had done. By the end of their conversations, he hoped he had convinced them of his sincerity. Certain ones, like Balen's longtime friend, Baron Thomas, were quick to voice their support.

After several such conversations, Daniel made his way over to Balen. He had only ever seen him in sturdy linens and leather, more suited for a woodsman than a king, but tonight he wore a coat of fine burgundy linen with gold embroidery. It wasn't as magnificent as something Daniel's father would have worn, but it did give him a kingly appearance. He certainly looked far more his part than Daniel did. It was good for Samara's lords to see Balen this way, especially with him having been in exile for so long and the queen now dead.

Daniel nodded in greeting and gestured with his cup to the mingling guests. "How does it feel to be home?"

Balen looked about the room as if only now fully taking it in. "I don't really know. Darham was never home to me. Though I know King Alton tried, I never felt like more than a guest when I visited. But I know that will have to change. As much as I would like to continue ruling from Westing, I can no longer do that. I fear that was, in part, the reason Samara fell. I need to be at the heart of the country where I can ensure we are moving forward according to Elôm's will."

"I know what you mean. If I could rule from a cabin in Landale, I would."

Balen smiled, showing his own affection for the camp they'd left behind. "Landale is the place that has bound us all together. I think all of us, who aren't able to return there, will miss it."

He was right. There was something special about Landale and the lives they'd forged there. It had not only created close friendships but, in a very real sense, bound them together as family. Though they strove for victory, it would be bittersweet to see the group disbanded and heading off to their various homes and responsibilities.

"At least we will still have people we trust around us to make wherever we are feel more like home." Balen nudged him with a sly grin. "And you'll probably have a wife."

Daniel looked for Elanor in the crowd and spotted her talking to a group of nobles' wives and daughters with Kyrin and Anne. Though she wore a simple, mossy green gown, she looked radiant, her smile dazzling. She appeared so comfortable mingling with the guests, reinforcing his belief she would make an excellent queen. And there he went with a sappy smile that surely made it clear how hopelessly smitten he was.

He dragged his attention back to Balen. "No doubt you'll have Samaran women clamoring at your gates once you've settled as king."

Daniel hadn't failed to notice the rather adoring gazes Balen received from some of the noblemen's daughters. A few had even been directed at Daniel himself, though said women would find themselves disappointed.

Balen shrugged, taking a cursory glance around the room, though he was probably more likely to find a wife amongst the common people than the nobility if they allowed him that luxury. "I only need one as long as she's the right one."

"I'm sure you'll find her. It wasn't like I was looking for Elanor when I showed up in Landale half-concussed. I still don't know how I didn't scare her off with the way I must have been gawking."

Balen laughed. "I remember."

It was only a year ago, yet Daniel felt as though he'd already known Elanor for a lifetime. He couldn't imagine a future without her. "I think I'll go see how she's doing."

Balen slapped him on the back. "You do that."

A couple of nobles were making their way toward Balen anyway. Tonight was for him to celebrate with his people, not talk women with Daniel.

Excusing himself, Daniel wove through the lords and ladies until he reached Elanor's side. They all turned to him, and Daniel greeted them politely. One young woman not-so-discreetly fanned herself, and another batted her eyelashes. Clearly, the women of Samara were the same as women in Arcacia. But Daniel only had eyes for one, and when she looked at him, lips tipped up in a knowing smile, he was the one who got a little breathless.

He offered her his arm. "Would you like to walk around the garden with me?"

Best show the nobles he was spoken for, lest they get any ideas about forming some sort of marriage alliance between him and one of their daughters.

Her smile spread impishly, and she wrapped her hand around his arm, excusing herself from the women. He steered her toward the open double doors out into the atrium. Lanterns flickered in the gathering darkness, giving the garden a romantic glow. A few couples strolled there already.

On the way out, Daniel caught Jace's sidelong glance from where he stood near the edge of the room with Elian and Holden. While Daniel could ignore the advances of other women, his relationship with Elanor did mean he had to deal with the highly protective men in her life, who wouldn't hesitate to overlook the fact he was a prince to ensure her wellbeing.

"I'm not sure your brother will ever be entirely happy with the two of us together."

Elanor shrugged, far less concerned than he was. "He'll get used to it eventually. It just might take a while to convince him you can truly make me happy and keep me safe."

"He probably hopes you'll lose interest." The thought of that left Daniel a little cold.

She just laughed lightly. "Probably." Then she looked up at him, holding his gaze for a long moment as if she could read his thoughts, and hugged his arm to her side. "But I won't."

Warmth returned, blooming through his chest. It was almost scary how much he loved her, because he'd be tempted to do anything, even give up his throne, just to ensure she was safe and happy.

The cool night air carried the scent of the ocean, mingled with sweet floral. Flowers bloomed all along the paths, the most predominant of which were exquisite burgundy roses. Daniel

would have liked to pick one for Elanor, but he didn't want to upset whoever tended them so faithfully. He was a bit surprised the garden was so well maintained. But then, Richard had always enjoyed finery and luxury. He'd no doubt demanded the palace be kept pristine.

A raised rectangular pool lay in the very center of the garden. Floating candles bobbed in the water and lit up the deep red, blue, and gold mosaic tiles that decorated the bottom and sides of the pool. Daniel could tell the servants had enjoyed making this evening memorable even if it wasn't an official celebration. Would any of the servants at Auréa be as happy if he returned home victoriously? He'd tried to treat them with respect, though he couldn't say he'd always succeeded, especially whenever they'd been caught in the crossfire between him and his father.

"What are you thinking about?"

He snapped from his thoughts and looked down at Elanor, only now realizing they'd stopped at the edge of the pool. "I was just wondering what my homecoming might look like. Balen is well-loved by his people. I was never in power long enough to discover how people in Arcacia truly felt about me."

"Considering what you're saving them from, I think they'll be quite welcoming."

Daniel snorted. "True. My sister's not a tough act to follow."

They shared a laugh. Daniel appreciated her humor—it was necessary sometimes to stay sane when things were bleak.

He turned to face her, watching the way the candlelight twinkled in her eyes and glowed on her skin. Her lips looked exceptionally soft tonight, and the sudden urge to kiss her nearly overpowered him. However, he just knew Jace would be watching if he did.

Those pink lips now lifted in a teasing smile. She knew him well. Resisting the urge, he turned to offer her his arm once more.

A black streak flashed in front of him. Elanor gasped and something splashed the water of the pool. She grabbed her arm. For a moment, they both froze in confusion, but when she pulled her hand away, blood coated her palm. A nearby shout shot ice through Daniel's veins.

"Assassin!"

Leetra wound her way through the injured soldiers, who still occupied blankets on the ground. Most, who were stable and could be moved, had either been taken to the barracks under guard or rested in their own tents amongst the rest of their army. Those remaining needed closer observation. Despite the fact these men posed little threat, crete riders still patrolled the area under Captain Darq's orders.

Recognizing a man from the Bear Clan, she nodded as she passed him and knelt next to one of the few members of the Landale Militia who had sustained severe injury. He slept peacefully, breathing more evenly than the last time she'd checked him. He'd taken a bad hit to the leg and lost a lot of blood, but if they could prevent infection, she was confident he would recover.

She lifted his head and let some water dribble into his mouth from the waterskin she carried. It was essential to keep him hydrated after so much blood loss. He stirred and swallowed the water but did not fully wake up. She rested his head back down and moved on to the next man. Once she'd worked through everyone, she returned to the tent where they had all their medical supplies set up and where Josef was mixing herbs. Liam and Cassie worked nearby. Cassie said something, and Liam smiled shyly. They were lucky to have each other close by.

"I thought you'd be up at the palace with your cousin."

Josef's voice pulled Leetra's attention away from Liam and Cassie. She'd heard about the celebration from Talas but had declined to join him. She would celebrate when they took down Davira…when she was able to do so with Timothy.

She fought back how much it ached to think about him. It had been hard to leave Landale knowing how far apart they would be and that she would not receive his letters until they returned. She'd kept his last one tucked safely in her vest and pulled it out more often than she would ever admit to anyone. In it, he'd expressed his heartfelt belief they would win this fight and be together again. She'd clung to those words since parting.

She opened her mouth to respond to Josef, but a shout cut her off. They both looked to see one of the Militia rushing toward them from the gate. A cold rock of dread formed in Leetra's stomach. The militiaman reached them a moment later and took a couple panting breaths before speaking, his words coming in a winded rush. "There's been an assassination attempt on Prince Daniel."

Now the air died in Leetra's lungs. All of their plans to liberate Arcacia rested on Daniel's claim to the throne.

Josef stepped forward and gripped the man's shoulder. "Is he all right?"

The militiaman nodded, relieving a little of the knot in Leetra's middle. "But Lady Elanor is injured."

And the knot was back in an instant. This time Leetra found her voice. "How badly?"

The soldier shook his head. "I don't know. I was just sent to get help."

Josef turned to Leetra. Though concern lined his face, he spoke calmly. "You go. With your dragon, you'll get there the fastest."

She didn't hesitate. Grabbing her medical bag from where it lay on the table just inside the tent, she raced toward the dragons.

Thankfully, Soka rested on the near side of the field. The dragon saw her coming, alert and always attuned to Leetra's moods. A nearby crete asked what was happening, but Leetra didn't pause to answer. She leapt up onto Soka's back and commanded her to fly before she'd even settled in. Soka launched into the air, flattening Leetra against her neck, but she'd flown without a saddle many times. Gripping tightly with her legs, Leetra held on until they evened out over the city and then commanded Soka in the right direction.

It took barely a minute to reach the palace, though it felt like ten times that by the time Soka landed, and Leetra jumped down. While she wasn't super close to Elanor, she would make a good queen for Arcacia, and Leetra didn't want Daniel suffering loss before they'd even taken back the country. Some people never recovered from such devastation.

She ran up to the palace entrance, where another militia-man waited. The soldier guided her through the halls before finally coming to a door guarded by several more men. One opened the door for her, and she hurried into a sitting room.

She spotted Elanor right away on a couch with Kyrin and Anne. Kyrin held what looked like a cloth napkin to Elanor's right arm. Though some blood stained her sleeve, she looked otherwise unharmed, thank Elôm.

This fact, however, didn't seem to comfort Daniel. He stood close by, his expression drawn, eyes a bit frantic as if he needed to be doing something to help. Just off to the right, Jace stood with Balen, Elian, Aric, and Trev. His stance was as stiff as an oak tree, one hand gripping the hilt of his sword, the other clenched at his side. The faint glow in his eyes held a fearful glint, but they turned a touch frosty when he glanced at Daniel.

The moment Elanor saw her, relief washed over her face, though Leetra suspected it had nothing to do with any pain or danger she was in.

"Leetra, thank Elôm. Will you please tell everyone I'm fine? It's not that bad."

By everyone, Leetra assumed she specifically meant Daniel and Jace. She stepped deeper into the room. "Let me see."

Kyrin moved aside to let Leetra in. Carefully peeling away the blood-dampened cloth, she inspected Elanor's wound through the torn fabric of her sleeve. "What happened?"

Balen took a step forward. "There was apparently an archer on one of the balconies overlooking the garden. We assume he was aiming for Daniel."

So Elanor had been grazed by an arrow that thankfully missed its intended target. The wound was deep enough to need stitches but not serious enough to cause any lasting damage.

"She'll be fine." Leetra heard Daniel release a long breath, and Jace relaxed the tiniest bit. "We'll need privacy for me to tend it."

Taking that cue, Anne got up and ushered the men out of the room. Once the door had closed behind them, Leetra helped Elanor slip her arm out of her sleeve before grabbing clean cloths from her bag. Elanor winced as Leetra went to work but turned her head to look at Kyrin.

"This won't make Jace very comfortable concerning Daniel and me, will it?"

"Probably not." Still, Kyrin gave her an uplifting smile. "Don't worry; I'll talk to him."

MARCUS RUSHED THROUGH the palace, Kaden, Talas, and several members of the Militia right behind him. General Mason had sent men to secure every exit, but they weren't sure which way the assassin had gone once he'd disappeared from the balcony. So they'd split up, General Mason taking a group to one wing of the palace while Marcus led his men to the other.

How had this happened? They'd combed the palace and had guards posted throughout, but an assassin had still managed to get close enough to nearly kill Daniel.

He rounded a corner into a long hall, and a flash of movement sent him lunging to the side out of instinct right as an arrow flew by him. He slammed into a door, frantically turning the knob to let himself into the room. The others dove back around the corner. Thankfully, no one appeared to have been hit.

Breathing hard, Marcus called out. "We have the palace locked down. Throw out your weapons and surrender. You have nowhere to go."

A deep, snarling voice responded. "I'll kill anyone who approaches."

Marcus grimaced, locking eyes with Kaden from his position at the corner. "You'll run out of arrows eventually."

The assassin snorted. "I'll still take several of you with me."

Marcus peeked around the doorframe to get a better idea of where the assassin was, but an arrow whipped past his face and thunked into the door near his shoulder. His heart jumped into his throat. He looked at Kaden again. His brother gestured to himself and Talas before making a motion that they would try to get around behind the assassin.

Marcus nodded. He hated letting them put themselves in jeopardy, but it wasn't like he could move from his position. Not without a high probability of getting shot in the attempt. The best he could do now was try to hold the assassin's attention so Kaden and Talas could sneak up behind him.

"Listen, this doesn't have to end in bloodshed."

The assassin laughed—a cruel, rough sound. "Why else do you think I was left here when everyone else fled?"

"It doesn't have to be this way. Emperor Daican wouldn't want this. He would want his son, his heir, on the throne. Davira is the usurper. You don't have to serve her."

The assassin scoffed loud enough for Marcus to hear even down the hall. "You think you can distract me so your men can get around behind me?"

Marcus winced. He'd been hoping. He chanced another peek down the hall. No arrow met him this time. The assassin's elbow poked out around the corner. No doubt he was watching for anyone sneaking up on him. If Kaden and Talas were going to have any chance, Marcus had to figure out a better way to distract him.

He glanced across the hall. He wasn't going to turn his back on the assassin and attempt to get back to his men. Just the idea made the skin between his shoulders crawl. But darting across to the other side would give him more cover. The assassin would have to give up his own cover to shoot, and if he thought Marcus was getting closer, that would divide his attention.

Marcus sucked in a breath and lunged toward a door across the hall a little farther up than he was currently hiding. The assassin cursed, and an arrow sliced the air somewhere over Marcus's left shoulder. Marcus flattened himself against the door, quickly opening it to gain more cover. He breathed out slowly. One less arrow to worry about.

But he couldn't let the assassin go back to scanning the halls. He needed to keep the man's focus fixed on him. He had no idea how much ground Kaden and Talas would have to cover. "Maybe I do have men working their way behind you. Or maybe I intend to take you out myself."

The assassin released a bark of laughter. "You'll be dead before you get near me, boy."

Marcus peered out of the doorway, calculating his next move. He could see a bit more of the assassin, who seemed to be trying to keep track of where he was without exposing himself.

"You think you scare me? My grandfather is General Marcus Veshiron, and I am captain of the Landale Militia. You really think I won't come for you?"

Before the assassin could answer, Marcus dashed for the next door. He heard the assassin scramble and caught a flash of him firing another arrow just before he ducked into the next room. His heart thudded his chest. Only another three doors and he would nearly reach the assassin. He wasn't sure if it was wise to antagonize the man, but if it helped distract him...

"I'm surprised Richard left such an incompetent marksman behind. Perhaps we'll return you to him as a gift. I'd be curious to see how he responds to the fact that you haven't hit one of your targets."

The assassin spat out a string of choice words. "I swear, I'll put an arrow in your gut, you pathetic traitor."

Marcus raced to yet another door. Though the assassin did

not fire this time, his growl told Marcus he was getting frustrated. Frustrated hopefully meant distracted.

"Try it again, boy," he spat. "I dare you."

Marcus had a feeling the next time he did try to move, the man would be waiting, and this time he wouldn't miss. He didn't even dare poke his head out of the room to check. He'd no doubt end up with an arrow in his eye socket.

But if he kept hidden too long, the man would start checking his surroundings again. Marcus moved as close to the edge of the door as he dared.

"If I'm so pathetic, why don't you come out and face me? Quit hiding behind your bow."

"You won't goad me. If you want me, you'll have to come and get me. Think you're faster than one of my arrows at close range?"

Marcus had to make a move. He glanced over his shoulder, looking for something he could use as a shield. If he had time, he might be able to tear a door off the wardrobe in the corner, but that would take too long. The assassin would probably just rush the room and shoot him before he could defend himself. He might even be thinking of doing that already.

Marcus was just about to dart a glance out to check when another curse exploded from the assassin. His bow twanged and then a mad scramble. Marcus looked out just in time to see Kaden, arms around the assassin's waist, tackle him to the ground. The assassin fought against him, and Marcus rushed to help at the same moment Talas did. The three of them wrestled the man to his stomach and wrenched his arms behind his back.

Once he was secure, Marcus looked over Kaden and Talas. Neither of them had any arrows protruding from their bodies or blood on their clothes. It appeared the assassin had, thankfully, once again, missed his shot.

Marcus grasped the man's shoulder. "Let's get him up."

They drew him to his feet. Marcus adjusted his grip, ensuring he and Kaden had a firm hold on the man's arms, and nodded at Talas.

"Take his arrows and search him for more weapons."

The rest of the men joined them as Talas searched the assassin. Marcus focused on one of his lieutenants. "Find General Mason and let him know we have the assassin. We'll take him down to the cells."

With most of the men still following in case of trouble, Marcus and Kaden led the assassin through the palace. He tugged against them, but most of the fight seemed to have gone out of him.

Below the palace, they entered a containment room. It wasn't a very big area—only enough room for a few cells. Nothing like what he'd heard of Auréa's dungeon. All the cells were empty save for one at the end. When the assassin spotted the other prisoner, he straightened.

"General Veshiron. We thought you were dead."

Marcus eyed his grandfather, who sat in the back of his cell. They'd brought him along with them from Landale in case they needed leverage. Barely a word had passed between them in the months following the attack on camp other than Marcus giving him orders. Would he speak up now that he saw a friendly face?

The General cast the man a slight frown, signaling the two didn't personally know each other, but didn't say anything.

Marcus and Kaden pushed the assassin into an empty cell and closed the door. The man immediately moved to the bars closest to the rear cell.

"I tried, General. I tried to kill the traitor prince."

Kaden scowled at him. "Tried and failed miserably."

He turned his heated look to their grandfather then but said nothing more. After all the pain and history between them, there wasn't anything left to say at this point.

Now that the assassin was secure, they turned to leave. Any questioning could wait until tomorrow. It was pretty clear Richard had specifically left behind the assassin with orders to kill Daniel.

On the way back up to the palace, Marcus looked over at Kaden. "So, just how close were you to getting shot?"

"Talas came the closest. He insisted he go first since he's quicker and had more chance of dodging an arrow. There was no time to argue. Thankfully, it worked."

There was a lot to be thankful for tonight. It was a miracle no one had been killed.

Jace opened the door to the room Balen had provided and told Kyrin to wait while he searched it—under the bed, in the tall wardrobe, behind the drapes. Anywhere an assassin could have hidden since they'd used the room to change in earlier. He'd done the exact same thing for Elanor one room over before reluctantly parting for the night. Satisfied this room too was safe, he motioned to Kyrin. She stepped inside and closed the door.

They met in the middle of the room, and she looked up at him, studying his face and no doubt reading the turmoil that must be etched there. She rested her hand on his chest over his heart as if trying to instill it with peace.

"Elanor will be fine. Marcus has men stationed up and down this hall, and Aric, Trev, and Elian all said they would take turns on watch tonight. No one could get by them."

Jace breathed out a long sigh. He wanted to be out there too, but he didn't dare leave Kyrin's side even if logic told him she was safe in this room.

"It's just hard not to worry about her."

"I know. I always worry about my brothers, but we all have to live our own lives. We can't protect each other from everything. Only Elôm can do that."

Wasn't this precisely what he'd had to learn last winter when Kyrin had nearly died from the fever? He'd almost made the gravest mistake of his life in his desperate attempt to save her instead of trusting Elôm. He should be better at trusting by now.

Her hand lifted to rest on his cheek, and he leaned into it.

"You need to rest. It's been a long day."

Between the attack on the city before dawn and now the assassination attempt tonight, it felt like more than a day had passed. No wonder his limbs were so heavy.

They got ready for bed, and his body thanked him when he finally crawled under the light covers. Though he hadn't received any real injuries from the battle, he did have some bruising and strained muscles that ached dully. Kyrin sat beside him, brushing out her long hair as they both quietly mused. Jace watched her for a long moment, a bit mesmerized by how the brush glided through the deep brown strands. If his arm hadn't been so weighted, he would have reached up and run his fingers through it.

Slipping back into his thoughts of Elanor, he sighed again. "Do you think I made a mistake in giving my blessing to Elanor and Daniel's courtship?"

Kyrin looked down at him, the hint of a smile quirking her lips, though he wasn't sure what was humorous about his question. "No, I think you made a perfect decision. I have no doubt Elanor and Daniel belong together."

"Then why don't I feel as confident as I did when I first consented?"

"Because things have gotten much more serious between them, and you know sooner rather than later, you'll have to let her go and fully entrust Daniel with her care and wellbeing. I know that's hard for you."

She was right, of course. He didn't want to let his sister go, especially when he'd known her for so short a time.

Kyrin reached out to rest her hand over his. "You just have to remember letting go doesn't mean losing her, and you did say yourself that Daniel is a good man. He'll do everything in his power to protect her, but it's not his fault if things like tonight happen. Nothing will happen to her that's not part of Elôm's plans. That's true whether she marries Daniel and becomes queen or not."

Her words soothed the uncertainty swirling inside of him. She'd always had that effect, and he nodded in acceptance.

Setting her brush aside, she leaned down to kiss his lips softly. Her hair fell around his face, and this time he did reach up and bury his fingers in it, pulling her in gently for a more lingering kiss that cleared his mind of anything but her. When they did part after a long moment, she blew out the candle before snuggling against him under the covers. He wrapped his arm around her and held her close, letting the peace of the moment wash over him.

THOUGH DAWN HAD broken some time ago, Daniel remained in his bed and stared at the ceiling. It had been hard to sleep well last night. Any little sound, real or perceived, had jolted him to alertness, and he'd gone over the attack far more than was probably healthy. It wasn't like someone hadn't tried to kill him before. Davira had certainly given it her best shot when he'd escaped from Valcré, but this was the first assassination attempt against him. He couldn't help thinking about his father's death. That was the thing about assassinations. They seemed to come right when least expected.

Elanor's injury, however, was worse than the attempt on his life. He had been the target, but she was the one who had gotten hurt. Had he been standing a few inches to the side before turning, that arrow likely would have hit her fatally. The thought was enough to cause a cold sweat to break out.

Though she'd assured him she was fine, he'd struggled to leave her last night. He hadn't been able to stop the visions of assailants creeping into her room during the night, though he knew the impossibility of that happening. Any attackers would have to take out the guards. No one could do that without an alarm being souhded by someone. That knowledge hadn't really helped, though. It was times like these he *really* wished he and

Elanor were married already. Then she'd be right beside him where he could see for himself that she was all right. Where he could put his arms around her and draw her close.

Before that thought could go too far, he shoved himself up and got out of bed despite how his body still craved sleep. He had a feeling adequate rest would be a luxury no one would be able to afford for a while. Taking Amberin was only the first step in a much bigger struggle that loomed ahead.

He got dressed and stepped out of the room. Guards still stood at their posts, just like last night. Elanor's room lay directly across from his, and Elian stood near the door. It helped settle Daniel's nerves a bit to see him there. He'd been watching over and protecting Elanor for longer than Daniel had known her.

Daniel gave him a nod and then turned. Aric was there to meet him.

"Is anyone else up yet?"

Aric nodded. "King Balen was up early and is meeting with the lords to decide how to best get Samara functioning again and who will oversee things here when he is away fighting."

It was a lot to think about and put into place. From what Daniel had gathered last night, many people had been displaced by Richard's men, and even more had nearly starved over the winter. Even now, they had trouble getting the necessary supplies the Arcacians had stockpiled for themselves. While cities and towns farther from the capital had fared better, Arcacia's invasion had still disrupted their way of life and sense of security. It would be difficult for them to see their king march away to battle so soon after his return.

If only Daniel could do something to help. After all, it was his people who had brought harm to Samara—but, until he was truly king, he found himself rather helpless to do much of anything.

He turned and started walking down the hall. Aric remained

at his side. After last night, he probably wouldn't be able to go anywhere without a guard now. He wasn't sure exactly where he was going since he'd seen very little of the palace, but he might as well take in some sights while waiting for the others to wake. He'd never even been outside Arcacia until they'd reached Samara a couple of days ago.

Downstairs, Aric gestured up the hall. "King Balen said he would have food prepared and set out for breakfast. I sent some of our men to ensure it was prepared safely and to guard it."

Good. The last thing Daniel wanted was to be poisoned like his father. He almost shuddered to think of it. If ever an assassin succeeded in taking him out, poison was not the way he wanted to go.

Exploring one of the central halls, Daniel first found a gallery filled with Samaran art. Next to it sat a library he took a little time to browse. It wasn't nearly the size of Auréa's library, but it did contain books concerning Elôm that neither Auréa nor Tarvin Hall did. He and Aric chatted while he browsed, discussing the future and what it might look like. Daniel's father had never been so friendly and familiar with his security, but Aric was more friend than staff at this point. He'd helped Daniel escape the palace and Davira's torture-happy clutches. After that, they'd fled the city together, barely making it to Landale alive. Daniel would be dead if not for him.

From the library, he found his way to the ballroom and stopped at the door leading out to the garden. He scanned what he could see of the balconies surrounding it, his gaze lingering where last night's assassin had hidden. A chill crawled up his back between his shoulder blades, but he walked out into the garden anyway. Best to face the memories of last night head-on.

He circled around to the pool before stopping. The floating candles had all burnt out. He half expected to see the assassin's arrow amongst them, but someone must have removed it. A little dark spot stained the pool's edge that could've been a drop of Elanor's blood, though he couldn't say for sure. Even so, his ribs constricted. Though she was not the target last night, someday she could be. He wouldn't be able to prevent that. He drew a deep breath, his soul reaching out to Elôm for Elanor's safety.

A moment later, he looked past the pool to the doors and saw her enter the garden as if she knew he was fretting about her. Elian followed close behind. Daniel quickly searched the balconies again, though both Aric and Elian would be hypervigilant. She approached him with a smile that never would have caused anyone to guess she could've been killed last night.

He put his hands on her arms, careful of her injured one. "How are you feeling?"

She gave a little shrug. "My arm is sore, but I'm all right. Nothing to worry about."

He grimaced. She shouldn't be hurting at all.

She stepped a little closer, resting her hands on his chest. "It's not your fault."

"You were still put in danger because I was the target." He rubbed his thumb over her sleeve, imagining the blood there, and sighed. "This time."

He looked back into her eyes. As much as he had wished earlier they were married, that would only pose more danger to her. "I remember once when I was a boy—seven or eight, I think. We attended some event in the city, and a couple of men took my mother. I'm sure it was for political reasons I couldn't understand back then. I don't even know how they managed it, but I remember how terrified I was when our guards rushed Davira and me back to the palace. They did get my mother back, but I've never forgotten the fear of thinking I would never see her again."

He paused. It had been so easy for their relationship to grow when they were safely hidden away back in Landale. So easy to overlook the hardships they would face if they were to become king and queen. The danger that would put Elanor in at all times.

"We'll always have enemies. No matter how well we rule or how much our people may love us, there will always be those who find a reason to hate us, and they will try to hurt us. It won't be just me, but you and any children we have. Even with the best security, I can't promise things won't happen—things like last night. Life at my side won't be easy. Things will be very different than they were in Landale."

Her face had gone sober during his speech, and his heart thumped, awaiting her response. He wasn't sure what he hoped for, but the little smirk that slowly lifted her lips was not what he expected.

"If you're going to try to tell me all of the reasons I shouldn't be with you, there's no need. I already went through them all before we started courting. I do understand the danger, and while last night was frightening, especially knowing how close you came to being killed, I'm not afraid to continue moving forward. I won't live my life ruled by fear."

A grin sprang to Daniel's face. He didn't deserve this woman. He brought her hand to his lips and kissed it. "You're one of the bravest people I've ever known. I don't think I'll ever quite understand how you're so willing to take on all of the challenges that come with this relationship, but I would hate to try to imagine a future without you."

Whoops, cheers, and hollering rose all around Kaden as he stepped up beside Talas to a gap in the crowd watching the latest wrestling match. Cretes got antsy when forced to be on the ground in wide open spaces for any length of time. These friendly competitions had broken out around mid-morning to combat the restlessness and had lasted most of the day. There'd been some foot races and sparring earlier, with wrestling matches now popping up across the crete camp. It hadn't taken long for the Landale Riders to jump into the competition. Kaden wasn't sure some of the cretes were thrilled to mingle with humans, but most were a good sport about it, especially since they won most of the time.

The current match between Naeth Tarn and Robbie caught his full attention. While Robbie was strong, wiry, and a bit taller than Naeth, Kaden was pretty sure he didn't stand a chance against the crete. Naeth had too much experience, and crete agility was hard to beat. Still, he cheered his man on, shouting encouragement as the two circled and grappled each other.

As expected, Naeth swiped Robbie's legs out from under him after barely a minute. Though Robbie put up an admirable struggle, it wasn't long before he tapped out of the fight. The cretes cheered, and some of Kaden's other men heckled Robbie a bit. He took it all with a good-natured smile. Kaden gave him a slap on the back as he joined them.

"Good effort."

Robbie shook his head, breathing hard. "Those cretes are fast." He flashed Kaden a grin. "You should give it a go, Captain."

The others heard him and immediately jumped in to encourage it. Even some of the cretes joined in. Kaden had participated in some of the sparring competitions earlier but hadn't intended to get roped into wrestling, considering the size discrepancy between him and the cretes. He looked over at Naeth, who stood, arms crossed, a challenging smirk on his face. Sometimes it was a little disturbing to see the family resemblance between him and Falcor. Still, he was nothing like his traitorous younger brother who had betrayed Kaden's father to Daican.

Naeth gestured to the men around them. "Willing to risk getting shown up in front of your men?"

Kaden raised a brow. Now how could he say no to a bit of friendly competition? "If you're willing to risk getting shown up by a human."

Laughter rippled through the cretes but was quickly drowned out by his men cheering when he stepped forward to face Naeth. The ring of spectators closed around them as they circled each other. Kaden eyed his opponent. Naeth was about a head shorter and probably at least twenty pounds lighter than Kaden. He'd know shortly whether or not that would work to his advantage.

Naeth lunged, going for Kaden's legs. Having learned from watching the previous match, Kaden jumped to the side. Naeth almost got one of his legs anyway, but he managed to keep his feet. An aggressive approach would probably be better than letting Naeth control the match, so Kaden lunged this time. He caught Naeth around the waist, dragging him to the ground. Naeth, however, used the momentum to his advantage and managed to roll on top of Kaden.

Robbie was right. Naeth was fast. Kaden scrambled to push himself up before Naeth could get a solid grip on him. This was where his strength worked to his advantage. He tipped Naeth off and tried to pin him, but Naeth slipped from his grasp.

They grappled back and forth long enough for sweat to drip from Kaden's forehead and into his eyes. Then, before he could shift away, Naeth's arm wrapped around his neck in a chokehold. He fought to break it but knew almost immediately it was pointless. Naeth was too strong, and once spots danced in Kaden's vision, he tapped Naeth's arm in surrender.

Naeth released his hold, and Kaden sucked in a lungful of air. He just lay there for a moment, breathing deeply. He hadn't had a wrestling match like that since Tarvin Hall. He'd probably feel it tomorrow too.

Naeth popped to his feet, his sweat-darkened shirt the only indication of how much effort had gone into the match. He offered Kaden a hand. Kaden gripped it, and Naeth hauled him to his feet.

"You're a worthy opponent." Naeth clapped his shoulder.

"Thanks, but I think I'll be sticking to dragon riding and swordplay from now on."

They shared a laugh.

Kaden turned back to his men. They applauded his effort, some thumping him on the back.

Talas gave him an approving nod. "Good job. You lasted longer than the cretes thought you would, considering Naeth is one of our best wrestlers. He dominates most competitions back home in Arvael."

"I believe it." Anyone who foolishly thought cretes to be weaker due to their slightly smaller stature had clearly never been in a wrestling match with one before.

One of the oldest and original members of the Landale Riders slapped them each on the back. "Hey, why don't you two give it a go?"

Talas held up his hands. "I can already tell you that our captain would likely win. Wrestling was never my strong suit. Knives, on the other hand…" He gripped the two on his belt and gave a wicked grin.

Kaden nudged him with his elbow. "Ironic, since you were very nearly killed with a knife."

Talas pulled out one of the knives and twisted it in his fingers so the sharp edge caught the sunlight. "Put Falcor and me in the same space again and that turns out very differently."

No doubt it would, if it ever came to that, but no one had even seen or heard from Falcor in over a year. Perhaps he would show up when they entered Arcacia, and Talas could put his words to the test. That is if Kaden didn't get to Falcor first.

Before Kaden could voice such sentiments, the onlookers parted to let Captain Darq through. If he were here to join in on the competition, he'd probably trounce all of them, except maybe for Naeth. However, he was all business when he reached Kaden.

"Glynn and your rider have returned from Stonehelm. I sent them on to the palace so King Balen can gather the others. We'll meet them there and see what they have to report."

Darq then headed off toward the dragon field, and Kaden turned with Talas toward the tent they shared. He should change into something more fitting for a meeting and not show up reeking of sweat. At the tent, he changed into one of his spare blue shirts and black uniform vest. Gold braid trimmed the edges and around the shoulders to show his rank. Talas also changed into his vest, though he did not wear a shirt underneath. Instead, he had a blue sash around his waist.

On the way to the dragons, Kaden rolled his left shoulder, which had begun to ache a bit. He must have strained it while wrestling. Hopefully, it would clear up quickly, considering whatever news their riders had brought could mean going into battle again shortly. Later he'd have to see about getting a liniment from Liam.

They didn't bother saddling the dragons when they reached them. While Kaden wouldn't attempt to go into battle without a saddle, he had trained himself to ride without one when needed. It helped to know Exsis would catch him if he somehow slipped off.

At the palace, they left their dragons with Darq's and the others and headed to the throne room. Balen was already there, speaking with Darq and Glynn, along with Daniel and Marcus. General Mason, General Torva, and the rest of those in charge of making military decisions arrived shortly. Once everyone was present, Glynn stepped forward.

"From what we observed, it appears the Arcacians intend to try to keep a foothold in Samara. They showed no evidence that they're preparing to leave. Based on what we were able to get close enough to see, they appear, instead, to be fortifying Stonehelm. They have a strong presence of firedrakes. The soldiers who fled the city yesterday will arrive by this evening, adding another hundred or so men to the garrison they have stationed there. I'd estimate the total to be no more than three-hundred men in their ground force and around seventy-five firedrakes."

The ground troops wouldn't be an issue, even within the fortress, once the giants and Saul's men were in place, and between Kaden's men and the cretes, they'd easily handle the firedrakes. The Arcacians would be better off just abandoning the fortress.

Balen looked at each of the leaders. "How soon can we be ready to march?"

Marcus spoke up first. "My men could be ready as soon as tomorrow if need be."

Kaden agreed, as did the others. The sooner they drove Davira's forces completely out of Samara, the better.

With everyone in agreement, they decided to march the day after tomorrow. Taking Amberin had been a major victory, but Stonehelm felt like the bigger prize, at least to Kaden. It was where he had faced his first battle as captain of the dragon riders two years ago when they had suffered such a crushing defeat. Reclaiming it would not only set things right, but it would be one step closer to Arcacia.

KYRIN BREATHED IN deeply and opened her eyes to the pale canvas of the tent. Birds twittered in the rustling grass outside. A pot clanked nearby, and wood popped and crackled. Others in camp must be up already, preparing for the attack on Stonehelm. Another battle. Another chance to lose someone. Her stomach ached, and she rolled over to snuggle against Jace for a few more minutes. However, she found his side of their makeshift bed empty, the blankets cool. She looked up.

He sat a couple of feet away, head hanging. His back was to her and drew her eyes to the crisscrossing scars marking his skin—some from before she had known him and others she'd had to bear witness to. Her heart squeezed over what he'd endured in his past.

She sat up and scooted closer to him. "Jace?"

He raised his head and looked at her over his shoulder. His expression was calm, but his vivid eyes gave away a deeper unease. Was he thinking of the battle too? Did he share her fears that this life they had only begun to build would end in tragedy?

She ran her hand down his back, over the raised ridges. "Are you all right?"

He nodded slowly. "I was dreaming. About Dane. Sometimes the things I did and saw just come back so clearly…"

She placed her lips against his shoulder in a soft kiss. "Once this is all over…once we've won, we'll find a nice, quiet, peaceful place, and we'll leave behind all the things we've suffered over the years. We'll just live and rejoice in where Elôm has brought us."

This was why they fought and risked everything.

A smile crept over his face and chased away the troubled look in his eyes. He turned to face her, sliding his fingers behind her head and into her hair, drawing her in for a deep kiss. Kyrin melted into his warmth and tenderness…until footsteps rustled the grass just outside.

They parted as whoever it was passed by the tent. Jace let out a sigh, and Kyrin giggled at the annoyance wrinkling his brow.

"I suppose we should get up. Everyone's starting the day without us."

He still didn't look amused. "I should have pitched our tent farther away from camp."

She giggled again but was cut short by one last kiss before Jace turned to grab his shirt.

She changed into a fresh short-sleeved shirt and leggings and then laced up her linen overdress. Once they were both ready, they left the tent, greeted by the scent of wood smoke and the sun's warmth. Though Kyrin missed the forest, Samara's open plains did allow one to enjoy the morning rays unimpeded.

All around them milled their soldiers. It had been quite a sight to see them all gathered for the first time when they'd marched away from Amberin. She prayed the Arcacians holding out in Stonehelm would surrender peacefully since they were far outnumbered. If not, this battle would probably be bloodier than their surprise attack on the capital. A lot more firedrakes awaited the clash; some perched on Stonehelm's walls like grotesque black sculptures even now. Loss was unavoidable without an immediate surrender.

Her spirits lifted when they found Anne and Trask working around the campfire not far from their tent. The two of them had only been married a few months longer than Kyrin and Jace had. Kyrin had appreciated having Anne around so the two of them could share their fears and the challenges of being newlyweds in the middle of a war.

They joined them at the fire, where a large kettle of porridge and a pot of coffee simmered. Jace poured her a cup, and after she'd taken a sip, she turned to Anne. "Have my brothers been by this morning?"

"Kaden and Talas came for coffee and then went to check on the dragons. I'm sure they'll be back soon for breakfast. I haven't seen Marcus or Liam yet."

Kyrin scanned the camp again, though it was impossible to find anyone in particular amongst the soldiers. However, others in their tight-knit group showed up before long, and Kyrin helped Anne dish out the porridge for everyone. As expected, Kaden and Talas arrived shortly. The two already wore their armor and uniforms. They looked strong and confident and even laughed as they shared a joke or story. It helped Kyrin feel more optimistic about the day.

She greeted everyone and made sure they all had enough to eat. At first, she declined food for herself, her stomach in knots, but Jace convinced her she needed nourishment for the morning ahead. So she forced down the porridge and prayed again for success. Once they secured the stronghold, Samara would be entirely under their control. Even if they did not go on to take Arcacia, they could still make a life here. She ached to settle down with Jace and build a home and family together.

As the final stragglers finished their breakfast, a tall, formidable figure approached. Kyrin didn't think she would ever get used to how fierce and warrior-like Sam looked, outfitted in traditional talcrin scale-mail and tooled leather. He carried with him a staff with a curved blade on one end. She couldn't imagine facing an entire army of the tall, stalwart talcrin men. Thank Elôm they had joined this fight on the side of the Resistance.

Her old mentor joined them at the fire. "King Balen has sent General Mason to parley with the soldiers in Stonehelm. If they don't surrender, Kyrin, you and Jace will be up to take word to Saul and Prince Haedrin and get them into position."

Kyrin looked out toward the stronghold in the distance, but Jace answered firmly. "We'll be ready."

The calm strength in his voice helped soothe her tangled insides. While the circumstances were not ideal, it was rather attractive to see him show more confidence in his abilities and his place in the group. It had certainly taken long enough to help him see his worth.

He turned to her. "We should prepare."

On the other side of Kyrin, Kaden gulped down a mouthful of his porridge. "Talas and I can saddle Ivoris and Gem for you."

Kyrin thanked him and followed Jace back to their tent, where she helped him slip on his chain-mail and secure his leather pauldrons and bracers. In turn, he helped her buckle on a leather cuirass and bracers she had acquired from the cretes with Leetra's help. Though she had no plans to do any fighting, Jace wanted her prepared, just in case. Once properly outfitted, she put on a belt with her dagger and the holder for the staff Jace had carved for her. If they did happen to meet unforeseen trouble, at least she wasn't defenseless.

Adjusting the strap for her staff, she caught a little smile on Jace's lips. She raised her brows at him. "What?"

"The armor looks good on you."

The warm way he looked at her caused her belly to flutter. "I don't think that's the purpose."

"As long as you're not doing any fighting, I can enjoy it."

His hands wrapped around her armored waist, drawing her to him as he bent to kiss her. Even now, it left her breathless and a little bit dizzy. She gave him a wry look once she returned to her senses.

"If you keep kissing me like that, you'll mess up my sense of direction and memory recall. We can't have that today."

He just smiled and straightened, making Kyrin want to pull him close and kiss him herself. However, she resisted and took his hand instead. Together, they turned toward the center of camp. Here, a large blue-trimmed pavilion tent stood as Balen and Daniel's command center. Talcrins, Samaran soldiers, and men from Marcus's militia patrolled the area, but no one stopped the two of them from approaching and entering the tent. Balen and Daniel stood around a central table with their commanders, including Marcus, as they awaited word from General Mason. Marcus shifted to make room for them around the table.

Jace gestured in the direction of the fortress. "We're ready to head out if we need to."

"Good. We should know shortly." Balen focused his attention on Kyrin. "You won't have any trouble finding your way through the caves?"

"No." She might have been uncomfortable and nervous during their escape from Stonehelm two years ago, but the memories of the path remained clear. Though navigating them again wouldn't be pleasant, she didn't doubt her ability to recall the way.

A half an hour later, one of the guards outside stepped to the tent flap. "General Mason has returned."

Mason rode up on his horse in another minute or two and dismounted in front of the tent. He strode purposefully inside and addressed Balen. "They refused to parley. They wouldn't even send anyone out to talk."

Though not unexpected, the news traveled coldly through Kyrin's veins. Bloodshed it would have to be.

All at once, the military commanders moved to prepare their men for battle. Balen was one of the last to remain inside the tent with Kyrin and Jace.

"We'll give you two hours to get into position unless the Arcacians decide to attack first. Once you hear the fighting start, move in."

Jace gave a firm nod, and he and Kyrin left the tent. Outside, they headed toward the dragons.

Along the way, Kaden jogged to catch up with them. "Be careful in there."

Kyrin cast him a quick smile though tension bound her muscles. "And you be careful up there." She tipped her head toward the sky. Every time he went up could be his last.

He flashed a confident smile back at her. "Don't worry, with all the cretes on our side, there's not likely to be much of a fight. Not like the last time we were here."

This gave Kyrin some comfort. Most of the losses would be on the side of the Arcacians, and they had brought it upon themselves with their refusal to surrender.

When they reached Gem and Ivoris, Rayad waited there with his own dragon. He wasn't as heavily armored as most of the men who planned to fight today, though he did wear a leather cuirass like Kyrin.

Jace greeted him and drew Kyrin closer. "Rayad is going with us and will wait with you in the tunnel so you won't have to be alone."

Warmth spread through Kyrin's chest and eased her anxiety. She'd been trying not to think about sitting alone in the tunnel beneath Samara's border wall while Jace and the others went into battle, but apparently, he had. And, as always, he'd made it his priority to make sure she was all right. She reached for his hand and squeezed it, thanking him before turning to Rayad to offer him thanks as well.

The three of them mounted their dragons and took off, heading east toward the mountains, out of enemy sight before angling south. The rolling hills and sunken valleys of the Graer Mountain foothills passed below them, void of life until they neared Samara's border. Coming up over a large crest, they found a familiar hidden valley full of canvas tents. Giants and ryriks milled about the area, but many stopped to look up as Kyrin, Jace, and Rayad landed at the edge of camp. Kyrin scanned the two armies as they dismounted. Everyone looked outfitted and prepared for battle, just waiting for the word to advance.

On the way to Prince Haedrin's command tent, which sat between the two armies, a familiar figure waved to them, and they met up with Saul. The ryrik greeted them kindly, and he and Jace shook hands. It had been a year since they had first met him in Dorland, changing everything they knew about ryriks. Because of this man, Jace had finally been able to fully accept his mixed blood, and Kyrin would always be grateful for his friendship.

Saul glanced back in the direction they had come. "I take it they didn't surrender the fortress."

Jace shook his head, and they continued toward the command tent, passing several other ryriks along the way. Though the army Saul had gathered over the winter came from many peaceful ryrik villages scattered across southern Dorland, they elected him as their leader in this fight. Kyrin still found the sight of so many ryriks a bit intimidating, but she thanked Elôm they were on their side and willing to help in the fight against Davira.

The four of them entered the tent that was twice the size of the one Balen and Daniel used. A few giants stood around the table inside, including Jorvik, who they had helped defend Dorland last summer in a battle that had nearly taken Jace's life. His two brothers, Halvar and Levi, must be around somewhere. As tall as Jorvik and other giants were, none quite reached Prince Haedrin's height. Standing almost ten feet tall, he loomed over Kyrin and Jace. His practical yet expertly crafted silver plate mail glinted even in the shadows of the tent. A burgundy cape pinned at his shoulder and trimmed with black bear fur contrasted against it and his dark blond hair and beard. He looked fierce enough to take out a large force of enemy troops all by himself. Unlike many giants, he wasn't prone to turning a blind eye when there was trouble. Dorland would have remained stubbornly passive in this war if not for him.

Jace stepped forward to address the prince, and Kyrin's heart swelled once again to see him step out of his comfort zone to help secure their victory.

"The Arcacians refuse to parley. We have a little less than two hours to get into position before King Balen and Prince Daniel begin their attack."

Prince Haedrin didn't seem surprised or particularly disappointed. After all this time, they were probably itching for a fight, especially since they'd arrived too late to help at the ford last summer. He ordered the giants to prepare to march and told Kyrin and Jace they'd meet them at the cave.

Everyone departed the tent. Haedrin and Saul went their separate ways, shouting orders, and Kyrin walked with Jace and Rayad to the yawning black opening in the rocky hillside on the western side of the valley. They stopped at the mouth of the cave, and Kyrin peered into the inky darkness beyond. She drew a deep breath of fresh air into her lungs. The air would become increasingly stale once they reached the tunnel underneath the border wall. Best to take in the clean air while she still could.

Jace's hand slipped into hers. "Will you be all right?"

She turned away from the cave to face him. "Yes. Better than last time, I think. At least I know what to expect."

Claustrophobia would surely do its best to take hold, but she knew the path this time. The first time through had seemed like an endless maze they could become trapped in forever.

Jace squeezed her hand and rubbed his thumb over her knuckles. "Remember, I'm right here, and Rayad will be when I'm not."

She smiled up at him and then lifted herself on her toes to give him a quick kiss.

He lifted one brow in a wry look. "I thought you needed a clear head."

She shrugged. "Maybe it'll help with the nerves."

"In that case…" He bent and gave her another kiss, slightly longer this time.

KADEN STRODE DOWN his line of dragon riders, checking that everyone was present and prepared. They would receive their call to battle any minute now. Talas waited at the end of the line. Here, Kaden mounted Exsis and adjusted the stirrups before looking ahead to Stonehelm. Black firedrakes perched on the walls, waiting for their attack. He counted about three dozen that he could see, though Glynn had estimated about twice that. Even so, it hardly matched the size of their army of dragon riders. This wouldn't take long.

Talas leaned casually on the grab bar of his saddle. "Doesn't seem like a very fair fight."

Kaden squinted at the firedrakes. "I don't know why they won't just surrender."

"Stubborn pride. Either that or they'd rather face us than Davira."

It wouldn't surprise Kaden to find they were afraid of Davira's wrath. Even before her father had died, she'd been crazy. He still shuddered to remember the one and only time he'd ever interacted with her down in the dungeon of Auréa Palace. "I met her once. She tried to seduce me into giving up Sam."

Talas snorted. "I imagine that ended badly. I'm sure she's not used to being told no."

"I was immediately thrown into the prison wagon that took me to Landale. I don't recommend it as a mode of transportation, especially when you've been beaten beforehand."

"If he's still here, maybe we'll capture Richard this time and be able to return the favor."

That would undoubtedly make today's impending victory sweeter. Kaden rubbed the white scar partially encircling one of his fingers—a physical reminder of when Richard had planned to cut him into little pieces to force Kyrin to give herself up. He also had a faint scar on his cheek from Richard threatening to take his eye. He touched the dagger attached to his belt. Richard's dagger. Warin had taken it from him when they'd rescued Kaden, Kyrin, and Trev from the man's clutches. After hearing what Richard had done, Warin thought it fitting for Kaden to have it. It would be tempting to use it on Richard when they finally captured him.

Kaden focused on the army of crete dragon riders ahead of them. Commotion amongst their ranks told him they were getting ready to take off. He looked over at his group of men and raised his voice so they could all hear him.

"Remember, keep close to your partners and watch each other's backs. If we all work together, we should have little trouble." And, Elôm willing, they wouldn't lose anyone.

A few moments later, the first of the crete dragon riders took to the air. With a command, Kaden, Talas, and the others followed suit. The sky filled with hundreds of dragons and their riders. The firedrakes launched off the border wall a moment later.

The two mismatched armies sailed toward each other. When the distance closed, the first line of dragon riders released their fire in a shimmering orange wall of heat. The firedrakes shrieked but didn't even get a chance to retaliate as a second line of dragons met them.

This wouldn't take long at all.

Though faint, the piercing shrieks of firedrakes reached the underground tunnel at the base of Samara's wall. Surrounded by flickering torchlight, Jace turned to Kyrin and the line of ryriks and giants stretched far down the tunnel.

"The attack has started. It's time to move."

He and Saul slowly opened the hidden doorway that led into the storerooms underneath the fortress of Stonehelm. Jace scanned the room for any Arcacian soldiers, but it was dark and empty, save for supplies. He motioned Saul and the others to pass through. As the two armies filed into the storeroom, he turned to Kyrin.

She looked him over as if making sure his armor was all in place and adequate to protect him before meeting his gaze. "Be careful."

Though she did rather well hiding it, he caught the tension lacing her voice. He stepped closer and rested his hands on her shoulders. "I will." He drew her near and kissed her forehead. "I'll come for you as soon as it's safe."

He forced himself to turn away and shared a look with Rayad, who nodded in a silent promise to watch over her. They would be safe down here in the tunnel.

Once everyone had gathered in the storeroom—a tight fit for the men Saul and Haedrin had chosen to accompany them— Jace closed the door to conceal the entrance to the tunnel and Kyrin's hiding place. Now that they were inside, firedrake roars and men shouting echoed more clearly above them. Jace turned and motioned to Saul and Prince Haedrin. They knew what to do. Saul took the lead and led the ryriks up the stairs first. Jace followed. Their job would be to work through the fortress to take control while Haedrin and the other giants secured and opened the gate for their army outside. If all went according to plan, they would have the fortress under their control within an hour.

They took the staircase swiftly but silently. No one met them at the top. Most of the Arcacian soldiers were likely outside preparing for battle. They spread out in groups, Jace joining Saul to search the fortress. Everything lay still and quiet inside, each room they came to holding nothing save for the Arcacians' personal effects.

Jace was beginning to think the fortress was empty when he caught a glimpse of movement down a short hall. He turned quickly and froze. Richard stood just a few yards away. Jace's shoulder radiated with phantom pain at the memories of what this man had done to him in the dungeon at Auréa. He tightened his grip around the hilt of his sword. Taking Richard captive would be a significant advantage to their army. According to Daniel, Richard was Davira's closest ally and confidant. It would be a severe blow to her to lose him.

They glared at each other. Jace lifted his sword and prepared to engage, but then Richard spun around and ran. Jace scowled. Coward. He wasn't so tough when he didn't have his opponent chained and kneeling defenseless in front of him. Jace sprinted after him. Footsteps echoed as others followed, but Jace remained focused on Richard, trying not to lose him in the shadowed fortress halls. He didn't remember the layout of Stonehelm nearly as well as he would have liked.

Around a sharp corner, a door burst open. Richard dashed out into the sunlight of the outdoors, and Jace charged after him. Behind the fortress, a group of Arcacian soldiers gathered, but none were close enough to worry about just yet. Not when Richard headed straight toward a waiting dragon. Jace pushed for more speed. He couldn't let Richard get away.

However, he skidded to a halt when Richard mounted the animal. It spun around with a menacing roar that produced a blast of heat. Jace held his arm up to shield himself and was buffeted by air and stirred up dust from the dragon's wings. For one heart-stopping moment, he thought fire would follow, but when he looked up, the dragon flew out of the courtyard. Jace gritted his teeth. If only he had his bow. He hadn't anticipated needing it in the close quarters of the fortress. He could do nothing to stop Richard from disappearing over the wall and into the safety of Arcacia.

Jace didn't have much time to experience the sting of disappointment. The soldiers closed in, and he had to turn to fight. Saul and the other ryriks who had followed joined him. Clashing swords rang out and echoed on the stone walls surrounding them. The sound alerted other soldiers, who rushed around from both sides of the fortress. Jace and the others would have quickly become outnumbered, but heavy footsteps brought nearly half of Prince Haedrin's army around to their rescue. The Arcacians didn't seem to know how to respond to the sight of the towering men, and most threw down their swords in surrender without even lifting them to fight.

Kyrin sat on the hard step near the secret door and leaned against the wall. The torch sputtered here and there but would hopefully keep burning for a while yet. It was their last one. She breathed a deep, measured breath. Sitting here, enclosed by stone and surrounded by only a small circle of light, reminded her a little too much of Auréa's dungeon. The cold dampness of the tunnel sent a shiver across her skin, and she rubbed the goosebumps on her arms.

Rayad stepped to the door and appeared to be listening before looking down at her. "I'm sure it won't be much longer. I don't hear fighting anymore."

That should comfort Kyrin, but she wouldn't completely relax until Jace returned. She drew a breath to steady her nerves and watched Rayad step back to lean against the opposite wall. "Jace has really stepped up the past couple of weeks."

Rayad cast her a smile that revealed his own pride in Jace. "He just needed someone to inspire him to be everything he could be. You've been that person since the moment you arrived at camp."

Memories flooded her mind of those early days. Her heart still pained to remember how deeply Jace had suffered back then, but there were many moments she cherished. "I still can't believe he let me go hunting with him the first time I asked."

"Neither can I."

They both laughed quietly and reminisced.

After a moment, Kyrin let a slow sigh seep out. "We've been through so much. There have been a lot of good times, but I want so much for us to know what it's like to just live and build a real home together."

"You will."

She latched onto the certainty in his voice. Only Elôm could guarantee such a future, but Rayad's confidence dispelled some of her worries.

The sudden grinding of rock and squeak of hinges propelled Kyrin to her feet. She reached for her staff just in case. The hidden door creaked open, and torchlight lit up Jace's face. All at once, Kyrin breathed easier than she had all day. She scrambled up the couple of steps between them and gave him a tight embrace before pulling back.

"How did it go?" She looked him over but didn't find any apparent injuries.

"The fortress is ours, and casualties are minimal as far as I could tell." His brows furrowed, sending a twinge through Kyrin's stomach. "I couldn't stop Richard from escaping."

Kyrin rested her hand over her middle, the discomfort fading. If that was the worst that today brought, she was happy. "At least you're safe, and we had an easy victory."

Jace murmured his agreement, though he'd probably stew over Richard's escape for a while.

Rayad grabbed the torch, and they closed up the no-longer-secret tunnel. No doubt Balen would have to figure out how to better secure it from now on. Perhaps even block the entrance entirely. Jace took Kyrin's hand, and she leaned close to him as they followed the stairs up out of the storeroom.

The fortress buzzed with activity as Samaran soldiers and their allies swept through to search for hostiles and marched groups of captive Arcacian soldiers through the halls. Seeing the familiar surroundings and bustle of activity brought many memories back to Kyrin, yet the atmosphere was entirely different. They were the victors this time.

Outside, they stopped in the courtyard where their diverse army milled about and prepared to set up camp just outside the fortress walls. She spotted Baron Thomas on his horse nearby. General Mason stood with him and seemed to be gathering soldiers—no doubt to go and secure Westing Castle, which lay about a mile west of the fortress.

When Jace gently tugged her hand, Kyrin turned to him. He wore a heart-melting little smile on his face.

"Remember the last time we stood here?"

Kyrin glanced around, and the memory returned immediately. This was almost exactly where they'd been standing when Jace first kissed her. The moment their feelings for each other had finally materialized. Of all her memories, it was one of her most cherished. She leaned closer to him and lowered her voice.

"Maybe you should remind me."

His smile deepened, and he reached up, cupping her face in his hands just as he had that day, and kissed her. She sighed as all the wonderful and surprise emotions of that first time flooded her mind.

JACE YAWNED AND SCRUBBED HIS hands over his face. The room Baron Thomas had offered them in Westing Castle was still dim; the sun not yet risen above the horizon. He rolled over and propped himself up on his elbow to look at Kyrin. Her peaceful, relaxed expression and slow breaths indicated a deep sleep. Smiling, he just stared at her for a long moment. He resisted the urge to hook his arm around her to pull her closer. Best to let her sleep after all the activity yesterday.

Instead, he slipped out from under the warm covers and got dressed. Kyrin didn't even stir as he let himself out of their room. She'd done an admirable job remaining calm while acting as a guide through the caves, but it had still drained her. By evening, she'd been quieter than usual and fell asleep quickly when they'd retired.

The hall was shadowed and silent. Having learned their lesson in Amberin, soldiers stood guard at either end. While it went against every instinct buried deep inside him to leave Kyrin alone, he knew he had to do better at trusting both Elôm and those around them. He glanced toward the sitting room a couple doors down. Memories seemed to drift from the open doorway. He had spent some of the lowest moments of his life in that room.

Moments he hadn't expected to survive. He whispered a silent thanks to Elôm for bringing him through it.

Though the castle seemed sound asleep upstairs, servants already bustled about their morning chores downstairs. Like at Darham Palace, there was a new life and excitement to the place. No one paid him much attention as he passed through the halls and outside. In the courtyard, the guards let him through the gate into the village. More signs of life greeted him. Doors opened and shut quietly on houses, and cows mooed in anticipation of milking. Though a large village, it wasn't as stifling as a city. Jace could get used to a life like this. He could see himself living here near Westing with Kyrin if Arcacia couldn't be won.

Just beyond the village, the tents housing their armies stretched into the open meadowland between here and Stonehelm. He arrived at the large field containing the dragons from the Landale riders. The rest of the dragons from the crete army occupied the area to the south at the forest's edge where their riders had hammocks dotting the trees. From here, they looked like some sort of giant, cream-colored birds roosting in the branches. He still shuddered at the thought of sleeping so high off the ground with nothing more than some canvas to keep one from falling to a likely death. Thank Elôm he hadn't been born a crete. He was more than happy to remain on solid ground unless, of course, he was with Gem. She was the only dragon he fully trusted.

Shaking off thoughts of heights, Jace headed in the direction of the forest. The crete army already buzzed with activity. Jace hadn't met a crete yet who didn't rise well before the sun. He nodded in greeting as he passed by those on the edges of their camp. Not all of them were particularly friendly, but at least they were united in their goals.

He breathed a deep breath of cool air when he passed through the first trees. The forest would always feel more like home to him than anywhere else. The open meadowlands of Samara and southern Dorland always left him a little anxious inside. Though he no longer used it as a hiding place from the world, the forest would always be where he found the most comfort.

Several yards in, he paused and looked around. The last time he'd visited here had been at his lowest. And he'd been stupid enough to wander off unarmed. He'd never had a chance when Falcor found him and took him captive to Valcré. He touched the hilt of his sword hanging from his belt now. He'd never make that mistake again. However, Elôm used such an error to change his life and transform him into someone he never dreamed he could be.

"Thank You, Lord."

The man he'd been then could never be a good husband to Kyrin now.

With her face in mind again, he scanned the forest floor and found what he sought amongst the springtime greenery—the pure white petals of trilliums. He smiled and bent to pick them.

Once he had a fistful of the tri-petal flowers, he hiked back to the castle. By now, the sun had climbed higher, and the village was alive with people on their way from one place to another. Everyone seemed to have a mission this morning.

Back inside, he let himself into the bedroom and closed the door. Kyrin still slept, though she stirred when he approached the bed. He moved around to her side, and her eyes blinked open.

"Good morning. I have something for you." He held the trilliums out to her, smiling at the way the sleepiness cleared and her eyes widened.

"Jace!" She pushed herself up and reached for the bouquet. He caught the glitter of moisture in her eyes and the waver in her voice. "They're beautiful. Thank you."

Jace knew the emotion was about far more than just him bringing her flowers. He took a seat on the edge of the bed and put his hand on her arm, rubbing his thumb over the soft skin where the trillium tattoo that honored her father was. "You're welcome."

He leaned in to kiss her and lifted his hand to bury it in her sleep-tousled hair. The rest of Westing might be up and tackling the day, but he wasn't ready to give up this time alone with his wife just yet.

Daniel straightened his jerkin for probably the dozenth time on his way to Westing Castle's meeting hall. How did he still feel so unfit for this position? He looked over at Elanor, who walked beside him. "Is it absurd that I still get nervous every time I attend a meeting like this?"

"No. It only means that you're human and understand the gravity of your position. It's better than arrogance."

That was true, but a little more surety wouldn't be unwelcome. "Still, I wish I had more confidence about this particular meeting. I know we'll have to decide whether to march into Arcacia or make Samara our permanent refuge. As much as I want to stop Davira, I know it won't be easy and will cost a significant amount of lives to achieve. I'm not sure what option I should push for."

"It is a difficult decision. Lives will be lost either way."

The weight of it pressed down on him, almost making it difficult to breathe. Either they fought and died to liberate Arcacia, or they left it to Davira's tyranny, in which case believers and other innocent lives would continue to be lost. If only Elôm could verbally tell him which path to choose.

They paused at the door to the meeting room, and Daniel turned to face her. Aric and Elian halted a few yards back, both pretending they weren't paying attention to the conversation. Ignoring them, Daniel looked down at Elanor.

"Will you still have me if it turns out I won't be king?"

Her smile was enough to soothe some of his nerves. "I'd still have you if you were a penniless beggar."

"Well, if we stay here in Samara, that's practically what I'll be. I'll have nothing but a very worthless title of Prince to my name."

She circled her arms around his neck, not caring at all that Aric and Elian were close by. "We'll have each other's love. That's worth a lot more than titles."

She then leaned in for a kiss, and he grinned against her lips. He was a very rich man when she put it that way.

The kiss was painfully brief, but he did have a meeting to attend. Before releasing him, she looked him in the eyes.

"Whatever decision is made, just remember Arcacia's future doesn't rest solely on your shoulders. It rests in Elôm's hands."

"Thank you for reminding me." He placed a quick kiss to the tip of her nose, drawing a laugh, and then turned to the meeting hall. He thought of Elanor's words as he stepped inside with Aric. *This is in Your hands, Elôm. Forgive me when I lose sight of that in my insecurities. Help me to remember I am Your servant, and guide me to make decisions that follow Your will.*

If only his father had sought Elôm and His guidance. The regret and sadness of knowing his father had died with his back turned to Elôm's love still stung.

A wide table stood in the center of the room, a bronze chandelier overhanging it. The tapestries adorning the wood-paneled walls appeared to depict various battles and victories from

Samara's far-distant past. Would their achievements at Amberin and Stonehelm someday find their way among them?

Conversation filled the room from all of the high-ranking military commanders and leaders. Daniel nodded to Marcus in greeting and joined King Balen and Prince Haedrin near the table. Their talk revolved around hunting, belying the gravity of the upcoming conversation, but the mood shifted once everyone was present and gathered around the table. All attention focused on Balen.

"Samara is back under our control. I've sent men out to gather our disbanded army and make sure Davira doesn't have any other footholds here in the country. I'm confident we'll have no more conflicts. We've had this victory, but now we must decide how to proceed. As I have said in the past, if Arcacia remains under tyranny, all those who are persecuted are welcome to seek refuge here in Samara."

The brief silence that followed settled heavily on Daniel because everyone looked to him now, waiting to see if he would ask them all to march into Arcacia with him. With another quick prayer and a fortifying breath, he straightened his shoulders. "I know for the past many years, both my father and sister have terrorized not only their own people but all of yours as well. If they'd had their way, they would've pressed forward to subject all of Ilyon under their rule. I'm sure my sister still aims for that end."

He paused, considering his conversation with Elanor. He realized now that the decision that lay before them really wasn't up to him. "As King Balen has said, we've had a great victory here. If Samara, Dorland, and Arda maintain this alliance, I don't believe Davira could mount any successful invasion into your countries. Because Arcacia has brought so much suffering to everyone, I will not ask any of you to march with me to take back the country. While it's my deep desire to liberate Arcacia,

I leave it to you to make your own choices. I'll happily accept King Balen's offer for refuge on behalf of the faithful believers in Arcacia and willingly give up my throne if this is what everyone feels should be done."

Silence settled once again, though Daniel felt lighter this time. At least now, he didn't feel as though everyone would live or die by his choice alone. This was a far greater decision than one person could make. Everyone seemed to be weighing their options, but Balen didn't wait long to speak up.

"I don't believe leaving Davira on the throne is wise. There's no telling what she may do in the future. Given her history, she very well could try to invade one or more of our countries. We are indeed strong if we maintain our resolve and alliance, but Davira's influence is like a poison. Nothing good can come from her enforcing the worship of Aertus and Vilai. We never know how it might seep into our own countries. Not to mention how many countless people will continue to die under her reign. I, for one, don't feel it is right to stand by and allow such evil to thrive when we have the power to put an end to it."

Around the table, the different leaders were nodding, and Daniel found himself a bit surprised. It would've been easy to claim the victory they'd just won and settle back into their lives, especially when most of those fighting had no ties to Arcacia.

"I say we press forward and take Davira down." Prince Haedrin's powerful voice resonated in the spacious hall. "I know it won't be easy and that lives will be lost in the process, but I trust Elôm to bring us victory."

Both Captain Darq and General Torva vocalized their agreement, and gratefulness swelled inside Daniel at their willingness to help. He didn't care if he was ever king; he just wanted to see his country freed from the tyranny and slaughter his family had imposed upon it—to see his fellow brothers and sisters in Elôm freed from their persecution.

He cleared his throat to loosen the clog that had formed there. "Thank you."

Everyone, who had become such close friends to him after his exile from his own city, nodded at him. It didn't matter that they had no ties to Arcacia. They had ties to each other.

Across the table, General Torva crossed his arms. In a long, slate blue tunic, he looked more like a typical talcrin scholar today, though still formidable. Even without armor, the flash of his copper eyes held the cunning of a warrior. "The question now lies in how to accomplish such a victory."

Daniel had a very simple answer for that. "We must take Davira down. She is the key. I believe once she is taken out, the hostility she has built will crumble around her. She rules with fear. From what we've heard from our friends around the country, particularly in Valcré, the people have no love or respect for her. They're terrified to speak out or oppose her, but I fully believe the majority will embrace me as king once the danger is gone."

Haedrin's voice rang with eagerness as if he intended for them to accomplish it that very day. "Then our main objective is to take Valcré."

"The problem is how to get there." Marcus gestured to a large map of Arcacia laid out on the table. "By sea would be the most direct course, but we don't have nearly enough ships to bring our full force against it to mount a strong enough attack. Ships are also dangerously susceptible to attack by firedrakes now that Arcacia is aware of the talcrin presence here. In order to attack with everything we have, we would need to travel south by land. The one thing standing in our way is Fort Rhall."

He pointed to a fort drawn on the map. It was a recent addition compared to the rest of the landmarks. Daniel couldn't accuse his sister of being stupid. Insane, yes, but not stupid. The most direct route for any army to reach Arcacia's capital from the north was through a narrow strip of land between the Sinnai Mountains and the large forest surrounding Landale. The mountains were impassable by foot and the forest would significantly slow and hinder a large army. Though a small fort had always been maintained there in the past, word had it Davira had significantly enlarged and fortified it over the winter, thanks to the slave labor of believers and other fugitives imprisoned in the last three years. Conquering it would be no small feat. They would have to mount a successful siege against the fort before they could even approach Valcré.

Prince Haedrin bent over the map but didn't seem fazed. "Leave the fort to me. My men will build siege weapons that can be assembled once we reach the fort. We'll get through. And once we have the fort, we'll have a strong foothold within the country from which we can plan our next move."

His confidence seeped into Daniel. They were really going to do this.

General Mason leaned past Balen to see Haedrin. "We'll need time to finish gathering our army if we are to be at our full strength. That will give you time to construct the weapons. However, I believe we should march as soon as possible while we have the upper hand. Davira won't be sitting around idly. She no doubt expects us to attack. We don't want to give her any more time to prepare than we have to."

Everyone agreed, and Balen addressed Haedrin next.

"Have your men start construction on the weapons. Use whatever timber you need from the forest. We'll start gathering provisions. As soon as we are ready, we march."

KADEN ROLLED UP his sleeves and scooped a full bucket of water from the river just on the other side of Samara's border wall. Three days had passed since they'd made their plans to march on Arcacia. The giants were busy at work near the forest, building the siege weapons while they waited for the rest of Samara's troops to gather. There wasn't much to do until then. Since it was a warm day, Kaden and a bunch of the other riders had decided to bring the dragons down to the river and give their scales a good washing. Might as well invade Arcacia looking their best.

He dunked a large sponge into his bucket and plunked it down on Exsis's back. The dragon turned his head to see what he was doing and snorted a hot breath into Kaden's hair.

"Hey, knock it off." He smoothed his hair back into place. "You need this bath."

A layer of dust and grime had built up on the dragon's scales that dulled their color. By the time Kaden finished, they would glisten black and green. Exsis released a low grumble but let Kaden keep scrubbing.

While they worked, he and Talas discussed what the next few weeks might bring—and even farther into the future. At one point, the conversation somehow turned to the fact that neither of them had a girl.

Talas shot him a conspiratorial grin from where he worked on his dragon, Storm. "You know, Trenna is still very much single. Comparing crete to human years, you two are about the same age now."

Kaden snorted. "Still trying to rope me into officially being family?"

"Why not? I want you to be stuck with me as your brother for the rest of your life."

Kaden held up his wrist marked with the Landale Dragon Riders tattoo. "I think this pretty much ensures that."

Talas shrugged. "But in all seriousness, I think you two would work well together."

Kaden paused now. Maybe he wasn't so opposed to the idea. He had liked Trenna, though he'd never looked at her that way, considering how Michael had taken a shine to her. Maybe if they got to know each other better…

He shook his head. They had a long way to go before he could even think about relationships. "Yeah, well, before you start trying to play matchmaker between your sister and me, let's take down Davira first. And if we're on a hunt for a wife for me, then you need one too. What about Darq's cousin?"

Kaden wasn't sure any of his men *hadn't* noticed the female dragon rider in the crete army. Typical Darq family characteristics—deep, midnight blue eyes and jet-black hair—did make her rather stunning. He couldn't say he hadn't noticed her striking figure, especially in an attractive set of blue and black leather armor

Talas gave a semi-choked laugh. "Have you *seen* her father? Or her brothers? She has six of them and is the only girl. If I even look at her too long, I'll need the entirety of the Landale Riders to rescue me."

"Come on; surely with Darq backing you up, you've got a fair shot."

"I don't think even Darq has that much sway. Like you said, let's just focus on taking down Davira. It's much less complicated…and probably safer."

Kaden had to laugh. It wasn't often Talas's confidence was shaken.

They let the subject drop and focused on the dragons. It took a few buckets of fresh water to clean them from head to toe, but the result was worth it.

He turned to see if Talas had finished but found his friend peering off to the south. Kaden looked, too, scanning the terrain and horizon of Arcacia in the distance. At first, he saw nothing, but then he picked out something dark dotting the sky. Though they resembled birds in the distance, Kaden knew better. His heart crashed against his ribs.

"Everyone, back to the fortress!" Talas shouted. "Firedrakes!"

The other riders along the riverbank sprang into action, abandoning their buckets. Kaden scrambled onto Exsis. They all launched into the air, and several dragons, including Talas's, released warning cries. Once over the wall, a couple of the cretes dove toward Stonehelm to warn those inside, while everyone else flew straight toward their army encampment at the forest's edge.

Kaden's heart drummed his ribs. None of them had anticipated a surprise attack, and they certainly weren't prepared for it at the moment. He and his men had to get their dragons saddled. They swooped down and landed where the rest of the men gathered with questioning looks.

Exsis had barely landed before Kaden leaped off. "Firedrakes! Saddle up, now!"

The men leapt to obey. Kaden raced to his tent and grabbed Exsis's saddle. He threw it onto the dragon's back and worked on the straps as quickly as possible. Good thing he'd done this a hundred times by now. Exsis sensed his urgency and grumbled anxiously but stood perfectly still.

Once Kaden finished, he dashed back to his tent, tugged his leather breastplate, and buckled on his sword. That was all he had time for. In the distance, a roar thundered like an approaching storm. The hair rose on his arms. Something about that roar didn't sound right. He'd faced countless firedrakes in the last couple of years. This sounded deeper, more powerful, more menacing.

He swung up onto Exsis and settled in the saddle. The moment his riders were all in place, he commanded, "Everyone, with me!"

He nudged Exsis, and they took to the air. Most of the crete army had taken off by now, and dragons filled the sky. He looked ahead to the fortress just as a billowing orange blast of fire cascaded down on top of it. His gut twisted, and his mouth went dry at the sight of the creature it originated from. Though black and shaped like all the other firedrakes he had faced, this one was bigger. At least half again the size of a normal firedrake, dwarfing their dragons. He counted over a dozen of these huge firedrakes, followed by a good hundred or more regular ones. Just one of the larger monsters could take out an army with a single breath of fire. He glanced down at all the tents housing their men. Taking out their army was probably exactly what these monsters were sent here to do.

Guttural roars pierced even the solid walls of Westing Castle. Jace gripped Kyrin's hand and held her close. Servants rushed about in a near panic. It was impossible to tell what was happening outside, but Jace's mind far too easily created a disturbing scene of death and carnage. He could only pray their dragon riders could hold back the surprise attack.

Near the castle entrance, Balen's voice rang out above the chaos. "Get the villagers inside!"

The castle doors opened, and guards rushed out. They would need help directing everyone. Jace turned to Kyrin and grasped her shoulders. "Stay here."

Her eyes widened, and she gripped his arms as if to keep him there. Her mouth opened, no doubt to voice protest, yet she closed it just as quickly. Though the same fear that pounded in his chest still flashed in her eyes, she nodded and let her hands slip from his arms. That alone made it all the more difficult to leave her, but others needed help. He squeezed her shoulders, pressed a quick kiss to her forehead, and hurried toward the entrance. There, he met Holden, and they followed the guards.

Outside, screams joined with the sound of airborne battle. The air above Stonehelm writhed with the shapes of dragons and drakes, fire streaking the air. Though no attack had reached the defenseless village yet, it didn't stop the panicked villagers from filling the roads in a chaotic mass. The guards ahead of them had already gotten the attention of some of the people, directing them toward the open castle gates. Villagers streamed toward it, toting their children in their arms or guiding them by hand.

Jace and Holden wove their way through the mayhem to another street to guide more people to safety. Jace didn't know how many could fit inside the castle, but it was their only shelter should the drakes make it past their army and turn their destructive force on the village. He prayed it would not come to that. Even the castle might not stand long against a concentrated attack.

Guiding a young family toward the castle, he glanced back at the battle. Multiple shapes of dragons fell from the sky. His stomach jolted. Any one of those falling dragons could belong to one of their loved ones.

"Elôm, protect them."

"*Roven!*" Kaden yelled, but his voice seemed swallowed by the constant roars and shrieks around him.

Still, Exsis followed the command, pouring fire down on one of the giant firedrakes. Three of his men followed behind with their own attacks, but while they may have injured or killed the beast's rider, it seemed to do little damage to the monster itself. The scales were too thick. Without prolonged and concentrated streams of fire, which were impossible in this airborne battle, they would never burn through the beast's hide. Kaden shouted in frustration. If they could not use fire, what could they use? Already the beasts fought to reach their army. Only persistence and the sheer number of dragons kept them at bay, but they couldn't keep it up forever. They had to kill these monsters, or their army would be destroyed.

Kaden looked at his comrades embroiled in battle. Nearby, two dragons attacked a drake, working in tandem to target its wings. The beast thrashed and spewed fire, but they managed to injure the wings enough that the drake fell from the air.

With renewed determination, Kaden signaled Exsis, who gave a call Kaden's men would recognize. Not everyone would hear, but a few of Kaden's men turned their attention toward him. Leading the way, Kaden dove Exsis toward a drake, and his dragon latched onto the beast's wing, shredding the membrane with his claws and teeth. The other men and their dragons followed his example.

It took a long struggle and several attempts before the drake floundered and lost altitude, a brief victory. Too many dragons and riders fell for every one drake they eliminated from the battle.

Fire blasted over Kaden's head, hot sparks raining around him. He swerved around and soared higher above the attacking firedrake. Below, dragon bodies and far too few firedrakes littered the open plains. They couldn't survive like this, let alone win the battle. He fought to ignore the sinking feeling in his gut that this might not be a battle they could win. Curse Davira and her hybrid monsters.

A ray of hope came in the form of several pairs of crete riders flying up from the fortress with thick chains suspended between them. Kaden dodged a firedrake and watched as one team of riders flew toward a giant drake, catching it around the neck with the chain. Before it could maneuver away, they swooped back down, crossing over the drake's back. The chain went taut, and they yanked it downward toward the wall. It struggled against the chain, but they managed to bring it down where several other dragons swooped in to kill the beast.

The battle raged on, men, dragons, and drakes raining down around them. Even the struggle Kaden had faced in Dorland didn't seem quite as dire as this one. He fought to focus on one opponent at a time, but ever in the back of his mind was the fact their entire existence rested on this battle. If they didn't win here, it would be all over. The drakes would ravage their armies, and no one would be left to fight. Davira would sweep across Ilyon with her massive army and giant drakes until none could oppose her.

He hardened his resolve. He and the other riders would not let that happen. They'd faced impossible odds before and won. Elôm willing, they could do it again.

He fought on, trying to block out the death and sense of loss when a couple of his men went down just ahead of him. He couldn't let their sacrifices be in vain.

By now, Exsis was almost anticipating his moves and extended his claws as they dove toward a firedrake's wing. Movement flashed at the corner of Kaden's eye. A smaller drake flew at them from the side. Kaden swerved, but the bigger drake did too. Its wing slammed into Exsis. The impact threw Kaden to the side and nearly from the saddle. He seized the grab bar and scrambled to right himself, and a terrible shriek exploded from Exsis. The firedrake had clamped its jaws over his neck and one of his wings.

Kaden reached for his sword, but the drake shook Exsis in its mouth. Kaden lurched from one side of the saddle to the other, only keeping his grip by some miracle. With a violent toss, the drake released Exsis. Kaden's head slammed against the saddle, and then he was falling. Everything rushed around him in a dark blur, sucking the air from his lungs. His head was numb and hazy. Something wrapped around him, slowing his descent, but not by much. He blinked hard to clear his vision and found the ground still racing toward him.

At the last moment, Exsis rolled so he hit the ground first. Kaden went flying and hit a second later, his body slamming the packed dirt. It knocked what little breath was left from his lungs, leaving him gasping and dazed. His head pounded, and he couldn't move for a second. Dragging air into his chest that seemed determined to repel it, he pushed himself to his hands and knees. His ears rang, and the battle seemed far away. He shook his head, and the sensation slowly faded. As his senses normalized, dread rushed in to replace the air he needed.

"Exsis," he choked.

He shoved to his feet, falling once to his knees before stumbling toward his dragon. Pain shot through his hip, and his knee throbbed, nearly giving out on him, but it all faded when he reached his dragon's side. Blood streamed from gaping wounds in the dragon's neck, and his wing was bent at an unnatural angle. His sides heaved with labored breaths.

Kaden fell to his knees and rested his hand on Exsis's neck. His throat squeezed in on itself as the dragon looked at him and groaned.

"I'm sorry." His voice rasped. He pulled Exsis's head into his lap, and his cheeks burned with tears. There was nothing he could do. As much as the desperate pounding of his heart screamed for action, he didn't have the power to do a single thing for this noble animal he had bonded with and dreamed of for so long. This animal that had just saved his life by giving his own.

"Thank you." Kaden's chest heaved along with his dragon's. He didn't want to say goodbye. Gritting his teeth, he rested his forehead against Exsis's cheek. The dragon took two more breaths before he went still.

Kaden didn't move for a long moment, frozen in time and grief. It shouldn't have to end like this. Exsis hadn't just been some animal; he'd been a companion, a friend. They had fought too many battles together. Still had battles left to fight. Kaden needed him.

Out of nowhere, firm hands snatched his arms. He jerked upright and struggled to yank away, but they held fast. He fought, catching a glimpse of Arcacian gold and black. Pain shot through his battered body, stealing his strength, and they wrestled him face-first to the ground, where they bound his wrists.

JACE HELD KYRIN tightly to him, huddled in the great hall of the castle with nearly the entire village of Westing. Outside, the roars of firedrakes and dragons seemed distant, but with every passing second, Jace feared one of the beasts would come crashing down on the castle and crush them under debris. The battle raged on and on. If only he could see what was happening, but he wouldn't leave Kyrin again. If it was their time to die here, he would remain at her side until the end.

Her arm tightened around his waist. He looked down at her face, which was nearly white, her lips moving in silent prayer. Jace sent up his own string of fervent prayers. It was the only form of battle he could do against the attack outside. He looked around the hall for the hundredth time. Balen and Daniel waited nearby, as powerless as he was. Daniel held Elanor much like Jace was holding Kyrin. For once, it didn't bother him. Others of their family and friends were present, but not everyone. He prayed those not fighting in their dragon force had found shelter somewhere from the attack.

He couldn't tell how much time passed—a half an hour, an hour, more—but it felt like an eternity before the sounds of battle quieted. In their place, a deafening silence settled inside the castle. No one dared move for a long moment. Did the silence mean they had won or lost? What would they find once they opened the doors? Jace held on to Kyrin, willing himself not to consider what might await them if their dragon riders had failed.

The charged silence gave way to rustling and murmuring. Villagers looked around at each other as if unable to believe they were still alive. Many turned to Balen at first, but then a guard entered the room, and everyone's attention shifted.

"The battle is over. The drakes fled back into Arcacia."

Jace released a long breath, mutual sighs of relief echoing all around him. However, just because they had won didn't mean they had not suffered loss. Just how much was the question.

Kyrin shifted in his grasp. "We have to find Kaden. And Talas and the others."

He took her hand. He would have preferred her to remain here while he checked the carnage, but how could he make her wait for news after what they had endured already? The unknown would eat away at her. Better to face it together.

The two of them worked their way through the crowd of villagers slowly filing out of the castle and back into the village. Once outside, they looked toward Stonehelm. While the fortress appeared untouched, dark bodies of dragons, firedrakes, and men littered the ground between it and the village. Jace's stomach recoiled at the sight. So many dead. Any one of them could be Kaden.

He slowed their progress, reconsidering. "Maybe you should wait here."

Kyrin's lips pinched, her eyes wide and watery. "I can't."

So they pressed on through the village. Rayad and Holden joined them from the crowd. They hurried to the fields at the outskirts where their dragons usually rested, but Gem, Ivoris, and the others were nowhere to be seen. No doubt they had taken to the sky to help once the fighting began. With no other choice, they hurried forward on foot.

Jace scanned the tents housing their army. It didn't appear they had taken any damage, which meant their ground army was still intact, thank Elôm. But such knowledge was little comfort as they passed the first of the fallen dragons. Kyrin peered at each one, and Jace could hear how her breathing turned ragged. He prayed with everything in him that none of them would be Exsis or any other dragon belonging to their friends. He held her close and tried to shield her from seeing the worst injuries, but that grew more and more difficult as they drew near the fortress.

Ahead, the surviving dragons and their riders gathered near Stonehelm's entrance. At least two-thirds of their force appeared to have survived, but that didn't erase how many were lost. There must be nearly a hundred, perhaps more, fallen dragons around them.

The moment they reached the dragon riders, Kyrin called out Kaden's name. Jace scanned the crowd for anyone taller than the army of cretes. He spotted a few Landale men, but not Kaden, and he tried to ignore the churning in his gut. Kaden had survived worse. Surely, for Kyrin's sake, he had survived this attack. *Please, Elôm.*

No one responded to Kyrin's call. Jace traded looks with Rayad and Holden, his own desperation rising up to clog his throat. He couldn't watch Kyrin lose another brother, especially not Kaden. It would destroy her.

She called out again, her voice rising to an unfamiliar pitch. This time, Talas broke through the crowd, and she rushed to meet him. "Where's Kaden?"

Talas's strained expression didn't offer any comfort. "I don't know. I haven't seen him since early in the battle."

Kyrin gripped her middle like she was about to be sick, her face ashen. Jace put his hand to her back to steady her.

"I'm sure he's around here somewhere." Talas's voice was a bit too light and forced at the end. "I'll look with you."

Unfortunately, the only place they had to look was amongst the fallen dragons. They all turned back to the body-strewn fields to search the tall grass. Though Jace had seen his share of battle and the aftermath, burned flesh and twisted limbs soured his stomach. Kyrin should not have such grisly sights seared into her memory. He tried to talk her into waiting at the fortress, but she wouldn't go. Not until they found Kaden. He couldn't blame her.

Most of the riders on the ground were dead, but some had survived. Cretes carried stretchers with the wounded to the fortress, while others helped their injured comrades limp along. Jace clung to the hope that even if Kaden had gone down, he had survived, somehow, just like these cretes.

It took an hour to scour the area, but they did not find any signs of Kaden or Exsis. They checked with the rest of their army once again, but no one had seen him, which meant they had to extend their search beyond Samara's border. According to Talas, more casualties lay beyond the wall.

They passed through the gate inside Stonehelm that led out toward the plains of Arcacia. The raised ground at the base of the wall gave them a disturbingly clear view of the carnage. Kyrin swiped her hands over her face as a couple of the tears she'd been fighting fell.

Jace put his arm around her. "We'll find him."

But the words probably brought little comfort. By now, they both knew the odds of finding Kaden alive were slim at best.

They trudged down the bank and crossed the river, where they split up to cover more ground—Jace, Kyrin, and Talas in one direction and Rayad and Holden in another. At every body they came to, Jace could hardly breathe for fear it would be Kaden. He tried to prepare himself for the moment. He would have to be strong for Kyrin, but the loss would hurt him too. Kaden was one of his oldest friends.

Sometime later, Talas halted ahead of them. His stiff posture flushed Jace's veins with ice and stabbed deep into his chest.

Talas's hoarse voice was barely audible. "It's Exsis."

Kyrin stood rooted where she was for a frozen moment before rushing forward. Jace hurried after her and reached her at the dragon's side. He grimaced at Exsis's still form and bloody wounds. If the dragon had sustained such damage, what about Kaden?

Tears streamed down Kyrin's cheeks now. She looked all around and called out Kaden's name, her voice breaking. Talas also shouted for Kaden, and Jace turned in a slow circle, searching. There. The dark mound of a body. His heart nearly stalled. *No.*

He slowly approached the figure in the grass. Already he could tell it was not a crete rider. How was he going to tell Kyrin? Tears burned his eyes. He reached the body, and the air gusted from his lungs. It wasn't Kaden. He hung his head, tremors passing through his legs, weakening them.

"Jace?" Kyrin's wobbly voice barely whispered behind him.

He turned around, witnessing the beginnings of sorrow about to crumple her face. "It's not him."

Her eyes closed, and her chest convulsed, rising and falling heavily. Jace approached Exsis again and searched the ground more thoroughly. Kaden could have fallen off anywhere, but the way the grass was trampled looked as if someone had walked around the dragon. A few feet away, he found a matted area about the size of a body. The crushed blades suggested something heavy had rested here. Either that or hit the ground with force. The trail through the grass led right to Exsis.

He hated potentially giving false hope, but he turned to Kyrin and Talas. "It looks like Kaden may have landed here and made his way to Exsis."

They rushed over to him and studied the signs for themselves.

"But where is he then?" Kyrin's voice wavered between hope and despair.

Jace shook his head and looked around again. Other trails wove through the grass, but they could have been from animals passing through. It was impossible to tell without footprints to identify.

A soldier yanked Kaden off the back of the massive firedrake, letting him fall hard to the rocky ground. Since they'd stripped him of his armor, he had nothing to cushion the impact. Pain speared through his leg and up his back into his skull. He bit back a groan and blinked, but blood seeped into and blurred his right eye. He must have gashed his forehead open when he'd hit it on his saddle during the fight.

Before he could even try to move, the soldier grabbed his arm and yanked him to his feet, nearly popping his arm out of the socket. Kaden shot him a glare, but the soldier just shoved him toward a grouping of small tents, bedrolls, and cold fire pits. Despite the way his senses had faded in and out during the flight, he was pretty sure they were somewhere a bit southeast of Stonehelm, hidden in a small, mountainous valley. Apparently, Davira's men hadn't retreated to Valcré like everyone thought.

Kaden looked to his right as a second soldier shoved another prisoner forward—Robbie. Three captive crete riders stumbled into view as well. While none appeared to have sustained any life-threatening injuries, one of the cretes limped badly, and another clearly had a broken arm. What their captors intended to do with them was anyone's guess. There weren't enough of them to make any big ransom demands or use as leverage.

The soldiers lined them up near a central tent and forced them to kneel. Kaden tried to resist, but his knee buckled, sending him to the ground with the rest. Situated at the end, he looked down the line. No one cowered, especially not the cretes, who looked as proud now as ever. Kaden traded a look with Robbie and gave him a firm nod. Kaden was still his captain, even as prisoners. It was his duty to encourage his men no matter the circumstances.

A few seconds later, a man ducked out of the tent. Kaden clenched his fists and strained against his bindings at the sight of Richard. If only they'd known he was so close all this time, they would've gone after him. Kaden thought for sure he would have flown straight for the safety and comfort of Valcré. He did look thoroughly put out by his current situation, which surely meant bad things for his prisoners.

He barely spared them a glance of disgust before turning to one of the soldiers. "This is it?"

"Most died when they fell. These were the only survivors we could find before we had to retreat."

Richard's expression soured even more. "It's not enough to be useful. Dispose of them."

Kaden's heart jumped into his throat as the soldier behind him reached for his arm and hauled him to his feet. In that same moment, Richard locked eyes with him. Recognition flared, and the man held up his hand.

"Wait."

Kaden drew himself to full height and scowled at the vile man. Richard approached him, his previous disinterest morphing into a cold satisfaction.

"Looks like you boys had a stroke of luck after all. This here is Kaden Altair."

If anyone reacted, Kaden didn't see it. He was too busy trying to burn a hole through Richard's skull with his eyes.

Unfortunately, he possessed no such ability.

Richard turned slightly to give the others a contemptuous

wave. "Tie them up and keep them under guard. I'll decide what to do with them later."

The soldiers led the other prisoners away. Kaden sent a quick, bolstering look to Robbie before Richard stepped back into his field of vision. Obviously, he wasn't through with him just yet.

Richard eyed him up and down as if measuring his worth and curled his lip. "Word has it you're a rebel captain now."

Kaden just mimicked his look of disgust.

"What are you and your army planning? Do you intend to invade Arcacia?"

Kaden snorted. "You're an even bigger fool than I thought if you really think you'll get any information out of me."

Richard plowed his fist into Kaden's ribs barely a second after the words left his mouth.

Kaden doubled over, crunching his teeth together to contain a wince. Drawing a hard breath, he straightened. "Haven't we done this once before? I don't recall you having any success then either."

He braced himself, but the next blow forced a groan from his chest. Even so, he would never give up anything. Richard could beat him to death, and he'd take everything he knew to the grave.

The sun neared the horizon, casting deep shadows over the courtyard of Stonehelm. Jace trudged across it and into the keep with Talas, Holden, and several of their other friends. They had thoroughly searched the area surrounding the fortress multiple times, checking every body, every thick patch of grass, but had turned up no sign of Kaden except for his fallen dragon.

He entered the main hall that had been set up as an infirmary just like the last time they had faced battle here. Kyrin stood across the room, helping with the wounded. Jace had insisted she do something to keep her busy while he and the others continued their search. He'd reasoned that, if Kaden was injured, someone would bring him here.

The moment she spotted Jace, hope flashed in her eyes, only to dim immediately when she saw Kaden wasn't with them. He walked over to her and put his hands on her shoulders.

"We didn't find anything."

She took a difficult breath, torchlight wavering in her unshed tears. "Why can't we find him? He can't have just disappeared. He could be lying out there injured."

This last bit was a desperate hope. The chances that Kaden was still alive were almost nothing. He would never say that, though. Deep down, he knew she was aware of it. He had to let her cling to hope for now. At least until they found a body. Then they would both have to come to terms with it.

Jace sighed and rubbed his eyes, feeling every minute of the long day and desperate search. "We talked to Darq on the way in. A few others are missing too. They're going to expand the search beyond the obvious battle area."

What else could they do? The missing riders had to be somewhere.

She looked past him, toward the door. "I should be out there."

Desperation thrummed in her voice.

Jace pulled her closer. "It's going to be dark soon. You won't be able to see well enough to search."

She gazed up at him, her tears about to overflow. In that moment, he watched the hope die from her eyes.

"He's gone, isn't he?"

She crumpled in his arms, sobbing against his chest.

KYRIN JUST STARED at the bedroom windows, her head resting on Jace's chest. Though it was a little after dawn, she hadn't slept all night. For the first couple of hours, she had hoped and prayed someone would come to joyously tell them Kaden had been found. But, in the darkest hours of the night, hope had faded once again.

Her body ached with weariness and loss. She couldn't even wrap her mind around losing Kaden. He had always been there. Always. Tears filled her eyes. A piece of her felt missing. She pulled her arm more tightly around Jace's chest as the pain swelled again. His hold on her tightened in response, and he rubbed his hand up and down her arm. She let a couple of mournful cries escape, too tired to hold them in. She wanted her brother back.

A teary half an hour later, Jace murmured, "Do you want to get up?"

Kyrin nodded against him. Lying there thinking about Kaden wasn't doing her any good. She wanted to know if the cretes, who had continued the search last night, had found any of their missing riders. At the same time, she was terrified of what news they bore. She sat up and bowed her head, her hair falling in her face. Pressure throbbed behind her eyes. Jace rubbed her back until she lifted her head again and drew a deep breath through her dry lips. It was a struggle to find the will even to move. She had borne so much loss in a couple of short years. In one way, she felt numb; in another, she wondered if she had any strength left to deal with it all.

When she looked over at Jace, she almost broke right there. His eyes were red-rimmed and tired. He'd tried to hide it during the night, but she knew he'd shed tears along with her. She'd heard it in his labored breaths and had noted every time he'd lifted his hand to wipe his face. Kaden was as much a brother to him as he was to her.

She reached for Jace's hand and squeezed it, hoping to offer even a small fraction of the comfort he so unfailingly provided her. He met her gaze in shared grief and weariness. No words could even come close to helping at this point, but Jace did squeeze her hand in return. Whatever happened, at least they still had each other.

They slipped out of bed and dressed quietly. Jace then held her close on the way downstairs, and Kyrin didn't know what she would have done without his strength.

In the main sitting room, they found most of their tight-knit group, including Talas. He was bent forward with his elbows resting on his knees. His long hair still fell in a tangled mess from the battle. He hadn't even taken time to clean up or change yet. He looked up when they entered, and his pained eyes stole her breath, as did the poorly concealed devastation on Marcus and Liam's faces. Their family had suffered so much.

Every sorrowful gaze she met cut deeper into her already aching heart. Barely holding back tears, her attention rested on Captain Darq. Emotion lurked in the crete's typically stoic expression. She licked her lips, forcing her voice past her swollen throat.

"Did you find anything last night?"

He shook his head. "We weren't able to locate any of the missing riders."

Kyrin squeezed her brows together, her thoughts sluggish. Nothing about this made any sense. "But how could they just disappear like that?"

Darq traded a look with Talas and a few of the other men. Silence stretched out far too long.

Kyrin's heart rate spiked. "Please, just tell me. I need to know."

Darq released a long breath. He was always so fierce and in control, but exhaustion and defeat broke through for once. "We fear they may have been…consumed by the firedrakes."

Nausea twisted Kyrin's stomach, flushing her limbs with ice. She was only vaguely aware of the hot wetness running down her face as horrifying images filled her mind.

Rough bark dug into Kaden's back through his shirt, and he twisted his wrists in an attempt to loosen the rope that strung his arms up to the tree limb overhead. The coarse fiber just bit deeper into his skin, further cutting off the circulation to his already numb fingers. He winced. Standing in this position all night did nothing to help his bruised ribs. Each breath reminded him of every fist blow he'd received yesterday. And he couldn't even try to wake up his legs with the rope bound around his ankles. It left him entirely exposed to any random attacks the vengeful soldiers wanted to throw at him.

Nearby, Robbie and the three cretes sat in a cluster with their backs together. The crete with the broken arm looked pale this morning. At least they could draw a little warmth from each other.

Kaden fought off a shiver. With the sun not quite risen over the mountains to the east, this rocky valley was chilly in the morning. Around camp, soldiers huddled around their campfires and prepared breakfast. None of the warmth reached Kaden, though the scent of food did. His stomach cramped and growled. No chance he'd eat any time soon, if ever again.

Struggling to ignore the tempting scent of frying meat, he looked over at the firedrakes resting at the edge of camp—the giant ones in particular. One of them had no doubt killed Exsis, and a fire burned inside him to destroy each and every one of them. This fire was the only thing that had kept him from dwelling too deeply on the loss of his dragon during the long hours of the night. Without a dragon, he wasn't even a dragon rider. His entire being rebelled at even the thought of having to replace Exsis.

Rocks crunched underfoot and snagged Kaden's attention. He wouldn't have to replace his dragon if he didn't somehow escape this current situation anyway. Richard strode toward them, a couple of his men in tow. Kaden stared defiantly at him. One uncomfortable night wouldn't make him any more willing to divulge information to the man.

Richard halted a few feet away. "As stubborn as ever, I see."

Kaden gave him a cool smirk. "That's what you get when you mix Altair and Veshiron blood."

One of the soldiers punched the air out of Kaden's lungs. He gasped and coughed, grinding his teeth together against the searing pain. He should just keep his mouth shut but couldn't help himself. "It's no wonder you lost Samara if that's the best your men can do."

Even though he anticipated it this time, the second blow tore a groan from his throat. It took him longer to catch his breath this time. He bit his tongue, forcing back any more goading remarks. For now, at least. He needed to recover first.

Unamused, Richard turned to the other prisoners and walked in a slow circle around them. When he reached the crete with the limp, he kicked the man's leg. The crete groaned and bared his teeth, more a snarl than a grimace. Hatred flashed in his eyes. Kaden had no doubt the crete would end Richard in a blink if he were free from his bindings. Cretes were like wildcats—quick, agile, deadly. Richard wouldn't get any further with them than he would with Kaden.

He made his way around to Robbie. Though Robbie glared up at him, Kaden caught a flicker of uncertainty. He was confident Robbie wouldn't talk, but Kaden would do whatever he could to protect him from Richard's torture.

"They don't rank high enough to know anything. I'm the only one with the information you want."

Richard stalked back over to Kaden and whipped out a dagger. In a blur, he had the blade pressed to Kaden's cheek just below his eye. Kaden sucked in a sharp breath, panic flaring from his chest, but he refused to flinch or even blink. He wouldn't give Richard the satisfaction.

"Why don't you start spilling some of that information?" Richard growled.

The man's eyes flashed with threats, but Kaden glared straight back at him. He leaned into the dagger just a little.

"Do what you want. I'm not afraid of you." The dagger threatened to slice skin, but all he had to do was think of Exsis and all the other dragons and riders killed in the attack. The anger and grief that still smoldered inside him burned away any trepidation. "Whatever you do to me, I'll never give you what you want."

Richard's jaw muscles tightened, a vein popping out on his temple. Kaden held his breath, using every ounce of strength not to pull back. This time, for sure, he would lose his eye.

"Lord Blaine!"

For a frozen moment, no one moved or even seemed to breathe other than the slight tremor Kaden felt in the blade of the dagger as Richard strangled the hilt. That vein bulged even more just before Richard whipped his head around to glare over his shoulder. The soldier gulped before his words burst out in a rush. "Some of our men are missing."

"What?" Richard snapped.

"I went to relieve one of the sentries, but he was gone. Upon further inspection, other men from camp are missing as well. About a dozen of them."

Richard's jaw ticked, and the point of the dagger dug into the skin just below Kaden's eye. Kaden gritted his teeth. Hopefully, Richard couldn't hear his heart thudding his ribs. A long moment later, Richard removed the dagger from his face and snapped it back into the sheath but speared Kaden with a promising look.

"We'll just see how strong you think you are."

He then stalked off after the soldier.

A huge breath gusted from Kaden's lungs, though he tried not to let too much relief show on his face in front of the remaining soldiers. And then he almost laughed. He may lose his eye yet, but once again, Elôm proved who was really in control.

Kyrin needed a moment alone. A moment to process and come to terms with the reality she wanted nothing more than to ignore. Tears blurred her vision as she retreated toward her and Jace's room, but at the bottom of the staircase, the full weight of the situation crashed in. Her legs wobbled, and she couldn't go on. Sinking down on the steps, she buried her head in her hands, and the tears gushed out. Waves of grief ripped through her, robbing the breath from her lungs, and she cried until she couldn't cry anymore.

When the tears had dried up, she just sat and stared at the floor. Her whole body ached as if fevered, and all she wanted to do was crawl into bed until the pain went away. She dragged in hard breaths, fighting to find her strength. She had always drawn so much from those around her, Kaden being one of the chief sources. Now he was gone. Despite the fact she thought she'd shed them all, tears overflowed once again, and she wept quietly over the loss of her twin.

Though she hadn't heard any footsteps, someone sat down beside her. She brushed her hair away from her puffy face with a trembling hand and looked up into warm and compassionate golden eyes.

"Sam," she whispered. He'd been her and Kaden's best friend for longer than anyone. Their one ally at Tarvin hall. If not for him, they never would have learned about Elôm and never would have become part of the Resistance.

"Remember when you and Kaden used to come to the library in the evenings back at Tarvin Hall?" His deep voice was soothing as always.

Kyrin nodded. The memories were as clear as if it had happened yesterday, yet it felt like a lifetime ago.

"You two were very different people then. You're a very strong and capable married woman now." He smiled gently, managing to draw a hint of a smile to Kyrin's lips. "And Kaden was rebellious, angry, and bent on defying everyone and everything around him."

She laughed a little now, though it was choked with tears. Oh, Kaden. He'd gotten into so much trouble back then. It was a wonder he hadn't been thrown right out of Tarvin Hall.

Sam rested a firm hand on her shoulder. "Kaden's life may have been cut short, but think of how far both of you have come. Kaden went out a hero—a captain of an army of dragon riders. I don't think either of you could've even imagined such a thing three years ago. I know it doesn't relieve the pain right now, but I hope someday it will comfort you to see the work Elôm did in his life and continues to do in yours."

Fresh tears welled up once more, and she bowed her head with a little nod. He was right. Kaden had accomplished so much in the last couple of years. At least his life had meant something important. He hadn't died the same frustrated and rebellious boy he had been.

Sam's arm wrapped around her, and Kyrin leaned into him. The talcrin had always had a way of making her feel safe.

Several minutes later, someone else entered the hall. Kyrin looked up to find Jace this time. His sorrowful gaze rested on her, and she could read in his expression the desire to be able to ease her pain. She rose to meet him, and he enveloped her in his arms, stroking her hair.

"Are you all right?" he murmured in her ear.

She nodded against him, not trusting her voice. She pulled away a moment later to wipe her eyes, and he reached up to gently brush back the hair sticking to her cheeks. He gave her one more look that said he was always there for her before glancing at Sam.

"Balen just received word. Apparently, some Arcacian soldiers deserted and gave themselves up at the fortress. They're being brought here."

Kyrin grasped on to this temporary distraction from her grief, and the three of them headed to the throne room. Most of their friends had already gathered there. A short time later, several Samaran soldiers led by General Mason escorted a group of fifteen unarmed and bound Arcacians into the room. Kyrin recoiled at the sight of their black and gold uniforms, too many painful memories flashing to mind. They were fortunate no one here would be bent on vengeance. She had a hard time not blaming them for what had happened to Kaden.

The group halted in front of Balen, their gazes darting between him and Daniel as if unsure which one would pronounce their fates. A familiar face popped out at Kyrin. Marcus must have seen him at the same time.

"Parker."

The man's gaze jumped to him, his expression lifting. "Captain."

Balen looked over at Marcus. "Do you know these men?"

Marcus eyed the group. "Parker was one of my lieutenants. Some of these are men I used to command."

Balen's attention swung back around to the soldiers. "What is your purpose here?"

Parker hesitated before drawing himself up, not arrogantly but as a soldier facing up to his actions. "We're done serving Davira. We served our emperor because it was our duty…even if we didn't always agree."

He cast a glance Kyrin's way, though not at her. She looked to her left, where Jace stood. Parker had been the one to whip him and Liam at Fort Rivor, though Kyrin never held him responsible. The General had given the command, and only Liam dared defy him that day.

Parker resumed eye contact with Balen. "His daughter is not someone we can serve. She's destroying our country. The throne belongs to Prince Daniel, the emperor's rightful heir, and we will serve him only." At this, he faced Daniel and dropped to one knee, bowing his head. The others followed his example. "We're at your service, Your Highness, though we understand if you choose not to trust us."

Kyrin scanned the faces of each and every man. She couldn't find any signs of malice or deceit, though she wouldn't just trust them.

For a long moment, silence hovered in the room. Daniel looked between the men and Balen. They were, after all, in Samara. Balen was the reigning king here, but he motioned to Daniel. "They are your citizens. It's your call."

Uncertainty crossed Daniel's face, though Kyrin was probably the only one who noticed. It disappeared when he took a step toward the kneeling men. "I will consider what you've said and discuss your future. Until then you will remain under guard."

Parker bowed his head. "Yes, Your Highness."

The men rose, and General Mason prepared to lead them out, but Parker spoke again.

"One thing you should know before we go. Lord Blaine has a small force encamped in the mountains southeast of here. That's where we came from. He has some of your dragon riders held captive."

A burst of shock and desperate hope exploded through Kyrin. She couldn't help herself. She rushed forward. "Who? Who are the dragon riders?"

Parker's attention swung to her. "Three cretes and two other men." He seemed to understand her desperation. "One is your brother."

Kyrin's knees nearly buckled. Her mind spun. "He's alive?"

"Yes, or at least he was when we left. I don't know what Lord Blaine intends to do with them. He was going to kill them all until he recognized your brother."

Kyrin stood in the midst of her whirlwind emotions, barely comprehending anything around her. She had spent all night believing Kaden was dead. All night mourning the loss and dealing with her grief. But Kaden was still alive. He was out there—still breathing, still fighting.

She became aware of a hand on her shoulder and blinked herself back into focus. The Samarans had led the Arcacians out of the throne room. She looked up at Jace, who stood beside her, and then spun to face Balen and Daniel with only one question burning in her mind.

"Can we save him?"

THEY'D BROUGHT PARKER back in for questioning to get all the details about Richard's camp and the number of men he had. It was still strange for Marcus to see him here after all this time—and as a deserter. He had served alongside Parker for over three years before they'd been promoted to captain and lieutenant. While he'd never been quite as close to Parker as he was to some of the people he knew now, they'd still been friends.

But whatever that meant going forward, the focus right now was Kaden and the other riders. Like everyone else, Marcus had truly believed Kaden was gone. He'd struggled through the grief of it last night. Struggled to maintain his poise as captain while breaking inside. He and Kaden had butt heads and faced their share of disagreements, but the past two years had brought them closer than they'd ever been. He'd already lost one brother. He wasn't about to lose another if there was even a slim chance he could do something about it. That made it difficult to maintain patience as they discussed their best course of action.

General Mason suggested a surprise attack before Richard realized the deserters had fled back to Samara, but Darq shook his head. "I wouldn't recommend mounting an attack against them. Even if it's a surprise attack, the first thing they'll do is kill their prisoners. Richard would see to that."

He was right. Richard was ruthless. One whiff of an attack and Marcus had no doubt he would cut the throats of his prisoners purely out of spite. General Torva, however, had different thoughts.

"Not to disregard the lives of Captain Altair and the other riders, but we should consider the opportunity this presents us. A chance to take them out and rob Davira of her right-hand man."

Across from Marcus, Kyrin stiffened. With her emotions so raw, it would be hard for her to understand that not everyone had a personal connection to Kaden and the other captives. General Torva was looking at the big picture. The military part of Marcus's brain knew he was right, though accepting it was just as hard for him. Kyrin probably shouldn't be here until they had formed a plan, but no one seemed to have the heart to ask her to leave.

"Are we sure we can't sneak the prisoners out at night?" At least Daniel didn't seem to like the idea of sacrificing Kaden and the others. "Then we'd have the opportunity to attack."

Marcus sighed. If only they could. "Richard's men will be on high alert, especially now that some have deserted. He'll make sure Kaden and the others are well-guarded."

General Torva shifted, and this time he did cast something of an apologetic look Kyrin's way before speaking. "If they are not dead already. Richard could have anticipated the deserters would bring us this information and chosen to dispose of the captives before we could respond."

Marcus watched Kyrin's eyes fill with moisture. She needed hope, not blunt facts, but so far no one had any to offer. As much as Marcus desired to drop everything and go after Kaden, this was in the hands of those above him.

It seemed Balen noticed the reaction as well. "We can't just assume they're dead. And I don't intend to sacrifice our men, even if it would mean taking Richard down. This may be war, but that's not who we are."

Marcus let out his breath slowly and sent him a grateful look. There was the hope both he and Kyrin needed.

Balen now turned to Daniel. "This is a decision you'll have to make, but I propose a prisoner exchange. General Veshiron for Kaden and the riders."

Kyrin couldn't stop pacing. In the end, everyone agreed to the prisoner exchange. She thanked Elôm for that, though her nerves were wrought so thin she was afraid they would break if she stopped moving long enough. Waiting might just destroy her. She needed to see Kaden's face—to see for herself he was alive and all right.

While the preparations were finalized, Jace waited with her. They had all more or less restricted her from going even though she had volunteered immediately. Jace had said he would go instead and promised to bring Kaden back to her. In spite of this, the danger of the exchange put her even more on edge.

"I think you should go talk to your grandfather."

Kyrin nearly stumbled, and her gaze shot to Jace. She wasn't sure she had heard him right. "What?"

"You haven't seen him at all since…last winter."

Coldness swept through Kyrin, the emotions of that time chilling her. To think of what they had lost a few months ago brought tears to her eyes in a heartbeat. Michael was gone, and she was far too close to losing Kaden too. She shook her head, but Jace pressed on.

"You may not get another chance to speak to him after this. I think…" he hesitated, but his eyes held an unwavering certainty, "I think you need to forgive him."

Every fragile and ragged piece of Kyrin instantly rebelled. How could Jace, of all people, even say that?

Her lips trembled. "It's his fault Michael is dead. He led the soldiers into our camp, our home. And what he did to you…" She swiped angrily at the tears that had made their way down her cheeks. "All I can see when I think of him is the pain you endured with your back torn up, and Michael—" She choked. "Michael lying there in the snow."

Jace stepped closer and put his arms around her. She collapsed into them, the memories searing her wounded heart. She could hardly breathe at the sight of him tied to the whipping post at Fort Rivor or the bloodstained snow where Michael lay and breathed his last breath. Jace let her cry as the memories ran their course and held her tight. When he did finally pull back, he rubbed his hands gently along her arms as he looked into her eyes.

"I know it's hard. And I would never even suggest it if I didn't think it would help you in the end. I think it will help bring closure. Holding onto your anger toward him won't help you heal."

Words of protest and argument burned on her tongue, but deep inside, she knew he was right. For a long moment, she said nothing, her sense of right and wrong warring with her emotions. Then, as she reached out to Elôm, she gave a surrendering nod. "All right."

It would be one of the hardest things she had to do, but she would do it.

Kyrin followed Marcus down the stone stairs to Stonehelm's underground containment cells. Jace had offered to go with her, but this was something she felt she needed to do on her own.

The history and pain between her and her grandfather were so deeply personal it had to be just the two of them.

She shivered, the air cooling and growing damp. Any place like this felt too akin to the dungeons underneath Auréa, but she forced that from her mind. She had to get this over with so they could get Kaden back. When they reached the cell block, her gaze locked on the cell at the far end of the hall, where their grandfather sat on a bench. Her heart drummed wildly. The last time she had seen his face was only moments after Michael had died. They stopped, and Kyrin closed her eyes against the uprising storm swirling inside her. *Please, Elôm, quell my anger toward him and give me the strength to forgive.*

Marcus turned to her and put a hand on her shoulder. "I'll wait here for you. Just call if you need me."

Kyrin looked at him. Though he handled his emotions far better than she was, she still caught a tortured look in his eyes. She marveled at how he could remain so strong in all of this.

With a fortifying breath, she left her brother and walked down the hall. Her grandfather watched her approach in complete silence. As she drew near, she found herself surprised by the sight of him. He wore ordinary clothing, something she'd never before witnessed, and he'd lost a good bit of muscle mass due to inactivity and lack of daily training. She'd never expected to see him look so…small, even a little frail. His age finally seemed to have caught up with him. He had intimidated her all her life, but the old man sitting in the cell before her didn't seem quite so daunting.

She stopped a couple of feet from the cell door. Intimidating or not, he was still the same man, and his eyes were just as steely as she remembered, albeit lacking their usual air of superiority. She tried to swallow, but her mouth had gone dry. The silence stretched out as she wrestled with her feelings. She had to take another deep breath before she could manage her words.

"My husband, Jace, the one you had whipped at Fort Rivor with Liam…he thought I should come down here to see you. He told me I should forgive you." She shook her head, her throat constricting. "If you had any idea of the life he has lived and what has been done to him, you would know what an incredible thing that is."

Her grandfather remained stone-faced. If not for the way his eyes pierced hers, she might have thought he hadn't even heard her. But what did she really expect him to say? She wasn't even sure what she had come to say herself. Tears threatened relentlessly, and she blinked hard to keep them at bay.

"You have done nothing but hurt me and the people I love. As long as I am breathing, I will never be able to forget any of it. Every moment of it will haunt me for the rest of my life. The sinful part of me doesn't want to forgive you because I don't feel like you deserve it." Her breath shook as she drew it in and then let it out slowly again. "But I know I didn't either, and Elôm offered it anyway. I know I will still struggle with it and will need Elôm's strength to change my heart but…" She cleared her throat and held her grandfather's gaze. "I forgive you."

While she didn't feel the words, confirmation whispered through her heart that she was doing the right thing. And maybe Jace was right that this closure would help.

She turned away from the cell, having done what she needed to do.

"Kyrin."

Her grandfather's voice was perhaps the softest she had ever heard it. For once he had said her name as if there could be love behind it. Slowly, she turned back to him. He was standing now.

"I never wanted to hurt you or your brothers. I just wanted what was best for you."

The earnest way in which he said it was foreign to her. He meant what he said, but he'd gone about it in all the wrong ways. If only he could have seen things differently when they were still children.

She had to swallow hard to work a murmured response loose. "Hopefully, you'll be able to save one of us this time."

Marcus watched Kyrin rush past him and hurry back the way they had come to leave the cell block. He didn't blame her for wanting to get away as quickly as possible. He'd dealt with the General's presence on many occasions since taking him captive, but it never truly grew any easier. He couldn't relive the details of his memories the way Kyrin could, but the pain of them still pierced him. The horrifying moment of walking up and realizing Michael was gone. Knowing he had failed to protect his little brother from the force their own grandfather had brought against them. Just like he had failed to protect Liam from the General's cruelty all those years.

He straightened his spine and pulled his shoulders back. Daniel and Balen would soon send guards to retrieve the General for the exchange. He shifted his attention back to the far cell. Should he say something? In truth, he had tried to put their family relationship and history as far from his mind as he could over the last several months. Pretending his grandfather was just a nameless prisoner had been what he'd needed to do in order to cope and do his job as their military leader. Once again adopting this mindset, Marcus strode down the hall and assumed his role as a soldier—his comfort zone.

"Yesterday, Kaden and a couple of our dragon riders were taken captive. We plan to propose a prisoner exchange. You for Kaden and the others."

The General's heavy brows shifted slightly upwards, but he said nothing.

"I assume, once you're released, you will resume your position as General of Arcacia's armies." Marcus didn't relish the possibility of facing his grandfather in battle again, but war wasn't pleasant any way you looked at it.

"I will do my duty to my country." His usual powerful timbre, which had once both inspired and frightened Marcus and could boom across a battlefield, now barely filled the cell, as if exhaustion weighed on every word.

Marcus sighed and lowered his guard just a little. He could pretend all he wanted, but his grandfather was still family. "Duty doesn't have to mean blind devotion. Daican was a tyrant. Davira is worse. She's a monster. She doesn't care about her people. Everything she does is fueled by vengeance. She doesn't care who dies in the process."

"She is my queen."

Again, Marcus had never heard his grandfather's voice lack such conviction, but he seemed bent on clinging to his loyalties.

"A throne she stole from her brother. Even Daican wouldn't have supported that." Marcus took another step closer, wrapping his fingers around the cold iron bars of the door. "Every man must decide for himself what is right and wrong. Following orders doesn't remove the personal responsibility and guilt for your actions. It took me a long time to learn that, and even though I know Elôm has erased that guilt, I still regret it. Consider that going forward after today."

SWEAT ROLLED DOWN the side of Kaden's face and along his neck, soaking into the collar of his shirt. So much for being chilled this morning. His stomach growled fiercely, signaling he was well past due for a meal. He hadn't seen Richard since his interrogation had been cut short, but he had overheard some of the soldiers talking. Apparently, some of their men had deserted. Good—for them, at least.

When Richard finally made an appearance, the taut set of his jaw and fiery gaze did not bode well for Kaden. He drew a deep breath while he still could and steeled himself. Speaking now was no doubt a terrible idea, but he would be tortured anyway. He'd just as soon face it getting in a few jabs of his own.

"I hear some of your men came to their senses and decided not to fight for a tyrannical witch like Davira anymore."

Richard glared daggers at him but maintained his composure this time. "Taunt all you want. You won't be the last one laughing."

"I wouldn't count on that. I'm heading to a pretty good place once I die. I wouldn't say the same of you."

Richard stepped closer, the coolness of his demeanor warning of some sinister plan. Kaden would rather see him raging, but the glint in his eye was far too smug.

"Have you ever heard of the Morvith viper?"

The question sounded conversational, and he gave Kaden a brief second to consider it. Kaden never had heard of it, but the almost smirk on Richard's face told him anything he needed to know.

"They're from the Krell Mountains. Our men brought some back when they went out for cave drakes to breed. The ryriks use them. That alone should give you some idea of their uses. This is the venom from one snake." Richard held up a small vial less than half full of milky liquid. "Doesn't look like much, but it's potent enough for ten people. It doesn't take much more than a drop to be effective."

Kaden kept his expression bland. Whatever Richard intended, he wouldn't show apprehension.

"The thing about Morvith vipers is that it's not the actual venom that kills you—it's the pain. Such intense pain your body can't withstand it and shuts down. They say it sets every nerve on fire. Very few survive it."

He tucked the vial back into his belt and reached out to tear open the front of Kaden's shirt. Then he yanked out his dagger. Slowly and deliberately, he dragged the sharp edge down across Kaden's chest, slicing deep into the skin. Kaden ground his teeth together, fighting not to flinch. Blood oozed and ran in thin rivulets from the wound.

Richard wiped the bloodied dagger on Kaden's shirt and slipped it back into the sheath. He then reached for the vial again and pulled the cork. "In a few hours, you'll experience the full effects of the venom. We'll just see how resistant you are to talking then."

Kaden's heart rate sped up as Richard poured the vial along

the gash in his chest. It burned the edges of the sliced flesh; a small hint of what he had to look forward to. He breathed unevenly, struggling not to display any fear over what was coming, but dread stirred deep in his gut. Could he withstand the pain? Or would he die a brutal death in which he couldn't hide his weakness from Richard? And what if it did make him talk? The thought sickened him. This was not how he wanted to go out. He would rather have died on the battlefield and maintained his dignity.

Marcus stared up at the mountains, a tense silence surrounding him and the others, who had come along to make the prisoner exchange—Jace, Captain Darq, Glynn, Talas, and a couple of other cretes. They would make an easy target if Richard decided to ignore their parley flag. Twenty minutes passed. Had Richard's sentries failed to spot them? They were plenty close to where Parker told him the camp was located. He rolled his shoulders. He wanted to trust his old lieutenant, but even though Kyrin had confirmed he was telling the truth, Marcus didn't like wondering if they had walked right into a trap.

Or maybe Richard and the others had already left the area. If so, had they taken their prisoners with them or left bodies behind for Marcus and the others to find? The thought of it twisted his stomach. How could he go back and tell Kyrin that Kaden was dead after the hope they had been given? *Please let him be alive.*

He'd just begun to weigh their options of what to do if no one showed up when he spotted movement ahead. A group of armed men emerged from behind a boulder a hundred yards away. Giant firedrakes also appeared on the slope above, peering down at them. Behind Marcus, the dragons grumbled, and he gripped his sword, little good it would do. However, the drakes remained where they were as the men approached with their own parley flag. Richard strode at the head. Marcus glared at him as the distance closed between their two groups. A charged moment of silence reigned before Richard spoke.

"To what do I owe the pleasure, *Captain*."

Marcus wouldn't be goaded by the sarcasm in his voice, but he did struggle to quell his hatred for the man. "We understand you have five of our dragon riders held captive."

Richard snorted, and his thin smile spoke of concealed anger. "I assume this information came from the deserters, who turned up missing this morning."

Marcus did not answer this question. Let him draw his own conclusions. "We want our men back and are prepared to make an exchange."

"And just what makes you think we're interested in an exchange?"

Marcus held his gaze for a moment before looking back and nodding to the men behind him. A moment later, Captain Darq led the General out from behind a boulder where they'd concealed him.

Richard's hard, dismissive expression changed to one more indicative of surprise. "General?"

"Lord Blaine." If the General was at all pleased to see him, it didn't reach his voice.

"We thought you were dead."

"Just captive."

Now Richard's attention returned to Marcus. His mouth pinched, and the way he sniffed gave away his aggravation that they actually had something to work with. Before he could say anything, Marcus laid out the terms.

"We will trade General Veshiron for our dragon riders."

Richard took a long moment, giving the appearance that he was mulling it over, before finally offering a slow nod. "Very well."

Marcus had expected at least some show of balking or negotiation. The lack of it, combined with the glint in Richard's eyes, reeked of duplicity.

"Alive," Marcus tacked on quickly. He wouldn't make this deal unless he saw all five of their riders still breathing.

Richard outright smirked now. "Of course." He turned to his men. "Fetch the prisoners."

Marcus almost missed it, but he also appeared to whisper to one of them. He was up to something, but they couldn't back out now. Marcus glanced at the others. Each one stood on high alert, ready to drag the General back onto the dragons and make a hasty retreat if necessary.

Richard casually rested his hands on the hilt of his sword and peered past Marcus. "Are you well, General?"

"Well enough."

Marcus looked between the two of them. He knew for a fact they had treated their prisoners far better than Richard had. They may have lacked proper rations over the winter, as everyone had, but at least they hadn't been tortured. The same surely couldn't be said for Richard's captives. Marcus suppressed a wince at what Richard might have done to Kaden, especially after learning of the deserters. But he couldn't think about that now. They had to get Kaden and the others to safety first.

Little more was said as the two opposing sides glowered at each other. Occasionally, one of the dragons gave a low rumble, sensing the tension. Marcus knew they were too well-trained to do anything unpredictable, but he wasn't so sure about the firedrakes. He kept a close eye on them just in case.

At last, Richard's men returned with their prisoners in tow. Marcus did a swift head count and then focused solely on Kaden. He and the others were all gagged. This set off warning bells in Marcus's mind, and he had to fight aside the burn of indignation upon seeing Kaden's condition. His brother was battered, bloody, and walked unsteadily. Marcus wanted to throttle Richard where he stood, but he fought down the impulse and maintained his composure.

Once they were close enough, the cretes brought the General forward. Trading wary, heated looks, they made the exchange. The moment it was done, Marcus ordered everyone back to the dragons. He didn't trust Richard not to attack now that they had the General and kept a close watch on them as he pulled out a knife and sliced through Kaden's bonds. Once free, he urged him toward the dragon he had borrowed from Rayad.

"Get on." There was no time for questions.

He helped Kaden up into the saddle and climbed on behind him. They were all in the air and on their way back to the fortress in under a minute. Only now did Marcus dare breathe a sigh of relief, although something uncomfortable still twisted inside him. He wanted to believe it was just lingering tension, but the sooner he could check Kaden over, the better.

The several minutes it took to arrive at Stonehelm stretched out particularly long. When they finally landed in the courtyard, Marcus slid down first and reached up to help Kaden, who moved slowly and gritted his teeth. No doubt he'd been badly beaten, not to mention any injuries he'd sustained when Exsis went down.

Marcus gripped his shoulder, looking for anything he had missed during the exchange. "Are you all right?"

He expected an affirmative answer. Kaden always downplayed his injuries. However, he looked Marcus in the eyes, the seriousness in his gaze sending a chill through Marcus's bones.

"I'm poisoned."

Marcus's heart lurched. "What?"

"Richard poisoned me with viper venom." He put his hand to his bleeding chest and winced.

A hundred different emotions crashed into Marcus at once, but he swiftly silenced the clamor as he was used to doing in these situations. The captain in him took over, and he gripped his brother's arm.

"We need to get you to Josef."

Kyrin sprinted around the side of Stonehelm toward the gate. Her heart thumped loudly in her ears. She was sure she had seen Kaden on a dragon with Marcus, but she had to see him face to face.

At last, she broke through the crowd already gathered near the gate. "Kaden!"

She rushed toward him and Marcus, though slowed at the sight of her twin's condition. He'd obviously been beaten, as she'd feared. Richard wouldn't have wasted an opportunity to inflict pain on anyone bearing the name Altair.

"Are you all right?" She sucked in a breath, winded from her dash from the wall.

For a pulse-stopping moment, neither Kaden nor Marcus spoke. In that silence, Kyrin caught all the visual cues that sent her stomach dropping toward her feet—Marcus's quick glance at Jace, the pain etched in Kaden's taut expression. She swallowed. Surely it couldn't be something so dire. After all, Kaden was standing here, alive, conscious.

Finally, Marcus spoke, his tone that of a captain. The tone he used when he was blocking his emotions so he could handle a hard situation with a clear head.

"Richard poisoned him. We need Josef."

Kyrin gaped at him, her mind freezing along with her body. She barely felt Jace touch her shoulder before his footsteps hurried away.

"What?" she gasped, her lungs barely refilling with air. She locked eyes with Kaden. He couldn't hide the pain and despair behind his.

"I'm sure Josef will figure out something." But even Marcus didn't look convinced of his own words.

He had his hand around Kaden's arm for support and guided him forward again. Kyrin took Kaden's other arm and walked with them. Her mind spun in circles, but she forced herself to focus on one thing—crying out to Elôm for her brother's life.

They neared the entrance of the keep, and Jace appeared again with Josef and Liam. The moment they reached them, Josef calmly questioned Kaden. "Do you know what type of poison Richard used on you?"

Kaden nodded. His face had a feverish sheen to it, Kyrin now noticed. "He said it was venom from a Morvith viper from the Krell Mountains."

Josef's brief nod and tight expression did not comfort Kyrin in the least. He focused his attention on Marcus. "Get him to a room back at the castle. I will gather my supplies and find Leetra. We'll be right behind you."

IT WAS AS though a fire had been built inside Kaden's chest, slowly burning through every vein in his body. How long before it consumed him completely? He crunched his teeth together, gathering every scrap of stubbornness he possessed. He would not let Richard take him out like this. Not if he could help it.

He stumbled, legs weakening, as they took the stairs at Westing Castle. Marcus's grip around his waist tightened and held him upright. He sucked in a breath, forcing himself to focus on something other than the pain growing closer to devouring him. Kyrin was several steps ahead of them with Jace, her stride and posture determined, but he'd read the fear in her eyes. She wasn't nearly as confident as her manner suggested. If Richard were standing before him right now, he'd be hard-pressed not to beat the man into oblivion. Not for what he'd done to Kaden but for what this was doing to Kyrin. What it would do to her if he died.

They turned into one of the guest rooms, and Marcus helped Kaden ease down onto the side of the bed. By now, his limbs shook, painful spasms darting through the muscles. He breathed raggedly, his heart thumping his ribs like a fist. He wasn't sure if it was from the venom, fear, determination, or a combination of all three. Sweat rolled down his face. He felt like he was sitting in front of a roaring fire in the middle of summer. If this kept up, he wasn't altogether sure his blood wouldn't actually start boiling.

Kyrin stepped in front of him a moment later and pressed a towel to the laceration slashed across his chest. Though she was careful, the touch ignited a fresh wave of pain that hit him so swiftly he couldn't bite back the groan that tore from his throat.

"I'm sorry." Her eyes welled with tears.

Kaden didn't trust himself to speak without the full extent of his pain bleeding out in his voice, so he only nodded. Gripping the edge of the bed, he focused on breathing through the waves of agony that slowly increased in intensity. He locked his teeth down on another groan as he thought of Richard celebrating his demise while welcoming the General back. They should have just let him die at Richard's hands. They'd given up one of their greatest bargaining pieces, and now he could very well die anyway. But then, the other riders would still live. Robbie would have the chance to see this all through, even if Kaden didn't.

A minute later, Liam, Josef, and Leetra rushed into the room. Josef and Leetra each set a medical bag on the table near the bed.

Kyrin twisted around to look at them while holding the towel over Kaden's wound. "Do you have an antidote for the venom?"

Josef and Leetra turned to them, looking between Kyrin and Kaden. Kaden read the answer in their faces before Josef even spoke.

"No."

Kyrin's eyes grew wider, far too bright with unshed tears. "Then what can we do?"

"We've brought a variety of painkillers." Josef's gaze now fell squarely on Kaden. "The only way to survive Morvith venom is to outlast it."

"How long?" Kyrin's voice wobbled.

"The venom should finish working its way through his system within twenty-four hours."

Kyrin looked from Josef back to Kaden, locking eyes with him. In them, he read her question. Could he last that long? Could he survive the pain of being burned alive for twenty-four hours? He straightened his shoulders and set his jaw. If that's what it took, Elôm help him, he would. He wouldn't give up until his last breath.

Kyrin's lips trembled, but a spark of hope ignited in her eyes. It was the best he could give her.

She moved back to let Liam take over tending his wound. Kaden watched her until she was busy saying something to Leetra and then nodded Jace closer. Jace bent down next to him, and Kaden drew a deep breath.

"You need to take Kyrin away. She can't be here for this. It'll be stuck in her head forever. If I don't make it, I don't want the next few hours to be the last thing she remembers of me. It would be too hard for her to bear."

Jace's jaw twitched as it went taut. Kyrin would certainly resist, but Kaden would not burden her with such awful memories that would never dull with time. Jace wouldn't want that either. He nodded, and Kaden breathed a sigh of relief. At least this he had some control over.

A fresh wave of pain seared through him, igniting every nerve from his head down to his toes. He squeezed his eyes shut and bowed his head, waiting, praying for it to pass, but it remained. He ground his teeth, forcing himself to cope with it before raising his head again.

Jace remained at his side, his expression one of shared pain, but when Kyrin rejoined them, he straightened and put his hand on her shoulder. "We need to go."

Her eyes flashed to his face, widening as if she couldn't believe he would make such a request of her. Before she could verbally protest, Kaden said her name. Her gaze jumped to him now, and he held it adamantly.

"I asked him to take you out."

She shook her head, but he kept speaking. "I will *not* let you see this and have it burned into your memory. I love you too much to let that happen."

"I can't just leave you." Her voice cracked.

"You have to." He released the final word with a gasp. "Please."

The tears in her eyes gushed over, rolling in two steady streams down her face. He was crushing her heart with this request, but it was better than letting her live with vivid images of him in anguish.

Jace put his arm around her and attempted to gently guide her away. She remained frozen in place until she bent down and put her arms around Kaden. He wrapped his own arms around her and hugged her tightly regardless of the pain it caused. This could very well be goodbye.

"I love you so much." She cried against his shoulder.

"I love you too." His voice carried an even deeper pain than the physical. He'd faced the possibility of goodbye every time he'd taken to the air to do battle, but that didn't make this moment any easier.

Kyrin pulled back and swiped at her face, but it did not slow the tears. If only he could leave her with something hopeful, but it was getting harder to think properly past the pain. He could only watch and silently pray this wasn't the end as Jace all but dragged her crying from the room.

The door closed behind them, and Kaden released a shuddering breath. He would keep fighting to remain strong, but with Kyrin gone, he didn't have to struggle so hard to hide the pain.

Josef approached him now. "Let's get your wound cleaned and bandaged."

Marcus helped him slip off his torn shirt. His wound was no longer bleeding, but the edges were badly inflamed. He didn't relish the thought of anyone touching it, let alone applying any healing ointment. He'd already spied Leetra pulling the too-familiar vial from her bag. When she arrived with a rag soaked in it, he fisted his hands in the blankets and crunched his teeth together. Unlike previous times, she cast him a truly apologetic look.

The moment she touched it to the wound, it was like a hot poker to his already burning skin. He gasped, a groan clawing up from deep within his chest. Lightheadedness descended, and shadows floated in front of his eyes. Marcus gripped his shoulder as he blinked the spots away.

The pain barely subsided even when Leetra finished, and Josef wrapped bandages around his chest. He was breathing harder now, tremors coursing up and down his arms.

"Drink this. It's one of the strongest painkillers we have."

Leetra held a cup out to him. He just short of snatched it from her, even though his hand shook as he brought the cup to his lips and gulped the bitter, syrupy liquid. At this point, any bit of relief would be welcome. He didn't want to admit the way fear wormed through his insides at the thought of the pain steadily increasing. It was one thing to project confidence to Kyrin, but entirely another to have to face the battle he had ahead of him. He could tell himself he would be strong enough to survive this all he wanted, but that didn't mean he would. He may very well succumb to the pain, something that could take hours. He suppressed a shudder. More than anything, he feared what the pain might reduce him to. *Elôm, give me the strength to endure this.*

"Kaden." Josef rested a wrinkled hand on his shoulder. "For your safety and ours, I think it would be best if we tied you down."

Kaden looked up at him, his stomach writhing at the thought of being trapped and unable to move while the pain ran its course. Yet, Josef was right, and even if he could move, he couldn't escape the pain anyway. The last thing he wanted was to hurt anyone in the midst of it. He nodded.

Marcus and Liam helped him get situated in bed, and Leetra wrapped a thick layer of bandages around his wrists and ankles to protect them from the rope. Kaden flexed his fists and struggled to breathe normally. At this point, the pain nearly brought tears to his eyes. If the painkiller was supposed to take effect by now, it wasn't working. Beside the bed, Josef, Leetra, and Liam quietly discussed their options while Talas appeared to be listening in. Kaden, however, found it difficult to follow their conversation.

"Hey."

He focused in on Marcus's voice. His brother leaned over the bed.

"You're one of the most stubborn people I know. It drove me insane when we were younger."

A strained smile briefly crossed his lips, and Kaden choked on a laugh.

"You're stubborn enough to beat this. Don't give up that stubbornness now."

Kaden drew the deepest breath he could manage. "I won't."

He felt Marcus take his hand and squeeze it firmly.

"Good, because I'm staying right here and holding you to that."

Jace watched Kyrin wring her hands, her pale face strained. If only he could do something to comfort her. But all that was left to him, or any of their friends, was to pray and to wait where they'd gathered in the sitting room just down from Kaden's room. An hour had passed since they'd left him. Every minute must be torture for both him and Kyrin. Jace had hated to take her out of the room. It didn't feel right, but things were different with Kyrin. She would be able to remember every excruciating detail as if she were right there reliving it. It would haunt her as long as she lived. As hard as it was, Kaden was right not to want her there. Jace just wasn't sure Kyrin would be able to understand and accept that for a long time, especially if Kaden did not make it. He begged Elôm to bring Kaden through this.

A pained, muffled cry from down the hall interrupted his prayers. Jace didn't even get a chance to pray Kyrin hadn't heard it before she stiffened, her face going another shade whiter. The others glanced at each other, and Jace shared a grimace with Rayad. It would only get worse from here. Jace couldn't let Kyrin sit and listen to Kaden's cries of anguish that would certainly become more frequent. He put his arm around her shoulders and drew her up with him.

"Let's go downstairs."

She seemed too traumatized to resist as they left the room. However, right as they passed Kaden's room, he cried out again. Kyrin stopped in her tracks and turned to the door. Jace grabbed her arms to guide her away, but she pulled against him.

"I have to see him!"

"You can't." It shredded Jace's heart to forcefully drag her away from the door.

By the time they made it downstairs, she sobbed uncontrollably. Before he could try to comfort her, she tugged out of his grasp and dashed toward the front doors and outside through the courtyard. He ran after her. Just outside the castle wall, she stopped, her shoulders heaving. He was afraid she was about to collapse. He reached out, and she turned to him, throwing herself into his arms and sobbing against his chest.

He wrapped her up tightly as if he could somehow hold together the pieces of her that were breaking. He was so achingly weary of having to see her cry like this. He looked up at the sky and then closed his eyes. *Kaden is in Your hands, Elôm. Give him the strength he needs and bring him through this. Please don't let Kyrin lose another brother. But I also pray that Your will be done, and that whatever it is, You will give Kyrin and the rest of us the strength to endure it.*

MARCUS RUBBED HIS eyes and glanced out the window where the sun had just cleared the horizon. He then returned his gaze to Kaden. By some miracle, he was breathing, albeit heavier than normal. For most of the past eighteen hours, Marcus had prepared himself to watch his brother slip away with each agonizing minute that passed. He had told Kaden to cling to his stubbornness, but listening to his raw, piercing screams during the night, he'd almost wished his brother would let go just so the pain would end. Thank Elôm Kaden had spent most of the night in a fitful unconsciousness. When he had been awake, Marcus had seen such pain in his eyes that he didn't know how anyone could endure it. None of the painkillers they'd tried seemed to do any good.

Josef approached the bed to examine Kaden and check his pulse. Marcus held his breath. Though he could see Kaden breathing, he was constantly preparing for bad news.

After a long moment, Josef straightened. "I do believe he has come through the worst of it."

Marcus's heart lifted in tentative hope. "He's going to make it?"

"I hesitate to make guarantees. He has been through a great trauma. However, I am optimistic now."

Marcus released his breath in a gust. *Thank you, Elôm!*

Josef gestured at the ropes, which were all that had kept Kaden from thrashing out of the bed during the night. "I think it is safe to remove his restraints."

It had been over an hour since Kaden had tried to move, though Marcus hadn't let himself become too hopeful over it until now. Josef and Liam went to work loosening the rope, and Marcus quickly rose to help. It had been terrible watching his brother strain against the bindings while the pain was at its worst. He'd been so delirious at that point Marcus didn't think he'd heard any of the encouragement they'd tried to offer him. Marcus winced at the chafing and bruises encircling Kaden's wrists, though it was probably more from his captivity.

Now that they had Kaden settled comfortably, and Marcus had a chance to think, someone else popped into his mind.

"I have to go find Kyrin." Their sister was probably sick with worry after all these hours.

Marcus left Kaden's bedside for the first time all night and stepped out of the room. Voices drifted from down the hall and drew him to the sitting room. Nearly everyone was there, and every set of eyes trained on him the moment he stepped through the doorway. They waited in heavy silence, their expressions pensive.

"Josef believes the worst is past. He can't say for sure yet if Kaden will recover, but he is optimistic."

Sighs filled the room, but one person, in particular, was not there to share in the relief.

"Where is Kyrin?"

Rayad stood and motioned to the door. "Jace took her downstairs last evening."

Good. No doubt she would have heard Kaden's screams from this room. He turned back through the doorway and headed downstairs to search for her. After asking a couple of the servants about her whereabouts, he ended up outside in the courtyard. Through the gate just beyond, he spotted Kyrin sitting huddled against Jace. Jace heard him coming first and looked over his shoulder. When he said something to Kyrin, she jumped up and spun around. Her red-rimmed eyes locked on him, her pale, tear-stained face nearly as disturbing as Kaden's appearance. She held her hand to her chest as though it were the only thing keeping her heart from breaking out, her gaze begging for answers.

"He's alive."

Her whole body sagged, and Jace put his arm around her.

Marcus's own body lacked strength after last night. "Josef can't say for sure he'll recover yet, but he's hopeful now that the worst has passed."

Fresh tears dribbled down Kyrin's cheeks, and her voice choked in her throat. "I have to see him."

She rushed past, and Marcus didn't try to stop her. He met Jace's eyes. His brother-in-law looked just about as spent as he was. It had to have been hard to face the unknown with Kyrin all night. Marcus glanced over his shoulder, but Kyrin had already disappeared inside. He looked back to Jace once more. "It's good she wasn't there."

Marcus didn't have his sister's perfect memory, but it would take a very long time before the images in his mind didn't turn his stomach.

Kyrin raced upstairs and down the hall, ignoring how her legs wobbled. Kaden's door stood open, and she paused for the barest second before entering. What would she find in the room? Kaden was alive, but in what condition? After that heartbeat of uncertainty, she rushed in, straight to Kaden's bedside. Her breath caught. His face was so gaunt and pale. Deathly so. Had he died before she made it up here? Her heart missed a beat, but the rise and fall of his chest halted that fear. He still lived. She sank to her knees at the side of the bed and put her hand over his. Tears blurred her eyes, but she blinked them away to stare at his face. She honestly hadn't believed she would see him alive again.

She looked up at Josef, who stood on the other side of the bed with Liam, Leetra, and Talas. "When do you think he will wake?"

Of course, he couldn't guarantee Kaden would, but she couldn't let herself think of any other possibility.

"Probably not for a while. But it's good his body has a chance to rest peacefully and recover from the strain."

As much as her heart yearned to see him conscious, his recovery was more important. Whatever that took, she would force herself to be patient.

Jace and several of the others entered the room behind her. Everyone remained quiet so as not to wake Kaden. They gathered around, making the room quite crowded for a few minutes before most dispersed after seeing for themselves he was on the mend. Jace tried convincing Kyrin to get some rest after the sleepless night, but she refused to leave Kaden's side. So, instead, he pulled up a comfortable chair for her beside the bed where she could be near him. Kyrin suggested that Jace should rest at least, but he chose to remain with her.

Once confident they wouldn't be needed, Josef and Leetra left to see if Cassie needed their help back at Stonehelm. Marcus, Liam, and Talas remained for a while, though they eventually gave in to her insistence to rest. And then it was just her, Jace, and Kaden. Jace pulled up another chair for himself, and Kyrin curled into her own.

She stared at Kaden, watching his steady breathing, and had

to laugh quietly at herself. "He'd probably tell me I was being creepy watching him like this."

Jace laughed a little too. "Probably."

But it was hard to shake the fear of losing him that had tormented her all night, especially coming on the heels of thinking they'd lost him in the battle. Hard to see just how close she really had come. Even being Richard's prisoner the first time hadn't left him in such awful shape. It was irrational, she knew, but she couldn't help feeling like he might slip away if she took her eyes off him now.

She wasn't sure how long they had been sitting there when someone entered the room. Turning, she found it was Rayad, and he carried a small tray. He set it on the bedside table near her. Two mugs steaming with coffee sat beside a plate of cheese, meat, and buttered rolls.

"I wanted to make sure you two had something to eat."

She smiled tiredly and thanked him as she handed one of the coffee mugs to Jace and balanced the plate on the arm of the chair between them. Only now did she notice the pinch of her empty stomach. She hadn't really eaten anything since yesterday morning.

Rayad pulled up a chair from the dressing table across the room to sit with them. He and Jace talked quietly, and their low voices soothed Kyrin while she waited for any sign that Kaden would wake. Part of her still feared he wouldn't—that the venom had taken too great a toll—so she prayed continuously for his recovery.

The hours passed into midafternoon. By this time, Marcus, Liam, and Talas had rejoined them. Though Liam assured Kyrin it was good that Kaden still slept, she was getting nervous that she hadn't even seen him move. One might have thought him dead if not for his breathing. He was still far too pale.

Kyrin leaned back in her chair and rubbed her eyes. They

burned with lack of sleep and so much crying. Rest would feel so good.

Jace nudged her arm. She opened her eyes and looked over at him, but he nodded toward the bed. There, Kaden shifted just a little, showing the first signs of waking. They all leaned closer, waiting, hoping. Then his eyes opened, pale blue and ever reminding Kyrin of their father. Her heart leapt.

He blinked sleepily a few times and opened his mouth as if to say something but then cleared his throat and grimaced. Kyrin jumped up to pour a cup of water from the pitcher beside the bed. Carefully, she slipped her hand under Kaden's head to lift it and put the cup to his lips. He took a long drink before releasing a sigh. His eyes closed again, and Kyrin wondered if he'd drift back to sleep. However, they opened a moment later and focused on her.

"I made it."

His voice was hoarse, but hearing it flooded Kyrin's eyes with tears. She took his hand and squeezed it. "You did. How do you feel?"

Kaden shifted as if to make sure all his limbs worked and winced. "Like every inch of my skin has been peeled off."

Liam straightened from where he'd been leaning over the other side of the bed. "Josef did say you'd probably still experience some pain when you woke. I'll get you a painkiller for it."

He turned to his medical supplies. While he prepared the herbs, Kaden's gaze returned to Kyrin. Seeing him awake and talking forced a couple of tears from her eyes. "I thought I lost you."

His lips tipped slightly upward. "I guess you'll have to put up with my stubbornness a while longer."

A small laugh bubbled up, a welcome sensation after such a terrible night. "Thank Elôm for that stubbornness. Richard should have known it would take more than a bit of snake venom to kill you."

Kaden breathed a quiet laugh of his own. "He should have." Then his smile faded, the mirth in his eyes dying as they filled with moisture. "Exsis is dead."

Kyrin's throat squeezed shut. She swallowed hard, an ache building in her chest. "I know. I'm so sorry."

Kaden's breath wavered as he released it slowly, tears close to overflowing. "He saved my life when we went down. He made sure he hit the ground first, not me."

Kyrin squeezed his hand a little tighter, shedding tears for both of them. What could she possibly say to help the loss? Kaden had dreamed of owning a dragon since they were little. No doubt he'd say losing Exsis was even worse than torture. What would he even do now that he had no dragon? It was hard to imagine him with a dragon other than Exsis.

Thankfully, Talas drew Kaden's attention, because Kyrin lacked the words to offer comfort. A crete would understand the loss better than any of them, and though sorrow robbed him of his usual upbeat manner, conviction rang in his voice.

"Exsis did his job. That's what makes dragons so special. Once bonded, they will defend their riders with their lives. Your bond was very strong, and we're grateful you're still with us, thanks to him."

"Now that he has awakened, Josef expects Kaden to make a full recovery given time and rest."

Daniel breathed a sigh of relief at Marcus's news, as did all the other leaders gathered around the table in the meeting hall. Losing such an integral member of their group before they even marched into Arcacia would have dealt a heavy blow to morale. The dragon riders were their first line of defense, as well as offense, and Kaden was a key component of that. Like many of the others, Daniel had sat up all night praying for his recovery, and he thanked Elôm for answering their prayers.

General Mason tapped a finger on a diagram of a catapult one of Prince Haedrin's builders had provided during their initial planning. "Since the giants are still working on the siege weaponry, Kaden and our other injured riders, at least those who didn't sustain significant injury, should have time to mostly heal without delaying our plans."

Across the table, General Torva crossed his arms, his expression more pensive than relieved. "This attack does raise questions. What of the new giant firedrakes? Where did they come from, and do they change anything?"

Silence echoed around the table, and all eyes seemed to turn to Daniel. After all, the drakes had come from his country. He should be the one with information, but he had none to give. In all of the chaos following the attack, he hadn't even had the chance to discuss the drakes and their potential impact on their plans, or give it much thought until now. Did this change things? Could they still march into Arcacia, or would Davira have a whole army of giant drakes waiting for them? What would it mean for their survival in general?

Before Daniel had to admit he had nothing to offer in the way of information or even speculation, Darq braced his hands on the table. Daniel might have been relieved if not for the grim expression the crete wore.

"Glynn and I have a theory. We don't think they're new drakes at all. I believe they're ones we've faced in battle before, probably here in Samara during last year's attack. Several of us noticed the drakes bear battle scars that look like they came from fights with dragons. If that is the case, it means the drakes we've faced for the past couple of years and assumed to be adults were not fully grown."

Everyone just looked at him for a long moment as this information and the import of it sank in. If he was right, that meant only one thing, and Daniel asked the question that surely ran through everyone's minds. "So all drakes will eventually be that size?"

"Or bigger." Those words settled like a proclamation of doom. How could they even hope to face something bigger? "There's no telling when they actually stop growing. I'm sure this is as much a surprise to the Arcacians as it is to us, and it presents more danger than ever. With a growing number of drakes that size, it won't take long before even the entirety of the crete army will not be able to withstand them in battle. Unless we put an end to it soon, it's only a matter of time before Davira could wipe out anyone who opposes her by simply sending an army of firedrakes."

She would be unstoppable. All of Ilyon would fall to her rule. She could wipe out entire cities if she believed them to be disloyal. Entire *countries*. Nowhere would be safe from her terror. Was it already too late? Daniel wasn't sure he wanted to know the answer. "Can you and Kaden's men handle them? What if Davira has more waiting for us?"

A heavy, deafening silence fell once more, but this time it did not stretch on for more than a moment.

"Yes, I believe we can." Darq's firm tone chased away the despair that had begun creeping into Daniel's mind at the prospect of Davira winning. They had fought too long and too hard for this to be the end.

Now Darq shrugged his tattooed shoulders. "If there were more giant drakes, why wouldn't she send them? I have no doubt she wanted to wipe out our armies here. I believe she reacted to our victory and sent what she had to make that attempt and failed. In a way, it worked to our advantage because now we know what to expect and how to prepare. But time is very much against us. That is why we must push on as planned and march as soon as the siege weapons are complete."

Everyone voiced their assent. The way it resonated in the room was like a rallying cry. Renewed purpose swelled inside Daniel. The attack had hurt them, but they would not falter. They couldn't. Otherwise, they were right on the verge of watching all of Ilyon fall to tyranny.

Now that they'd confirmed their path forward, the others began to disperse. Daniel waited while Marcus answered a few questions about Kaden and then motioned him to follow. Part of looking toward the future they fought for was preparing now for how Daniel would take over once Davira was deposed. At times, the sheer weight of everything he had to consider over-whelmed him, and while some decisions would be difficult to make, the one before him now came easily.

They stepped away from the table off to one side of the room where they could talk a bit more privately. Daniel turned to face Marcus, who stood straight and tall, the image of discipline and professionalism in spite of the toll Kaden's near death must have taken on him. This only confirmed Daniel's decision. He spoke accordingly, trying to get used to his "king voice." If all went well, he'd soon use it far more often. Might as well start now.

"I've been giving a great deal of thought to the fact that each army marching into Arcacia will do so with a strong general at their head. Each one except for ours. I know our militia hardly constitutes a true army, but that doesn't mean they shouldn't have a general. In light of that, and considering everything we've been through, I've decided, as prince and heir to the throne, that you should be our general."

Marcus's expression barely changed, only mild surprise in the lift of his brow, and he did not hesitate to respond with a firm nod. "I'd be honored to lead the men as general."

But Daniel didn't think he understood the full ramifications of the decision. This wasn't simply a superficial change in title that would cease with their victory. "Before you fully accept, you need to know that this is not a temporary position. I expect you to keep it after we have taken back Arcacia. I will need someone at my side to help me with military matters that are sure to be a mess once this is over. But the choice is yours. You are free to decline if you wish."

Marcus's eyes widened now, his cool composure slipping just slightly, and he seemed at a loss for words. Daniel had just offered him the highest position in Arcacia's military. A position soldiers worked their whole lives for and few achieved. One that held high honor, but also heavy responsibility.

All this seemed to flash across Marcus's face, but he regained his composure a heartbeat later. Standing tall, he dipped his chin in a firm nod. "I will accept the position."

Daniel reached out his hand and clasped forearms with him. "Congratulations, General Altair."

Hearing the title seemed to leave Marcus dumbfounded again.

Daniel dropped all kingly pretenses and grinned. "I admit, I didn't pay much attention to my history studies, but I'm pretty sure this makes you the youngest general in Arcacian history."

A brief smile flashed across Marcus's face. "I'll see that you won't regret it."

"I know you will." Daniel clapped him on the shoulder. The two of them were both far too young for the responsibilities they faced, but at least they could face them together.

KYRIN FINISHED BRAIDING her hair and glanced at Jace in the dressing table's mirror. He stood at the door to their room, waiting for her to go down to breakfast together. The warmth in his eyes sent a flutter through her stomach. If only every day for the rest of their lives could begin with such simple peace. How she prayed the future they fought for would make that dream a reality. Every day that passed brought them a little bit closer.

She stood up and walked over to him. He reached for her hand, but instead of turning to open the door, he drew her close. He reached up and let his fingers trail gently over her face before leaning in for a kiss. Kyrin sighed and melted into it. Yes, every day could start just like this.

Jace broke the kiss with a smile and opened the door. Out in the hall, Kyrin motioned to the room two doors down from theirs.

"I want to check on Kaden. I just know he'll go out to see his men today. I almost had to tie him down to keep him resting yesterday."

Though a few days had passed since the attack, she could clearly see he was not yet at full strength. He still grew fatigued easily, something Josef said could last for weeks yet. Kaden, of course, wasn't about to let that stop him, no matter how much Kyrin wished he would rest more.

Jace shrugged, though he wasn't known for resting when he should either. "Josef did say there was no harm in it if he takes it easy."

"I don't think Kaden knows how to take it easy."

"Altairs can be very stubborn when they set their minds to something." He cast her a quick glance, humor twinkling in his eyes.

She smirked at him. "In Kaden's case, it's probably more the Veshiron blood kicking in."

At his door, she paused and knocked lightly. She half expected not to receive an answer and to find Kaden had been up early to flee the room before she could stop him. However, it swung open a moment later. He stood on the other side, fully clothed, as if he'd just been about to walk out. He'd probably gotten dressed at the first hint of dawn just so she wouldn't have a chance to try to keep him bedridden for a moment longer. Though his face was still a bit pale, the gash to his forehead, surrounded by a yellowing bruise, had scabbed over, and his eyes were alert and eager.

"Morning."

It did Kyrin good to hear him sound so normal. She never wanted to see him so near to death again. "How are you feeling?"

"Desperate for a change of scenery." He smiled, but it lacked its usual brightness. Sorrow over Exsis's death still hung heavily, and that hurt Kyrin. Still, he was alive. "Josef was already here this morning. He said other than fatigue, there should be no lingering effects of the venom, and I don't have any significant injuries, so I'm only limited by my energy level and pain tolerance."

Kyrin gave him a look. Neither one of those would be much of a limit. But, if Josef was comfortable letting him resume his normal activities, she would trust him. "Just be careful. Don't ignore your body's need to rest."

"Yes, Mother."

She waved her finger at him. "You're lucky Mother isn't here, or you'd still be in bed."

He chuckled, some of the usual mischief returning to his eyes, and the three of them headed down to the dining room to join everyone.

Around the huge table, the men discussed the progress of their preparations in between bites of breakfast. General Mason shared the growing tally of men who'd arrived from around Samara to rebuild their army, and Prince Haedrin updated them on the construction of their siege weapons. While they would still have to leave quite a few of their wounded behind, others like Kaden had rested long enough to begin their march. Only a few more days and they would set out for their biggest challenge yet.

They were scraping the last of their breakfast from their plates when Baron Thomas's butler entered and approached Balen. "My lord, visitors have arrived from Landale."

Kyrin's breath died in her chest. Had something happened back home? They'd moved their main camp much deeper into the forest, but that didn't mean Davira couldn't find it the way she had their last camp. Mother and Ronny flashed to mind, and she fought to keep her fear at bay. There were any number of reasons someone from Landale had come to Samara.

They rose to follow the butler. Inside the main drawing room, three men awaited them. Kyrin's fears drained, and a grin sprang to her face. "Aaron!"

She hadn't seen him in months. Not since he and Timothy had visited for her and Jace's wedding. He greeted her with a hug, and Kyrin only now felt the true measure of how much she had missed him. Their group just didn't seem quite complete without him and Timothy.

She was going to express these sentiments when they parted, but something pained lurked in his eyes, and shadows surrounded them. She knew he'd been released from two long months in a workhouse a little over a month ago, but she would have expected him to have recovered from that by now, and her fear that something was wrong returned. However, before she had a chance to question him, the man to Aaron's left snatched her attention, temporarily eclipsing her worry. Jace's uncle, Charles.

He greeted Jace with a huge smile and a back-slapping embrace. Two years had passed since they'd last seen each other the night Jace had fled his mother's estate. Joy warmed Kyrin at the reunion. Jace often spoke of how much he missed his uncle. Though Kyrin had never had the chance to get to know him, she'd heard such wonderful things about him.

So caught up in seeing the familiar and loved faces, Kyrin barely noticed the third man standing apart from them until their gazes met. His indigo-blue eyes held hers for a heartbeat before lowering, but it was like a blow to the stomach as she took in his black hair and the scar on his cheek just above the short beard he'd grown. James.

A shiver streaked up her spine and along her arms, a phantom hand covering her mouth. Shaking herself loose, she dragged a deep breath into her depleted lungs. She was safe. Jace was less than five feet away. She was here in Westing with her friends, not back in Ashwood alone with James. And last they'd heard, he had turned to Elôm. Why would he even be here otherwise?

Still, he'd tried to assault her. Just because he'd changed and time had passed did not mean her memories of that night had grown dull. Even if she could forgive him, it would take time to work through the emotions of that night. Emotions she'd never really thought she would have to face again.

Jace's strong hand came to rest against her back, his presence at her side like a shield. She glanced up at him. He stared James down, a bit of a war going on in his expression. James was his brother, but Kyrin was his wife.

James continued to hang back from the group, enough guilt in his expression to convince Kyrin he truly had changed. But she needed time to come to terms with him being here and figure out how to proceed. Right now, there were others she preferred to focus on, and she forced her attention back to Aaron and a smile to her face.

"How have you been? How are Lacy and baby Isaac?"

Everyone had been surprised by the news that Aaron had married the former tavern girl in Valcré, becoming both a husband and a father to her infant son. Of course, Kyrin wasn't as surprised as some. Not since Jace had told her all about Lacy and Aaron's connection to her. From Aaron and Timothy's letters, Kyrin knew there was quite a story involving their relationship and Lacy's turn to faith, and she was eager to hear the details. Considering how recently they'd been married, she was a little surprised Aaron was here in Samara. She hoped the troubled look she'd noticed didn't mean something had happened between them.

The completely smitten smile that grew on Aaron's face allayed those fears. "They're doing well. Both of them are healthy. I brought them and Lacy's mother and sisters out to camp before I came here."

"What about Timothy?"

In an instant, his expression fell, his eyes filling with a pain sharp enough to stab into Kyrin's own chest.

"That's why I'm here." The rawness in Aaron's voice spoke of unshed tears. "Timothy is missing."

Kyrin put her hand to her mouth, a cold sensation washing over her. The room went instantly silent as all eyes fixed on Aaron.

"A couple of weeks ago, soldiers raided the warehouse where we gather. Some of us were able to escape. I got Lacy and her sisters out, but…" He swallowed hard and had to clear his throat. "I lost track of Tim. As soon as Lacy and Isaac were safe, I went back to look for him, but no one could find him. Several others are missing too. We can only assume they were arrested. If they're not already dead, the only way we'll ever find them is if we take Davira down."

Kyrin couldn't breathe. Timothy couldn't be dead. They couldn't lose one of the strongest spiritual leaders they had.

No one seemed to know what to say. Kyrin struggled to find something—anything—that might relieve even a small portion of the misery Aaron must feel. After all, she knew too well how it felt to lose a brother. Before she could find words, Aaron's tortured gaze shifted past her. She looked over her shoulder. Leetra stood there, staring at them as if Timothy's dead body were lying at their feet. Tears welled, turning her eyes violet. She stood frozen for a moment before spinning around and fleeing the room.

"Lee," Talas called, his voice breaking a little. He traded a pained glance with Aaron before hurrying after her.

Aaron followed as well but paused near the door where Daniel stood. His shoulders drooped as if the internal weight he'd been carrying all the way from Landale was too much. Kyrin almost didn't hear the words he murmured to Daniel.

"Ben and Mira are missing too."

Daniel's face fell. Though Kyrin had never met the couple, Jace had told her about them. They had been Daniel's closest friends right after he turned to Elôm and had sheltered both him and Aric when they'd escaped Davira. Not only that, but they were the driving force behind bringing together the believers in Valcré.

Elanor walked over to him and put her hand on his arm. "I'm so sorry."

He nodded slowly but appeared dazed by the news as he reached up to give Elanor's arm a squeeze.

Kyrin turned back to Charles, who gave them all an apologetic look.

"I'm sorry we come bearing such ill news. Aaron told us all about Timothy and the others. I can't imagine how difficult it must be not to know what has happened to them."

Elanor rejoined them, standing at Jace's side. "It is, especially for some of us." Her brows bent questioningly. "Why is it you're here? Did something happen that you had to leave home?"

"No, nothing like that," Charles assured her. "When word reached us of your victory here, we guessed you would try to take Arcacia and put Prince Daniel on the throne. I decided to come help, and James wanted to join me. We just happened to arrive in Landale at the same time as Aaron and were able to make the journey with him."

"What about Mother? Will she be all right at Ashwood with the two of you gone?"

Charles glanced at James, and Kyrin caught something in the exchange that tied a knot in her stomach. Had something happened to Jace and Elanor's mother? She couldn't bear to see Jace have to face that loss.

"Your mother is very well and will be just fine."

Charles's brief smile allowed Kyrin to breathe a little easier. Still, he did hesitate again, and this time Elanor seemed to have picked up on whatever he wasn't saying. "What is it?"

James took a step forward. Kyrin had to fight not to shrink back, but his attention focused solely on his sister. "Father is dead."

The words fell like an executioner's blade. Conflicting emotions swirled up inside Kyrin. Rothas had been a cruel-hearted, wicked man, who had caused much pain in his household and even threatened to hang Jace. So in that way, relief whispered inside her. Yet, at the same time, he was still Elanor's father. Kyrin would never wish the pain of such loss on her sister-in-law.

"How?" Elanor's breathless question hung between them, her expression slack.

"The fever." James's voice carried little emotion, but it did lurk in his eyes. Kyrin just wasn't sure whether it was only for his sister or his father too.

Elanor drew a slow breath, her lips thinning. Tears glinted in her eyes, though none fell. She looked just as conflicted as Kyrin as to how she should feel.

Jace reached out to lay his hand on her shoulder. "I'm sorry."

She cast him a weak smile. Charles stepped forward, putting his arm around her. "Why don't we go sit somewhere and talk? I'd love to hear how you've been."

The two of them turned and left the room, others following until only Kyrin, her brothers, Jace, and James remained. Deafening silence blanketed them. Kyrin glanced at her brothers, who stood a few paces behind her. All three of them glared at James as if contemplating the morality of throwing him off one of the castle turrets. Even Liam managed to look impressively fierce. She looked at James again. He stared at his feet like he hoped the floor would swallow him up, and she *almost* felt sorry for him. The silence was oppressive.

Then James cleared his throat, his discomfort palpable, and lifted his gaze to hers. She leaned a little closer to Jace, but the look in his eyes was nothing like the way he had leered at her back at Ashwood. Remorse weighed on his entire being, and his eyes even grew a little watery.

"I'm sorry." Two very simple words, and yet they held immense weight. He shook his head, unable to maintain eye contact. "I did terrible wrong to you and others. I constantly wish I could go back and change it. And I pray every day for Elôm to heal all the damage I did."

The night at Ashwood replayed once more in Kyrin's mind, but she prayed that, after today, she could leave it behind. "I forgive you."

The memories would never be gone, yet with Elôm's help, she knew she could move forward and see James as the changed man he was. She had to, not just for her sake but for Jace. James was family. She wanted Jace to have a relationship with his brother, and she wouldn't stand in the way of that by refusing to forgive.

Her brothers, on the other hand… That would probably take a little more doing. She turned to Jace, who had barely spoken a word. He searched her face as if seeking an answer on how to proceed. She squeezed his hand and gave him a little smile to assure him she was all right.

"I'll let you two talk." She needed time to process her own feelings, and it would probably be best to get her brothers out of the room to cool off a bit.

Jace let his gaze trail off after Kyrin, torn whether or not to follow her and make sure she was all right. She seemed to be, though she could be concealing her true feelings. His own emotions tangled in a complicated web. The last time he and James had been face to face, it had come to blows. At least

Kyrin had her brothers with her. They would make sure she was all right.

He turned to face his own brother again. James looked very different now than when they'd first met. Perhaps not much had changed in his appearance, but his manner was completely different. Though he'd heard the news of James's change of heart, it was shocking to witness after all this time. It probably shouldn't be. Elôm had changed Jace's life just as drastically.

Before the silence could linger, James drew his shoulders back as if preparing to face judgment. He'd probably contemplated this moment during the entire journey to Samara. "I truly am sorry for what I did to Kyrin. I know this can't be easy for you. Mother told me how much you care about her."

"She's my wife." They were the only words Jace could think of at the moment. Kyrin wasn't just his friend anymore. She was the love of his life. His partner.

James swallowed convulsively. "Oh."

He hung his head again and seemed at a loss now.

"Why are you here?" Jace fought to quell the paranoid suspicions that flitted through his mind. He knew James had changed. He had no reason to doubt his sincerity or Charles's confidence in him. But he still had to hear from his brother's lips why he had come.

"After all the wrong I've done, I just want to do something right." James's shoulders now sagged, a slight tremor to his voice. "I know nothing I do now can erase what I've done. I've found it as hard to forgive myself as I'm sure it is for you and Kyrin to forgive me. I just know that, going forward, I want my life to look very different from my past."

Jace released a breath and remnants of suspicion along with it. "I know what you mean. My past is not one I'm proud of either."

"Mother mentioned that your life after my father and grandfather took you away was very difficult. But she said it was your story to tell."

"We'll talk about it sometime." And they would if they both managed to survive what lay ahead of them.

James nodded, and finally, something like hope seemed to lift the weight from his expression. "I didn't know if you would be able to accept me being here, but I'm glad I came. Though, I wasn't completely sure I'd end up coming once I found out we'd be taking dragons." He shrugged and ducked his head a little as if embarrassed. "I'm not too keen on flying."

A small laugh escaped Jace, freeing the last of the tension that had built in him the moment he'd walked in and seen his brother's face. Maybe his own fear of heights and flying wasn't only from a childhood trauma. "I can't say I'm very keen on it either. It helps if you're bonded with your dragon."

The first of a smile lifted James's lips, and Jace caught a glimpse of their mother in it. It strengthened the growing desire to truly get to know his brother despite the past and their history. He studied James's face, focusing on the thin, pale line along his cheekbone.

"Sorry about the scar." Jace gestured to his face.

James touched his cheek. "Don't be. You made a point that struck deep. It made me think in a way I hadn't before and saved me from continuing down the path of my father." He stepped closer to Jace, looking him in the eyes. "Whatever my future holds, I hope it will include getting to know my older brother."

He held out his hand. The back of Jace's throat grew thick. Back when they had first met, James had looked at him in disgust, seeing him as an animal and an intruder. To hear James call him brother was nothing short of a miracle. He reached for James's arm and gripped it firmly.

"I'd like that."

LEETRA COULDN'T BREATHE. It was as if her lungs had been ripped from her chest, leaving nothing but a hollow, searing pain in their place. She needed fresh air. She needed home.

She needed Timothy.

Tears scalded her eyes as she escaped the suffocating confines of the castle and all but ran through the village. She blinked rapidly, choking on the attempt to swallow the lump in her throat. The clamor of emotions all rising inside her at once nearly sent her to her knees. She clenched her fists. No, she couldn't fall apart. She had to stay strong. She would not let herself break despite how her own body fought to betray her.

At last, she left the village and reached the crete encampment, where she found Soka. She had always drawn a certain strength and comfort from her dragon and was desperate for it now. Still struggling for air, she put her hands on her dragon's neck and rested her forehead against her warm scales. Squeezing her eyes shut, she labored to drag in deep breaths. But the flood inside her she fought to tamp down continued to rise and suffocate her.

A concerned grumble vibrated through Soka. All Leetra could do was ball her fists as both grief and anger exploded inside her like a lightning storm. She wanted to fly to Valcré and rip that witch of a usurper queen's throat out. She trembled with the intensity of how much she hated Davira at that moment.

"Lee." Talas's gentle voice broke through the haze.

All at once, the breath-snatching fear and pain of a possible lifetime without Timothy doused the anger. She gulped a breath, shaking as her protective walls crumbled faster than she could build them. It was what she had always feared. Every time she opened her heart, it ended up broken—first by betrayal and now by the actions of a madwoman. How could she bear such loss?

Slowly, she turned to Talas and found Aaron there too. She wasn't sure how to handle the pitying looks they gave her. She wanted to scream, and to fight, and to do *something*. Anger and action were better than falling apart. Yet even this seemed to abandon her, leaving her stripped of all strength and more like a scared little girl than the warrior she fought so hard to be.

Talas stepped closer, putting his hands on her shoulders. "We'll find him. In just a few days we'll be on our way, and when we get to Valcré, we'll find him."

"What if he doesn't have that long?" Despite her most courageous effort, her voice wavered, and a tear broke free. "What if he's already gone?"

More tears rushed in. Timothy was the only person who had ever truly succeeded in helping her open up and be vulnerable. Though she'd resisted it mightily at first, once she'd let go of her pride and shame, she felt safe to be vulnerable with him. But he wasn't here, and breaking down without him, without knowing if she would see him again, was terrifying.

Her defenses shattered anyway, and she collapsed against Talas's chest, unable to fight the pain, the fear, the loss. He wrapped his strong arms around her, and she clung to him as she cried harder than she ever remembered crying. In the midst of it, she felt Aaron's firm hand grip her shoulder.

Though the pain remained, she found comfort in letting herself break in their presence.

Daniel slumped in a chair in one of the empty halls of the castle. He hadn't really been sure where to go once he'd left the drawing room. He'd only known he needed time to process the news Aaron had brought. Swallowing hard against his constricted throat, he tried to rub away the stinging in his eyes.

To possibly lose Ben and Mira now when victory was nearly in their grasp would be a devastating blow. They were family to him. More so than any actual family he had other than his mother. They were the ones Elon had sent him to. Without them, Davira may very well have succeeded in killing him.

"Elôm, wherever they are, please protect them until we can stop my sister. Them, Timothy, and the rest of the believers Davira has captive."

If only they could act now. If only they didn't have a long march and a massive army yet to face.

"Give me patience and wisdom as well. We're so close now, but that makes the wait all the more difficult. Help us all to remain focused on You and Your leading. Especially me. So many look to me now. I don't want to let them down or stray from the path You've laid before me."

He sat for a while in continued prayer, fighting not to think about where Ben and Mira could be and what might be happening to them. His only consolation was that Davira wouldn't know they were the ones who had helped him escape the city. He couldn't imagine the horrors she would inflict on them if she knew. It was enough to make him ill.

He was about to get up when voices caught his attention. Marcus, Kaden, and Liam turned a corner into the hall, and he stood to meet them.

"Where are you three headed?"

Marcus traded a look with Kaden, something hinting at

chagrin in his expression. "Kyrin insisted our time would be better spent on war preparations than hovering around her brooding."

Daniel almost laughed at the image of Kyrin ordering his general about. "I take it I'm correct in assuming the young man, who showed up with Viscount Ilvaran, is Elanor's brother, James?"

"Yes."

"I'm sure that's difficult." Elanor had told him all about the family drama and the encounter between Kyrin and James. Even he felt the prickle of animosity to think of what could have happened to Kyrin.

"Especially for those of us who were there." Marcus cast another pointed glance at Kaden, whose smoldering expression suggested he might be working to tamp down some vengeful impulses. Not that Daniel could blame him.

Marcus was a little better at hiding any such feelings. "We know he's changed, but it's not as easy to forget what happened now that he's here and around Kyrin."

"I'm sure that will take time, especially if he's ever to earn your trust."

Daniel hadn't been with the group then, but he still found his view of James a bit tainted. He couldn't let it grow into anything too judgmental, though. Like Marcus had said, James had changed and would be Daniel's brother-in-law one day.

Movement beyond the three caught his attention. Elanor walked toward them. When Marcus noticed, he motioned to his brothers, and they went on their way. Daniel studied Elanor's face as she drew near. Her cheeks looked a bit damp, and moisture glistened in her eyes. It hurt to see her in any pain. Yet, before he could say a word, she was the one who asked, "Are you all right? I know how much Ben and Mira mean to you."

That she would be concerned about him after just receiving news of her father's death swelled his heart to a near painful degree. "It is difficult, but there is still hope we'll find them."

He stepped closer and cupped her shoulders with his hands. "What about you? I'm sorry about your father."

Two tears wavered on her lashes before spilling over, and a painful band tightened around Daniel's chest. It wasn't often he saw her like this. She was one of the most joyful and strongest people he knew.

She swiped her fingers delicately across her cheeks, but moisture remained on her lashes. "I don't know why I'm crying. He was a terrible man. He made my mother's life miserable and did horrible things to our servants, not to mention wanting to hang Jace…"

Daniel rubbed his hands along her arms. He knew well the tenuous and complicated relationship with a father like hers. "He was still your father. I cried when my father died."

"Did you?"

Daniel nodded, his mind going back to that night in Auréa. The night his father was assassinated. To this day, the memories were surreal. "Yes. I remember feeling angry he'd been too stubborn to see the truth, and we never got to experience a true father and son bond."

Elanor nodded, sniffing quietly. "I keep wishing something could've been done to change him, but if even the change in James had no effect, then I don't know what else anyone could have done. I think the two of us had some of the most stubborn fathers in Ilyon."

Daniel chuckled quietly. "Us and Mrs. Altair."

A small smile blossomed on Elanor's lips, tempting Daniel to lean in for a kiss, but now was hardly the right time. The smile grew, and the twinkle in her eyes told him she could read him like a boldly-written scroll. It was far better than her mournful tears.

He drew her a little closer to him. "So, did you tell your uncle about us?"

"Not yet." She tipped her head. "Would you like to meet him?"

Daniel sucked a breath, the air suddenly feeling a bit thin. Sure, he was the prince of Arcacia and heir to the throne. He could technically have anything his heart desired, yet facing Elanor's family left him feeling like a pauper. All the riches and prestige he could offer Elanor if he reclaimed the throne would mean nothing to her family. It was who he was as a man that would matter to them. What if they found him lacking?

She grasped his hands and offered him an encouraging smile, once more guessing exactly what he was thinking. "Don't worry; he isn't nearly as scary as Jace or Elian. You already have the approval of the two most intimidating men in my family, except maybe for my grandfather. My uncle will love you, and I'm sure James will be pleased."

A little of Daniel's nerves quieted. "Lead the way."

They returned to the drawing room and found that Trask and Anne had joined Kyrin, Jace, Charles, and James. The group parted to welcome Daniel and Elanor into it. Charles stepped forward first and bowed at the waist. "Your Highness."

Daniel had spent so much time as an exile and fugitive that having someone bow to him now was almost uncomfortable. In many ways, he'd begun to feel more like a common man than royalty.

"Lord Ilvaran, please, call me Daniel. At least when we're among friends and family."

Would Charles find it strange he'd said family? After all, Daniel had no family here just yet. But if Charles picked up on the term, he didn't show it.

"Very well, if you will call me Charles." He wore a kind smile that reinforced all the good things Daniel had heard about him.

Elanor introduced James next, and Daniel took care to greet him kindly. One would never guess the young man's past based on his humble and rather quiet manner. Daniel could see how this would cause a lot of conflicting emotions for Kyrin's brothers.

A slight pause followed the introductions, and Daniel's heart beat a little faster than normal. All that was left was to announce the relationship between him and Elanor. He tried to cast her a surreptitious glance. Would she tell them now, or would she wait a bit? Should he be the one to say something?

Elanor slipped her hand into his, effectively cutting off his thoughts and no doubt saying more than words ever could.

She grinned at her uncle. "So there is something I didn't mention when we were talking before. For the last few months, Daniel and I have been courting."

The lift of Charles's brows made Daniel's breath grow shallow, but who wouldn't be surprised to hear their niece was courting a prince? The question was, would that surprise turn into disapproval?

"We did get Jace's blessing," Elanor was quick to add.

Charles looked over at Jace, who wore a thankfully mild expression as he answered with a nod. That was all it took for Charles's warm smile to return.

"Well then, I am very happy for you—both of you—and wish you the best." His eyes crinkled even more when he focused on Elanor. "Your mother hoped you would meet someone."

She wrapped her free hand around Daniel's arm and hugged it to her side, sending him an adoring look. "Though I'm sure she never imagined that someone would be Prince Daniel."

Charles laughed now. "No, I'm sure not."

He eyed Daniel appraisingly, and Daniel held his breath. Hopefully, upon second inspection, he wouldn't be found lacking. But nothing in Charles's smile dimmed.

"I think she'll be pleased, though."

At last, the nervous tension cramping Daniel's stomach and squeezing his chest eased. To have the approval of someone as well respected as Elanor's uncle meant a great deal. It also cemented what he'd been feeling for days. It was time to ask Elanor to marry him.

THREE DAYS.

In three days, they would march into Arcacia.

Jace could feel the thrum of anticipation and excitement as their lords and leaders discussed the final preparations within the meeting hall. Whether the anxious undercurrent that ran along with it was just his or shared by the others, he couldn't say. It would be hard not to be at least a little uncertain about the future. None of them truly knew what to expect, except perhaps for Marcus, who had firsthand knowledge of the Arcacian army.

But, regardless of what they faced, Elôm was on their side and would guide them. That was certain. And there were those in Arcacia who needed them. He suspected the news of Timothy's capture two days ago had spurred the decision to leave so soon. He prayed they were not already too late and that Elôm would protect and preserve Timothy, Ben, Mira, and others, for however long it took to reach them. A long march lay ahead, and perhaps a long siege. Then battle. A battle that would decide the fate of Ilyon going forward.

With their plans in place, the men began to depart, the anticipation propelling them each toward their last-minute preparations. Jace turned to go as well. While he had no specific duties, he could make himself useful somewhere.

Someone called his name before he could exit the room, and he turned to find Daniel striding toward him.

"Could I have a word with you before you go?"

Jace nodded, and they stepped away from the door, out of the way of the others. The room grew quiet as it emptied. This reminded him of a different day back at camp last winter. The day Daniel had asked for permission to court Elanor. The same anxious look crossed Daniel's face, but it faded into a more collected and determined one, and he did not waste any time.

"With your permission and blessing, I want to ask Elanor to marry me before we leave Samara."

The direct way he asked was different than the day back at camp. Then, Jace had been able to make him squirm. Now, he didn't sense the same uncertainty, at least not to such an extent. He had noticed a change in Daniel in the past few weeks. Though subtle, he had transitioned from prince to king somewhere along the way. A king who, in reality, did not need his permission for anything yet sought it anyway.

In many ways, this was the moment he'd been dreading since that morning in camp, but as much as it scared him, he knew the choice he had to make. "You have my blessing."

Daniel didn't try to hide the breath that gusted from his chest, suggesting he'd been more nervous than Jace thought. "Thank you. I know this is difficult for you. I shudder to think of the day I may have a daughter and have to let her go."

Jace held back the laugh that jumped to his throat. He and Daniel both. This was hard enough.

The silent humor between them faded as Daniel's expression grew more serious. "I'm sure what happened at Amberin makes it worse, but I want you to know I'll do *everything* in my power to protect her. I love her with all my heart and, believe me, I know the life I'm asking her to join me in will have its dangers. It terrifies me more than I can tell you to think of something happening to her, but I hope both of us can trust that Elôm is ultimately in control and will prevail wherever I may fail."

It was just as Kyrin had said, and it was one of Jace's greatest struggles. He did hold onto his loved ones more tightly than he should. After growing up with nothing and no one and then having Kalli and Aldor ripped away from him so violently, it was hard not to. But he couldn't live that way. They all had their lives to live, and it was not his place, nor was it within his ability, to make sure those lives were secure.

"I know you will take care of her."

A tentatively hopeful smile claimed Daniel's face. "Maybe, instead of seeing this as letting Elanor go, you might see it as gaining a brother?"

The suggestion settled deep inside Jace with the realization that he'd never truly contemplated that aspect before. At least not with any lingering consideration. With Elanor's marriage, his family would only grow. The unease that had dwelt inside him for too long slowly released, and he smiled in return. Brothers they would be.

Daniel fidgeted worse than a little boy at a formal dinner party, only now his mother wasn't there to send him stern glances, warning him to stand still. So much for not acting suspicious. A servant girl passed by where he waited at the base of a spiral staircase in one corner of Westing Castle and cast him a quick smile. Everyone else would be about ready to sit down for the evening meal in the dining room. Anyone not in on this plan probably wondered what in Ilyon he was doing just standing here.

He rocked on his heels. Any minute now. He tugged at the collar of the leather jerkin Balen had loaned him. It was just slightly big on him, so why did it feel so tight around his throat? He shook out his hands, which were starting to get tacky. He really had to get a hold of himself.

A graceful figure entered the hall, and his heart gave a solid thump against his ribs. So much for that. His pulse thundered on as Elanor walked toward him. Her forehead puckered in the most delightful look of confusion and curiosity.

"What's going on? Jace said you wanted me to meet you here."

Despite their heart-to-heart earlier this morning, Daniel had half expected Jace not to relay the message to her and leave him standing here half the night. Daniel probably would have been tempted to do so if he'd had a sister he loved so much. Of course, he could have asked someone else to carry the message, but it seemed better to keep Jace involved in the process. He had to show Jace he meant what he'd said about being brothers.

Now that Elanor was actually standing in front of him, a little of Daniel's nerves settled. It wasn't as if he had any qualms about this decision. With his most charming smile, he offered her his arm. "I thought we could have a quiet dinner together before we have to march out. Just the two of us."

They'd barely had more than a moment to themselves since they'd left Landale. It didn't exactly lend itself well to courtship.

Her brows lifted delicately, her lips quirking into a delighted grin. She wrapped her hand around his arm. "So, where exactly are we going?"

Daniel turned her toward the staircase. "Up."

Her grin widened as they started up the stone steps. How he loved her childlike joy over simple things. A woman like that was hard to find, and he had no intention of letting her slip away.

They wound up and around until they reached the top of the castle's southern turret. The sky to the west was turning deep pink, and the moons had already risen to the east. Torches burned at intervals around the turret, casting a warm glow. In the very center sat a lone table draped in burgundy linen. Daniel heard Elanor's breath catch. She looked up at him, her eyes wide and twinkling. She bounced a little on her toes.

"This is so beautiful!"

It was just the sort of reaction he had hoped for. He grinned and guided her to the table, where he pulled out a chair for her.

"Thank you." She suddenly seemed to grow a bit shy as she dipped her chin and tucked a stray piece of hair behind her ear.

For some reason, it just emboldened him. It would be mighty hard to wait through dinner to ask her, but he forced himself to take the seat. He wanted this to be an evening to long remember. That involved the proper lead-up, not just dropping the question two minutes in.

"Balen had the cook prepare something special for us." He gestured to the covered plates laid out before them.

Together, they uncovered their meal, finding tender slabs of meat—black deer, most likely—covered in a glaze scattered with peppercorns as well as an assortment of roasted vegetables. A small basket of fresh rolls sat to the right, along with a bottle of wine, and there was even a plate of still-warm honey cakes between them.

He picked up the wine bottle. He wouldn't be surprised if it was from Baron Thomas's personal wine cellar. "May I?"

"Please."

He poured a little into each of their goblets, and they set their attention on their plates. The food was every bit as delicious as expected, particularly the meat. The castle cook was quite skilled. Daniel, however, found himself very much distracted from the meal by the woman across from him.

Between bites, she gave him that adoring look that made him want to spend every moment of the rest of his life with her.

"This was really sweet of you. I've never had a sunset dinner before, let alone a rooftop one."

"Neither have I."

Elanor tipped her head, a little smirk claiming her lips. "No? Seems like you would have brought all those nobles' daughters, who visited Auréa, to the palace roof to stargaze."

Daniel shook his head. "No." Thank Elôm. He may have done his share of romantic stargazing from the gardens, but this rooftop dinner was something only shared with Elanor.

She seemed to understand the significance of this, her smile growing warm and making him all the more impatient for the day they were wed.

For the next while, they enjoyed their meal and conversation about their pasts and the future that lay ahead. Daniel could have spent all night just happily staring at the way the torchlight flickered in Elanor's dark eyes. He probably looked like a besotted idiot, but he didn't even care.

Once they'd finished their meals and the honey cakes, they walked to the parapet to look out over Westing. The view was quite spectacular. Light glittered in the village below and from hundreds of campfires lit by their army, mirroring the stars that had awakened overhead.

Elanor breathed in a deep breath. "It's beautiful, isn't it? You know, if you look past the fact it's an army prepared for war."

Daniel nodded, though his mind had already shifted away from the view. His heart skipped. It was now or never. He swallowed hard, his dratted collar getting tight again. A madman might think it was actually trying to strangle him.

"Elanor."

She turned to face him, her lips quirked and just begging to be kissed. He cleared his throat. Focus. There'd be plenty of time for kissing if this went right.

"I have something to ask you."

"Yes?"

His tongue stuck to the roof of his mouth. Why was he so blasted nervous? It wasn't like they hadn't already talked about marriage. If she turned him down in the end, then he'd just have to deal with it like a gentleman. Sure, his heart would be broken, but he'd probably have bigger issues to deal with in a few days. Life and death issues. Not that such thoughts actually calmed his nerves. But if he couldn't ask her a simple, life-changing question, how did he expect to rule a country?

He sucked in a breath and forced his tongue to stop playing dead. "In three days, we'll march into Arcacia. I don't know what will happen after that. I pray for success, but only Elôm knows. In light of that uncertainty"—he took her hands in his, hoping his palms weren't sweating too much—"I wanted to ask you, Elanor, if you will marry me. Will you be my wife and my queen?"

Her eyes grew wide before crinkling once again into a glorious smile. She pulled her hands from his to wrap her arms around his neck and held his gaze with a steady confidence.

"Yes."

And then she leaned in to kiss him. He put his arms around her, pulling her close and falling deeply into the kiss. He would happily have stayed in the moment for the rest of time, but he broke it off before it could linger overlong. He rested his forehead against hers, his pulse racing and his breaths a little ragged.

"I wish we had time so I could marry you before we leave."

She pulled away just enough to look into his eyes again. "We have three days."

He straightened a little, still holding her close. "You want to get married within the next three days?"

She shrugged. "Why not?"

He couldn't tell if she was serious, but her words definitely tugged at him.

A little grin slowly lifted her lips. "Unless, of course, you want a large royal wedding."

She was teasing him now, and he snorted.

"Do you know how much drama would be involved in a royal wedding? I would very happily skip that headache unless it was something you wanted. If you want a fancy wedding dress, feast, dancing, I'll give you that. Whatever you want, it's yours."

"I simply want to be your wife. It doesn't matter to me what it takes to accomplish that."

Heaven help him, he could hardly contain his love for her. "And I, more than anything, want to be your husband."

"Then let's get married tomorrow."

Words momentarily failed Daniel. He'd never imagined she'd be so eager or that they could make this happen so quickly.

She lifted her brow at him, though her lips still quirked playfully. "Too soon?"

A laugh bubbled from his chest. "I mean, I'd marry you tonight if that were an option." He reached up, brushed his fingers over a strand of her silky hair, and let them trail down her soft cheek. "Tomorrow it is then."

In twenty-four hours, this miraculous woman would be his wife. He could hardly wrap his mind around it. The urge to kiss her again flooded over him, but he held it in check. He'd wait until tomorrow. Until the moment she was pronounced his wife. Then he probably wouldn't be able to stop kissing her. That was an intoxicating thought.

"I suppose we should go and let everyone know." They'd have a lot of preparation to accomplish in a very short amount of time. "Jace is probably waiting at the bottom of the stairs anyway, ready to have my hide if he suspects I've done anything to jeopardize your honor."

Elanor laughed lightly. "Either that, or he's been hiding just around the corner, keeping an eye on you this whole time."

Daniel's gaze darted to the stairway. It would be easy for someone to hide just out of sight. He narrowed his eyes. Why hadn't he thought of that?

She laughed again and took his hand. "Come on."

They headed back down the turret's spiral staircase. Of course, Daniel could find no evidence of anyone eavesdropping on them. At the bottom, it was just as he'd expected. Jace waited, leaning back against the wall, his arms crossed. Daniel cast him a suspicious look, searching for any signs he had rushed down just ahead of them. But his breathing wasn't even slightly elevated.

"Jace, we have something to tell you." Elanor wore a brilliant smile that radiated all the joy and excitement still bursting in Daniel's own chest. Even the thought of Jace potentially spying on them couldn't quell that. "Daniel and I are getting married. Tomorrow."

Jace's brows shot up. "Tomorrow?'"

Judging by his reaction, he probably hadn't been eavesdropping, at least not at that point of the evening. Daniel struggled not to squirm when Jace's gaze turned to him. They'd made so much progress this morning. He would hate for this to ruin it. It wasn't actually his idea, after all, though to say so probably wouldn't help.

But Elanor remained undimmed. "Yes. We want to make it official before we leave Samara. Considering the uncertainty of the future, we don't want to lose our chance."

If Jace held any lingering reservation, this seemed to calm it. He had nearly lost Kyrin before they got married. He could hardly blame them for wanting to avoid a similar situation.

With enough of a smile to reassure Daniel, Jace nodded. "Congratulations."

They thanked him, and Daniel did his best to convey just how deep his gratitude was. He'd lived with enough family drama in his life. The last thing he wanted was to invite more in marriage. Instead, he prayed that, by marrying Elanor, he could build the tight-knit and loving family he'd never had. One that extended beyond just the two of them.

Bubbling with excitement, Elanor nudged both of them down the hall. "Let's go tell the others. We have a lot of planning to do."

Daniel reached for her hand, the same thrill and anticipation propelling him. He didn't remember the last time his heart had been so light. Even the unknown of the coming days could not diminish it. For tonight and tomorrow, he would focus only on Elanor and their union and thank Elôm for such a blessing. Not long ago, he'd feared he wouldn't even find a wife, let alone one who shared his faith, and one he loved so deeply.

The three of them headed toward the center of the castle, where everyone had gathered in the drawing room. Though Jace was the only one Daniel had included in his plans tonight, more than one set of eyes focused on them expectantly when they entered. He let Elanor share the news, relishing the way her voice lifted as though she could barely contain her excitement. Celebration, hand shaking, back slapping, and the chatter of happy female voices ensued. Charles offered hearty congratulations. Elian's was more reserved but no less sincere, and Daniel was grateful for their acceptance of him. The women jumped into planning immediately, and Balen freely offered whatever they would need for a ceremony.

In the midst of it, Daniel caught Trask giving Anne an impish look. "Now, how come you refused to marry me so quickly after we were betrothed?"

Anne just smirked at him. "We're married now, aren't we?"

This set off a round of laughter, and warmth filled Daniel. He couldn't wait to marry Elanor surrounded by such a good group of people. It was more than he'd ever dreamed.

JACE WAITED NEAR the front of the great hall, where all their closest friends had gathered. At some point in the whirlwind of a morning, servants had filled the grand room with festive flowers, garlands, and rows of chairs. He had also heard they were cooking a dinner feast at Balen's request. For such a rushed event, this wedding was turning out to be quite well prepared.

And he was glad. Despite the shock of going from giving his blessing to Elanor and Daniel's betrothal to about to watch his sister get married in the course of little more than a day, he was at peace with it. His conversation with Daniel yesterday had calmed his misgivings, and he was ready to celebrate the union and the expansion of their family.

Kyrin entered the room a moment later and wound her way toward him. He let his gaze trail along the pale blue dress she wore. She must have borrowed it from someone because he hadn't seen it before. It reminded him of the one she had worn for her birthday a couple of years ago. He loved that dress and the way the color brought out her eyes. This one did the same.

Pink faintly dusted her cheeks when she drew near and realized how intently he was staring. It drew a smile to his lips. He put his hands around her waist to pull her closer and dropped his voice to a low murmur. "I like that color on you."

The pink deepened, and she grinned up at him. "I know."

Casting his usual self-consciousness aside, he bent down to kiss her. This was a wedding, after all, with all its romantic atmosphere. He did keep it brief, however. The focus today was on a different couple, and he dragged his mind back to them.

"How is Elanor?"

In their mother's absence, she had asked Kyrin and Anne to assist her in preparing for the wedding. Jace hoped everything was going smoothly for her.

"She's beaming. She's a radiant bride."

Good. He wanted this day to be everything she had ever dreamed of, especially with the unknowns ahead. If only their mother could be here. She would be so happy.

Kyrin wrapped her arm around his, hugging it to her side. "I'm glad you're feeling better about this."

"So am I. Thanks for always reminding me to trust Elôm."

"You're welcome." Her loving smile washed over him, and she tugged him gently along with her. "Let's go sit down. It won't be much longer."

Jace followed her to one of the front rows of chairs. At a pair of empty ones, she took a seat next to Aaron. Jace hadn't seen much of him since his arrival, except at meal times or when the whole group gathered in the evenings. It had to be difficult not knowing where Timothy was or if he was even alive. Jace wouldn't know what to do with himself if Elanor was missing. Just letting her get married had stressed him enough. He could very well imagine how having to wait these last couple of days to return to Arcacia ate at him.

Kyrin greeted Aaron with the gentle and understanding kindness Jace loved so much about her. It was that same kindness that had drawn him out of some of his darkest moments and captured his heart so thoroughly.

She gestured around them. "I bet all this makes you miss Lacy."

A wistful smile claimed Aaron's face. Focusing on something other than Timothy was probably just what he needed. "Very much. Our wedding was fast, too, though not this fast." He chuckled. "I had no idea I'd become a husband and father on the same day."

"It sounds like it was perfect timing."

Aaron nodded. "I thank Elôm all the time I didn't miss Isaac's birth. I could've missed out on so much. I just hate that I even have to miss out now."

By Jace's calculations, Aaron had only been married for about three weeks when the warehouse had been raided. He couldn't imagine how hard it would have been to leave Kyrin after only a couple of weeks of marriage. No wonder Aaron had been withdrawn.

"Elôm willing, you'll be able to return to them soon, and we'll get to meet them."

Kyrin's earnestness managed to brighten Aaron's smile. "I hope so."

By now, the rest of their friends had found their seats to provide a small and intimate gathering for the ceremony. James slipped in to take the seat next to Jace. While they hadn't had much one-on-one time in the last couple of days, Jace was glad to share this moment as brothers. He looked over at Kyrin to ensure she was comfortable, and she answered the silent question with a smile. Trust toward James might be far in the future, but at least there was acceptance and understanding.

Satisfied that all was well, Jace turned his attention to Daniel, who stood at the front of the hall with Trask. He kept shifting from one foot to the other, and Jace couldn't help the smirk that claimed his lips. He remembered that feeling.

Was this really happening? Daniel rolled his shoulders and wiggled his toes inside his boots. It felt real enough, but he couldn't seem to wrap his head around the fact he would be married within the hour. He'd barely slept last night in his euphoria.

He shrugged his shoulders again as if it could calm the jitters in his stomach and the thudding of his heart. Was it possible to be elated and downright terrified at the same time? Elanor was giving up a wonderfully normal life and stepping into that of royalty just to be with him. What if he somehow let her down? What if being queen made her miserable?

"You're more jittery than Jace was at his wedding."

Trask's amused tone drew Daniel out of his head. He had chosen Trask to officiate the wedding. He was, after all, rightful baron of Landale. It seemed appropriate for Arcacian nobility to oversee the joining of the future king and queen.

Daniel drew a deep breath and lowered his voice. "I'm just afraid I've drawn Elanor into a life that will make her miserable."

Instead of giving those words any serious consideration, Trask snorted a laugh. "If I've learned anything about women in the years I've known Anne, it's that they know their own minds. I highly doubt you drew Elanor into anything."

The churning in Daniel's stomach abated. Trask was right. Elanor had experienced too much struggle and hardship to make decisions naively. Though she couldn't know exactly what life would be like as queen, she understood the challenges.

Any further thoughts on the matter flew from his mind the moment the doors at the far end of the hall opened, and Elanor entered on her uncle's arm. Daniel couldn't feel his heart beating anymore—couldn't feel much of anything really, except for a breath-stealing flood of emotions. Was he really going to marry the incredible, gorgeous angel walking toward him? Moisture burned his eyes, and he had to blink hard to bring her back into focus. Despite the wedding's short notice, their female friends had dressed Elanor in a stunning white gown with draped sleeves and silver embroidery befitting a future queen. The only moment in his entire life he'd seen anything so pure and breathtaking was when he'd met Elon on the cliffs of Valcré.

Ever since he was a boy, he'd known it was his duty as the prince to marry well. He'd always expected a marriage based on political advantage, not love. As much as he'd rebelled against those facts, he'd always known that that was how it had to be. Yet here he stood, about to marry a woman he loved more than life itself. It was a miracle only Elôm could have wrought. No words would ever be able to come close to expressing his deep gratitude to his King.

When Elanor reached him, her smile somehow managed to both nearly buckle him and make him stand taller. She was the kind of woman who inspired a man to be the best version of himself he could possibly be—the perfect attribute for a future queen. If Elôm gave them victory, Arcacia would be incredibly blessed by her influence.

Daniel shifted and met Charles's gaze. Unspoken communication passed between them, and Daniel silently vowed to love and defend Elanor until his dying breath. He then took Elanor's hands in his, once more becoming immersed in her loving eyes.

"Friends." Trask's voice reminded Daniel they actually had a ceremony yet to perform, but he did not take his gaze from Elanor's.

"Today, we gather not only to celebrate a union of two people but to celebrate our future. A future every one of us is fighting to achieve."

Murmurs of agreement filled the room, and Rayad said, "Hear, hear."

It was true. Daniel and Elanor would be at the head of their new lives if they succeeded in ending Davira's bloody reign. People would look to them to shape Arcacia's new future. That did not scare him as much as it once did. Not now that he'd have such a wonderful partner by his side.

Trask continued, and before Daniel knew it, it was time for the vows. He promised from this day forth to love and honor, to protect and provide, and to rule and to reign with Elanor until the final moments of this life. She promised the same, and Daniel thought his now-thumping heart might burst.

A brief moment of expectant silence followed as if the whole room held its breath before Trask spoke again. "Then, as rightful baron of Landale and in front of Elôm and these witnesses, I pronounce you husband and wife." He gave Daniel a broad grin. "You may kiss your bride."

Daniel barely waited for him to finish. He reached up to cup Elanor's face in his hands and capture her in a kiss. His blood thrummed at the way she kissed him back. She'd definitely been holding back before.

They broke the kiss amidst thunderous applause and cheers, and Trask called for quiet. Daniel raised a brow at him, unsure of what more there was to say, but Trask looked out at all of their gathered friends.

"It gives me great pleasure to present Their Majesties, Daniel and Elanor, the true king and queen of Arcacia."

JACE WATCHED DAWN light paint an increasingly bright square across the ceiling. Kyrin still slept peacefully beside him, their shared warmth captured under the light blanket. He should have tried to go back to sleep when he'd awakened an hour ago, but he had too much on his mind. Besides, this still early morning peace might be the last he saw in a while. So much was changing and happening. His sister was now married and their rightful queen, and today they would begin their southward march into Arcacia. Sounds of activity already floated through the open window. If Kyrin didn't stir soon, he would have to wake her. But not yet. Let her have a few more minutes of uninterrupted peace.

These few minutes passed fleetingly, and the growing commotion outside finally roused her. Jace rolled onto his side to watch the wakefulness slowly overtake her expression. With a deep breath and a yawn, she rubbed her eyes before opening them. After blinking a time or two, she looked over at him. A tiny crease formed between her brows.

"How long have you been awake?"

"A while." He propped himself up on his elbow. "I didn't want to wake you until I had to."

Kyrin smiled softly and breathed another deep breath. "I guess we better not tarry too much longer. I imagine it will take most of the day to get such a large army moving, but we don't want to keep anyone waiting."

Now it was Jace's turn to sigh. He deeply missed the quiet mornings back at camp when he and Kyrin didn't have anything or anyone waiting on them. Leaning over, he gave her a long kiss that would just have to satisfy this morning and then got out of bed. They dressed in silence, though Jace could almost feel how her thoughts must be racing. Buckling his jerkin, he turned to her. She rubbed her hand over her stomach, her face a bit gray.

"Are you all right?"

Her pinched expression smoothed, though her eyes betrayed her discomfort. "I'm just a bit nauseous. Everything we've done and fought for the last three years has led to today. What happens when we march into Arcacia will determine Ilyon's future. This is the biggest challenge any of us will ever face."

Jace crossed the short distance between them and put his arms around her. He didn't know what to say that could take away the fear behind her words. So he just held her, willing her some bit of comfort. He was afraid too. This was so much bigger than all of them. He knew Elôm was in control, but he desperately missed Elon's physical presence at times like these. It would be so much easier if they could see Him leading them into battle. But he supposed that was where faith came in. It wasn't faith if you could see it.

A minute later, he pulled away slowly. Kyrin didn't seem as pale anymore, and he brushed a wisp of hair from her cheek. "Let's go see if breakfast is ready. Then we'll pack our things."

He took her hand, and they left their room. Downstairs on the main floor, they spotted Kaden. His determined stride toward the front entrance said he was on a mission.

Kyrin hurried to catch up. "Where are you going?"

He stopped and faced them. Faint bruises still shadowed his face. "I'm meeting Talas to choose a new dragon."

His voice was flat, masking the painful emotions that must be boiling underneath the surface. Unlike most of them, Kaden had dreamed of having a dragon for most of his life. Jace could not imagine the pain he must feel having lost Exsis after the bond they'd formed. It would be like losing Tyra. His wolf had been with him through so many of his best and worst times. It surely only added to the pain to have to think about finding a replacement. The sort of bond Kaden had with Exsis didn't just form overnight, at least not normally, even if it had technically happened between Jace and Gem.

Jace snapped from his thoughts, sensing a change in Kyrin. Tension stiffened her shoulders, and a frown pulled her brows together. "Are you sure you're up for this? You almost died barely more than a week ago."

Kaden straightened his stance as if preparing to fight a battle. "I'm fine." He gave her a stubborn look that no doubt came from the Veshiron side of the family. Jace had witnessed it a time or two from Kyrin as well. "I won't let my men go into battle without their captain. Not now."

Kyrin drew a deep breath, pressing her hand to her stomach again. At this rate, she probably wouldn't even be able to eat breakfast. Jace made a mental note to make sure they had food easily accessible for later.

Kaden seemed to read her distress and let the stubbornness fade from his expression. "I need to do this."

Slowly, Kyrin nodded, her own expression grim. "I know."

The day Talas and Leetra had shown up at camp and given Kaden a dragon was a day he would never forget. It had fulfilled a childhood dream he never believed could come true. He'd also never believed he'd have to choose a new dragon now. Exsis was supposed to be his for life. They'd fought and survived the most harrowing battles together. Exsis had sensed Kaden's moods and had even been able to predict his commands before he made them. Part of Kaden's confidence in battle had come from his trust in his dragon—trust they had built through countless hours of flying together. Trust he would not have going into the next battle with a new dragon.

His breaths grew shallow as he followed Talas to the dragon field, and his throat ached. He didn't want a new dragon. It was too soon. No dragon could replace Exsis. But he had no choice. He would not leave his men to face their greatest battle alone. They'd been through far too much together, and they looked to him to lead them. And for that, he needed a dragon.

In the field, cretes were busy at work, saddling and preparing for the flight into Arcacia. Off to the side, however, milled a group of more than thirty dragons whose riders had been killed in the firedrake attack. While some merely rested, others looked around as if searching.

They paused at the perimeter, and Talas motioned to the dragons. "They're all well-trained and experienced." He was far more subdued than usual this morning. The devastation that came with the loss of a dragon was something a crete would understand on a deep level. Dragons were the lifeblood of their people. "You're free to choose any one you wish. Take all the time you need."

What Kaden needed was a lot more time than they had, which was why he had put it off until this morning. But a choice must be made before their army marched.

He walked into the midst of the dragons, not even sure what he was looking for. He'd been drawn to Exsis immediately, but that memory did not help him. Instead of the excitement of that day, everything inside him rebelled. Maybe he would just have to let Talas choose for him.

"I don't know if I can do this," he murmured, more to himself than his friend. His eyes smarted, and he had to blink hard.

Talas gripped his shoulder in a firm, strengthening grip. "You can't replace the bond you had." He paused, grimacing, sharing Kaden's pain. "But in forming a new bond, you may save one of these dragons from becoming despondent and dying."

Kaden dragged in a fortifying breath. Talas was right. Exsis was gone, but perhaps another dragon might be saved. The bond between rider and dragon was not one-sided. To some degree, each of these creatures was suffering through loss as well, even if they could not understand why.

He moved amongst them slowly, noting their reactions to him. Some were curious, while others were too distracted to notice him. None really pulled at him until one rose to pace and stare toward the army of cretes, his head held high, searching, waiting. Scars marred the black scales on his face, slashing down his neck and through the dark green membrane of one of his wings. He'd obviously seen battle before.

"What is his name?"

Talas stepped to his side. "Rhune. He and his rider fought with us during the first attack on Samara. He was one of the dragons Elon healed on our way back to Landale."

Thinking back, Kaden did have a vague memory of seeing Rhune and being shocked the dragon could still fly, wounded as he was. It would be a shame if the creature died now after Elon had healed him.

Kaden strode toward him and called his name. At first, the dragon didn't respond, just kept staring off at the army. Kaden tried again, with more authority in his voice. This time, Rhune responded and turned to him, lowering his head to Kaden's level.

"*Ami.*" He held out his hand for the dragon to take in his scent and then ran it up the dragon's face. Both of them were scarred and had lost. Perhaps they could help each other heal.

"*Réma,*" Kaden commanded him to follow.

With one last glance in the direction of the cretes, Rhune followed Kaden toward where their men were gathering.

Marcus stood in front of the mirror in one corner of the room he'd shared with Liam and Kaden for the past week and straightened his blue and gold Militia surcoat. Sometime in the last few days, Kyrin had found enough materials to add the trimmings of a general to it. It still didn't seem real. After all, nothing had really changed. He still commanded the same men and had the same duties. The full import of his promotion would only sink in if and when they took control of Arcacia.

He didn't let himself think that far ahead yet, to a time when he'd be one of the highest-ranked commanders over all of Arcacia's armies. Probably *the* highest until they could figure out who would have unwavering loyalty to Daniel. It would be his biggest challenge yet. He'd surely face some resentment, especially from older, more seasoned soldiers, for gaining such a position when he was only just past twenty-five. What would his grandfather think when he found out? Would he resent it, or would there be some pride deep down?

Liam joined him, his simple, muted garb coming into stark contrast with Marcus's uniform. It was as it always should have been. They both were in the positions where they belonged and thrived. He could be thankful this struggle had shown them that much, if nothing else.

Liam inspected the uniform in the reflection, and Marcus stood as straight and tall as if it were a superior officer. He concluded with a nod, but then something glinted in his eye, and a teasing smirk rose to his face. "It's a good thing we're leaving. You'd have half the women in Westing following you around by nightfall dressed in that outfit."

A laugh burst from Marcus's chest. Typically, Kaden was the one with such quips. It just proved Liam was in his element now and free to be himself. And clearly, much more observant than most would give him credit for if he'd picked up on how a couple of the servant girls had been looking in Marcus's direction.

"A military uniform will only get you so far." He turned and clapped Liam's shoulder. "Remember, you're the one Altair brother in a committed relationship."

Liam's ears turned a bit red as Marcus noticed they had a habit of doing whenever someone mentioned him and Cassie. Marcus would never have guessed Liam would be the first to find love, but he couldn't be happier. He prayed both Liam and Cassie and Kyrin and Jace would be able to live their lives out in peace once this war was over.

With one last glance in the mirror, Marcus turned for the door. Back to his duties as general. "I'd better get downstairs. It's time to decide what to do with Parker and the others."

They left the room and parted ways, each to their own responsibilities. By this time, several of Marcus's men had gathered and followed him down to the holding cells, where they had kept the Arcacian deserters. Marcus opened the cells, and the Militia formed an escort back upstairs.

Now came an even greater task. Daniel was counting on him to help decide whether or not these men could be trusted to fight with them. It might be wiser to just leave the men here and deal with them once this war was over, yet they needed every able-bodied man willing to fight. According to Parker, these men were willing.

They entered the great hall where Balen had set up a throne of sorts for Daniel. The prince, however, stood with Kyrin and Jace. Balen and the rest of their leaders gathered to the side, speaking amongst themselves. At least Marcus wasn't the only one who had to advise Daniel on whether or not to trust the Arcacian soldiers. He only wished Kyrin wouldn't have had to be dragged into it. No doubt this would dredge up all her old memories of her time serving Daican. She might not hate her previous service as much as he did his own, but it surely couldn't be comfortable for her. She was, however, their best hope at accurately deciphering the soldiers' intentions.

The sound of their approach drew everyone's attention. Daniel turned in their direction, drawing himself up to stand squarely in front of the temporary throne. Though he wore no crown or royal robes, he possessed enough of his father's bearing to appear kingly without them, which was exactly what these soldiers needed to see.

Kyrin stood to his left and a pace behind him, with Jace directly behind her for support. They'd all decided to keep Daniel's marriage to Elanor a secret for now. No sense in providing their enemies with a particular target they could use against him.

Marcus led the men down the center of the room until they reached Daniel. Here they stopped, and he bowed before turning to the men. "If you wish to fight with us to reclaim Arcacia from tyranny, you must swear your allegiance to your rightful king. As I'm sure most of you know, my sister once served the former emperor to advise him who was loyal and who was lying. She is here now serving Prince Daniel in the same capacity, so choose your actions wisely."

He gestured to Kyrin. Many sets of eyes darted to her. Marcus scanned the group, looking for anyone who appeared particularly nervous. Most seemed a bit on edge, and he couldn't pick out all the subtleties in their demeanor that Kyrin could. He looked at her then. She stood very poised, her gaze seeming to sweep over every person. If she was uncomfortable, no one would be able to tell.

Daniel took a seat on the throne, sitting tall and proud, and spoke in a commanding voice he must have been practicing lately. "One at a time, step forward to give me your name and swear your allegiance to me and our goal of bringing peace back to Arcacia."

Marcus shifted his focus back to the men and nodded to Parker, who stepped forward first. He dropped to one knee and bowed his head, swearing his allegiance without hesitation. Kyrin might tell Marcus otherwise once this was over, but of all the men here, about half of which he had once personally commanded, he trusted Parker's sincerity.

One by one, the men stepped forward to swear fealty to Daniel without incident. When the final man stepped back into the group, Daniel rose again. "Thank you for your loyalty. You will be informed once I have made my decision."

Marcus motioned to one of the senior members of the Landale Militia, who he had chosen to replace him as captain. "Return them to their cells. I will come down once I have the decision."

They moved out in an orderly group. Once the door closed, Balen and the others drew closer, and everyone turned to Kyrin. Some of her poise had slipped, her expression strained and tired. While he was used to having so many people counting on him and watching him, she was not. And it had to be exhausting to watch people's reactions and mannerisms so closely.

At least Daniel seemed to understand this, judging by the seemingly apologetic look he gave her. "Were you able to pick up on anything?"

"Well, from what I noticed, I would say all but two are truly loyal and dedicated to our goals. I wasn't able to pick up any signs of deception or malice. And the two I'm unsure of aren't necessarily disloyal; they just seemed more hesitant to swear their loyalty. My guess is that, while they don't want to serve Davira anymore, they may not fully want to serve you either."

She named the two, and Marcus found relief wash through him that it wasn't Parker or any of his former men. Relief and a bit of pride. It wasn't like he'd had any direct hand in their change of heart, but at least he'd led a good company of men.

Daniel gave a decisive nod. "We'll leave those two here. We can't take risks on uncertainties. If everyone else agrees, I will allow the others to join us under the watchful eye of the Militia."

No one spoke in opposition. Just over a dozen men might not make a difference in the battle to come, but perhaps their influence could help sway favor toward Daniel in the future. That is what Marcus hoped, anyway. What they needed now was a leader to help make sure they remained on the right track. While he hoped they would integrate well into the Militia, that wouldn't happen overnight. Perhaps not even before they were thrown into battle together. The Militia, up to this point, had consisted entirely of fugitives fleeing the tyranny enforced by Arcacia's military. Hard feelings might arise, and that would require strong leaders on both sides working together.

"I know the group is small, but if you agree, I would like to make Parker their captain. He served me well, and I have no doubt he'll report and help resolve any potential issues that may turn up."

The look Daniel gave him was one of full support and confidence. "I trust you to make whatever decisions you see fit, General."

Marcus's breath caught, the title suddenly feeling more real and holding more weight than it had up to this point.

Jace strapped the last of the supplies to Gem, including an easy-to-reach bundle of bread and cheese for Kyrin. As expected, she'd barely touched her breakfast. Agreeing to help read the Arcacian soldiers hadn't helped, though she'd done so without hesitation. If he had his way, it was the last time she'd be called upon for such a task.

He patted Gem on the shoulder. She curled her head around and blew a steamy breath into his face that reeked of raw meat. The cretes had made sure every dragon was well-fed for the start of their journey. He turned his face away and wrinkled his nose. "Thanks for that."

He patted her cheek anyway and shifted to scan the area. He spotted James nearby, checking the saddle of a sturdy gray horse. Kyrin was preoccupied with talking to Anne, so he walked over to his brother. "Not flying this time?"

James looked up from his work with a half-smile. "Charles and I were asked if we would mind riding so that our dragon could be used to transport extra supplies. I was more than happy to accept the arrangement."

Jace chuckled and ran his hand down the horse's neck. "If I didn't have Gem, I would have done the same."

There were certainly times he missed riding Niton. As much as he loved Gem, horses always held a special draw for him.

James reached up and attached his sword to the saddle, pausing and letting his hand slide down the scabbard. He looked at Jace again.

"You know, the only time I've ever used this outside of sparring was against you." He shook his head, no doubt reliving that night like Jace was. Then Jace noticed the way his throat moved in a hard swallow. "I don't know if I'm prepared to face what's ahead."

The raw honesty sunk deep into Jace's chest, dredging up all the times he had experienced the same doubts and fear. He put his hand on James's shoulder. "I don't think anyone is ever truly prepared for their first battle."

He breathed out a long breath under the weight of so many memories. They hadn't yet talked about his past, and now part of him wished they had. Perhaps there would be time yet on their journey, but some he would share now. "You know I was a slave, but you probably don't know I was a gladiator."

James's black brows lifted some, but he remained silent.

"I was sixteen the first time my master forced me out into an arena. Everything I'd been taught disappeared in the terror of facing my opponent. I was sure I would die, but the training kicked in, and I survived. If nothing else, I'm sure your father made sure you were well trained."

James nodded solemnly.

"Then try to hold onto that. Everyone is afraid to go into battle, but try not to let it drown out the training ingrained in you. You'd be surprised how much your body remembers without you having to think about it."

James stood a little taller, head held a little higher. "Thanks. I'll try to remember that."

It struck Jace then how much he hated the thought of his brother going into battle. One more person he could lose before this fight ended. But that was the way of war, and all he could do was pray and hope his advice would help. He squeezed James's shoulder and then turned back toward Gem. Now Kyrin waited there for him.

She glanced toward James, her tone genuine. "Is he all right?"

"He's just anxious like we all are." Jace looked over Gem and their supplies before returning his gaze to her. "Ready?"

A tentative smile that held all their hopes and dreams tipped her lips. "Ready."

She stepped back to let him mount Gem first, and then he reached down to hoist her up behind him. Ivoris lingered nearby, loaded with extra supplies. Jace prompted Gem forward, drawing more closely to the others from Landale. All around them buzzed a sense of anticipation. He looked toward the bright banners flapping in the breeze nearby, marking where Daniel, Balen, and the rest of their leaders gathered. Any moment now, they would give the order to march.

Holden and his dragon moved up alongside Gem. "You know, I really never thought I'd live long enough to see this."

They peered at the sea of soldiers surrounding them, waiting to march into Davira's domain. The culmination of three years of struggles, battles, loss. None of them had probably believed they'd live to see Ilyon come together like this. Not after everything they had faced already.

Before Jace could respond, a loud, clear horn blast echoed across the meadows. A chill raced through Jace. It was time. Time to reclaim Arcacia.

Time to return home.

THE SINNAI MOUNTAINS rose tall and majestic to Daniel's right, the admittedly impressive Fort Rhall standing obstinately about a mile ahead. Behind him, their army waited with just as much resolution. After a long march across Arcacia's northern plains, they were eager for a fight. Daniel, however, wasn't ready to let them at that fight without one final effort to preserve lives.

When they had arrived two days ago, he'd sent messengers to the fortress. Messengers with an offer to parley with Davira. If he could speak with her face to face, just maybe he could talk her down and avoid bloodshed altogether. He'd love nothing more than to send everyone home to their families without any more casualties.

He looked to the clear sky and then closed his eyes, calling out to Elôm for a miracle. Last word from the fortress was that Davira had arrived and agreed to speak to him. He wasn't sure whether to find any spark of hope in this or not. His sister had proven to be too unstable for him to truly believe she had any real desire to negotiate—as much as the parley pavilion her attendants set up a couple of hundred yards away might suggest otherwise.

He shifted, his traditional Arcacian plate armor creaking along with his horse's saddle. He looked to his right. Marcus waited there with him. To his left was Aric. Daniel appreciated having them both with him.

Marcus had chosen a dozen of their best militiamen for further security, standing in formation behind them. And a couple of hundred yards beyond them waited a line of dragon riders. It was a risky move to meet with Davira face to face, but one he believed necessary. If there was even the slightest possibility of avoiding further conflict, he had to pursue it. Not that he particularly wanted to face her. During their last encounter, he'd been dangling from the dungeon ceiling while she watched her men take turns beating him. He rolled his shoulders, phantom pain darting across his ribs.

"My lord."

Daniel's attention snapped to Marcus, who motioned toward the fort in the distance. Daniel shifted his gaze and spotted two dragons rapidly drawing closer. He'd been too busy brooding to notice them. He straightened in the saddle and dug his fingers into his horse's reins. They'd never attack with only two dragons, but that didn't make him feel any less exposed sitting in the open. He was tempted to glance back and see how their dragon riders responded, but he kept his eyes glued to the approaching dragons. Even if they couldn't see him well, he didn't want to give the slightest appearance of doubt or weakness.

The two dragons glided downward, landing on the other side of the pavilion. He couldn't see for sure, but he had no doubt one of the riders was his sister. If he had to guess, the other dark figure was Sir Richard.

Now that his sister had arrived, Daniel gave Marcus a nod, and his general raised their parley flag. With a deep breath and whispered prayer, Daniel nudged his horse, and they rode forward. Marcus and Aric remained on either side of him. The pavilion doors were parted on both sides, and it did not take long to get a good view of Davira standing at the table in the center. His heart gave a solid thump that continued with a heavy beat, and his scalp prickled. He couldn't make out her emerald green eyes just yet, but he could certainly feel them boring an invisible hole into the center of his forehead.

A few yards from the pavilion, they dismounted. Daniel took great care to do so without fumbling due to his armor. He wasn't used to the cumbersome pieces even though he'd started wearing them daily once they had drawn deeper into Arcacia.

Steeling himself, he led the way into the shade of the pavilion. His gaze tangled with Davira's. Her eyes simmered with such intense loathing he struggled not to look away. Any hope he'd had for this meeting rapidly dwindled, and they hadn't even spoken a word yet.

Once he'd held her gaze long enough to show her he wouldn't be intimidated, he glanced over at Richard. The man focused on Marcus, a smug tilt to his expression. No doubt, he believed Kaden had died from the viper venom and had come, in part, to gloat. Daniel barely held back the urge to wipe the smirk from his face with the truth, but he might as well keep Kaden's recovery a secret for now. It was always good to have the element of surprise.

Daniel's attention returned to Davira. Now that she wasn't pinning him in place with her eyes, he had a moment to take in how awful she looked. Oh, she stood tall and proud in her gaudy black and gold finery. However, her cheeks were sunken, and her skin looked as though she spent most of her time avoiding daylight. She wasn't exactly skeletal, but everything about her face was sharp and severe, a contrast to her typically more rounded features. Perhaps she had been unwell? Either that or just so consumed with hatred it took that much of a toll on her body. Why couldn't she see the damage she was doing to everyone, herself included?

"Davira." He spoke tentatively, praying for even the smallest inkling of softening. Of reason. Of anything sane.

Her jaw only clenched harder, and she shot him such a menacing glare a shiver traced down his spine under the thick layers of clothing and armor. So much for that.

He braced himself, falling into the commanding tone he'd been working on so hard lately. "We have come to discuss your surrender. All I ask is for you to step down peacefully and transfer your rule to me, Father's rightful heir. No one else has to die in this war."

She bared her teeth at him. "Never."

Daniel released a great sigh. She was more stubborn than their father, and he could shake her for it. No one had ever aggravated him the way his family could. And family they still were, despite everything. Nothing could erase that fact. He glanced at Marcus and then locked eyes with Richard.

"I want to speak to my sister alone." He left no doubt in his voice that he wouldn't take no for an answer. This was no time to be timid about representing himself as king.

Richard's brows furrowed, his arms crossed stubbornly, but then he turned slowly to Davira. Daniel studied his sister again. Was she actively trying to kill him with just a look? No doubt praying to her false gods to smite him. He almost snorted.

At last, she snapped to Richard, "Leave us."

Richard did nothing for about two seconds before he unfolded his arms with a grumble and slowly turned to leave.

Daniel looked over at Marcus. "Go."

Marcus cast a wary glance at Davira and traded a look with Aric, but neither one questioned him. Still, Daniel read their hesitance. He wasn't even entirely sure what he was hoping to accomplish by this. It wasn't like there was any real chance Davira would respond to a private family conversation, but he had to try at least. Chances were she had weapons hidden somewhere on her person, despite the parley agreement, and would try to kill him right here and now. But if he kept her from reaching his neck or face, he was relatively confident in the security of his armor. He'd keep a safe distance between them in any case.

Once both parties stood several yards away, offering some privacy as long as this didn't turn into a shouting match, Daniel focused his full attention on Davira. At least the table acted as something of a safety buffer between them. The way she glared at him from across it convinced him she truly was trying to kill him with her gaze. He rolled his eyes. It was one of the most ridiculous things he had ever seen, and right now, this whole ghastly struggle seemed to shrink down to his little sister throwing a temper tantrum.

"Seriously? You're going to stand there and waste energy hoping, by sheer willpower on your part, I'll drop dead where I stand?"

Her face turned crimson. "The gods can still strike you down."

Daniel folded his arms. "And how many times have your gods actually done that for you?"

Her eyes would pop out of her head if she glared at him any harder. He leaned toward her, bracing his hands on the table. "Davira, please, can we just stop this? All of it? Too many people are dying. Our country is dying. You know Father would have wanted me to be king. You *know* that. Aren't you tired of all this anger and hatred? What is it costing you? What could you possibly gain? We just want peace. I don't want any more of our people to die. We could end it all right here if you would just let go of this darkness and hatred."

With every word, she seemed to recoil as if it were the most loathsome and disgusting thing she'd ever heard.

"I will never surrender to you," she spat. Now she leaned toward him, and he kept half an eye on her hands in case she reached for a weapon. "You will not have my father's throne. I'll send every soldier in Arcacia here to cut you down until every man and woman standing with you is lying dead in this field."

Daniel let his shoulders slump, the last tiny spark of his own foolish hope dying in his chest. He'd known it would never end except through violence. Their entire life Davira had seemed intoxicated by death and destruction. Why should now be any different?

He looked her straight in the eyes. "And what of all the Arcacians who will die? What army will be left to help you maintain your throne? Because even if you manage to stop us here, this won't end. The more pain you cause, the more people will rise up to oppose you."

Her lips curled. "Let them try."

With a whirl of her black skirts, she spun around and marched out of the pavilion. That was it then. Now they would fight.

Marcus and Aric were at his side in a moment, and Marcus all but pushed him toward the pavilion entrance.

"We should get moving. I have the feeling she won't wait long to unleash her drakes on us. We need to get you to safety."

Daniel clenched his fists and sent a glare after his sister as she stormed off. Unlike her gods, Elôm was real, and Daniel couldn't help wishing He would just strike her down so that no one else would have to die. No one else should die because of her unbridled wickedness and quest for vengeance. But no lightning came from the sky. No crack appeared in the earth to swallow her up.

Releasing a great sigh, Daniel heeded Marcus's warning and left the pavilion with them guarding his back. At his horse, he paused to look toward the fort as Davira and Richard flew away. Dark firedrakes dotted the wall, ready to attempt to decimate their army just like they'd tried in Samara.

He mounted up and turned his horse toward their men. No sense in waiting for Davira. He would give the order to begin the siege.

KYRIN BRACED ONE hand against a tree and fought to convince her stomach not to upturn for the third time in five minutes. It rolled and churned but slowly started to settle. She brushed the cold sweat from her forehead, wincing a little at how her head ached. The shriek and roar of dragons and firedrakes close by for the second morning in a row didn't help, though it couldn't explain the intense bouts of nausea lately.

Slowly, she straightened and turned around once she was sure she wouldn't empty whatever little remained in her stomach. Jace stood not six feet away, arms crossed. He looked quite fierce in his chain-mail and leather, though she knew the deep frown on his face was due to worry. She'd already told him she was fine. Other than weariness from their long journey and the strange bouts of nausea she'd experienced every day since leaving Samara, she felt normal. That didn't stop him from hovering whenever he noticed her queasiness.

She attempted a weak smile. "I'm feeling better now."

If anything, his brows only lowered. "Why do you keep getting sick?"

She shrugged. "Probably the stress. Same reason I have been getting more headaches lately." She rested her hands on his arms and looked up into his eyes, which seemed to be trying to pinpoint a reason for her suffering. "If it makes you feel better, I'll talk to Josef when he isn't busy."

At last, some of the tension released from his expression. "Good."

She probably should have days ago, but she really did think it was only stress. They had so much depending on this siege and whatever battles came next. It was hard not to let the fear build up inside of her.

"I think I'll head out and join the Militia." Jace's low tone said he was as reluctant as she was for him to go. Not that he would fight today. None of their ground forces had done any fighting yet. Only those manning the siege engines and the dragon riders. There wasn't likely to be any ground fighting until they breached the fort or unless Arcacia's forces decided to march out and meet them. Because of this last possibility, their army remained ready for battle each and every day. Though not officially part of the Militia, Jace always joined them.

Kyrin's stomach cramped again. Even if he wasn't fighting, she still couldn't stop worrying. Though the dragons managed to keep the firedrakes at bay, one still could break through and destroy part of their army. "Be careful."

He unfolded his arms to rest his strong hands on her shoulders. "I will." He pressed a kiss to her forehead.

She sent him a smirk as he pulled away. "You don't want to kiss me on the mouth?"

He smirked back but then bent to give her a soft kiss on the lips. "I'll see you later."

He squeezed her shoulders before walking off to join some of their friends heading to the battlefront. Kyrin watched until he disappeared into the trees and then looked around camp. Everyone not on the front lines had set up their tents within the small forest. It provided basic protection for their medical base, command headquarters, and supplies just in case any firedrakes got past their dragons.

She focused on where Josef and their other physicians had set up. She would talk to him at some point, but she wanted to give her stomach a little more time to settle. The scent of blood had already caused her to lose her lunch when she'd volunteered to help two days ago.

Instead, her eyes snagged on Elanor and Anne near the royal pavilion. Kyrin set out along the path through the rows of canvas tents toward them. She passed several guards, including Trev, who Daniel had placed in charge of Elanor's security, which he took very seriously. Elanor and Anne smiled when they spotted her, and Kyrin thanked Elôm for the blessing of having such wonderful women in her life. She needed that camaraderie, especially when she had to say goodbye to Jace every morning.

As she drew near, Anne's expression pinched a little. "Are you all right? You seem pale."

Kyrin waved off the concern. "I'm fine. I've just been getting nauseous lately for some reason."

"Oh? Have you talked to Josef?"

"Not yet. I will today. I just wanted to wait a bit. Two days ago, the smell of blood was too much."

Anne scrutinized her more closely now. "How long has this been going on? Is it only the smell of blood or other things?"

"Well, I first felt ill the morning we left Samara. And anything strong seems to trigger it. Even coffee." That's what had set her off yesterday morning.

Anne looked over at Elanor for a lingering moment. There was something…odd in their expressions like they were sharing hidden information and coming to the same dawning conclusion. For once, Kyrin couldn't figure out what such silent communication meant.

Her heart gave a nervous thump. "What?" She looked between the two of them. Anne faced her with a gentle, almost mothering look while Elanor seemed to be trying not to smile. "What is it? Is something wrong?"

Anne put her hand on Kyrin's arm, which only sent a panicky sensation into her already sensitive stomach. What were the two of them not saying?

"What you're describing sounds a lot like morning sickness, and… that's a common early pregnancy symptom."

Everything inside Kyrin grew very quiet, followed by a sudden rush to her head. She wobbled, but Anne held her more tightly. Her heart pounded loudly in the airiness in her head.

Anne nudged her gently toward the pavilion. "Let's go sit down."

Elanor took her other arm, and they guided her inside. Kyrin's mind spun around that one last word Anne spoke.

Pregnancy.

They led her to a chair and helped her ease down into it. Kyrin gripped the wooden armrests in an attempt to anchor herself. So many emotions rushed through her at once she couldn't even identify one to grasp onto.

She looked up at Anne and Elanor, a little breathless. "You think I'm pregnant?"

Anne knelt alongside her and rested her hand over Kyrin's. "Have you noticed anything else? Are you late?"

Kyrin hadn't thought of that. "Well, yes, I just thought it was all stress." She shook her head. How had she not figured this out? Not that they'd really taught about pregnancy at Tarvin Hall. It wasn't as if she'd grown up like a normal young woman with her mother around to explain things like this when she was young.

Kyrin laid her hand over her stomach, and the full import of it sank in. She knew—hoped—it would happen someday, but she'd never expected it now. Not in the midst of this war. But it had. She breathed out slowly, the end forming into a laugh as tears filled her eyes. She and Jace were going to have a baby!

Elanor bounced on her toes, her hands clasped under her chin. "I'm going to be an aunt!"

Kyrin stood up and was immediately enveloped in their arms. They all laughed now, tears in their eyes and on their cheeks. Kyrin's mind still swirled, trying to comprehend everything that had happened and changed in the past few moments. The tiny little life growing inside her. The fact that, in less than a year, it wouldn't be just her and Jace anymore. They would be a family of three.

Just as quickly as the love and excitement had grown, fear joined in. Where would they even be several months from now? Would the war be over? Would they even survive? A cold wave rushed through her, tingling in her lips and fingers. Above all else, she had to protect her child any way she could.

She slowly pulled out of her friends' embrace. They both looked at her, their brows lowering at what must have been a distinct lack of joy on her face. She drew a deep breath to get a hold of the racing fear and breath-stealing protectiveness she couldn't believe was already so strong. She'd only known she was going to be a mother for less than five minutes and already every instinct and impulse screamed at her to do whatever she must to protect her baby.

"I can't stay here. It's not safe." It had never been safe, but now it wasn't only her own safety she had to consider. She winced. The thought of leaving Jace, not knowing firsthand what was happening here, tore at her heart, but her priorities shifted in the last few life-altering moments. Jace would wholeheartedly agree.

"I should go to camp where it's safer." At least her mother was there. And Lenae. She was suddenly desperate for their wisdom and experience as mothers. She rubbed her stomach again. If only Jace could be there too! But as much as he would want it, he wouldn't leave the fight now. Not when it held the key to the future they both prayed so fervently for. Especially once he learned it was their child's future too.

Anne's hand rested on Kyrin's arm again. "I'll go with you."

Kyrin's gaze shot to her friend's face. Before she could speak, Elanor clasped her other arm. "So will I."

Kyrin looked between them, shaking her head. "I couldn't ask you to leave Trask and Daniel just for me. I'll go myself."

Anne simply smiled. "I can guarantee you Trask and Daniel will be thrilled to know we are safely away from this battle. It might be difficult for us all to be apart, but we'll do it together."

A fresh flood of moisture gushed into Kyrin's eyes before she could even try to fight it. She loved these two women so much. She hugged them both again, the tears now streaming down her cheeks. "Thank you so much," she all but blubbered, not quite sure what had come over her.

Finally getting hold of the surge of emotion, she released her friends and swiped her fingers across her cheeks to dry the tears. "I'll start packing my things. We'll leave as soon as we can all say goodbye to our men."

It would be tough. She'd cry again the moment she saw Jace, but it had to be this way. Each of the men would trickle in at some point during the next few hours to grab a bite to eat as long as nothing was going wrong on the front lines. If not, she would find someone to get a message to them before it grew too late to leave. They still had plenty of daylight hours left.

Kyrin headed back toward her and Jace's tent. She really didn't have much she would have to pack. Mostly she would just need to gather enough rations to last a few days. By her estimate, they may make it to camp late tomorrow evening if they traveled into the night. Suddenly, she found herself analyzing everything she had been eating lately. Was she eating enough? She'd never had the kind of appetite her brothers had. Should she be eating more? What about variety? Field rations weren't exactly fresh. Not as fresh as foraged food at camp would be. There was so much she didn't know. Maybe she would still try to see Josef before she left. She had so many questions.

Inside the tent, she divided her and Jace's spare clothing into two packs. She hated having to separate them. Their lives had become so meshed into one these past few months of marriage. She couldn't imagine not being here with him, not seeing him every day, for however long this war lasted. Just thinking about it was like an iron grip around her heart that squeezed painfully and set her eyes to stinging. She blinked hard. He would be fine, and they would be together again to raise their baby. She couldn't let herself think of any other possibility or the time in between.

When she finished, she ducked out of the tent and looked around. The queasiness had left her for the moment, so now might be a good time to find Josef. She headed toward the medical area, which was set up under a group of awnings. About two dozen cretes, who had been injured in the fight so far, rested on cots. A couple, who were sitting up, looked like they would be rejoining the other dragon riders in another day or two, whether or not Josef thought that was wise. Others looked like they were barely hanging on. Kyrin tried not to focus on them or any of the bloodied bandages.

Josef, Liam, Leetra, and Cassie were all at work, but Cassie was closest and the first to notice her. She had the perfect, calming smile for a physician. It was no wonder Liam was smitten with her.

Kyrin beckoned her closer, hoping Liam wouldn't notice. She didn't want to share the news with her brothers until she had a chance to tell Jace. "Could I talk to you about a private matter?"

She sent another glance at Liam, and Cassie nodded in under-standing. "Come with me."

She motioned Kyrin into one of the tents they had set up around the perimeter of the medical area. This must be Cassie's tent, judging by the personal items and neatly-made bed inside. It was only just big enough for the two of them to stand upright.

"How can I help?"

Kyrin took a breath, the overwhelming emotions building again. She spoke in a quiet voice just in case anyone was nearby. "I'm pretty sure I'm pregnant."

Cassie's soft eyes widened and took on a joyful sparkle. Kyrin shared all her symptoms and answered a few questions, and Cassie confirmed that it all pointed toward pregnancy.

"Based on your information and symptoms, I would say you're around eight weeks along."

"Is there anything I should do? Should I be eating more? I just want to make sure the baby is healthy."

Cassie's smile helped calm her racing thoughts. "Yes, eating well is important. You should also try to limit your stress as much as possible."

Kyrin winced, her stress levels much higher than she wanted to admit, and Cassie gave a sympathetic look. "I know it's not easy, but do your best."

"I'm planning to leave for camp. It will be much safer there for the baby and me."

"That's good. And I'm sure Lenae can help you even more than I can. Medically, I know about pregnancy, but she also has the experience of being a mother herself."

"I was thinking the same thing."

Cassie's smile widened once more. "Your brothers will be so happy."

Kyrin allowed herself to smile and experience the joy as well. "I can't wait to tell them. I have to tell Jace first, though."

"I will keep the secret."

"Thanks, Cassie." Kyrin gave her a quick hug and hoped her belief that Cassie would soon become her second sister-in-law was correct. She would make a wonderful addition to the family. It was growing so quickly. Kyrin smiled at the thought, though it made her sad, too. Her father would have loved to see it.

The two of them stepped back out of the tent. This time Liam noticed them, and Kyrin gave him a quick smile. She was sure Cassie would think of a good excuse if he wondered why she was there.

As she left the makeshift medical area, her stomach growled, and she realized how empty it was. She hadn't been able to hold down any breakfast she had eaten. She should probably get something to eat now while the nausea was gone. There were still some dried berries left from breakfast, so she turned back toward her tent.

An ear-shattering shriek and snapping limbs exploded overhead, and Kyrin fell to her knees.

KYRIN COVERED HER head and ducked. Branches splintered and cracked overhead as if the whole canopy was about to collapse on top of camp. Another thunderous roar blasted through the trees, echoing in her chest. Her first thought was of the baby, and she gasped a desperate prayer for protection.

Another moment passed without anything crushing her, and she chanced a glance up. The leaves and branches shuddered and thrashed, though she couldn't see much more than flashes of black scales. Dragons roared now. Sparks and smoke fell around camp. Everyone rushed around as if not knowing where to go or what to do. The sounds of men shouting and women screaming warred with the struggle overhead. Kyrin couldn't tell if the firedrake right above them was trying to get through the canopy to the camp or if it was just stuck there being attacked by the dragons.

She looked around frantically. Was anywhere safe in camp? Her thoughts jumped to Elanor and Anne, and she turned back toward the royal pavilion, not knowing where else to go in the chaos. People dashed across her path, slowing her down as the firedrake continued to roar above them. At this point, she could only hope the dragons would kill the creature, and it would remain suspended in the trees instead of crashing down into the camp.

As she drew nearer to the pavilion, a face caught her eye. It seemed out of place, yet familiar at the same time. She stopped for a better look. A blast of phantom cold flushed through her body. She had seen that man before. Scerle, an interrogator who had worked for her grandfather. Something flashed in his hand. He reached out to grab someone and drove the blade right into the unsuspecting man's chest.

A gasped cry broke from Kyrin, and she couldn't move for a moment, frozen with the shock of it. What was an enemy soldier doing deep within their campsite?

Getting hold of herself, she rushed to the nearest man, a Samaran soldier.

"We're under attack!" She grabbed his arm and pointed to Scerle, who appeared to be hunting for his next victim. "That man works for Davira and just killed someone."

The soldier pulled out his sword and motioned her back. "Stay here."

Kyrin watched, unable to breathe. What was going on?

Before the soldier reached Scerle, a tall figure stepped out from around a tent just behind him. Kyrin barely caught a muffled gasp, and the soldier fell to his knees. The tall man turned, and Kyrin's heart lodged in her throat.

An enemy ryrik.

She took an unsteady step back as their eyes locked and then turned to run. Footsteps thudded behind her, and she reached for the dagger on her belt. Right as strong fingers closed around her arm, she spun around and drove the blade into the man's side. He let out a roar and released his grip. She yanked her knife free and fled.

Her heart raced as her gaze darted everywhere, frantic for a place to hide. How many enemies had infiltrated camp? How badly had she wounded her pursuer? Would he still come after her? Of course, he would. He was a ryrik. The wound wouldn't stop him.

That's when the screams registered, rising up in panicked clamor all around her. The cries of the helpless being attacked. They didn't have enough fighting men in camp.

The army.

Kyrin dashed between two tents, changing direction. She had to get to their army. It was the only place of safety from whatever stealth attack Davira had mounted against them.

"Kyrin!" The shout came from somewhere to her left.

Her heart skipped a beat. "Jace!"

She couldn't see him through the chaos and tents. Swords rang out now. She hurried toward the sound, frantically seeking him, calling his name.

Then he appeared several yards away. She rushed toward him. She'd only taken a couple of steps when something tripped her. She crashed to her hands and knees. Someone grabbed her by the hair. She turned and slashed upward at the arm hovering above her. The man cursed and released her, but a swift backhand across the face nearly sent her to the ground. Her ears rang, and her eyes watered.

A fist closed around her wrist and wrenched it sharply. Pain shot up her arm, forcing a cry to her lips, and the dagger slipped from her fingers. The captor yanked her to her feet, twisting her other arm and holding it securely behind her back.

Jace's voice cleared the lingering buzzing in her ears. She looked for him, only to find him embroiled in a battle with two ryriks.

Her captor hauled her backward, away from the fight. Kyrin dug in her feet and resisted him all she could. She would not let herself be taken from Jace again. He caught her gaze and realized what was happening. He fought with increased fury. He would come to her rescue. He had to. Kyrin was going to fight her hardest to see that he had time.

But then a third figure appeared just behind Jace. Kyrin had no chance to warn him before a sword hilt smashed into the back of his head.

"No!"

Jace fell to his knees, Scerle standing behind him. He fought to get up, but one of the ryriks kneed him in the stomach, sending him to the ground. Still, he struggled to rise, only to be met with a solid kick this time.

Kyrin begged them to stop, tears flooding her eyes.

Scerle knelt, digging his knee into Jace's back, and wrenched his arms up, binding them tightly. When they dragged Jace to his feet, he met Kyrin's gaze again, his eyes blazing but pained with defeat.

Jace stumbled up the steep incline leading into the mountains. The back of his head throbbed. His only consolation was that he didn't think he'd suffered a concussion. He needed all his wits about him if he was going to get Kyrin to safety. He glanced over his shoulder to see her struggling up the hill just behind him, prodded by a ryrik. The very same one who had left her lip swollen and bleeding. His own blood still burned hot for a fight.

Just beyond Kyrin staggered a ragged line of eight other captives taken in the surprise attack—two women and the rest men. Jace didn't know any of them except for Holden. He, too, had somehow been taken in the ambush. He glanced up and met Jace's eyes. Understanding passed between them. Whatever it took, they would try to get everyone out of this mess.

A shove forced Jace to focus back on the path ahead and at

Scerle, who was in the lead. Jace had recognized him as soon as he'd been dragged back to his feet in camp. He remembered all too clearly the sight of the man with a dagger to Kyrin's neck back in the forest between Mernin and Fort Rivor. He'd heard of the man's reputation for cruelty—had seen it in his eyes.

Elôm, please don't let him harm Kyrin. Help me get her to safety.

Despite the heat in his blood, icy cold sank deep into his chest. This wasn't the first time he and Kyrin had found themselves captives. And each time, he'd been powerless to do anything to protect her. Elôm had always intervened in the end, but what if this time was different? What if, this time, they would not see freedom again?

Jace breathed hard, trying to tell himself he trusted Elôm no matter the outcome. If only his mind and fears were more cooperative. *Please give me strength.*

Sweat rolled down Jace's neck. Dragon and firedrake roars echoed in the distance. He looked back once more, but a ridge line hid their army from view. Their captors had taken precautions to remain out of sight. Jace looked up at the sky, praying to see dragon riders searching for them, but not even a cloud marked the perfect blue. Maybe no one in camp even realized they were gone yet, still trying to sort through the attack no one had seen coming.

Jace's leg muscles burned from strain, and he could hear Kyrin huffing for breath by the time their captors finally jerked them to a halt on a small plateau surrounded by shrubs. Before he had a chance to take in much else, his captor shoved him to his knees. Sharp gravel bit into them through his pants. Kyrin was at his side and on her knees a second later.

Holden dropped next until every captive formed a semi-circular line at the edge of the plateau. Heavy breaths and the crackle of rocks surrounded them as their captors ensured they were secure.

Jace leaned toward Kyrin, their shoulders pressing together. "Are you all right?"

It took her a second to respond. Though she nodded, her face was pale, bringing her bloodied lip into sharp contrast, and her eyes were too wide. Jace tested the strength of his bonds for the hundredth time. He couldn't take on these men alone, but it did not stop the fire inside him from screaming to do whatever he could to get Kyrin to safety. The rough rope refused to budge.

Scerle stepped in front of them, and Jace craned his head back to look up at him. The man swept his cruel gaze over Jace, Kyrin, and then Holden. "You three will make a fine gift for Her Majesty."

A chill prickled Jace's skin. It was just as he'd feared. If they didn't find a way out of this very quickly, they would have to face Davira. He shifted a little closer to Kyrin. Davira held a particular hatred for the Altairs. His blood ran cold to think of Kyrin at Davira's mercy.

Scerle moved on then, slowly following the line of captives. "As for the rest of you, do any of you belong to the traitor prince's inner circle?"

Tense silence reigned. Jace wasn't sure if it would be better if they were or not. He recognized one of the women from Landale but did not know her personally. The others were either from one of the other camps or from Samara.

"So it's a no then." Scerle waved to one of the ryriks. "Kill them."

Gasps and pleas for mercy erupted. One of the men tried to rise, but a ryrik knocked him to the ground. Another ryrik closest to Scerle scowled. "Even the women?"

Scerle sneered at him. "Yes. You'll get your rewards once the queen's rule is no longer challenged."

With some reluctance, the ryrik motioned to the others. Cries and screams rose again. For once, Jace's blood froze as the ryriks carried out their orders. His stomach lurched, and he focused on Kyrin. Her eyes were squeezed shut, tears streaming down her cheeks.

A heavy, chill silence settled after a moment, though Jace's thudding heart promptly drowned it out. He glanced over at Holden, trying not to look at the still bodies beyond him. It could easily have been the three of them, though he had a terrible feeling their fates might be much worse.

Scerle snapped his fingers. "Get them up."

A rough hand grabbed Jace's arm and hauled him to his feet. They left the clearing and bodies behind, following a narrow path through the brush. Not far away, they reached another clearing crowded with firedrakes. Jace swallowed hard, the moisture abandoning his mouth. He'd found himself in this position before, hauled off to Valcré against his will, bound to a firedrake. This time he didn't have just himself to worry about but also Kyrin and one of his closest friends. They probably wouldn't survive this. Not this time.

A ryrik shoved Jace toward one of the drakes and up onto its back behind the saddle. He looked for Kyrin. She, too, was lifted onto a drake. She looked his way as she settled in. Her face was set, yet a shadow of anguish he was not expecting filled her eyes. During past captivity, she'd always been so strong, but for some reason, any hope she may have clung to seemed dim this time. It twisted his insides into knots. He was her husband, yet found himself powerless to do the number one thing he vowed to do. Protect her. If only he had made it back to camp sooner.

Evening was upon them when they landed in the courtyard of Auréa Palace. The deep ache in the pit of Kyrin's stomach intensified so much she almost doubled over. She had not seen the palace this close since she had fled it nearly three years ago, and had not anticipated seeing it again unless they were victorious against Davira. She certainly had not been prepared to face Davira again in her domain. Just the thought of her bone-chilling eyes robbed the breath from Kyrin's lungs.

She gulped. Why this? Why now? Her heart cried out to Elôm. She had literally just found out she was pregnant. Jace didn't even know yet! Now that her life was in danger, so was their child's. All she'd needed was a couple more hours, and she would have been safely on her way to Landale.

Scerle reached up and pulled her down from his drake. His eagerness to deliver her to Davira had grown more evident the closer they'd come to Valcré. She looked for Jace. One of the other men was just leading him around his drake. They locked eyes, and Kyrin's heart constricted. She knew how hard it was for him to be powerless. He always fought so hard to protect her, and if he knew she was carrying their child…

Scerle's hand locked around her arm, his fingertips digging into the muscles, forcing her toward the palace. She glanced up at its towering walls as they climbed the front steps. Her mind flashed back to the very first time she had come here. She'd frozen, right here on these steps, terrified to face the unknown. It was Collin's teasing that had gotten her moving again. It felt like a lifetime ago. Even now, her legs shook and threatened to buckle.

They passed through the wide double doors and into the grand foyer. Kyrin shivered, the spasms darting through her limbs. There had never been a time since escaping that she missed this place. It seemed colder than she remembered. Perhaps because anyone who had ever been a friend or ally no longer inhabited it. Now only Davira's dark influence permeated it like a sickness.

A palace guard led the way toward the throne room. The huge hall soon opened up to them, their footsteps clapping against the tiled floor and echoing in the vaulted ceiling high above. They stopped at the far end, where Scerle ordered them to kneel. Kyrin obeyed, though Jace and Holden were slower to comply. She was terrified to do anything that would jeopardize the safety of the baby. Terrified to even think of it.

Swallowing hard, she looked up at the throne that rose above them. Once, she'd sat right beyond it, watching people who were in the same place she was now. A chill shuddered through her, and she fought to breathe slowly.

Footsteps echoed from the hall just outside the throne room—a sharp and distinct tapping of heels too light to belong to a man. Kyrin's mouth turned to dust as she looked to the doorway. With a swish of gold and black brocade, Davira stalked into the room. Kyrin's heart struggled to beat. However, it was not the same Davira she remembered. The usurper queen's face was far too thin, her cheekbones jutting and giving her a skeletal quality. Daniel had mentioned she did not look well, but Kyrin wasn't prepared for how great the change would be. Her eyes, however, were as cold and sharp as shattered emeralds, exactly how Kyrin remembered. With merely a look, she spewed all the hatred and darkness Kyrin could only imagine took such a brutal toll on her body.

Those piercing eyes locked on Kyrin, and some of that hatred ignited a cruel satisfaction. "At long last, someone has finally brought me Kyrin Altair. Scerle, you never disappoint."

Her insidious gaze snaked its way to Jace. "And you brought the ryrik as well." She cast Kyrin a savage grin that held nothing but loathing. "I'm told congratulations are in order. You actually married the monster."

Kyrin forced her shoulders to remain straight. She would not cower even if her insides quaked.

When she failed to spark a reaction, Davira switched her attention to Holden. "You, I do not know."

"That was one of my most promising informants before he betrayed me."

Kyrin had been so focused on Davira she hadn't noticed who else joined them in the room, but now her gaze snapped to Richard. She swallowed hard, her breath catching as images of Kaden flashed in her mind. This man had hurt her brother far too many times, and Jace as well. The cold way he now peered at Holden raised the hair along her arms.

Worse was Davira's response. "Then he's yours to do with as you please."

Holden did not react except for a barely perceptible elevation in his breathing. He only glared up at Richard, his expression otherwise like stone. Even so, Kyrin cried inside for him. He was one of Jace's closest friends. She shuddered to think of what torture Richard would inflict on him for his betrayal.

Davira's attention swung back to Kyrin, and she struggled not to flinch. What Davira would do to her and Jace might be even worse. If Davira knew they were married, she would know how to hurt Kyrin the most. Tears burned Kyrin's eyes, though she fought with all her might to hide the fear clawing up her throat. She begged Elôm for courage but even more for deliverance.

Davira took a step closer. Jace shifted beside her as if to put himself between them, but a guard must have held him back. Kyrin couldn't stop herself from shrinking when Davira reached toward her. With a stinging tug, she yanked something from Kyrin's neck. The breath froze in Kyrin's lungs when she saw her father's stone necklace dangling from Davira's fingers. The rope dug into her wrists as she instinctively tried to grab for it.

Davira's eyes narrowed as she peered at the necklace. "I recognize this. It belonged to your father." A bitter, cold smile twisted her lips. "Perhaps I'll have it ground to dust and sprinkle it on the altar in the temple."

The lump in Kyrin's throat grew infinitely more painful. Already the torture had begun.

DANIEL RAN HIS hand through his hair as he paced within the small circle of his guards, trampling an ever-widening path in the grass. He'd received word of the attack, but Aric and the rest of his men would not allow him to enter camp until they were sure it was secure and clear of attackers. If he had to wait much longer to find out if Elanor was safe, he would be hard-pressed not to try to barrel his way through them.

He dragged in a breath and worked to calm himself. Everyone was just doing their jobs, protecting him above all else, but he *really* hated being a prince right now. How had this even happened? He'd thought the camp was safe, else he never would have left Elanor's side.

At last, they received the all-clear. Daniel rushed forward, his guards hurrying to keep up. He headed straight toward the pavilion. Bodies littered the ground along the way, and his lungs struggled to draw in enough air. Most were enemies, some ryriks, but as he neared the pavilion, a few he recognized as men Aric had chosen for the royal guard. He hardly dared to breathe, terrified to find Elanor amongst the dead.

Hands shaking, he brushed aside the flap of the pavilion and stepped inside. His breath left his lungs in a gust, his legs going a bit wobbly. Elanor was there, crying in her uncle's arms.

James and Elian stood nearby, along with Trask and Anne. Anne's face glistened with tears as well.

"Elanor," he gasped her name.

She pulled away from Charles, her face still crumpled in anguish, and rushed into his arms. He held her tightly, assuring himself she was alive and well, yet something was obviously very wrong. He glanced around, his gaze focusing on Charles. "What happened?"

The deep worry lines on his face were not comforting. "Jace and Kyrin are missing. Others are unaccounted for as well."

This declaration socked Daniel in the gut with the same force as a rock from one of their catapults. It was Samara all over again. A surprise attack. Missing loved ones. He looked about the tent, hardly able to comprehend. Only now did he notice Trev standing near the door with a grim look. "How did this happen?"

"A stealth attack, it seems. From what I can gather, a firedrake caused a distraction and allowed some of Davira's men to sneak in from behind. They went through camp killing at random, and it seems they took some captives since Jace and Kyrin weren't found among the dead."

A small sob escaped Elanor, her tears leaving wet splotches on his surcoat. He gripped her more tightly, fighting the way his mind was racing. He needed calm. He needed to be the leader. "We must find them. Have a search started at once. We must find out where they went."

"Already underway. Rayad and several others are searching as we speak."

Charles crossed the tent, pausing at Daniel's side to give Elanor a pained look before meeting Daniel's gaze. "Now that you're here, I'll join them."

He, James, and Trask all left the tent. Daniel stared after them. The same helplessness as before descended and weighed on his shoulders. He should be out there with them. But all he could do was try to comfort Elanor and pray their loved ones would be found safe.

Jace held Kyrin tightly as the dungeon's cold, damp darkness pressed in around them. The last time he'd been here, he'd been suffocating in his own blood. He would have died if Elon had not saved him. As terrifying as that was, he would go through it again in a heartbeat if it meant Kyrin was safe. To have her imprisoned with him when he could not protect her was one of his greatest fears. Davira would be ruthless when it came to a member of the Altair family. Jace begged Elôm to intervene on their behalf once more.

He prayed for Holden too. He did not know what had become of his friend in the hours since they had arrived in Valcré. Richard had led him off elsewhere in the dungeon while Davira's guards had brought Jace and Kyrin to this cell and stripped Jace of his armor.

Kyrin shifted a little, nuzzling into his chest. He wrapped his arms tighter. She hadn't said anything for a long while. At times, he'd wondered—hoped—she was asleep. She would need the strength. After another long silence, she sniffled. She wasn't sleeping. She was crying. It wasn't the first time, and it stabbed pain through his heart because he couldn't do anything to truly comfort her. He wanted to say something, but words had little effect on their situation.

Something about her tears worried him. He could not figure out why such a heavy dread churned in his gut to see them. Perhaps Kyrin really believed this time they would not escape. He did not blame her. This could well and truly be the end for them, right when they were so close to victory.

The ache in his chest compressed his lungs, and he had to close his eyes to ward off the sting of his own tears. They'd been so close to living out their lives in peace.

Kyrin stiffened in his arms. She pulled away from him and scrambled to her feet, crossing the cell. In the corner, she bent over and retched. Jace shoved to his feet and rushed over to her as she leaned against the cell bars. He laid his hand on her back, that dread pulsing throughout his body. Why did she keep getting sick like this? She kept saying it was stress, but this had never happened before. Something was wrong. He could feel it in his gut. He should have gone straight to Josef himself. He should have…

Her soft weeping cut off his thought process. She slowly turned toward him with a look of such distress that his heart stalled for a moment. "What? What is it?"

She shook her head, the tears rolling heavily down her cheeks, pain written in every line of her crumpled face.

Jace could barely breathe with the weight pressing on him. "What's wrong? Are you sick?" Still, she did not answer, and he reached out, taking her face in his hands and tipping it up so he could look into her eyes. "Tell me what's wrong."

She stilled and stared at him for a moment that speared his chest with panic before barely more than whispering, "I'm pregnant."

A silent and invisible bolt of lightning struck Jace, robbing him of the ability to breathe or even think as it sank in. Pregnant. Baby. They were going to have a baby. But how? They were trapped. Davira was going to kill them. Kill the baby.

The pain that scorched through him at that thought stole any remaining air from his lungs, igniting such a raging fire in his blood he could have taken on an entire army. But it died just as quickly with the knowledge that he did not have the power to save

Kyrin or their unborn baby, leaving only his eyes and throat burning as he tried to swallow the lump that had lodged there.

"Please, Jace, tell me what you're thinking. I can't see you."

Snapping from the suffocating flood of emotions, he gulped a ragged breath. Kyrin was still staring at him, but he forgot she couldn't see in the dark the way he could. He struggled for a reply and finally managed a rough, "I don't know."

How could he? Unless Elôm provided a miracle, he, Kyrin, and their baby would all die. He wouldn't even get to see his baby's face before they were all with Elôm.

Kyrin let out a long breath, her entire body sagging. "I know."

She was no longer actively crying but looked so fragile, like she could shatter right there.

Gently, he led her back to the far side of the cell. They sat down, and he gathered her into his arms, holding her close as if he could somehow protect her and the baby. He could hardly wrap his mind around it. They were parents. There were three of them in this cell. Once, the fear of ever having children had nearly crippled him. Now his greatest fear was that his child wouldn't even be born. That he wouldn't be able to see what he or she looked like. Wouldn't get to hold them.

He struggled to work his voice past his swollen throat. "So, these mornings you've been sick, that's why?"

She nodded against him.

"And it's normal? There's nothing wrong?"

"According to Anne and Cassie, yes. Unpleasant but normal."

He released a slow breath. At least that worry was gone, little good it did. "How long have you known?"

"Just since this morning." She paused, and when she finally spoke again, her voice wavered. "I was going to leave. I was going to go home to Landale, where the baby would be safe. Just as soon as you came back and I could tell you. I didn't know we'd be attacked." A small, hitching sob gripped her.

Jace rested his head on hers, his eyes burning with a vengeance. He should have been there. They weren't even fighting a battle yet. He should have stayed with her. Should have insisted they go see Josef. Should have found out together. Should have been there to protect his family.

A tear scalded his cheek and then another. The pressure in his chest choked him almost as much as the last time he'd been in this cell. He begged Elôm to save his wife and child. Even if he had to die to do it, they had to live.

Kaden knew something was wrong. He could feel it twisting in his stomach as he unsaddled Rhune at the end of the day. Even in the gathering gloom, he caught groups of soldiers talking, pointing toward camp, shaking their heads with looks of bewilderment and pity. His gut ached with dreadful anticipation that eclipsed even the exhaustion dragging heavily at him after another day of fighting. He glanced at Talas, but his face betrayed the same unease. They rushed through taking care of their dragons before hurrying toward camp, unsure what they'd find there.

Things seemed deceptively quiet and normal when they crossed into the forest and spotted firelight and tents ahead. There was no damage to suggest some unforeseen catastrophe had occurred, yet a cold hush seemed to hover over camp. Kaden lengthened his stride, and it soon brought him to the gathering of tents belonging to their group. Most of his closest friends huddled around the fire, but he noticed immediately that Kyrin was missing. So was Jace. He tried to tell himself they were likely with Daniel and Elanor or Marcus and Liam, but his stomach lurched regardless.

"What happened?"

The brief but deafening silence that met his question only solidified his fears.

Trask, his face weary and downcast, was the one to answer. "The camp was attacked by Arcacians and ryriks."

Kaden's heart missed a beat. "How?" It wasn't as if they'd left the camp completely defenseless. Surely they'd been able to withstand such a thing. The camp was still here, after all.

"We can only speculate, but…they took captives." He paused, and Kaden held his breath. "Kyrin, Jace, and Holden were among them."

A choked gasp broke from Kaden's chest. "Has anyone gone after them?" Why was everyone just sitting here? Where was the rescue party?

This time, Rayad answered, his voice pained. "We tracked them up the mountains to a hidden plateau. We found most of the captives dead—slain. Jace, Kyrin, and Holden were not there. We believe they must have been recognized and taken to Davira."

Kaden still struggled to draw a decent breath, his chest cold and weighted with the horror of what Davira would do to them—all the fury she would expend on them for their march into Arcacia. "What is the plan to get them back?"

Rayad's heavy, resigned sigh drifted above the crackle of the fire. "I don't think there is one."

A fire sprang to life inside of Kaden. They couldn't just give up. He spun around, brushing past Talas, and marched toward the commanders' tents near the royal pavilion. Kyrin had done too much—sacrificed too much—for everyone to just be given up as a loss. So had Jace and Holden. Someone had to be doing something to rescue them.

He intended to march straight into the royal pavilion but swerved when he caught sight of his brother's tent and the two figures there. Marcus and Liam sat around a small fire. They raised their bowed heads when they heard him coming. Liam looked tired and defeated, while Marcus straightened subtly as if preparing for a fight.

"What are we doing about Kyrin?" Kaden demanded. *Surely*, his brother had a plan.

But Marcus's bleak answer was like the fall of a hammer. "Nothing."

Shock exploded inside Kaden. "What do you mean, nothing?"

"There's nothing we can do."

"There has to be something."

Marcus stood now, still fully outfitted for battle. "We have a fortress we have not yet breached and thousands of men between us and Valcré. We cannot reach her." His controlled tone didn't quite mask the turmoil in his eyes.

But Kaden wasn't willing to give up that easily. "What if I take the dragon riders to Valcré?"

"Then you'll likely be facing an overwhelming number of firedrakes. For all we know, Davira is trying to draw us into doing something reckless. The strength of our dragon force will mean the difference between victory and defeat. You and the cretes are the only ones keeping our armies from being annihilated. Whoever controls the skies controls everything. We can't risk losing a large chunk of our force"—his voice cracked—"not even for Kyrin."

The truth of it hit Kaden like a slab of ice. He was right. Of course, he was. But Kaden couldn't just give up. Not on Kyrin. "Can't we find something to trade for them?"

Marcus stared at him, the firelight wavering in the moisture in his eyes. "Unfortunately, we don't have anything more to bargain with."

Because they had already traded away the one thing they had to save Kaden. He hung his head. They should have just left him to Richard.

"There is nothing we can do." The quiet resignation in Marcus's voice destroyed the last of Kaden's resolve. "Our only hope is to take Valcré and pray Kyrin is still alive when we do."

Kaden tried to find even a glimmer of hope in that, but there was none. They were weeks, maybe months, away from taking Valcré. Even if they breached the fort within the next couple of days, the entire might of Arcacia's army would be waiting for them on the other side, ready to lay a siege of their own. Davira would never keep Kyrin alive that long. Even if she did, she'd kill her the moment she knew she was losing control.

The weight of reality and a long day of fighting descended on Kaden at once. All strength seemed to abandon him, the weakness from the viper venom shaking his limbs. He sank into an empty chair near Liam. That fighting spark that pushed him to do anything necessary to protect his loved ones slowly diminished. His voice scraped past his throat.

"I'm so tired of watching our family get taken out one by one."

DIM LIGHT HAD only just started to filter through the canvas of the pavilion as Daniel listened to the camp awaken. Elanor lay beside him, her back to him. He hadn't expected his first couple weeks of marriage to be spent in a tent in a war camp, and he dreamed of the day they could wake up every morning in the quiet and privacy of an actual bedroom. That dream, however, seemed a little more distant and clouded than it had before the attack yesterday. Everything had been going according to plan, and victory seemed within their grasp before reality had dealt them a cruel reminder of just how tenuous the situation was.

A sniffle told Daniel that Elanor wasn't asleep like he'd thought. His heart squeezed and ached just as it had all the other times she'd cried yesterday and through the night. She'd only just learned of her father's death, awful as he was, and now she had to deal with losing her brother. He'd do anything to take away her pain, including marching straight up to his sister and demanding Jace back if he could. Jace and Kyrin were his family now too. If only he could figure out how to save them. But all he could do right now was try to comfort his wife.

He rolled over and wrapped his arm around her, holding her close against his chest. She said nothing at first, only wove her fingers into his and held tightly. Her breath hitched with quiet tears. He could almost feel the pain radiating from her.

Was it selfish of him to be thankful she had not been taken yesterday? He did thank Elôm their marriage was still relatively secret, at least from Davira. Elanor likely would have been the primary target if his sister's men had known. He wanted to believe he'd be strong enough to continue to stand and lead as king despite such a loss, but the thought of it put a stranglehold around his throat.

Elanor's tear-choked voice cut through the stillness. "Kyrin is pregnant."

Daniel's heart gave his ribs a painful thud, his blood running cold despite the warmth of their bed.

"She just realized it yesterday. It's supposed to be a secret until she can tell Jace and her brothers. Now…" A sob broke loose and cut her off.

Daniel closed his eyes against the sting of tears. He had already lost nieces or nephews to Davira's depravity. Would this be another? *Elôm, if there is any way to save them, please show me. Protect them and the baby from my sister's evil. She has taken too much already.*

Unknown hours passed in the darkness of the dungeon. No one came or went, nor was there any sign of Holden. Long stretches of silence drew out between Jace and Kyrin. They didn't talk much about the baby. Jace was almost afraid to, as if talking about such a future would jeopardize it. The hope was too fragile, just like the life of their child. But he thought about it constantly. Often he found himself wondering what the baby would look like. He'd only known one other half-blooded ryrik, and in both of them, their ryrik traits were dominant. Would it be the same for a child born to a half-blood? Or might the child favor Kyrin? He smiled to himself, thinking of a child with her blue eyes and brown hair. He'd like that. In fact, he hoped it would be so. People would be less likely to hold prejudices against a child who didn't so clearly have ryrik blood. If the child even had a chance to live…

He swallowed hard to quell the burn in his throat that kept rising up. Why hadn't Elôm held back the attack until Kyrin left? Why allow her to be captured when she had only just found out she was pregnant? Jace gritted his teeth and bowed his head. It was so hard not to question the situation. So hard not to despair. But he knew he must trust. Whatever happened, Elôm was in control. He had proved His faithfulness time and again. If Jace did not cling to that now, he would have nothing left but hopelessness. He grasped for words from the Scrolls, and they soon trickled in. *But as for me, I trust in You, O Lord; I say, "You are my God." My times are in Your hand; Deliver me from the hand of my enemies, And from those who persecute me.*

A door shrieked open somewhere far down the hall and echoed against the cold stone. Torchlight appeared, illuminating a group of six guards. Richard marched at the head. Kyrin went rigid in Jace's arms. He squeezed her tight and drew her up with him to face the guards. As they neared the cell, he stepped in front of her, ready to do anything he could to shield her.

One of the guards stepped forward to unlock the door, and Jace eyed Richard. Dark spots that glinted wetly in the torchlight spattered his already dark clothing. Blood. Holden's, no doubt. Jace shuddered for him but couldn't bring himself to ask whether his friend was dead or alive. Knowing Richard, he wouldn't have killed him just yet. He would want to prolong the suffering.

The guards filed into the cell, watching Jace closely and ready to draw their weapons. He tried to prepare for whatever was about to happen. Was it their turn to face torture? What would that do to the baby? Could it survive? A desperation like nothing he'd ever experienced before clawed up inside him, and he found himself pleading. "Please, I beg you, don't take her."

Nothing but contempt twisted Richard's cold expression. "We're not here for her."

Two of the guards seized Jace by the arms. The desperation blasted heat through his body. If he was separated from Kyrin—from their baby—he could not protect them. He yanked against the guards, but they tightened their hold and hauled him toward the door. Kyrin cried out behind him, and he fought harder. The other guards drew their swords. One of the blades jabbed into Jace's neck, nearly breaking skin. He stilled, chest heaving.

Richard raised his hand as if preparing to give a signal. "Struggle, and you will die right here."

Jace had no choice. Unless he wanted Kyrin to watch him bleed out right in front of her, he had to comply. He did not resist when the guards wrenched his arms behind his back and fit a tight pair of shackles to his wrists.

Richard lowered his hand with a sneer. "Wise choice."

The guards gripped Jace's arms once more and shoved him out of the cell. He strained to look back at Kyrin. She stood alone, tears streaming down her face, her arms wrapped around her middle. Every instinct screamed for him to fight to get back to her, but the guards still had their swords ready to destroy any attempt.

His last glimpse of her was like one of those blades shoved right through his chest. Would he ever see her again? The unknowing choked him as the guards half dragged him through the dungeon and up a staircase. They entered the palace at the top, but he felt as though he had left his heart behind in the cell with Kyrin. Only a sharp ache pulsed inside him.

They marched through the stark palace halls the same way they had come, straight back to the throne room. Davira waited there for them. Her cruel gaze raked over him, prickling his skin. He may have the blood of a ryrik, but she was the monster.

The guards halted him near the throne. Each one remained vigilant with their weapons. Davira sidled toward him, continuing her perusal with a far too satisfied look. Though they were metal, Jace tested the strength of his shackles. He couldn't stop himself from imagining how he could use them to strangle her.

Her blood-red lips smirked as if she knew exactly what he was thinking. The guards' already firm grips tightened around his arms. Perhaps his intentions were showing more clearly on his face than he intended.

"I've learned a lot about you since the last time you were here, Jace." The hissing sound of his name from her lips sent a shiver down his back. "You were once a gladiator and a rather famous one at that. In fact, I believe I saw you fight once in the old arena."

He tamped down a reaction, but the reminder of his past twisted his stomach and left a sour taste in his mouth. He remembered exactly when that would have been. Could remember the lifeless eyes of the opponent he'd fought and defeated that day. The blood oozing on his hands. He gritted his teeth, forcing the memories away.

"And then you quit doing as you were told."

Jace stiffened, Jasper's voice an unwelcome phantom in his head. *When will you learn to do as you're told?* How did Davira know all this?

"You disappeared after that." She reached out to touch his chin with icy fingers, and he yanked his head away. She snorted. "That is until you showed up again, fighting for the rebellion. I'm told you never lost a fight as a gladiator. Impressive. I wonder if such luck will still favor you when you fight tomorrow."

What? A cold wave crashed through Jace. No, not again. He could not fight again. He shook his head, but his voice seemed snatched away. The protest built in his chest, pressing against his ribs. No, this could not be.

Davira stepped closer. Too close. Her deceptively light voice pierced like a knife. "I imagine the prospect of seeing the famous half-blood fight again will draw people from all over the city. See that you give them a good show."

Something raw and desperate burst inside him, and he yanked against the guards. "No! I will not fight."

An utterly compassionless shrug met his declaration. "Then die." She flicked her hand at the guards. "Take him to the arena."

Their hands dug into his arms, leading him through the palace and outside before he could even wrap his mind around what was happening. His thoughts spun in a thousand different directions. He felt trapped in his own body as they hauled him through the streets. The blood flowed hot in his veins, pulsing from his pounding heart. He looked left and right at every intersection and building, seeking an escape. He had to stop this. He had to get away.

And then the arena loomed before him. For one stuttering heartbeat, numbness encased his entire body. His breaths grew rapid and shallow. He'd escaped this life. For years, he'd lived in fear of ever facing it again. He gasped for air. He couldn't do this. He couldn't be that killer again.

At the tug of their hands, fire exploded through his veins. Digging his feet in, he struggled against the guards. They couldn't make him do this. The cold shadow of the arena fell over them, and they dragged him inside. Stale air, heavy with dust and sweat, smacked into him, sucking him back into the past. The clang of swords echoed in his head.

He twisted and wrenched against the guards. A desperate cry ripped from his chest. He had to get out of here. One of the guard's hands slipped. Jace lunged to pull free, but three others jumped in to subdue him. His feet skidded and scraped against the stone floor, not giving him any firm footing.

Between all six of the guards, they wrestled him into a cell, nearly throwing him to the floor. He scrambled to the door as it shut and slammed his shoulder into it. But it had already locked, trapping him in the nightmare. The guards sneered at him and marched away.

Despite the sweat soaking through his shirt, Jace shivered uncontrollably, violent tremors racing up and down his body. His lungs heaved, but he couldn't seem to get enough air. Numbness tingled in his hands, and he couldn't feel the ground beneath him. His vision warped. Pain tore across his chest, his heart thrashing like it was about to burst. Why couldn't he breathe? It was like he was drowning and fighting for the surface.

Dizziness crashed into him, stealing the strength from his legs, and he all but collapsed against the cell bars. He hung his head, shoulders shuddering. Breathe. He had to breathe. He forced himself to drag in a slower lungful of air and then another. Though his body continued to shake, his heart rate eventually started to slow.

Five, maybe ten, minutes later, he breathed almost normally. His heart beat a heavy, sluggish beat now, no longer racing, and the sharp pain in his chest had faded to a dull ache. That was when he heard a voice call his name from the next cell over.

He lifted his head, and his gaze caught on a familiar face. "Timothy?"

His friend knelt at the bars separating them, concern written in his taut expression.

Jace drew another deep breath, not sure what had come over him. The panic still gnawed somewhere at the back of his mind, but he managed to quell it for now. He cleared his throat and swallowed hard. His tongue felt dried out and sticky as he forced it to form words. "We were afraid you were dead."

"Not yet." Timothy offered a small smile, though it died as he studied Jace's face. "What happened? How did you get here?"

Jace shifted, using his feet to push himself up and sit straighter. His legs still felt shaky, and his entire body had grown cold and heavy. "Kyrin, Holden, and I were captured and brought here to Valcré."

Timothy's face fell, his eyes sliding closed for a moment. That's when it struck Jace how rough Timothy looked. Concerning hollows shadowed his cheeks, and his shirt hung on him. What appeared to be a nearly healed burn scar followed one side of his jaw. Jace winced. He had little doubt Timothy's clothing hid other wounds and scars.

"What happened to you? Aaron said the warehouse was raided. We assumed you were captured, but he never saw it happen."

Timothy's expression lifted with tentative hope. "Aaron is well? What about Lacy and Isaac?"

"Yes, they all made it out, including Lacy's family," Jace assured him. "Aaron took them all to Landale."

Timothy breathed an audible sigh. "Good. I had hoped since I didn't see any of them here, but I never knew for sure." Now that Jace had eased his mind, weariness settled once again in his eyes. "But yes, I was taken with the others. Davira knew who I was. I don't know if we had an infiltrator or if the information was pried out of someone. I spent a couple of weeks in the palace dungeon. Once she got tired of physically torturing me, she had me brought here to work and watch as other believers are killed."

His words trailed off into heavy silence. To repeatedly witness the deaths of other believers would be worse than any physical torment for Timothy.

Jace hung his head. "I'm sorry."

"What she didn't foresee is the comfort Timothy brings to those of us here."

Jace's head snapped up at the second familiar voice coming from beyond Timothy. He hadn't even realized the next cell held half a dozen people, including Ben and Mira. They, too, looked rough and half-starved. It was a miracle they hadn't been killed already, but Davira probably had so many captives it took a while to get to them all.

Timothy glanced over his shoulder at Ben. "If my suffering can help bring others peace, then I am thankful." His tired but compassionate gaze turned back to Jace. "How did you get captured? Were you able to take back Samara?"

Jace maneuvered to his feet, his knees a bit wobbly, and moved closer to Timothy's cell, where he could better see the others. Sitting once again, he recounted their victory in Samara, the siege on Fort Rhall, the attack on the camp, and details of their capture.

KYRIN HUGGED HER knees to her chest and fought not to let the tears overwhelm her again. They had been relentless since Jace was taken away. But hysterics would not help the baby. She had to stay calm, even if calm was the last thing she felt. Instead, everything inside her wanted to break down as she wondered where Jace was and what they were doing to him. After everything they had been through, her mind was entirely too good at creating horrifically vivid possibilities. Would they bring Jace back to her broken and bloodied? Would she even see him again at all? She choked on a sob. She needed her husband.

Before the black wave of despair slowly rising out of the darkness around her could fully take hold, she forced her mind to the only place she could draw true comfort—the Scrolls. At first, even with her perfect memory, she struggled to recall the verses through the hold of fear, but words slowly pieced themselves together in her mind.

The Lord also will be a refuge for the oppressed, a refuge in times of trouble. And those who know Your name will put their trust in You; for You, Lord, have not forsaken those who seek You.

While fear and despair still clamored, Kyrin pictured herself back at camp, in their cabin reading the Scrolls with Jace as they had many times since their wedding day. Tears continued to slip down her cheeks at random, and the ache in her chest was still present, but she found comfort in the memories and the verses she quietly recited to herself. As bleak as the situation was, she knew Elôm had not abandoned her because He never had before. Whatever happened, she had to hold onto the truth that giving her and Jace a child and still allowing Davira to capture them was part of His plans.

The shriek of hinges snapped Kyrin's head up. Light glowed in the hall as footsteps approached. Her heart jolted. Were they bringing Jace back? Or were they coming for her? Could the baby even survive if she was tortured? She gripped her stomach, tears ever threatening, but she blinked them away. She had to try to be strong.

That proved difficult when she saw the guards half dragging someone between them. Jace! Her heart stalled. But the captive's short hair belonged to Holden, not Jace. She pushed to her feet as they approached the cell beside hers. Holden's head hung, but even so, she could tell his face was dark with bruises and blood. His shirt was gone, his torso riddled with deep red splotches that would surely turn into a myriad of bruises. They opened the cell door and practically threw him in. He stumbled before falling to his knees, raising his arm to cradle his ribs.

Before the guards left, they jammed their torch into the holder across from the cell. As much as Kyrin welcomed the light, the only reason she could imagine they'd left it was so she could see Holden's wounds. It was just the sort of cruel thing Davira would do. Did she want Kyrin to anticipate Jace being returned to her like this? Anticipate what awaited her?

Struggling to force such thoughts away, she walked to the bars separating her from the other cell and lowered herself to her knees. She wasn't sure what else to do but ask, "Are you all right?"

Holden nodded, taking a hissing breath before looking over at her. His face was swelling, especially around his left eye and split lip. His brows lowered, his gaze shifting from her to the rest of the cell and back. "Where's Jace?"

She swallowed with difficulty, the knot in her throat nearly robbing her voice. "I don't know. They came and took him a while ago."

Holden let out a long, hitching sigh and hung his head. Slowly and with effort, he pushed to his feet, and they both moved to the back of their cells, where they sank to the floor. Kyrin pulled her knees to her chest again, desperately missing Jace's arms around her.

They were mostly silent as the hours slipped by. Kyrin kept praying for Jace's return, but the dungeon remained silent. The torch eventually died, and Kyrin drifted off several times, exhaustion too hard to fight. But she always woke with a jolt of fear and dread.

After what seemed like a lifetime, the sound of a door and footsteps came again. She shoved to her feet, her heart beating wildly. Would it be Jace this time? She wasn't sure she was prepared to see what they had done to him. However, only two guards appeared. She fought to quell the sheer disappointment that he was not with them, but her eyes burned anyway. She blinked hard to keep the tears at bay. Without a word, one of the guards set a bowl next to Holden's cell and another next to hers. They replaced the torch before they both left.

Kyrin shared a glance with Holden and then walked over to inspect her bowl. She reached through the bars and picked it up, eyeing the lumpy, sticky substance inside.

"Looks like porridge." She caught a whiff of it, and her stomach instantly soured. Nearly dropping the bowl in her haste, she lurched for the corner where she'd been sick before and emptied what very little her stomach had to offer.

Trembling, she walked shakily back to her place at the rear of the cell and sank down. Shoving the bowl away, the tears she'd held back for the last several hours all rushed in at once. How would she ever survive this and keep her baby alive? It was impossible. She would lose Jace and their baby, and there was nothing she could do to stop it. Her shoulders shook as a black tide of despair once again swallowed her. She let the tears and the sobs run their course. At some point, she thought she heard Holden try to console her but was too consumed by the pain.

At last, the tears slowed, and she wiped her face as best she could with her sleeves. Her chest ached from crying, and heaviness weighed on her limbs.

Several minutes of silence stretched out before Holden spoke. "I know it's difficult and not very appetizing, but you should eat to keep up your strength."

Kyrin gave a short exhale of breath. He had no idea how right he was. "I should."

He cast a questioning look at her bitter tone. Kyrin sat quietly for a long moment. Jace should be the one to tell him, but carrying the weight alone when he wasn't here was too much. She needed support—someone to share the burden with. More tears prickled her nose as she met his gaze. Deep sadness welled inside her, sharing news that should have been announced with joy.

"I'm pregnant."

Holden's right eye, which hadn't swollen shut, widened. He seemed to struggle for words at first. "Does Jace know?"

Kyrin sniffled, her voice almost failing her. "I told him before they took him away. I only just figured it out right before the attack."

Holden sat silently, processing the news. When he did speak again, his tone was both encouraging and protective. "You really should try to eat. For the baby."

Drawing a deep breath, Kyrin reached for the bowl of porridge. Her stomach gurgled, and she tried to avoid smelling the food. She brought a spoonful to her mouth. It was just as sticky and bland as it looked, but she forced herself to swallow it. Her stomach threatened to rebel, but she held it in place.

Over the next while, she managed to keep down one bite at a time until the bowl was half empty. That was as much as she could take without making herself ill. Holden kept a close eye on her while she ate but didn't say anything when she set the remaining porridge aside. He didn't appear to have finished his either. How could they eat with so much fear and uncertainty hanging over them? Kyrin just prayed it was enough, for now, to keep the baby healthy. She would try to eat more next time.

If there was a next time.

It couldn't have been more than an hour later when yet another set of guards returned. Once again, Jace was not with them, but Kyrin's breath did catch to see a familiar face. "Collin?"

She had not seen him since the day she'd been dragged to the city square and humiliated three years ago. He'd been so vibrant and self-confident back then, but when their eyes met, she found something broken in them. The spark and charm of the boy she used to know were gone. He only held her gaze for a moment before bowing his head as if he couldn't bear to look at her. Or couldn't bear for her to look at him.

They came straight to her cell. She rose to her feet, though her legs trembled as they unlocked the door. The other man stepped inside. She backed away from him but quickly ran out of room. He grabbed her arm and yanked her forward. Out of the corner of her eye, she saw Holden push unsteadily to his feet, following their progress.

"Leave her alone." Despite his injuries, his voice rang with the command, but they paid him no heed.

Collin clamped a rough set of shackles around Kyrin's wrists, still avoiding her eyes. The cold metal sent a shiver up her arms and back down her spine. This was it. Now she would discover what pain Davira had in store for her.

Holden rattled the door of his cell and demanded they take him instead. The other guard just sneered at him. "Your turn will come soon enough."

Kyrin looked over her shoulder as they dragged her past, meeting Holden's gaze. She hoped he could see through the fear gripping her how much she appreciated his effort to protect her, especially with Jace absent. She lost sight of him as the guards tugged her forward, down the dim tunnel toward an unknown fate.

KYRIN'S HEART BATTERED her ribcage and echoed in her ears. She looked for signs of Jace, but the doors of the rooms they passed were shut. Though tempted to call out for him, she worried about riling the guards. Not that the possibility of torture and injury wasn't already looming before her, but she had to protect her child however she could. Besides, even if Jace responded, she wouldn't be able to get to him. And hearing her cry out would only cause him further torment.

Instead of entering one of the interrogation rooms as expected, they led her up a staircase. One she knew led outside into the courtyard. The last time she'd climbed these steps was when Daican had brought her before the people as a precursor to her execution. Prickles crawled up her back and raised the flesh on her arms at the vivid memories of that day. Daican had been cruel, but Davira was demented. What could she possibly be planning now?

Sunshine momentarily blinded Kyrin when they opened the door, though she dragged in a breath of the fresh air. She squinted to take in the surroundings as Collin and the other guard led her around toward the front of the palace. Here they found the royal carriage waiting. Kyrin stumbled as they shoved her toward it. Did they mean to put her inside? It didn't make any sense.

At the carriage, they did indeed push her toward the open door, barely giving her time to step up and avoid banging her shins on the jutting step. She ducked inside, and the other guard followed, sitting her down on the rear-facing bench. He took a seat beside her, resting his hand on the dagger on his belt. It would take less than a second for him to yank it out and drive it into her chest. She gulped in the tense silence that followed. Though she peeked through the windows, she couldn't even imagine what was happening.

After long, nerve-racking minutes, footsteps approached, crunching in the gravel outside. Then Davira stepped into the carriage, her heavy silken skirt pooling around her as she took a seat across from Kyrin and her guard. Kyrin's entire body went rigid as Davira's devilish eyes pierced hers. Her lips curved in satisfaction as if she were reading from a book just how much her presence unnerved Kyrin.

The door shut, and the carriage rolled forward only a moment later. Kyrin held Davira's gaze though her insides quivered. Only one thought rose to the forefront of her mind.

"Where is Jace?"

That cold, cruel smile of Davira's grew, and she gave a spine-chilling little laugh. "Consider that a surprise."

Kyrin's stomach convulsed, threatening to make her sick again. It was on her tongue to beg for answers, but she couldn't give Davira that satisfaction. She had to be strong no matter how weak she found her resolve to be. She glanced toward the window as they passed through the palace gate. "Where are we going?"

"You will see soon enough."

The pleasure Davira seemed to be drawing from this was terrifying. *Elôm, only You know what is happening. I need all the strength, grace, and protection You can give me.*

They traveled the streets of Valcré now, though she couldn't tell which ones without leaning forward to see better, and she didn't dare get any closer to Davira. Less than ten minutes later, the carriage stopped. Voices hummed outside. The door opened, and Davira disembarked first. Next was the guard, who turned and reached for Kyrin.

Careful not to trip on the step, she scrambled out and looked up. Her breath died in her lungs, her heart lodging itself in her throat. The arena loomed above her, its arched balconies like a hundred gaping mouths. She tore her eyes downward to the crowds pouring into the lower entrances. So many people here to witness the shedding of blood. Would they see hers? Was that why Davira had brought her? Sweat slicked her palms, her heart quavering with the thought of being torn apart by wild cats or some other ravenous beast—of her baby being torn and consumed along with her. Tears bit her eyes. *Elôm, please rescue me, for my baby's sake!*

The guard shoved her forward, and she nearly fell, her legs turning to water. She took a stumbling step after Davira, who approached an entrance cordoned off from the others.

"Is this how you mean to kill me?" Kyrin's voice trembled but gained strength as a spark of defiance finally found ground inside her. "Throw me into the arena to let the city watch animals tear me apart?"

Davira glanced over her shoulder with a biting laugh. "As entertaining as that sounds, no. When I decide to kill you, it will be far more personal than that. Today, you're here as my guest."

The flash of a taunting grin accompanied that last declaration. Kyrin didn't have a chance to voice further questions until they arrived at what must be the royal viewing box. She took a tentative step toward the edge and sucked in her breath. The sand-covered floor of the arena stretched out before her, stands filled with people rising in every direction. Thousands of men and women packed in tightly, the drone of their conversations buzzing in her ears. Not even a whiff of a breeze cut through the stifling early summer heat.

Davira's dark shape moved into her periphery, and she half turned to look at her. "Why have you brought me here?"

Davira lifted her chin to gaze upon the crowd, the picture of vicious satisfaction. "Because today is a grand occasion. People from all across the city have come to witness the famous half-blood fight again."

All the blood drained from Kyrin's body. Her knees nearly buckled as she grasped weakly at the edge of the viewing box to hold herself upright. She could barely breathe past the pain engulfing her heart as the words sank in.

Jace was being forced to fight again.

Jace's blood thrummed with a heated current as the din of voices from the stands above filled his cell. He paced from one end to the other, unable to keep still. Memories and old emotions swirled about him. His heart raced, the same panic that had assaulted him yesterday barely held in check. What would he do when they forced him out into the arena? He'd sworn to himself he would never fight like that again. Not for the entertainment of a crowd.

He glanced at the other cells. Ben and Mira, and even the others he did not know, were on their knees praying for him. Timothy had prayed for him, too, right before guards had come to lead him away for work. Jace shuddered to imagine what Timothy had endured the last few weeks, forced to cart their brothers' and sisters' broken, mangled bodies from the arena floor every day. Would Jace's body be one of them? If he refused to fight, then yes. *What do I do, Elôm?*

"I never would have believed it had I not seen it for myself."

Tension shot through Jace's body at the voice, igniting a fresh burst of heat even as part of him recoiled. He spun around. Two figures approached the cell, the lead man dwarfed by the one behind. A piece of the boy Jace used to be wanted to shrink farther back into the cell, but he fought the impulse. Letting the heat in his blood burn away apprehension, he met the man's mud-colored eyes. He would not give his former master the satisfaction of seeing how his presence unnerved him. "Jasper."

The man sized Jace up like caged livestock. That's all Jace had ever been to him. "Look at the magnificent creature you've become. Perhaps I was hasty in selling you."

Jace clenched his fists and conducted his own study of the man. Jasper appeared to have gained a good twenty pounds since they last met and still had a tendency for garish clothing a size too small, judging by the way his orange velvet doublet strained around the buttons. He was a bit shorter than Jace remembered, though Zar was still the bear of a man he always was. Jace caught Zar's eye momentarily but, as always, couldn't really tell what he was thinking.

Jasper's low chuckle grated on his raw nerves. "As angry as ever, I see."

Jace gritted his teeth and forced himself to take a breath. He was nothing like the broken boy he'd been as Jasper's slave. He fought to speak calmly. "You know nothing about me."

Jasper just smirked. "We shall see. It's a pity the queen has no intention of letting you live. I'd pay good money to get you back."

Banishing the fears that had been resurrected from his past, Jace stepped closer to the bars to look down on Jasper and spoke very evenly. "I would never fight for you again."

There must have been something in his eyes that caused Jasper's smirk to fade. Jace held his gaze without wavering until Jasper glanced away. A small surge of victory coursed through him. He would never again be cowed by this man.

Jasper sniffed. "Well, whether for the queen or for me, you will fight, or you will die."

Jace just continued to watch him with a flinty stare. Finally, Jasper backed away with a scowl and snapped his fingers at Zar. "Let's go find our seats. I don't want to miss the spectacle." He spat the last word in Jace's direction.

Jace, however, was no longer governed by the insecurities and uncertainties of his past and gave no reaction.

Once Jasper had marched out of sight, Jace allowed himself to release a shaky breath, his chin dropping to his chest. He had not been prepared to meet his past head-on. Some part of him had always hoped and prayed Jasper had met with some sort of calamity in the past years. He certainly deserved no less.

"Are you all right?"

Jace looked over at Ben with a nod. A couple of years ago, he didn't know how he would have faced his old master, but Elon had given him enough peace to stand strong. Now, he prayed Elôm would show him how to face the rest of his past in the arena.

He'd barely finished that prayer before four guards approached his cell. They unlocked the door and motioned him out.

They all watched him closely, two with swords drawn. If he didn't comply, they'd simply drag him from the cell. With a deep breath, he stepped out, and they closed in around him. Marching forward, they led him through the tunnels of the arena. They passed many cells, all of them full. Timothy had told him how many people Davira had locked up awaiting execution, but to witness it himself was staggering. There had to be hundreds, most of them believers. Jace's heart ached as he met the bleak gazes of those who appeared to have been there the longest. They were so close to freedom if Daniel and the armies could take the fort and march on Valcré. But even that could take months. Many of these people, himself included, didn't have that long.

Leaving the cells behind, they entered a large waiting area that reeked of leather and sweat, triggering memories from other arenas. A wide variety of armor and weapons arrayed the walls and tables. Other gladiators—large, battle-hardened men—moved about in various stages of preparation. They all shot him shadowed glances, some sparking of mere curiosity, others with outright hostility. Jace made a quick study of each man. Would one be his opponent?

He didn't like how quickly fighting tactics and opponent weaknesses sprang to his mind. How quickly his body seemed to jump back into fighting mode. Not here like this. These men weren't his enemies. Most probably had no more choice than he did. How could he fight them knowing that? They were just as precious to Elôm as he was. The uncertainty warred within him. What was he supposed to do when he set foot in the arena?

The thunderous roar of the crowd outside rushed over him like a chilled wind that carried an avalanche of memories. Sweat prickled his neck, slowly making its way down his back. His lungs squeezed around each breath, and he had to choke down the panic reaching for his throat. Moments from past fights flashed in his mind. Bloody, despair-filled moments. *I can't do this, Elôm. Not again.*

He flinched when one of the guards seized his arm and removed his shackles. They then shoved him across the waiting area to a tunnel. Bright sunlight and sand waited at the far end. A man held out the hilt of a sword. Jace stared at it. What would happen if he just refused to take it? No doubt they would shove him out weaponless. It already appeared he would get no protection in the way of armor.

Struggling for clear direction, Jace finally reached out and took the sword, his clammy fingers wrapping around the grimy, cracked leather hilt. The blade at least appeared sharp, though Jace would not have been surprised to be given a blunt weapon.

Then they nudged him forward, and Jace's heart rate spiked. Just like the first time he'd been forced into an arena, the guards pushed him toward his waiting doom.

JACE HALF-STUMBLED INTO the arena, blinded by sunlight. He raised his hand to block it as his eyes adjusted. The roar of the crowd was like a wave crashing over him. His breath caught in the back of his throat. The arena was more than twice the size of the old one he remembered. Thousands of people packed the stands all around and high above him. More eyes fixed on him than he'd ever had to endure before.

He slowly swung his gaze around, and it caught on one of the viewing boxes not far from the tunnel entrance. This time his heart nearly failed him.

"Kyrin." The gasp barely made it past his lips. She stood there staring at him with wide eyes, so close yet completely unreachable. Pain knifed through his chest. Whatever happened in the next several minutes, she would see it all. He could hardly bear the thought of her seeing him struck down in this place.

Movement flashed at the corner of his eye. He looked over to where two men slowly made their way toward him, about fifteen feet apart. Both wore leather armor, one carrying a broadsword and the other a short sword and buckler. Recognition struck him when he focused on the one with the broadsword. He was one of Jasper's men. One of his best if he'd survived long enough to be still fighting. The other, younger man was probably one of Jasper's too. Either Davira wanted a good show or a swift end for Jace by sending two men against him at a time.

He glanced back to the viewing box, catching sight of the queen lounging in her seat, a cruel smile twisting her lips. He then locked eyes with Kyrin once more, despair and indecision feeling as though they were about to rip his chest open. He'd sworn never to do this again, but how could he let himself die with her watching?

Sensing the men drawing near, he tore his eyes away from her and faced them. *Elôm, I don't know what to do. I don't want to be this killer again.* The men increased their pace. He stood frozen, unable to breathe as the man with the broadsword raised his blade. One more step would bring him close enough to cleave Jace in two. Should he let him?

The sword arced toward him. A sudden but quiet internal voice echoed in his head. *Defend yourself.*

Jace lifted his sword just in time to block the opposing blade. Metal screeched against metal. Before the other gladiator could make his move, Jace spun away, putting distance between them. Heat surged in his blood, sharpening his focus and kicking it into fight mode. He'd fought this moment with everything he had, but if Elôm had commanded him to defend himself, he would. *Guide my sword. I don't want to kill unless I have to.*

The younger gladiator attacked first this time, charging in, his eyes alight with bloodlust. No doubt, he wanted the distinction and honor of being the one to defeat Jace. Jace blocked, doing his best to keep the other man in view. The seasoned gladiator approached more slowly, biding his time for an opening. Jace would have to be wary of him. He wouldn't have gotten this far being reckless. The man tried to sneak in and take Jace out from the side while he was distracted, but Jace managed to knock the younger gladiator back just in time to parry the other's blade.

Jace recognized Jasper's, or rather Zar's, training techniques in these fighters. He'd had the same training and used the same moves, but now he had far more diverse teachers and opponents since his last time in the arena. He drew on all of that experience as the men grew bolder.

At first, the younger gladiator seemed focused on being the one to claim victory, but after Jace managed to slice his arm, he must have thought better of it. Now the two men worked together, targeting Jace's blind spots. It took every bit of concentration and skill he possessed to avoid their blades.

When the older gladiator's sword nicked his shoulder as he spun away from him, pain and then heat flared. Vaguely, he heard the reaction of the crowd. This emboldened the gladiators. He had to take one of them down before they wore him out. But to incapacitate one of the men, he may have to kill him.

Sweat rolled down Jace's face, and he blinked the sting from his eyes. Any hindrance to his concentration would be deadly. He had to be in constant motion to avoid being caught between the gladiators and keep them both in view. After several minutes, he picked up the patterns in how they fought and worked together.

Taking advantage of this, he faked inattention toward the younger man, keeping his gaze on the older. The young gladiator jumped at the opportunity, just as Jace predicted, stepping forward without properly guarding himself. At the last second, Jace back-stepped and swung to his right in a wide horizontal swipe. The younger gladiator had just raised his sword for an overhead blow, and Jace's blade sliced across his exposed thighs. The man's arms and sword dropped as he doubled over and went to his knees, nearly tripping the older gladiator.

Jace took a few steps back to prepare to face the remaining fighter, who would surely step up his efforts. Skirting around his fallen comrade, the man stalked toward Jace. Their swords met in a violent crash. The man pushed forward more viciously now that he was the only one still standing. Jace tried to keep a wary eye on the wounded gladiator. He'd seen men continue to fight with gruesome injuries before, but the man remained kneeling, clutching the deep wounds to his legs.

After barely avoiding a decapitating blow, Jace slashed downward and connected with the gladiator's leg. The man stumbled, and as quickly as Jace could shift his momentum, he stabbed his sword. This time his blade punched through the man's leather breastplate just below the ribs. With a groan, the man toppled.

Just like that, it was over. Both of Jace's opponents lay or knelt, bleeding into the sand. That's when the roar of cheers and applause registered, cutting through the muting rush of his blood, which only now started to cool. The sound reverberated around him, beating against his skull, but of the thousands that watched from the stands, he sought only one face. He turned to the royal viewing box. Kyrin stood at the edge, her face ashen, her eyes shining with unshed tears. If only he could reach her. If only he could hold her. He hated Davira for forcing her to watch. It was the worst kind of torture.

He shifted his gaze momentarily to the queen, letting his hatred show before softening his expression to focus on Kyrin again. He prayed she could see how much he loved her. It was all he could do before guards appeared. They grabbed the sword away from him and gripped his arms to lead him away.

Back inside, the driving heat in his blood cooled completely. It left his limbs weighted, and tremors passed through his body. Even though he was no longer exerting himself, his heart wouldn't stop pounding. It was all sinking in now. He'd really just fought as a gladiator again. Even his hands were shaking, and he was afraid he would be sick. But he forced himself to draw in slow, deep breaths and remember the prompting he'd felt just before the fight.

When they reached his cell, Ben and Mira's anxious gazes fell on him, and relief engulfed their expressions.

"Praise Elôm," he heard Mira murmur as the guards pushed him into his cell and locked the door.

Ben and Mira watched him, though they didn't ask any questions. Jace took a moment, flexing his hands, which felt ice cold. He drew a few more breaths before facing them again.

"I felt Elôm wanted me to defend myself, so I did. I tried not to kill anyone, but I'm not sure how well I succeeded."

"I am sure you made the right choice. We were praying the entire time."

"Pray for Kyrin. She was there with Davira." Jace squeezed his eyes shut. He knew very little about babies and pregnancy, but the anguish Kyrin must have felt watching him fight couldn't be healthy. He'd seen many a slave woman miscarry under strain during his lifetime.

"We will."

Jace thanked them but kept the pregnancy to himself. There were far too many people around who might overhear and relay the information to Davira, who would surely use it to her advantage. She didn't need any help devising torture methods.

Stinging pain began to throb in his shoulder, and he only now noticed the large splotch of blood on his sleeve. Carefully peeling the fabric away, he checked the damage. The slice in his shoulder was thankfully shallow, though it had begun to bleed again now that he'd disturbed it.

"Here." Mira reached down and, with Ben's help, tore a strip of fabric from her underskirt. Rolling it up, she tossed it to him through the bars. "I'm not sure how clean it is, but it will help stop the bleeding."

"Thanks." Using one hand and his teeth, he managed to wrap the makeshift bandage around his shoulder and tie it.

Now that his adrenaline had worn off, exhaustion set in. He'd forgotten just how drained he'd always felt after a fight. With a heavy sigh, he sank down at the back of his cell and leaned against the wall, trying not to think about being forced out into the arena again.

Kyrin was one more carriage jolt away from being sick as they returned to the palace. If she did, it would go all over Davira's dress. Only the intense fear of what Davira might do in retaliation kept her stomach in place. The fierce, splitting pain that throbbed in her head didn't help, nor the sting of unshed tears. Watching Jace fight, not knowing at first if he would defend himself, was one of the worst things she'd ever had to experience. She couldn't imagine what he was feeling. His past had left him broken before he'd found peace in Elôm, and in his rawest moments, she had witnessed him express his fear of ever fighting in an arena again. Even Davira couldn't know just how cruel a torture she had wrought.

It made Kyrin sick to beg, but she had to try. "Please, let me see Jace."

"Oh, you'll see him. Tomorrow. When he fights again."

In that moment, hatred boiled up, burning the back of her throat. She couldn't help it. She hated this woman and her desire to cause pain.

Hanging her aching head, she slumped in her seat as despair rapidly overtook the hatred. Back at the palace, she was almost relieved to return to her cell, where she didn't have to endure Davira's vile company any longer. Once the guards had left, she let tears have their escape while she huddled against the back wall of the cell.

Holden gave her a moment before asking, "What happened?"

She wiped her sleeves against her cheeks, but the tears kept falling. "She made Jace fight in the arena."

Holden breathed in sharply. "Is he…"

"He's alive, but he'll have to fight again tomorrow." And probably every day after that until he had no strength left and fell to his opponent.

Holden released a sigh that was somewhere between relief and pain. No doubt, he'd wondered if Jace had refused to fight. It was the same stabbing fear she'd experienced while watching the gladiators approach Jace. In that brief moment, before he'd defended himself, Kyrin had truly believed she was about to see him die. While it pained her to think of what he must be feeling right now, she also thanked Elôm she hadn't had to bear such loss. Not today, anyway.

WITH A THUNDEROUS crash, the catapulted stone tore through the already weakened supports of the gate, and all at once, it came tumbling down in a rain of dust and debris. Cheers rose all around Daniel, competing with the falling rock. After nearly a week of besieging the fort, they had finally overcome their first major hurdle to taking back Arcacia. If only he shared the same exhilaration as the surrounding army, but summoning such excitement had been difficult since Jace and Kyrin had been captured.

Four days had passed since the surprise attack. Another had occurred just two days ago, but they'd been more prepared this time. Only two soldiers had died in the brief skirmish that ensued. But Daniel's mind was constantly on his brother- and sister-in-law, as well as his unborn niece or nephew. It was hard to face Elanor's sorrow every morning, knowing there was absolutely nothing he could do about it. She handled it bravely, already conducting herself as a queen. It made Daniel both proud and pained.

Forcing his mind back to the matter at hand, he cast a glance at the sky from where he sat on his horse, surrounded by his men. Dragons circled, but no firedrakes this morning. Captain Darq reported that the drakes and Arcacia's ground force had pulled back from the fortress during the night. Everyone had known the gate would be breached today, and no doubt they would find the fort empty. There wasn't much point in Davira's men defending it anymore. No, the might of Arcacia would allow them to take the fortress and would regroup and position themselves between Daniel and Davira. Somewhere between here and Valcré, their two armies would clash, and their fate would be decided. This was merely the first step toward either victory or catastrophic defeat.

Daniel drew a deep breath. *I don't look forward to what's coming, Elôm. Not with the losses we've already suffered. Today the men celebrate, but so many are going to die as we move forward, and the closer we get to the battlefield, the more uneasy I feel. We all knew there would be losses, and I know I can't make emotional decisions, but if there is a way to avoid the bloodshed we all sense coming, show me. I know every life is precious to You.*

The dust cleared from the destroyed gate, and their first group of soldiers, led by Marcus, marched toward the rubble. Daniel nudged his horse forward to follow. The ruined gate wasn't passable to the animals, so he dismounted when they arrived. Marcus and his men were already scaling the debris, picking their way over the jagged stones and watching closely for any danger. Daniel and his guards followed a short distance behind. The rest of their armies waited at their back to help secure the fort should they discover it wasn't as abandoned as it appeared.

At the top of the hill of rubble, Daniel paused to peer down into the fortress courtyard, which was indeed empty save for Marcus's men. The door to the keep stood open and silent. Marcus stationed soldiers outside, taking a dozen men with him into the keep. Daniel joined the men in the courtyard, and a few minutes later, Marcus returned.

"I want to do a more thorough sweep, but it does appear abandoned." He motioned to the ruined gate. "I'll talk to Prince

Haedrin about getting a team together to clear rubble to make it easier to bring in supplies. There should be plenty of room for Josef and the others to set up an area for the wounded inside the keep."

"Good."

As Marcus turned to give out further orders, Daniel's focus shifted to the opposite wall of the fort. Beyond it lay their next challenge. Though Captain Darq had warned him Arcacia's army was amassing to oppose them, Daniel needed to see what they were up against for himself. He set off across the courtyard toward the nearest stairs. Aric followed.

The beginnings of dread threaded through his gut as he climbed the steps, but it was nothing compared to the gut punch that hit him when he reached the top and looked southwest. Though some distance away, the biggest army he had ever seen stretched far into the horizon. He'd heard of Arcacia's military might all his life, but even as its prince, he'd never realized just how big an army they commanded. He braced himself against the parapet and released a heavy sigh. So many were going to die.

The stands were starting to fill with people. Jace could hear the hum of voices and the thump of feet above them, all getting ready for another day of slaughter. If only he felt more prepared. He'd struggled to sleep last night, as worn out as he was. During the brief times he had slept, nightmares had tormented him. Some involved the arena, but the worst were those that involved Kyrin in peril and his inability to save her. He longed to see her, though not if it meant the possibility of her watching him slain by whatever opponents Davira threw at him today. *Protect her, and for her sake, don't let me fall.*

He couldn't stand the thought of her sitting in the dungeon back at the palace by herself or facing what Davira had in store if he was killed. *When* he was killed. At this point, it was only a matter of time unless Elôm provided a miracle, and it would take more than one to get both of them through this alive.

The heavy thump of footsteps sent Jace's heart plummeting toward his stomach, where it twisted violently. He never thought he'd have to be this horrific spectacle again.

"Our prayers go with you, Jace."

He gave Ben a grateful nod just before the guards opened the cell and motioned him out. As much as he wanted to resist them, it would only waste his strength and energy, both of which he would need. They led him to the waiting area, where dread mounted in a chill sweat across his back.

A few minutes later, a guard handed him a sword and pushed him into the tunnel. He drew a steadying breath and called to Elôm for guidance and protection. When he stepped into the arena, he first swept it for opponents before looking straight to the royal viewing box. Kyrin stood there just as expected. Bittersweet pain crashed in at the sight of her. Would he ever even get to hear her voice again before death?

Though he was loathe to take his attention away from her, cheers erupted from the crowd. He spun around to find the cause but was still alone in the arena. That could only mean the cheers were for him as if he were some hero. He scowled. He knew for a fact that if he met any one of these people on the street, they would recoil in fear or disgust. But, as long as they were safe in their seats and he was down here participating in this blood sport, they lauded him.

Movement drew his attention across the arena to where another gate opened. Out strode two men, though not gladiators like yesterday. Ryriks. Cold pooled in his gut at the same time as heat ignited his blood. So Davira's game was to pit him against increasingly difficult opponents until he fell to one of them. He took his sword in both hands. It wouldn't be the first time he had to face more than one ryrik at a time. At least these men weren't armored, which led Jace to believe they were as much prisoners as he was. Not that their drive to kill him would be any less potent.

He raised his sword, and the men stalked toward him, their eyes aglow. To stop them, he would probably have to kill them. Ryriks didn't go down due to pain or injury like other men, and they certainly didn't give up a fight. They would fight until their last breath. So would Jace.

They rushed him, coming at him from each side. He sidestepped, barely avoiding one blade and blocking the other. He attempted an attack of his own but failed. He would have to be aggressive to win this fight. These men would not tire before he would.

They fought in a fury, each one trying to catch him off guard while he was busy with the other. Jace had to move constantly to avoid their blades. His only advantage was that they were reckless and sloppy in their attacks. They didn't have the discipline or patience of a soldier or a trained gladiator.

His heart hammered, heat pulsing in his blood, spiking every time a blade nearly found his flesh. He was vaguely aware he'd been nicked in the side, but he barely noticed the pain.

Greedily, they both tried to attack at once, and one caused the other to stumble just enough to give Jace an opening. He drove his blade forward in a move more instinct and survival than choice. It pierced the one ryrik's chest, and he fell to one knee as Jace's sword pulled free, slicked with crimson. Jace took a couple of quick steps back to reestablish his footing. He had no confidence the wounded ryrik would stay down, but maybe it would slow him at least.

Sure enough, the man shoved back to his feet, murder

glowing in his eyes, but the blood rapidly soaking the front of his shirt didn't bode well for him. Dragging in deep breaths, Jace raised his sword as the two came at him again.

At first, the wounded ryrik didn't seem fazed, but he grew sluggish after a minute or two. Shortly after that, he swung widely at Jace, the momentum sending him to his knees. He tried to rise but ended up falling into the sand. This time he did not move. Now Jace was down to one opponent.

The remaining ryrik bared his teeth and attacked like a raging pickerin boar. Each hammering blow jolted up Jace's arms. It was like fighting Ruis again in Dorland, but there were no trees or a river to get in his way this time. A recklessly wide attack left the ryrik open, and Jace quickly slashed his sword across the man's middle. While not fatal, it caused the man's arms to drop, leaving him open again, and this time Jace swung higher. The man grabbed at his throat. While he looked like he was going to try to attack Jace one-handed, even a ryrik couldn't fight such rapid blood loss. He took one step and collapsed at Jace's feet with a gurgle.

Jace looked at him and then the other, sweat pouring down his body, and hung his head. The cheers roared around him. He looked to the royal viewing box, the heat in his chest crackling with hatred. He wasn't sure he'd be able to stop himself from driving his sword through Davira's heart if she were close enough. He gritted his teeth and looked away. *Lord, help me. I'm not a killer.*

Then a change swept through the crowd. The cheers died to murmurs of confusion, and a cold warning shivered across his skin. He turned quickly to find another gate had opened. This time one man stepped out, one very familiar figure, who stood several inches short than Jace. Long dark hair fell over his shoulders, and he peered at Jace through large, sapphire blue eyes. Falcor.

The last time Jace had seen the crete was at the first battle of Samara, but he was not the same proud man who had put a noose around Jace's neck and dragged him around like an abused dog. His sagging posture was like no crete Jace had ever seen, his long hair straggly, his clothing ragged and filthy. He appeared to have gone hungry more times than not in recent days. Was he a prisoner? He must be. Maybe Davira hadn't had the same patience as her father, who had allowed Falcor his delusional belief he held any kind of power.

Tension coiled Jace's muscles as every memory of Falcor flooded his consciousness. The man had hurt not only Jace but many others as well. He'd broken Leetra's heart, murdered Josan, and tried to kill Talas…but above all, he'd betrayed William Altair to the emperor. He was the reason Kyrin's father was dead.

Jace tightened his grip around his sword as the crete approached him. He hadn't had a weapon the last time the two of them had faced each other, but he did now. He'd never fought a crete, but he had sparred with Talas and Darq. He would have to draw on that experience.

Though Falcor had a sword in hand, how he approached Jace lacked any resolve. And while his expression was hard, there was no fire or determination in it. Even so, he attacked swiftly, just as Jace anticipated. A fresh burst of heat rushed through his body in response to the rapid attacks that forced him back several steps just to maintain some distance between them. Falcor, being shorter, would have to get in close to land an attack. Jace couldn't let him accomplish that.

So, he gave ground whenever Falcor got too close, trying to learn his fighting style and adjust his own. It was very different from fighting the ryriks. Now he might be able to bide his time and let his opponent tire. Falcor's appearance and the fact that he didn't have ryrik blood told Jace it was possible, just so long as he didn't wear out first. He had to be careful with his own attacks. Falcor would undoubtedly be too quick to take advantage of any opening.

They ranged around the arena, no doubt giving the crowd a good show. Jace's breaths were soon gasping again with exertion. Though the guards gave him a bit of food every day, it wasn't enough, and he could feel its negative effect on his energy. Even so, his blood continued to burn hot, keeping him going. For now.

Soon, the sweat rolled down Falcor's face just as much as Jace's. His attacks were getting just a little slower. Seeming to know this, he rallied and came at Jace in a flurry. Jace blocked and dodged, barely managing to avoid the whirring blade. It brought Falcor in too close. The crete lunged, blade aimed for Jace's gut. With barely time to react, Jace twisted sideways. The blade darted just past him, nearly catching flesh. Jace reached out and grabbed Falcor's arm, pushing it away and slamming the hilt of his sword into the side of Falcor's head. Both the crete and the sword fell to the ground.

Panting for breath, Jace scooped his opponent's sword out of the sand as Falcor pushed dizzily to his knees. Blood rolled down the side of his face as he blinked sluggishly and looked up at Jace. Jace raised his sword level with Falcor's neck, but the crete did not try to get to his feet. Resignation settled in his expression.

"Just do it. Do everyone, including me, the favor."

The bite of self-loathing in his tone caught Jace off guard. Perhaps Falcor had finally realized what so many had tried to tell him: that everything he had done, all the betrayals and death, had not given him or his people the power he'd desired. Instead, it had only empowered their enemies, endangering the very people he had convinced himself he fought for.

Jace, however, couldn't summon much in the way of sympathy. Falcor had hurt too many people far too deeply. To kill him would bring justice for those people. For Kyrin's father. He looked to the viewing box where Kyrin stood watching him. She was too far away for him to know exactly what expression she wore, but he could give her family justice.

With a heavy breath, he turned back to Falcor, who waited, almost eagerly, for him to act. But Jace had been in this position before when he'd fought Dagren last winter. It wasn't his place to dispense judgment or vengeance. Killing Falcor now that he was defenseless would be murder.

He took a couple of wobbly steps backward and turned for the exit, carrying the swords with him. Along the way, he looked at Kyrin again. This time, she gave him a little nod before the guards met him at the gate.

KADEN LEANED AGAINST the parapet of Fort Rhall and peered out at Arcacia's army. The sun had set, and soon only distant campfires would be visible to mark the army standing between him and his sister. If she was even still alive.

An ache burned in his throat, and he had to clear it lest it forced moisture to his eyes. This was much easier said than done. He and Kyrin had fought too long and too hard for it to end like this. She should be here with them, not at Davira's mercy, because there was no such thing. Davira would torture her—*was* torturing her, perhaps even at this moment. A hot tear rolled down his cheek, and he rubbed it away with his shoulder.

Sensing movement, he glanced to his right. Rayad approached him slowly, his expression as heavy and tired as Kaden felt. "Mind if I join you?"

Kaden shook his head. If he tried to speak right now, his voice would fail him. He cleared his throat again as Rayad joined him at the parapet and worked to get his emotions under control.

Rayad, too, just stared out at the army in silence. What could either of them say anyway? The battle ahead of them would be unlike anything they had ever faced. Most of them would probably die, and Kaden would never reach Kyrin in time, even if he did survive. Just like with his father and Michael, he would have to find a way to go on without her. But that was a loss he didn't know if he could handle.

The silence stretched out until Rayad turned. Though Kaden kept his gritty eyes trained on the horizon, he could feel how Rayad studied him. Finally, he asked, "How are you holding up?"

Kaden gave that question several seconds of consideration before shaking his head once more. "I'm tired," he breathed out heavily. "Tired of fighting, of struggling, of loss. I just want it to be over."

Every bone and fiber of his body had had enough, and it wasn't just because he still found his strength lacking since the venom. His soul was tired. He'd lost too much. Seen too much. Any sense of adventure and excitement he had experienced when this all started had died. At this point, he wasn't even sure how sweet victory would feel…if he survived that long.

"I know." Rayad's heavy, worn voice reflected everything Kaden was feeling. But then his firm hand gripped Kaden's shoulder. "It's hard to still have hope, but…I think we should hang on to it. Elôm has worked many miracles. He can still do that now."

Kaden hung his head. It was true he was feeling pretty hopeless. He let Rayad's words sink in. As hard as it was at times like this to hold on to hope, he was right.

He looked over at Rayad, into his wise, weathered face, and thought of his father. If he couldn't be here with them, then Kaden was glad Rayad was. "Thank you."

Daniel just stared at the documents and maps strewn across the table in the war room. Everyone else had left some time ago for supper, but Daniel had stayed sitting in the solid stone room that muted all sounds of outside life. Just him and Elôm and his circling thoughts.

As it stood now, the plan was to remain at Fort Rhall to give their wounded dragon riders time to heal before pushing toward Valcré. It was a solid plan. They had defenses, shelter, and the forest to provide provisions. Really, they could hold out here indefinitely. But, no matter how long they waited, it didn't change the fact that Arcacia's army was out there, ready to attack as soon as they moved and no doubt gaining men as the days went by.

He rubbed his forehead. Everything was going according to plan, so why did it just feel so wrong? He'd always known this fight was coming, but part of him now wondered if they should have just stayed in Samara and avoided the bloodshed. Had he lost his nerve? Was he not as committed to this fight as everyone else? That was a scary thought. He shook it away. Just because he didn't want to see people die didn't mean he wasn't committed to their goals. What if this unease was actually Elôm trying to get his attention?

"Show me Your will, Lord." His voice seemed swallowed up in the shadowy, cavernous room, but he pressed on. "We've made our plans, and we have a goal before us. Everyone is committed to it, but I have no peace. Show me the way. How can I lead if I have no confidence in our decisions?"

If only Elon would show up in the room as He had on the cliffs of Valcré two years ago. Daniel longed for the face to face interaction and reassurance. Now he would have to rely on prayer to find the answer to his persistent unrest.

"There you are."

Daniel looked up to see Elanor in the doorway. She adjusted a light shawl around her shoulders as she approached him. The inside of the fort was cooler than they were used to, being outside in a tent for the past couple of weeks. Just the sight of her soothed a little of the turmoil inside of him. He reached for her and drew her into his lap. A little smile claimed her lips as she wrapped her arms around his neck and leaned into him. It was good to see her smile.

She glanced from him to the table, that smile shifting to a more concerned expression. "Have you had anything to eat?"

"I haven't."

Now she turned serious, her voice gently chiding. "You shouldn't skip meals. It's important we all maintain our strength."

Didn't he know it? "I'll go find something in a bit."

"What are you doing in here all alone anyway?"

"Praying." He smiled sheepishly. "Worrying."

She tipped her head, her thumb brushing the hair at the base of his neck. "Share with me."

He hated for her to worry on top of everything else. He'd much rather just enjoy her company. But it would be better to share the burden. After all, they would both be ruling this country.

"I'm afraid of how many lives will be lost in the battle to come. Arcacia's army is…" He forced out a hard breath, seeing the vastness of it in his mind. He could hardly imagine the destruction that would be left in its wake once this was all finished. "I know they can be defeated if that is Elôm's will, but how many will die in the process on both sides? The numbers could be catastrophic. Honestly, part of me wishes I had tried to take Davira out during the parley when I had the chance. Maybe all of this would already be over."

Not that he'd had a weapon on him to make such an attempt, and assassinating his sister probably wasn't the best way to begin his reign.

"Well, what can we do? Is there any way we can avoid battle?"

"There doesn't seem to be, but…" He hesitated. Was he crazy for even letting his mind go here? Was it his fear moving him or Elôm? He forged on, needing to share. "I do have something of an idea. I'm not sure, though, if it's Elôm's guiding or desperation on my part. I've prayed about it and can't seem to shake the idea off."

"Have you talked to Marcus or one of the others about it?"

"Not yet."

That lightly scolding look was back on her face. "Well, isn't that what a general is for? To assist you in military matters?"

"Yes."

"Then I think you should share your idea with him. If he thinks it's crazy and desperate, then maybe it is. But maybe he'll think it's a good idea. Sitting on it won't do any good one way or the other."

Daniel just stared at the marvel of a woman Elôm had brought into his life. "Have I ever told you how much I love you and how blessed Arcacia will be to have you as its queen?"

Her lips curved in a perfect little smile. "You may have mentioned it a time or two."

He drew her close for a kiss he did not want to end. These moments between them were so much less complicated than matters of the future. It was almost physically painful when they parted, though he was quite happy to stare into her eyes and at the way her lips lifted in a soft smile.

She placed a warm hand on his cheek. "Should I send someone for Marcus?"

His thoughts were a little fuzzy, but he nodded. "That would be a good idea."

She got up and turned for the door, leaving him feeling a bit bereft of her presence, but the sooner he talked to Marcus, the better. He didn't dare let himself wonder if there was still time to save Jace, Kyrin, and Holden, but deep down, that desire stirred in his heart. A desperate hope Elôm would preserve them until help arrived.

With a renewed sense of purpose and urgency, he stood up and looked over their battle plans, all of which wouldn't even be needed if his half-baked plan amounted to anything. Though he'd been mulling it over for days, he needed to get his thoughts in order now that he was about to discuss it with someone. He'd just finished praying for Elôm to guide the conversation clearly one way or the other when Marcus walked in.

"You wanted to see me?"

"Yes. I need your honest opinion and perspective."

Marcus stepped closer so they were standing face to face. "I will do my best."

"The thing is, I've had no peace about our long-term plans for days." Daniel waved his hand at the maps on the table. It was all so cold and calculated laid out like that. Paper and ink could never prepare one for the mass casualties involved in war. "When we took the fort this morning, and I saw what awaited us, I had only one thought—we can't face that army head-on."

"I don't see that we have any choice unless we turn back and return to Samara." When Daniel didn't respond, Marcus's brows raised in question. "What are you thinking?"

"I think all of this could be avoided if I could just get to Davira and take her out of power."

"That's exactly what that army is out there to prevent."

Here it was. The moment of truth. "What if some of us managed to sneak around it and into Valcré?"

Marcus didn't appear to know what to say at first. Daniel didn't blame him. On its own, what he was proposing was a little crazy, but if Elôm was behind it, then it wouldn't matter.

Marcus spoke slowly as if he were trying not to show how much he was questioning Daniel's sanity. "And what then?"

"Then, if we can sneak undetected into the palace, I think we can stop all of this. All we have to do is establish that Davira is no longer in power, and I am. Unless that army out there has some sort of blind, unwavering devotion to her, what would they have to fight for if she was gone? Any sane individual should know surrender is the only option."

Silence echoed between them as Marcus took it all in. Daniel did feel bad for springing it on him like this. As far as everyone else knew, their plans were straightforward and set. Marcus seemed to let the scenario play through his mind before focusing on Daniel again.

"The problem is, we have no idea what kind of defenses Davira has at Auréa. We may be able to reach it undetected, but it's doubtful we would get inside without an alarm being raised. She will surely have firedrakes ready for an attack."

"That is the biggest challenge." And the one thing that could bring this whole idea crashing down. "We would have to take some dragon riders with us. I know it can't be many because they are the only ones keeping our army from being decimated, but hopefully, enough to keep Davira's drakes busy while we get in."

Marcus's eyes narrowed slightly. "You intend to go yourself."

Daniel gave him a firm nod. Here was where he anticipated the most opposition to his plans, but it was the one element he was steadfast on. "I have to be there to take control. It's the only way to shift momentum in our favor."

"And what if the plan fails and you are captured or killed?"

Daniel could hear the note of uncertainty, perhaps even fear, in his voice. They'd all placed so much hope on his claim to the throne. It was everything they had been fighting for since he'd limped into their camp last summer. But he could not be the only key to their success.

"Then everyone would either return to Samara to live their lives or press on. I will name a successor before I leave in case the worst should happen. I know everyone has rallied around me, but all of our hopes for the future can't live and die by me.

Others can take up the mantle if I fall, and if I'm not willing to die for my people, then I shouldn't even be king."

The hesitancy remained in Marcus's expression, though he didn't seem to know how to voice it. Daniel gripped his shoulder. Marcus was his general, but he was also his friend.

"Listen, I know the risks, but I'm struggling to accept the fact that the land from here to Valcré will be littered with tens of thousands of men and women if we continue on this course. I've had no peace about it. I've prayed for both peace and direction. Taking a small force to Valcré to end this is the only thing I am confident about. I just need to know if you think the army will stand down if Davira is no longer a threat."

Marcus let a long breath seep out as he shifted to stare at a map of the area as if he could look down on the army and know their minds. "My gut says yes, but I don't know what it has been like amongst the men since Davira took over. Parker could probably answer that better than I can."

"Send for him."

Marcus nodded and turned for the door.

"Send for Aaron and Kaden, too," Daniel called after him.

# 31

MARCUS COULDN'T BELIEVE they were really considering this. Back when he'd been a captain in Arcacia's army, everything had been structured, calculated, executed with precision. This plan to infiltrate Valcré was desperate. And bold. And relying far too heavily on hopes rather than facts. Yet, how many of their other plans had been executed the same way over the last couple of years and brought them to this very moment? Elôm didn't need precision to accomplish His plans.

After sending men to search out Kaden, Parker, and Aaron, he rejoined Daniel in the war room. There was much they still needed to discuss. Even desperate plans should be as well-thought-out as possible. Daniel had found a map of Valcré amongst the documents strewn on the table. If only it could tell them what sort of defenses Davira had.

Lowering the map, Daniel gave him a pointed look. "You think I'm crazy, don't you?"

Marcus took half a second to consider an answer to that. He wasn't about to call his future king crazy, even if they were friends. "Daring. It's a daring plan, but…" He glanced at the inked representation of Valcré on the map. While it held no answers, the same peace Daniel had talked about settled inside him. "I believe it can work."

"Do you?"

"I do, because I believe Elôm will give us victory, whether that means fighting our way to Valcré or taking it by stealth."

He could see in Daniel's expression and the hint of a smile how that declaration bolstered him. Marcus couldn't imagine having the weight of the country on his shoulders. Heading the army was heavy enough.

While they waited for the others, Marcus asked questions and posed suggestions that would better prepare them to take the city. By the time Kaden, Parker, and Aaron entered the room, they were on their way to a fleshed-out plan of action.

Kaden, eyes brimming with questions, looked between the two of them. Marcus knew his brother, and he wouldn't hesitate for one second to accept this change of plans.

"You sent for us?"

Daniel nodded but focused on Parker first. "Captain, I have a question."

Parker bowed before standing at attention. So far, aside from some initial suspicion from the Militia, no trouble had arisen between the men. Marcus attributed this, in part, to the capable way Parker led his small company. Already, Marcus looked ahead to him being a strong asset when it came time to unite their army.

"Yes, Your Highness?"

"If Davira was captured or killed, and I had control at the palace, would Arcacia's army stand down?"

Marcus caught the way Kaden's brows lifted. His gaze darted to meet Marcus's, and it must have taken all his self-control not to cut in and ask what this was about. Last he'd heard, their army was going to rest here for a while before making a move on Valcré. Though he hadn't spoken against it, Marcus had seen the restlessness on his face and fully understood the reason for it. To wait destroyed any minuscule amount of hope to rescue

Kyrin. But Daniel's plans restored some of that. While he couldn't let it cloud his decisions, he could not say it wasn't the first thing that sprang to mind when Daniel had first shared his plans. The chances of finding Kyrin alive, even if they did succeed, were still slim to none, and he tried to prepare himself for that reality, but he couldn't help but hope.

He forced these thoughts to the back of his mind when Parker spoke. He had to focus on the challenge before them. It wouldn't do Kyrin any good if they failed due to poor planning.

"I don't know if I can say for certain, my lord, but from my experience, I think it's a likely outcome. The high-ranking officers might not be so quick to shift allegiance, but when it comes to the average soldier, I haven't found many with true loyalty to the queen. Given a choice, I think most, like me, would rather fight for you than Davira. They're just too afraid to speak out or leave."

Daniel shared a look with Marcus. This was the key. If the army chose not to back down, it wouldn't matter whether they defeated Davira now or later.

Daniel turned to Aaron, and Kaden swallowed as if tamping down his rising questions yet again. Marcus had to give him credit. By now, he had to have some idea of where this discussion was headed.

"How many men does Avery have at his command in Valcré?"

Aaron crossed his arms, tilting his head as if calculating. Like Kaden, he had to be eager to know what was going on, though he hid it much better. "I don't know the exact number, but best guess is around a hundred. Could be more now. He's always recruiting, and people are eager to join him."

"That could be just what we need." Daniel seemed to say this more to himself than anyone in particular.

Kaden, apparently, couldn't hold back any longer. "Not to interrupt, but what are we discussing? Are you going to Valcré?"

"Yes. I am going to try to infiltrate the palace and take Davira down before this standoff with Arcacia's army can become a bloodbath."

Kaden's shoulders straightened, a spark igniting in his eyes, which was a welcome sight. Ever since Marcus had to tell him that rescuing Kyrin was impossible, it was as if the fight in him had died. It was disturbing after everything they had been through, but this small chance had brought it back—it and that stubborn, willful look that had irritated Marcus to no end at times.

"I'm going with you."

Marcus shook his head to himself. For being captain of the dragon riders, Kaden really should work on properly addressing Daniel as their sovereign, but he couldn't blame him for his boldness. With Kyrin involved, Marcus would have insisted on going too, though in a more tactful way.

Daniel nodded, and a little of the stubbornness faded from Kaden's expression. No doubt he'd been prepared to fight to go along.

"That's why I sent for you. I'll need a small group of dragon riders to join me and take on whatever firedrake force Davira has guarding the city. However, you and all who join you need to be fully aware we can't afford to take many, and I have no idea what you'll face in Valcré. For all we know, there could be a hundred firedrakes waiting for us. It could very well be a suicide mission."

Kaden, of course, didn't take any time to mull it over. "I'm willing. I know my men will be too."

Daniel turned to Marcus once more and tapped the city map that now lay on the table. "Then we will take the Landale Dragon Riders and the Militia. This is our city, and we should be the ones taking the greatest risk to free it. That will still leave the vast majority of our dragon force here to defend the army.

We'll have to travel through the forest to avoid detection. We need to maintain the element of surprise. Davira can't know we're coming."

Aaron stepped closer now, uncrossing his arms. "And what's the plan when we reach Valcré?"

"That is what Marcus and I were starting to discuss before you walked in." Daniel leaned against the table, his brows pulling together in thought. "It will be hard to make a solid plan without knowing what we'll face there, but we'll need to infiltrate the city quietly. Once there, I would appreciate your help locating Avery. I hope to recruit him and his men. That would give us a decently-sized force to work with on the ground. We just have to decide how best to use it."

Though they hadn't had long to discuss it, potential strategies had begun to develop in Marcus's mind. "I do have some ideas about that. We can't get that many men to the palace without detection. If you want the element of surprise, you will have to do it with a smaller force. The problem is the fort is nearby. They will march out immediately if they know the palace is under attack. I propose that, while you lead a group to the palace, the Militia and I form a distraction. We can march on the city as if we intend to claim it. That will draw out the city guard and keep them occupied while you take the palace."

He paused to run it through his mind again and calculate the risks. "This, of course, will put the palace on alert, but they won't be expecting a surprise attack there. It may even draw out some of the guards if Davira thinks they are needed to hold the city. I hate to turn the streets into a battleground, but I think it's our best option, and we'll try our best to keep it to the outskirts. There aren't as many homes near the main gate as there are to the north and south sides of the city."

Daniel nodded slowly, as if he, too, were playing it out and searching for flaws. "It's a good plan."

Aaron joined in again, an eager hum to his voice. Marcus and Kaden weren't the only ones with a sibling trapped in Valcré. "I would also suggest bringing a couple of cretes with us, but not as dragon riders. Getting past Auréa's outer wall will be a challenge unless you have someone on the inside to take out the guards and open the gate. I can climb the wall and get in, but I will need help with the guards."

"Good idea. I will talk to Darq about it." Daniel motioned at Kaden. "You and the riders will have to do your best to hold back any firedrakes and keep them from wiping out either group. If all goes according to plan, we'll secure the palace and spread the word Davira is no longer in power. Hopefully, that will quell any opposition, and we can then fortify the city and prepare to negotiate the army's surrender. It's a risk, but if we are successful, it will spare thousands of lives on both sides."

"When do we leave?" The way Kaden shifted his feet looked as though he were ready to dash out and prep his men immediately.

"Ideally tonight, before dawn. We can't leave during the day and risk being seen. No doubt Davira and her men expect us to hole up here for a while as we planned and won't expect any sort of an attack. I think it's best to hit them when they least expect it."

It took more effort to convince the other leaders of the plan than it had for Daniel to convince Marcus. But Balen quickly took his side and helped sway the rest. Daniel had no doubt he would have done the same thing had their places been switched.

Once everyone was in agreement and all questions had been exhausted, the men filed out of the war room—all except for Trask, who Daniel had asked to stay. They waited in silence until it was just the two of them, and then Daniel gestured to the empty chairs around the table. This was probably a conversation best had sitting down. They both took a seat, and Daniel shifted his chair to face him.

"I know you expressed your desire to join me, but…I have reasons I would like you to remain here."

Disappointment flashed across Trask's face, but he nodded in acceptance. "Whatever you require."

He might not be so eager once he learned the specifics, but Daniel would be forever thankful for such loyalty. He hardly felt he'd done enough yet to deserve it. "While I'm confident in this plan to go to Valcré and believe it is Elôm's will, there is still a chance I could be killed in the attempt."

Trask's face sobered. Daniel didn't like it either. It was disconcerting to have to plan for the possibility of his death, but it must be done.

"I know that is what everyone is worried about, and it does bring up the subject of succession. There is no one next in line for the throne unless Elanor happens to already be carrying a child."

It was, of course, possible, though this was the first moment he'd given it any real consideration. If he died in this mission, he'd never know, and that left a cold sensation in his chest. But he had to let it rest in Elôm's hands.

"To avoid any confusion or possible issues, I think it's best to have a contingency in place. I've actually given this a good deal of thought, even before tonight, and am confident in my decision. So in the event of my untimely death and no heir, I'm appointing you as my successor."

"What?" Trask stared at him openmouthed for a moment. "Surely there are others more qualified than I am. Someone like Lord Ilvaran would make an obvious choice."

Daniel knew the weight he was placing on Trask's shoulders and the feelings of inadequacy, but he had no doubt this was the right decision. "No, I believe it should be you. You're the one who has kept the Resistance fighting for the last three years. None of us would be where we are without you. The truth is, you're far more qualified to lead this country than I am. I'm merely a prince by birth. You are a true leader, and someone I know could lead this country where it needs to go. I understand it's a heavy burden, but I did not make this decision lightly."

Trask exhaled a drawn-out breath and considered it for a long moment. Daniel did not rush his response. Anyone who answered too eagerly or too quickly would not have been right for this responsibility.

Trask straightened in his chair and dipped his chin. "If that is what you will, then, should the worst happen, I will lead our people to the best of my ability."

A smile reached Daniel's face as a weight he'd been carrying for a while lifted. "Thank you. I will put my wishes down in an official document and give it to Elanor for safekeeping. Providing I survive, you will be let off the hook once I have a son."

The spark of humor so often found in Trask's eyes returned with a grin. "Then I will pray for that outcome."

"You do that." Daniel took a moment to consider such a future. He would like to have a son he could bond with like he never had with his father. If it were up to him, he'd have a bunch of children. He could think of nothing more satisfying than a large, loving family. He'd always envied the Altairs a bit with all of their siblings.

Realizing he'd been caught up in this dream for the future, he shook it off and gave Trask a purposeful look. "I'll pray the same for you."

Trask and Anne had been married for about a year now with no signs of pregnancy, and Daniel had a feeling that wasn't intentional.

Trask's wistful expression confirmed it. "Thank you."

Now that everything was settled, Trask left him to finish his preparations. Daniel grabbed a blank parchment and set about recording his wishes for succession. By the time he'd signed and sealed it, it had grown late. Aside from preparing himself personally to leave, everything was in order. He just had to tell Elanor he would be leaving. She would support his decision, but it still wouldn't be easy for either of them.

He made his way to the private room that had been set up for them and quietly opened the door. Considering how late it was, he'd almost expected her to be asleep, but instead, he found a couple of candles still burning where she sat at a small desk reading what he assumed to be copies of the Scrolls. She looked up, her face already set in acceptance.

"When are you leaving?"

Of course, news would travel fast, especially since Marcus and Kaden had begun preparing their men immediately.

"As soon as we're ready."

She rose from her chair. "I wish I could go with you."

Closing the distance between them, he wrapped his arms around her and pulled her close. "I know."

He bent his head, and she welcomed his kiss. Right now, he wanted to savor every moment of it. A couple of weeks was far too short a time to be married, but he was glad they had not waited. If these were their last moments together, he would make them count.

Leetra made another round, checking on the most seriously wounded cretes while Josef, Liam, and the other physicians got some much-needed rest. She should probably try to sleep as well before too long, but that was hard to do with the presence of such a large army so close. It crawled under her skin and made her fingers itch for her swords. She couldn't stop herself from imagining the number of wounded who would need care once the fighting began. They wouldn't have nearly enough physicians to tend them all, even with the extras who had joined them from Samara. It was a bleak, stomach-turning fact of war.

"Lee."

She spun around at the sound of Talas's low voice. He and Josef stood near the door across the room. Fear prickled her arms, but she shook it away as she wound through the cots toward them. Surely nothing terrible could have happened, or an alarm would have been raised. Still, it didn't help that he put his hand on her shoulder as if she would need comfort.

"What is it?" She held her breath.

"Daniel is taking the Militia and Landale Riders to sneak into Valcré. He hopes to stop Davira and end all of this without a battle."

Leetra barely caught the very end, a thousand thoughts rushing into her mind but just one rising above them all. Timothy. To be so close to the city yet unable to fly out and find him had been eating at her relentlessly all day. This was her chance.

"I'm going with you." And no one was going to stop her.

Talas's lips twitched with the hint of a smile as if he'd somehow read that last thought. "I know. Darq went to saddle Soka for you. We're gathering outside the fort. Grab your things, and I'll meet you there."

JACE LEANED BACK against the cell wall with a deep sigh. Two days of intense fights and fitful nights had left him drained. The cuts on his shoulder and side throbbed, and if not for his ryrik blood, they would probably be infected by now. Not that they wouldn't be in a day or two if he couldn't clean and properly bandage them. Once infection did set in, it would deplete his strength even faster. Unless Elôm intervened, his chances of surviving the week were pretty slim. Then Kyrin would have to watch him die.

He rubbed his eyes, fighting to mentally prepare himself for what this new day would bring, but his mind was as worn as his body. If only he could talk to Kyrin for even a brief moment. He didn't want to die without one more chance to tell her how much he loved her, even though they would probably be reunited in death much sooner than he wanted to think about.

He struggled to shut out the commotion of the stands filling above him and let his mind wander back to when he and Kyrin first met. He'd been such a mess then, but she had gotten through to him when even Rayad could not. In spite of every-thing, a quiet laugh rumbled in his chest. All those mornings she would stand outside her cabin, waiting to try to go hunting with him. He'd lurked in the trees watching her, annoyed at how it pricked his conscience until he'd finally given in. They had been through so much since then. Tears burned the back of his throat, and he had to clear it.

Elôm, help me trust You even though things seem hopeless.

Another memory came to him, like a gentle reminder—the days he'd been held captive by Daican. All hope had seemed lost then too. He'd been convinced he would die in that cell, but Elon had rescued him. While another miraculous rescue seemed unlikely, the memories bolstered his waning strength. Elon hadn't abandoned him to the darkness then, and He wouldn't now, even if the end was death.

Thudding footsteps approached, but Jace was ready. He pushed to his feet.

Davira rounded the corner with her guards, and his confidence wavered. What was she doing here? Hatred scorched the inside of his chest, and he fought to tamp it down even as the burn of it flowed into his veins. But then his attention shifted to the man between two of the guards—Holden. Dried blood caked his friend's swollen face. He walked a bit hunched, dark purple bruises splashed across his ribs and stomach. Why would Davira bring him here?

When they reached the cell, he braced himself, and Davira's eyes roved over him. Like Jasper, she probably saw him as little more than an animal.

"Impressive yesterday, taking down two ryriks and a crete." Her voice carried no true genuineness, and she shrugged. "But not unexpected. Today we'll try something different. Let's make a deal. If you accept, I'll let Kyrin stay here with you."

He couldn't stop the way his heart skipped at the possibility of being with Kyrin, but he knew better than to believe it wouldn't come at an unpayable cost. "What deal?"

She motioned to the guards, who shoved Holden forward. "Today, you fight him."

Jace recoiled. "No."

Her voice lilted in mock concern. "You don't want to spend time with your wife before you die?"

Jace would do almost anything to see Kyrin, but not something like this. Holden could barely stand by the looks of it, and Davira wouldn't be satisfied unless Jace killed him. That wasn't going to happen, no matter how desperately he longed for Kyrin.

He grabbed the cell bars, the rough surface digging into his skin as he squeezed them and stared Davira down. "I will not fight him."

"Well then, you'll both have a surprise in the arena."

Something sharp and demented flashed in her eyes, her smirk enough to freeze even his blood. Either way, she won this, and Jace's gut twisted with the implications of her words. Whatever she had in mind was no doubt intended to bring an end to both him and Holden. He had a feeling if even one of them survived the day, it would be a miracle.

Davira nodded to the extra guards, who opened the cell and led him out. He was more than a little tempted to lunge for her and snap her neck. It wouldn't be difficult. But the guards' firm grips told him they were ready for such an attempt. She did keep her distance now that he wasn't behind bars or shackled.

"Enjoy today's opponent. Kyrin will be watching."

Heat burst from Jace's chest and into his limbs. He jerked against the guards. Davira scrambled back against the wall with a squeak. A fist plowed into Jace's ribs, driving the breath from his lungs. He doubled over, though the surging heat quickly dulled the pain. Every bit of it was worth it just to witness the brief terror that had replaced Davira's smirk.

He straightened. By this time, Davira had drawn herself up, her spine stiff as if trying to hide just how much he frightened her. Her lips curled in absolute loathing, and her hand was tucked into one of the folds of her dress. Probably reaching for a hidden blade. He locked his gaze with hers, daring her to use it. Her hand slowly dropped back to her side, balling into a fist, and she clenched her teeth. She wouldn't dare get that close.

He maintained eye contact with her until the guards yanked him down the hall. Only then did his attention shift to what lay ahead. The guards led both him and Holden to the waiting area. They gave Jace a sword and offered another to Holden. Holden just looked at it for a long moment before releasing a heavy, halting sigh and taking it in one hand. He wrapped his free arm around his ribs. As dark as the bruising was, Jace would be surprised if some of the ribs weren't broken.

The rough edge to Holden's voice only proved how much pain he was in. "I'd say you should have just accepted the offer, but I wouldn't have either." He gave a half-hearted shrug and winced. "Though being killed by you would be a lot more pleasant than whatever awaits us out there."

He was probably right, but Jace shook his head. "I'm not murdering one of my best friends. Not even to see Kyrin."

Holden released something like a choked, wheezing laugh, and Jace frowned at him. "What?"

"I just find it ironic, considering I used to imagine you murdering me and everyone else in our sleep."

Jace snorted. Holden had been horrible to him then, though it wasn't as if Jace had made any effort to change his mind. He could never have guessed they would become such good friends after that. Friends who would likely die together in the arena today.

Holden appeared to struggle for a full breath before looking at Jace again. All humor had faded from his expression. "Listen, whatever happens out there, don't risk your life to save mine. Kyrin needs you to survive."

Jace's own breath caught. He did not like where the conversation was going. "I don't think Davira intends for either of us to survive, and I won't just let you die."

Holden's gray eyes bored into him. "In this condition, I'm no match for whatever we'll face. I won't have you trying to fight for both of us. Don't worry about me. If I don't die out there, Richard will happily torture me to death anyway. So just focus on keeping yourself alive."

Kyrin didn't know why Davira had left the viewing box or why she'd taken Holden with her, but it left a tight feeling in her chest. Whatever it was couldn't possibly be good. Nausea threatened. She'd already lost her breakfast back in the cell, but that wouldn't stop her stomach from upturning again. She laid her hand over it as tears bit her eyes. She closed them tightly and tried to form a simple prayer, but she was so tired. She'd never had a harder time trusting in Elôm's presence, and she hated the despair that clung so heavily. It was getting so hard to fight when she had to endure this torture every day.

She sensed movement and opened her eyes. Collin stood a couple of feet away, looking out into the arena. He glanced at her and then over his shoulder at the other guards standing farther back. He made a point not to focus on her.

"I'm sorry."

She barely caught his murmured words but felt the weight of them. She leaned slightly toward him to hear better, watching him only from the corner of her eye.

"If I could find a way to get you out of here, I would, but…" She noticed the way his throat moved with a hard swallow. Something between fear and despair contorted his features. "She would know. Neither one of us would make it out alive. I think that's the only reason I'm here. She's hoping I'll do something stupid. I'm surprised I've lasted this long. I doubt I'll last much longer."

His voice echoed with the defeat of someone who had been fighting for too long to survive without hope. She resisted the urge to reach out to him.

"If you have the chance to go, take it. Join Prince Daniel and the rest of our army." As hard as it was to think of not living long enough to see the culmination of everything they had fought for, at least she could encourage him to seek what was out of her grasp. "You would be welcomed, I promise you."

Footsteps approached, and one of the guards growled, "What are you whispering about?"

Kyrin held Collin's gaze for a brief moment, urging him to run the first chance he got, and then gave the guard a cold look. "He was just telling me there's no way to escape."

The guard sneered. "He's right."

Collin moved away from her then, and Kyrin found the energy to pray he would escape and not only find Daniel and the others, but faith in Elôm as well. He needed it desperately. Daniel had told her how Davira used Collin as her plaything. Kyrin couldn't imagine how deep the mental and emotional scars must be for him after all this time.

Commotion drew her attention to the rear of the viewing box, and she turned as Davira and Richard entered. Holden wasn't with them this time. Anger simmered in Davira's eyes, but her hands fluttered around her dress, smoothing non-existent wrinkles. Was she flustered? Her gaze pinned Kyrin, and she froze, her fists clenching instead.

"Apparently, your husband doesn't want to see you. I offered to let you stay here with him, but he didn't accept."

Kyrin narrowed her eyes. "And what was the catch?"

Davira stiffened her posture and tipped her chin. It was almost as if she was trying to hide whatever strange discomfort Kyrin had witnessed. "All he had to do was fight that pathetic excuse of a traitor he calls friend. He refused. Now they'll both be sorry."

The ache in Kyrin's stomach deepened. "What are you planning?"

"Watch and see." Davira gestured to the arena.

Kyrin turned back to the edge of the viewing box and dug her fingers into the rough stone. A moment later, the main gate opened, and Jace and Holden walked out to the eruption of cheers. As always, Jace turned to find her in the crowd. Her eyes burned. If only she could be near him. She clutched her stomach and fought a wave of nausea, not ready for the intense fear of watching him fight.

Jace and Holden stood in the sand, waiting, though Holden looked barely capable of standing upright, let alone wielding a sword. He'd never be able to fight anything that came out of the next gate, which meant he would die, and she would have to watch. Two tears spilled over. She couldn't do this.

The panic only mounted when one of the larger side gates lifted. From deep within the shadows beyond, a beast emerged, its long, lean body covered in black scales. Kyrin covered her mouth to stifle the sob. Jace and Holden were never going to survive.

JACE COULDN'T SEEM to swallow past his too-dry tongue. He'd known whatever Davira had planned wouldn't be good, but this was even worse than he'd anticipated. He traded a look with Holden. It would be hard enough to take on the cave drake at full health, and neither one of them were prepared for such a challenge.

Holden finally gripped his sword with both hands as the drake spotted them and slunk their way. "Focus on the threat and not on me."

Jace gritted his teeth. He couldn't make that choice. "Just stay back. I'll try to bring it down."

Holden's expression hardened with stubbornness, and he opened his mouth, but Jace cut him off. "We both know you can't fight. To try would be suicide and serve no purpose. The only chance of us both walking out of here is for me to handle this. I can't focus if I have to worry about where you are."

An argument still brewed in Holden's eyes, but with a growl, he backed away. Jace breathed a quick sigh and concentrated on the approaching drake. It closely resembled a firedrake, though its neck and legs were shorter, its belly almost dragging on the ground as it moved. Its scales would likely deflect any sweeping sword attacks, and the thick horns curving down toward its snout would protect a large portion of its head. Precise stabs between the scales were probably the only option. He'd never expected to find himself in this situation, or he would have learned more about the creature's weaknesses.

A low growl rumbled from the drake, its forked tongue darting past its lips, which glistened with saliva. Jace took another step back, but they couldn't just circle the arena all day. He would have to fight it. If only he'd been armed with a spear instead, he wouldn't have had to get so close to cause damage.

The drake ended any deliberation by charging toward him. It moved surprisingly fast for such a bulky creature, its claws flinging up sand. Jace held his ground until the last second. He jumped to the side and swung his sword down at the same time. The blade connected at the base of the drake's skull. It felt like hitting a rock, but there was a little bit of give to it. Not nearly enough to do any real damage, though, which destroyed his remotest hope of just cutting the beast's head off and being done with it.

The drake released an ear-piercing shriek and turned on him as he scrambled backward. Thankfully, it wasn't as agile as a dragon and seemed clumsy without wings. All his concentration poured into avoiding the beast's snapping teeth and sharp claws as he repeatedly dodged its attacks and searched for where its scales were the weakest. A couple of his swings managed to draw dark blood that oozed between the scales, but nothing to mortally wound it. The closest he came was a swing to the underside of the animal's neck near its head. The scales seemed thinner there, as well as where its limbs met its body. If he could just find an opening to stab his sword into one of those spots, he might be able to kill it. But the monster wouldn't stop moving long enough, especially now that he'd angered it.

The drake just kept coming at him and showed no sign of tiring. Jace, however, could feel the strain in his muscles and each panting breath. If he didn't find a way to end this soon, the drake would outlast him.

He dove again for its neck. The beast roared when his blade split some of the scales but failed to deal lethal damage. Instead of turning on him like it usually did, it spun in the opposite direction. Jace didn't have a chance to duck before its tail whipped into him. The blow caught him in the chest. He barely felt his body hit the sand. His ears rang as he gasped for breath, but his lungs didn't seem to work. Nothing did. *Get up!* The internal warning flushed heat through his body. His lungs finally opened. He took a gulping breath and pushed himself to his hands and knees.

A shout echoed in his ears. He looked up. The drake loomed over him, mouth gaping to snap his head from his body, but the noise distracted it. Holden rushed in to stab at the beast. The drake swung its head around like a giant mace, nearly slamming one of its horns into him. He stumbled back, but it wasn't far enough. The drake lashed out with its claws.

"No!" The rest of the fog cleared from Jace's mind as Holden fell. He shoved to his feet. Lunging for the drake, he drove his blade into the beast's side, where its shoulder met its body. He met with brief resistance, but then the blade sank in, and he shoved it in up to the hilt.

The beast shrieked, the terrible sound ringing in his ears. It spun toward him, ripping his sword from his hands. He ducked and scrambled away, narrowly avoiding its jaws. The beast pursued him with fury, but after a few yards, it started to slow. Its gargling breaths told Jace his attack had succeeded. With a few more wobbling steps, the animal collapsed. It continued to gasp for a few seconds before quieting and lying still in the middle of the arena.

Jace raced back across the sand, his own breaths burning. "Holden!"

He dropped to his knees beside his friend. Holden clutched at his chest, but there was blood everywhere. Four diagonal lines slashed across his ribs and bled freely. One had barely missed his throat, and another had come dangerously close to ripping open his abdomen. Jace froze, his mind scrambling. Shaking himself, he yanked off his shirt and pressed it to his friend's chest. Holden groaned, breathing hard against Jace's hands. The shirt grew warm with soaked-up blood. He needed a physician.

Jace cast a desperate look around, but Davira would never provide one. She'd wanted them both to die here. He lifted his head to look up at the viewing box and met Kyrin's gaze. Tears poured down her face. Then her eyes shifted, and Jace looked over his shoulder. The guards were just behind him.

They grabbed his arms and pulled him away from Holden. Fresh heat exploded through his body. He shoved to his feet to ram into one soldier and shrug off the other. They retreated a couple of steps and reached for their swords as Jace glared at them.

"I will not leave him here to die."

He turned back to Holden and knelt to slip his arms beneath him. Sand clung to his bloodied hands. He gritted his teeth and used all his remaining strength to lift his friend. Holden gasped in pain. When Jace turned, he caught the soldiers casting questioning glances at the viewing box, but they did not stop him from carrying Holden toward the gate.

Back inside, he brought Holden to his cell. His legs nearly buckled as he tried to lower Holden to the floor as gently as possible. He brushed as much sand from his hands as he could and reapplied pressure to the wounds, praying to Elôm it wasn't as bad as it looked.

"What happened?" Ben's taut voice rang from the other cell.

Jace glanced at him and Mira. "She made us fight a cave drake."

For the next half an hour, Jace focused on stopping the bleeding. When it finally slowed, he carefully peeled back the saturated layers of his shirt. The four ragged lacerations cut deep, maybe even to the ribs. Swallowing down a reaction, he covered them back up.

Holden gritted his teeth. "How bad is it?"

Jace hesitated, but lying wouldn't help anything. "You need stitches."

Holden released a shuddering breath, squeezing his eyes shut. Without a physician, the wounds wouldn't even get cleaned, let alone stitched, and, in these conditions, infection would set in quickly.

Kyrin swiped at tears that would not stop falling as she huddled in the back of her cell, all alone now that Holden wasn't there with her. It had been at least an hour since they'd returned from the arena, but she couldn't stop seeing the images of Jace getting knocked down and Holden falling. Was he even still alive? She hadn't been able to tell how bad the wounds were from the viewing box, but she'd seen the blood. For all she knew, he had died already, and her heart broke for Jace if that was the case.

She prayed the wounds weren't as bad as all the blood suggested, but her prayers felt empty. Did Elôm even hear her? She fisted her fingers in her hair, disgusted with her weakness. Of course, He did. How many times in her life had that been proven? She'd been face to face with Elon—seen the love in His eyes.

"I'm sorry. Forgive my lack of faith. I just feel so weak, and it hurts so much." A small sob escaped her throat and died in the unrelenting darkness. "Please give me strength like You did when I stood up to Daican. I don't know how to bear this otherwise."

The tears fell heavier for a time, but somewhere deep inside, she found the stirring of strength she so desperately needed. A tiny spark in the dark despair that threatened to take over.

"Thank You," she whispered.

She forced her mind back on passages from the Scrolls. She'd managed to read all of them in the years since they'd been recovered from the palace, and it gave her much to draw on as the hours passed.

Sometime later, approaching footsteps drew her out of her concentration. A guard appeared with a torch and a bowl. He set the bowl next to the cell and stuck the torch in the holder across from it before striding away. Kyrin didn't think enough time had passed for an evening meal, but maybe she'd been more engrossed in the Scrolls than she'd thought.

She walked to the bars and picked up the bowl. The soup inside looked heartier than the cold porridge or watery broth she was used to receiving. It even had large chunks of chicken and plump carrots. Though the knots in her stomach never released, and she didn't have much appetite, she forced herself to eat. For the baby. Maybe it would be pointless in the end, but she had to do anything she could to stay healthy. She actually found a little of her appetite returning after the first savory bites. She hadn't had a warm meal in days.

"Enjoying the soup?"

Kyrin jumped at the sound of Davira's voice several minutes later and nearly dropped the bowl and what little soup was left. When had she even shown up? Kyrin hadn't heard a door or any footsteps.

Davira emerged from the shadows just beyond the ring of torchlight and walked to the cell. "Go on, finish up," she coaxed. A grin slowly stretched across her face, her teeth too white in the dim light. "You need to eat for your baby."

Kyrin's face and limbs went numb with the cold that flushed through her. How did she know?

Davira's voice wrapped around her like a smothering blanket. "You didn't think you could hide it from me, did you? My guards have reported how you keep getting sick, and I've seen the way you hold your stomach at the arena like you're trying to protect something. It didn't take much to piece it all together."

Kyrin couldn't move or breathe. She should have been more careful. She should have known Davira, of all people, would see the signs. Now she knew Kyrin's greatest weakness.

Davira's gaze dropped to the bowl in Kyrin's trembling hand, her tone sickly sweet. "Finish your soup. You don't want any going to waste."

White hot realization jolted through Kyrin, nearly sending her to her knees. "You poisoned it."

It was just the sort of thing Davira would do. Poison her so she would lose her baby. Rip away everything precious to her. Her stomach heaved into her throat, and fresh tears gushed into her eyes. She shook as if caught in one of last winter's blizzards, blasted with the chilling cold of Davira's grin. The floor tipped beneath her, a buzzing filling her ears.

Davira's cruel laugh was a hollow echo. "No. I did consider it, but then I had a better idea."

Kyrin gulped, the cell still spinning around her. She squeezed her eyes shut, barely keeping the soup down. Had Davira told the truth? Was it not poisoned? The bowl must have dropped from her hand because it was gone when she wrapped her arms around her middle. Fear still pulsed at the very core of her being with the thought she was about to lose her baby.

Fabric rustled. Kyrin dragged in a breath and lifted her head, her gaze fusing with Davira's. The princess stood right at the bars now, silhouetted by red torchlight.

"I have decided to let you live long enough to have your baby. Maybe longer, if it suits me. Once your baby is born, I will see that it's raised to serve the gods and me. It will never know you, it will never know about its father, and it will certainly never know about your pathetic God. It will be my possession to do with as I will. And for however long I decide to let you live, you will know you have absolutely no influence in its life."

Tears left burning trails down Kyrin's cheeks, and darkness like she'd never known robbed her of breath. For one bleak moment, she nearly drowned in it, but then a spark ignited amidst a flush of anger. Though her voice failed her, she shook her head. Whatever she had to do, she would fight to protect her child, and Elôm would be right there with her.

Davira scoffed. "You think you have any power to stop me? I could snap my fingers and have my guards kill you right here. You and your baby. There is nothing you or anyone can do to stop me." Her eyes sharpened, revealing the full measure of her hatred. "So tell me, where is your God now?"

Kyrin leaned in, holding that menacing gaze, the strength she had so desperately prayed for rising in her voice. "I can't answer why He has allowed me to be here or is allowing you to do this, but I can tell you exactly where He is. He is right here with me in this cell. He is with Jace in the arena. He is with your brother as he prepares to take back our country. I can also tell you, even if I don't understand His plans, I do know you can't lift a finger against me without Him allowing it for some greater purpose."

The arrogance in Davira's expression faded with every word, replaced by ever-growing darkness. But, for that very brief moment, Kyrin lost her fear of her.

With a whirl of her skirts, Davira spun around, snatched the torch, and stormed away. Once the light had faded, Kyrin released a heavy breath, suddenly worn to her bones. With shaky steps, she returned to the back of her cell and slid to the floor. Though the darkness weighed on her once again, Davira's threats left behind something completely unexpected. Hope. Daniel and the army were coming. It might take a few weeks, but they *would* reach Valcré. It wouldn't help Jace, but Davira's plan to keep her alive did provide hope for their baby, and Kyrin chose to cling to that while everything else crumbled around her.

Jace shifted, the cell wall cold against his back. Pain darted across his chest. He winced. Over the last several hours, he'd become increasingly sore from being struck by the drake's tail. His ribs were the worst. He didn't think any had broken, but it still hurt to breathe. His neck was sore, too, and he rolled his shoulders before returning his attention to Holden.

His friend seemed to be asleep since his breaths were more even and not quite as labored. Jace had asked passing guards for bandages or even some water for Holden to drink, but they'd just sneered or laughed at him. He didn't want to think this way, but some part of him wondered if Holden would have been better off dying in the arena instead of this slow death of neglect.

It was near evening when another set of guards returned. This time, instead of just making their rounds, they dragged Timothy with them. Blood ran from his nose and lips. The guards shoved him into his cell, where he stumbled and fell to his knees. The cell door slammed shut, and Holden groaned as he jolted awake.

Jace pushed to his feet, and Ben asked, "What happened?"

Timothy just breathed hard for a moment before straightening, a wince crossing his bruised face. "They caught me trying to get medical supplies for Holden." He carefully wiped the blood from his face with his sleeve and looked over his shoulder before turning to Jace. "Thank Elôm, they didn't find everything I had on me."

He reached into one of his boots and withdrew a roll of bandages and a small vial. The first bit of hope sprang to life inside Jace. It wasn't much, but that bottle of antiseptic could be all that stood between Holden and deadly infection.

Timothy handed them through the bars. "I wish I could've gotten more. But I did tell everyone I could what happened. I know they will be praying for Holden and for you."

MORNING ALWAYS CAME too fast these days. Especially when Jace wasn't able to get the sleep he so desperately needed to face a new opponent every day. But sleep was nearly impossible when Holden lay there so seriously wounded, and his own body hurt too much to get even semi-comfortable. Though he didn't hear spectators entering the arena yet, he was getting used to the subtle morning routines of the guards. It wouldn't be long before they came around with meager rations for their prisoners.

They hadn't brought any for Holden last night. Jace had tried to give him his, but he'd refused it. His friend had only given in when Timothy offered them his supper, insisting they needed it more than he did right now.

Jace tried stretching out his stiff muscles, but his body responded with a chorus of aches and pains. He wiped sweat from his brow, though he was chilled without his shirt. That wasn't right. He checked the wounds on his shoulder and side. The edges were inflamed, almost purple, and bright red mottled the skin around them. Though scabs had formed, they oozed. He let a long breath seep out and hung his head. He couldn't fight infection and fever with a sword.

Forcing himself to his knees, he crawled closer to Holden and lifted the bloodstained shirt he'd used to hide the bandages around Holden's torso. Some blood had seeped through, but not a lot. This, at least, was comforting. At this rate, Holden might even last longer than he did.

Holden drew a halting breath and opened his eyes. He blinked several times to focus before squinting up at him. Jace wasn't sure how much he could see in the dim light cast by a lantern farther down the hall, but apparently enough.

"You're sweating."

Jace wouldn't meet his gaze. Holden needed to focus on his own healing. However, he looked Jace up and down, his brows drawn into deep lines. Hopefully, it was too dark for him to spot the infected cuts. But even if that were the case, he knew Jace was wounded.

He noticed Holden swallow hard, and with so much blood loss, he needed water. "You have to use some of the antiseptic for yourself."

Jace looked away from him. "We only have enough left to treat you once more."

As long and as deep as Holden's wounds were, it had taken half the vial to treat them. He reached to cover the bandages with his shirt again.

Holden grabbed his wrist in a surprisingly tight grip. "Jace, I am not asking." There was a sharpness to his voice Jace had not heard since they were enemies.

Jace crunched his teeth together, refusing to respond at first, but huffed. "Fine."

He reached into his boot, where he'd hidden the vial, and pulled it out. He just stared at it for a moment. How could he use it when Holden's needs were so dire? But then he caught Holden giving him a stubborn and expectant look. He sighed. What would it really matter in the end anyway? Neither one of them would leave here alive. This tiny vial only prolonged the inevitable.

He pulled the cork and raised it to his shoulder first. Careful not to waste a drop, he poured a little onto the cut. Pain flared, and he sucked in his breath. His side was even worse, and he had to bite back a groan. Once he finished, he tucked the vial under the shirt next to Holden where it wouldn't get broken or lost when the guards came for him.

Holden caught his wrist again. The edge to his voice had softened, and he held Jace's gaze as if this were the last time they would ever speak. "You need to be able to keep fighting. For Kyrin…and your future."

Those quiet words and the emphasis he put on *future* hung in the silence between them. He knew about the baby. Kyrin must have told him. A knot burned at the back of Jace's throat and stung his eyes. He struggled to draw a breath, a deep ache throbbing in his chest with every thump of his heart. That future seemed so dim. He tried to swallow the lump but could only nod. Holden squeezed his wrist before letting his hand drop back to his side.

Before long, footsteps and the wooden creak of a cart echoed in the hall. The guards arrived to pass out stale chunks of bread to the prisoners. As expected, they offered none for Holden. Jace's stomach growled traitorously as he tore his chunk in half to share, but when he knelt beside Holden to help him eat, his friend raised his hand.

"No. And I'm not taking Timothy's either."

Jace should have expected no less. "You have to eat to heal."

Holden's breath hitched, and he shook his head against the stone floor. "We both know, without a physician's care, it's only a matter of time. You're the one who needs it."

Jace hung his head, not wanting to accept what he knew to be true.

Holden tapped the back of his fist against Jace's knee. "Please, just eat it. You can't go out there hungry."

Though his stomach ached, Jace did as he asked and ate the bread. It caught on the thickness in his throat, and he swallowed hard. He tried to pray while he ate, but the presence of darkness just seemed so strong in this place. After yesterday, the thought of what he might have to face today brought more fear than he wanted to admit—the sort of fear born of utter helplessness that he'd experienced so often as a slave. This battle to simply survive one more day drained him.

It was as if Timothy read his mind or, perhaps, the hopelessness in his expression. "Elôm is still in control. He still has a plan. I don't know what it is, but I know He has not forgotten or abandoned us here."

A desperate, raw cry to ask why Elôm had allowed this caught in his throat, but a smaller voice whispered after it, reminding him of just how far Elôm had brought him. From his bleakest moments as Jasper's slave to now, he was an entirely different person. Once, he had lived in constant fear, but now he knew beyond any doubt that if he died today, he would see Elon again. This temporary life, as painful as it could be, was only fleeting compared to the eternal future he had to look forward to. He might not understand what happened here, but what lay beyond was a certainty he had once never even hoped to possess. And that certainty would give him strength no matter what came.

He met Timothy's gaze with a firm nod. Whatever he faced in the arena, he would not face it alone.

When the guards came for him, an almost peaceful acceptance had replaced much of the fear. They led him to the waiting area as usual, but they didn't just stand quietly this time.

One of the guards sneered in his face. "You're going to die today, half-blood."

That term had once cut so deeply. Now, instead of cursing it, he thanked Elôm for his mixed blood. It had kept him alive more times than he could count, including in this arena.

He looked the guard in the eyes. "Maybe. But if I don't, you'll know it's because Elôm has different plans."

The man snorted and scowled. Jace glanced at the second guard, but he said nothing. In fact, he looked like he wanted nothing to do with the conversation.

A loud cheer from the crowd outside distracted them. The signal came a moment later, and the guard handed Jace a sword, an ugly expression still on his face. The blade felt heavier today. Once again, they offered no armor or even a shirt to replace the one he'd used to staunch Holden's bleeding. They ushered him forward through the tunnel, and he breathed a prayer.

He squinted in the bright sunlight as he emerged and took in the crowd. The stands were packed to near bursting with people. They were pressed in so close to each other he wasn't sure even one more person would fit in the arena. How could there be so many day after day? They must be invested now, to see how many days he could last, and something about today drew them especially.

After a glance around the arena floor to make sure his opponent wasn't present yet, he looked for Kyrin. She stood where she always was, watching him. Today the longing to spend even one more moment with her stole the breath from his already aching chest. But all he could do was hope she could see the love in his eyes.

A blast of cheers warned him to focus on his surroundings. He turned around. A man had just exited one of the gates. His glistening armor and gold helmet told Jace one thing—he was a champion gladiator. A sinking feeling descended on him. Had this been the first or second day, he might not have been overly concerned, but today he had no strength for such an opponent. For the man to have made it far enough to become such a popular champion, he had to be the best. He wasn't one of Jasper's brutes or a group of fierce but undisciplined ryriks. He was a man who had fought and survived long enough to earn that shining armor and the love of the crowd. A man like that would require Jace to be at his best—not half-starved and already injured.

The gladiator strode toward him, wielding a short sword and round shield. Jace raised his sword defensively, the sore muscles in his arms protesting, and waited for the gladiator to make the first move. The man did not slow his approach. When a mere couple of feet separated them, he lunged and crashed his shield into Jace's sword, forcing him back a step.

Before Jace could recover, the man slashed with his blade. Jace barely had time to block before it would have taken his head off. He scrambled back another few steps to regroup, but the man did not let up. He pursued him, delivering one attack after another, though mostly with his shield. Each battering blow forced Jace backward. Though heat flared in his blood, dulling the pain in his chest and warming his weary muscles, it did little good when he tried to attack. The man blocked every attempt with ease.

There. The briefest opening. Jace lunged to attack. The shield swung around and rammed into his side. His bruised ribs exploded in pain, his lungs seizing. Black spots mottled his vision. A fresh burst of heat freed his breath, but it lacked its usual ferocity. The man could have taken him in that moment, but he held back. So that's how it would be. He would wear Jace down to the delight of the crowd and then finish him off.

Despite the heat in his veins, Jace's limbs were growing heavy. His head throbbed as if someone was trying to cave it in, and sweat already slicked his entire body. The fever must be getting worse. He shook away the remaining spots in his vision. He could not give up. Not while he had even a drop of strength left in him. He planted his feet and called up every bit of ryrik heat he possessed. If he could just get that shield away from the gladiator, it would help even things up. Jace would have the longer reach and could find more openings for attack. So he focused on the shield, doing everything he could to wrench it from the man's arm.

It did not take long for the man to realize what he was doing and counter him. After a few minutes of back and forth, the gladiator launched a furious string of attacks that sent Jace scrambling backward. Every shattering blow jolted up his arms until his hands were numb.

Even so, he knew the exact instant one especially vicious attack ripped his sword from his hands and sent it flying. That's when his strength finally abandoned him. Thrown off balance, his knees hit the sand hard. He fought to rise, but he had nothing left. His legs collapsed as if made of straw. All his energy was spent. Even the fire in his blood that usually carried him beyond this point had gone cold.

His lungs burned as he gasped for air and looked up. The gladiator stood over him, his sword hovering near Jace's chest. So this was it. This was the end. He swung his gaze around to lock on Kyrin. She stood, white hands gripping the edge of the viewing box, her eyes huge and watery in her ashen face. Terror flashed in them, but he saw something more in her expression—a quiet acceptance and a steady strength. Somehow he knew even if he was gone she would be all right, and that gave him peace.

"I love you," the words rasped past his lips.

She wouldn't hear them, but she saw and understood. Her own lips echoed his.

That's when a chant rose from the crowd, echoing from every direction. "Live! Live! Live!"

He had no illusions they cared at all for his life. They simply wanted to watch him keep fighting. He was the spectacle that drew them here in droves. They weren't ready to give up their entertainment.

All eyes locked on the viewing box, where Davira approached the edge next to Kyrin. Her gaze settled on Jace, her lips curling in a hateful smirk, and she jerked her thumb toward her throat.

Death.

Kyrin's eyes closed, and Jace hung his head. Of course, Davira wouldn't have any desire to please the crowd. All she cared about was inflicting as much pain as she could.

Jace's attention shifted back to the gladiator, who released a heavy breath, his shoulders sagging. It seemed he wasn't happy with Davira's decision either. Perhaps that was why he had let Jace survive the fight when he'd had ample opportunity to end his life. He'd wanted to give the crowd a good show and reason to spare Jace, though why was a mystery. But it didn't matter now. The gladiator could never defy Davira. Jace didn't blame him for what he had to do.

He held himself as straight and steady as possible and stared up at the man, who slowly turned his helmeted head to face him. Jace could see his pale blue eyes through the eye holes. The man cast his shield aside and removed his helmet, revealing his stern expression and fair hair. He adjusted his grip on his sword.

Jace drew a breath, expecting it to be his last. But instead of dealing the death blow, the man asked, "Do you remember me?"

It took Jace a second to process the question. He studied the gladiator's face, and recognition flooded in. He'd fought this man before. He was the very last opponent Jace had ever faced in the arena before Rayad had rescued him. An opponent Jace had been supposed to kill and refused.

"Yes."

The man leaned closer. "You let me live that day. Because of that, I am here."

Jace couldn't tell if it was an accusation or a simple declaration, but the man's firm features softened with something nearing a smile. "Because I'm here, I heard the words of Elôm for the first time through many who are now dead because of it. You spared my life in more ways than one. I won't take yours."

With these words, he drove his sword into the sand and extended his empty hand toward Jace. Dumbfounded, Jace stared for a moment before he reached out and took it. The man pulled him to his feet, holding his arm to keep him steady. That's when it struck Jace—the absolute silence of the arena. He looked to the stands. The entire crowd sat unnaturally still, some leaning forward in an attempt to hear what was spoken. Not one person moved or even seemed to breathe as the man turned Jace toward the exit and helped him across the arena floor.

Jace shot a look toward Davira. She stood watching, murder flashing in her eyes. Icy cold blasted through the heat of fever. He turned and gripped the gladiator by the armor, forcing him to stop. "She's going to kill you for this."

The man just looked at him for a moment and then gave a firm nod. "I know."

Without hesitation, he continued. But how could Jace let that happen? He was the reason the man now faced a death sentence. "I can't let you do this."

"Then it's a good thing you can't stop me."

And he was right. Jace had no power to resist his help. He could barely stand on his own.

Near the exit, half a dozen guards rushed out. Two grabbed Jace, dragging him out of the arena. In the tunnel, he fought to look back. They paused just long enough to let him watch as the other guards forced the gladiator farther back out into the arena. The lead guard looked to his left, toward the viewing box. *Please, Elôm, no.*

A moment later, he yanked out his sword.

"No!" Jace struggled but couldn't break free.

The gladiator's voice rang out as he looked up into the stands. "Elôm sees what is happening here. He sees all of you."

He then faced the direction of the viewing box. "And He won't forget."

The guard lunged at him, and the gladiator crashed to the ground, blood pooling around him. It filled Jace's vision, paralyzing him. His own blood pounded in his ears, joining the echo of his ragged breaths.

A guard jerked him forward, breaking him from his frozen state. He stumbled after them, but something cut through the hum in his ears. The arena was no longer silent. A deafening wave of boos rose from the crowd and echoed in the tunnel. They knew it was wrong—knew Davira was wrong—and it seemed they'd found the courage to show it.

Davira was livid. More so than Kyrin had ever seen in all of the time she'd had the displeasure of sharing the princess's company. She stormed out of the arena, the guards rushing Kyrin along just to keep up.

"How dare they?" she seethed as they marched toward the carriage. Her voice reached a near screech. "How *dare* they!"

If she'd been able to throw every last person from the stands down into the arena and kill them in one fell swoop, no doubt she would have. Though Kyrin still shook from believing Jace had been about to die and then watching the gladiator who had spared his life murdered, a grim satisfaction welled up inside her.

At the carriage, Davira must have seen it in her face. Either that, or she just needed something to take her anger out on. She grabbed Kyrin by the throat and slammed her against the coach. Kyrin gasped for the air that was forced from her lungs, but Davira squeezed her windpipe. She grabbed Davira's wrist and tried to pry her hand away. The pressure just increased.

Spots danced in Kyrin's vision. Her fighting instincts flared. She pushed against Davira and kicked her hard just below the knee. Davira nearly toppled to the ground with a shriek. Kyrin desperately wanted to kick her again, but every guard except for Collin, who reacted a little too slowly, yanked out their swords. She raised her hands in surrender.

Righting herself, Davira whirled on Kyrin and punched her in the face. Kyrin stumbled, dazed, but a sharp blade pressed against her midsection, forcing her back against the coach. She hardly dared to breathe even as blood rolled from her nose and over her lips.

Davira leaned in close, her hot breath spewing over Kyrin's face. "I should just gut you right here."

Kyrin held her gaze, tempted to ask her why, when she had already tried to kill Jace today, and Elôm clearly intervened, did she think she would succeed with her? But even as that boldness eclipsed much of the fear of dying here on the street, Kyrin held her tongue. She couldn't put her baby at more risk. Still, seeing Davira lose even the smallest bit of control was just the kind of victory she needed.

DARKNESS HAD JUST fallen when Daniel stepped out of the woods and set eyes on Valcré for the first time since he'd fled the city last summer. The towering walls rose in the shadows, both a threat and a welcome. He paused. So much had happened since he'd left, and part of him hadn't been sure he'd ever return. But this was his city—his home. Once, he had longed to leave it all behind, his heart yearning for adventure and change and something…more. Yet, over the past year, Elôm had worked in his heart, showing him his duty as heir to the throne wasn't just dull responsibility and endless paperwork. It was a duty to the people who looked to him to lead them and provide an environment for them to thrive. Such leadership and care had been absent for far, far too long.

Aaron passed him, leading the way toward one of the smaller gates on the southern side of the city. Daniel followed along with Aric, Marcus, Kaden, and Trev. Though Daniel had wanted to leave Trev behind as Elanor's head of security, Elian had assumed the position when Aric suggested it would be better to have Trev along since the two of them were so familiar with Auréa and its security. They would need that knowledge to secure the palace and ferret out any threats. Once Daniel had thought about it, he'd admitted they probably knew the palace even better than he did.

He drew a deep breath as they neared the gate and the two guards stationed there. With the size of their group, he hoped no one who might recognize him would pay too much attention. The riskiest part of tonight was their entrance into the city. Things could go south quickly if a guard grew suspicious and tried to detain them. They'd all dressed like simple woodsmen so, Elôm willing, they would look like they were just coming in from a day of hunting.

The guards moved to block their path as soon as Aaron reached them. "State your business."

Daniel's heart thumped, though the man's tone didn't even carry suspicion. If anything, he looked a little bored by the routine check. Daniel maintained what he hoped was a casual appearance and let Aaron do the talking.

"We're just headed home for the night. We didn't have much luck with game today. That winter sure made our jobs hard. We'll probably hit up the nearest tavern on the way home." Aaron leaned in a little as if sharing a secret, his mouth quirked in a conspiratorial smile. "I'd invite you to join us, but that probably wouldn't go over well with the queen."

The guard scoffed, exchanging an eye roll with his partner. "You have no idea."

They parted to let them pass.

Aaron nodded to each of them. "Evening then, gentlemen."

Daniel stopped himself from shaking his head. He'd had no idea Aaron was such a good actor.

They walked on through the gate, and Daniel let out a long breath once they were out of earshot. They'd made it inside.

Passing by the first few buildings, he caught a glimpse of the palace up on the hill, bathed in moonlight. He sucked in a breath, not expecting the tangle of emotions that struck him at the sight—anger, fear, anticipation, even homesickness. Davira was up there. All he had to do was get inside and stop her. They were close now. So close.

Aaron led them along with more familiarity than Daniel had with this particular part of the city. The streets were dark save for what light filtered through various windows. Only sporadic lanterns were lit, unlike the center of the city near the palace. They did cast enough light for Daniel to notice how run-down most of the buildings were. Garbage littered the streets, collecting in corners and dark alleyways. He wanted to blame Davira, but he had a feeling this side of the city had fallen into disrepair long before her rule.

Though not nearly as bustling as the city's center, people did pass by and crisscross their path. Most were heading home from a long, hard day of work if Daniel were to guess. Their appearances were just as run-down as the buildings around them. A few people, men mostly, glanced in their direction, and Daniel's skin prickled, but most kept their heads down, not deviating from their paths. The women tended to scurry past on the farthest side of the street. Considering their large group, they probably did appear threatening. Daniel had heard all too much about how lawless Valcré had become. It would certainly provide a challenge to fix once he was king, along with a mountain of other issues.

Before long, they turned off into a narrow alleyway. Just ahead, the double doors of a two-story building stood open, spilling out light and rowdy voices. They strode inside, and the pungent scent of ale laced with a musty sweet note of pipe tobacco engulfed them. A couple of dozen patrons occupied the tavern tables scattered throughout the dim interior. Barmaids squeezed between them, carrying tankards back and forth from the bar. Daniel couldn't say he was surprised Alex had made such establishments his bases of operations, considering some of the exploits of their youth. He scanned the room. Sure enough, at one of the largest tables near the back, Alex sat facing the door, half a dozen burly men surrounding him.

Aaron must have seen him, too, because he barely paused before making his way through the tavern. Alex picked up the movement immediately, his dark eyes training on Aaron. A welcome smile had just begun to grow on his face when his gaze shifted to Daniel. The smile stalled, his brows rising. Even so, he maintained a cool demeanor as he leaned over to one of the men at his side and murmured something before rising from the table to meet them.

For being an outlaw and smuggler, his sense of style certainly hadn't suffered. His deep red brocaded vest and tailored black coat were almost as fine as the clothing Daniel used to wear before his exile. A few rings glinted on his fingers. It called to mind a sudden memory of when they used to play pirates as boys. Daniel had an idea his old friend was enjoying his roguish role just a tad too much.

"Good evening, gentlemen." His tone was that of a smooth businessman, lacking any familiarity with them. "Perhaps we should take our business somewhere more private." He tipped his head to the back of the tavern, his gaze briefly catching with Daniel's again before he and the other man led the way toward a staircase.

They followed, and Daniel appreciated the discretion. Alex could have outed him in front of everyone. Though he'd heard the patrons of these taverns were no supporters of Davira, one never knew where his sister had her spies.

At the top of the stairs, they followed a dark hall, and everyone crammed into a private room. Alex and his friend lit several candles, bathing the walls in a warm glow as the rest of them spread out around a small table. When Alex finished and turned to them, his attention landed first on Aaron. "Welcome back."

Aaron nodded to both him and the other man. "Avery. Tavor."

After all this time, Aaron probably knew Alex far better than Daniel did. Once, Alex had been his best friend, but so much had changed. Neither one was the rambunctious, carefree youth they'd once been.

At last, Alex faced Daniel across the table. The openness and familiarity he'd shared with Aaron turned pensive. He seemed uncertain, which was unusual for Daniel's typically self-assured friend. Then he inclined his head. "Your Highness."

To be addressed so formally and respectfully by Alex made Daniel realize he hadn't prepared for this meeting. In plotting through every possible scenario on their march through the forest, he hadn't once taken time to consider this moment. The last time he'd seen Alex had been when he'd snuck from the ballroom after poisoning Daniel's father. Daniel would never have Kyrin's capabilities, but that night would be forever burned into his memories. It had never occurred to him to figure out how he felt toward Alex before coming face to face.

The silence between them drew on too long, and Daniel caught the exchange of glances out of the corner of his eye. He took in a breath. Stepping around the table, he extended his hand toward his longtime friend. "Alex."

While Daniel couldn't excuse murder, he knew Alex's actions had been to avenge his father. If someone murdered Daniel's mother, he couldn't honestly say he wouldn't struggle with a need for vengeance as well. Besides, Alex had provided the remedy for the fever over the winter and had gone out of his way to help Aaron and his wife. Right now, they needed him to help take back the throne.

Alex sagged a little, his dark features relaxing and changing into a genuine smile. He gripped Daniel's arm.

"Welcome home."

Daniel was sure he heard more than one sigh as the tension left the room. Alex was a powerful force in the city. None of them wanted him as an enemy. They would have to address the past at some point, but for now, Daniel was happy to simply accept him as his old friend.

Alex gestured to the table. "I'd offer everyone seats, but I'm a little short."

Daniel shook his head. "That's all right. We have a lot to discuss but not a lot of time."

Alex crossed his arms and leaned against the edge of the table. Despite his casual stance, his eyes were sharp. "Last I heard, you had thousands of soldiers between you and the city. What are you doing here?"

"Hopefully taking Davira down before those thousands of soldiers become thousands of dead. My sister is willing to bathe the land from here to Fort Rhall in blood to keep her throne. I'm trying to stop that from happening, and I need your help."

Daniel watched Alex's reaction closely. Though it had worked out in the end, he had initially refused them the remedy. Would he again withhold his aid?

However, a smirk took hold of his face, one that had driven both their parents to distraction at times because it always spelled trouble. "I'm all ears."

"How many armed men could you gather before dawn who would be willing to distract Davira's men while I take over the palace?"

Alex traded a look with Tavor, both sporting an eager glint in their eyes. "Oh, with a goal like that, I think I could get you close to one hundred fifty. They've just been itching for a chance to deal real damage to the queen."

That was even more than Aaron's estimate. With the Militia, it would bring their number to around four hundred men. But would it be enough?

"Would you know how many soldiers are stationed here at the fort and how many guards Davira has?"

Alex flashed a full grin this time. "Lucky for you, that is just the sort of information I like to have handy. Right now, we figure there are about three hundred soldiers at the fort. Your timing is perfect because two hundred of them headed out just a couple of days ago to join those at Fort Rhall. The palace is a little harder to get an accurate count, but best guess is fifty to seventy-five."

Those numbers were doable and better than they'd hoped, especially since so many had just left. Davira's overconfidence that they couldn't get past her army would be her downfall.

"That works perfectly." Feeling even better about their plans than when he'd left Fort Rhall, Daniel laid out exactly how they intended to take control of the city.

Alex gave a slow nod and fiddled with one of his rings. "Sounds like a solid plan, but what about firedrakes? My men are certainly willing to risk it all to stop your witch of a sister, but a fiery death could put a damper on things."

Quite a damper. Daniel winced. The firedrakes were still the biggest unknown of this whole plan. "We did bring a number of dragon riders. Hopefully, they can keep us from being slaughtered long enough to take Davira down. We had to leave the majority at Fort Rhall to protect our armies. Do you know how many firedrakes are here?"

"Unfortunately, no. They are housed somewhere outside the city and come and go frequently. It's impossible to get a count, though if Davira is willing to send the majority of her men to battle, there's a good chance the same could be said for the drakes."

"I pray you're right, because our only option, beyond giving up, is to move forward and trust our dragon riders." Daniel traded a quick look with Kaden. He didn't appear the least bit concerned about possibly being outnumbered. Daniel then turned back to Alex. "Would you have a way of getting about fifty of my men into the city undetected?"

Alex shrugged. "Sure, that wouldn't be a problem. I know a guard who should be on duty tonight and owes me. He'll turn a blind eye if I ask him, and the other? Well, he can be detained."

"Good, I'll need them here to march on the palace once the fort empties. I thought your men could provide backup at the gate, perhaps as a surprise attack from behind."

"They'd be happy to. And if you want to up the odds even more, you could probably pick up some more men at the arena. It's full of Elôm believers like you. Most of them are malnourished, but I'm sure many would join you. There are plenty of weapons there for them. Before the games start in the morning, only about a dozen guards are on duty. Tavor could take a group to liberate them." Alex's calculating expression morphed into something much more sympathetic as he turned away from Daniel to focus on Aaron instead. "Your brother is there."

Aaron straightened, his eyes going wide. Daniel could hardly believe it. Knowing his sister, he really hadn't expected Timothy to still be alive.

Aaron gripped the back of the chair across the table. "You found him?"

Alex nodded. Daniel wasn't used to seeing this caring side to him. Maybe Alex had matured more than he thought.

"We did. It took a while. Davira kept him at the palace at first. Then he was brought to the arena and forced to work there hauling bodies after the daily games."

Aaron's knuckles turned white, and his jaw clenched. Such a torturous job would significantly hurt someone with Timothy's compassionate soul.

"Jace and Holden are there too."

Daniel sucked in a sharp breath. He hadn't thought they'd

learn of Jace's fate until after this was all over, and even then, he'd been dreading it. Before he could formulate a response, Kaden jumped into the conversation, a painful desperation in his tone. "They're alive? What about Kyrin?"

"I know Jace is for sure, despite Davira's best efforts. She forces him to fight every day. Kyrin is kept at the palace, but Davira brings her to the arena to watch."

If Kaden wasn't a disciplined soldier, Daniel might have been afraid he'd attempt to storm the palace right now. It did present a tough situation that would leave Kyrin vulnerable during their attack. The way Kaden met his gaze told Daniel he was just as aware of the danger. Marcus put his hand on Kaden's shoulder and squeezed it. Though Marcus had always been more skilled at hiding his emotions, the taut lines on his face betrayed his concern. Daniel wished he could say something to assure both of them, but his attention shifted back to Alex, who wasn't finished.

"Last I saw Holden, he was badly wounded. Davira threw him out into the arena with Jace yesterday and set a cave drake on them. Jace killed it and carried Holden inside, but I don't know what happened beyond that."

Daniel's stomach turned, bombarded by unwanted memories of being forced to sit while a cave drake slaughtered fellow believers during his father's birthday celebration. It was a horrifying, gruesome way to die. He wasn't sure how he would have been able to live with the knowledge of losing his brother-in-law that way. Having to go back and tell Elanor would have destroyed him. But this was exactly why they had to stop Davira here and now.

With only hours left before dawn, they had no time to waste if they were going to pull this off. Daniel sent Marcus with Tavor to start bringing militiamen into the city while Aaron, Aric, Trev, and Kaden remained behind to make final preparations.

To aid them, Alex produced a map of the city and laid it on the table so they could plot their best route to the palace.

Daniel rubbed his hand over his chin as he stared down at it. "Ideally, I'd get my men in position at the palace before dawn, and if we had a smaller group, maybe we could. But trying to get fifty men that close runs too great a risk of being spotted before we're ready. We need the majority of Davira's soldiers already busy at the gate before she realizes the palace is under attack."

Alex tapped the large square on the map that represented Auréa. "And just how do you plan to get inside? It's no fortress, but they're not just going to open the gates for you."

Daniel motioned to his right. "Aaron and a couple of our crete friends will go on ahead of us and scale the wall before dawn. They'll lie in wait inside the courtyard, and once we're in position, they'll take out the guards and open the gate for us. We must be ready to rush in before more guards can secure it. As for the palace itself, we can break in through the windows if we have to."

Kaden cleared his throat, and Daniel looked over at him, though he could already guess what he was about to say.

"Is there any way Aaron and the others can get to Kyrin before we attack?"

Daniel released a sigh. He'd already been turning it around in his mind but didn't have a good answer. "I don't think so. The outer entrance to the dungeon will be locked for the night and, no doubt, heavily guarded. The only other way down is from inside the palace."

He had thought about sending Aaron and the cretes into the palace during the night, but it posed too great a risk. It would only take one guard catching a glimpse of them for their entire plan to fail. Their best chance of success was going in all together. And as badly as they needed to stop Davira, they weren't assassins.

"I'm afraid there's nothing we can do until we're inside." It pained Daniel to have to say it. He didn't want to think about it, but Davira would surely try to kill Kyrin the moment they attacked. That was how her mind worked, always lashing out when she felt she was losing control. He thought of the baby. Kaden likely had no idea Kyrin was pregnant, and the secret ached inside Daniel, knowing the likely outcome of their plans. He wasn't sure how he would even face Kaden and the rest of Kyrin's brothers if she died. *Protect her and the baby, Elôm. You are the only hope they have.*

Kaden's jaw muscles ticked, and he looked like he was struggling not to say something. It had to be especially hard for him knowing he wasn't even going to the palace with them. Trev turned to him before Daniel could think of something to say that was even remotely comforting.

"As soon as we're inside, I'll find her."

While he was technically part of Daniel's security now, he was originally Kyrin's bodyguard. Daniel could understand his desire to rescue Kyrin and nodded his assent. Someone should be dedicated entirely to Kyrin's safety.

Leetra wiped a rag over one of her short swords. The bit of moonlight that filtered through the forest canopy glinted on the edge of the blade and the amethyst embedded in the hawk-head-shaped pommel. It didn't really need to be polished, but it helped keep her busy while she waited for the next stage of their plans. Talas sat on a log across from her, doing the same thing.

"I don't have to worry about you putting that blade through Davira's throat when I'm not around to stop you, do I?"

Her gaze flashed to him. His smirk and twinkling eyes said he was teasing. Mostly. Typically, she would be disappointed not to join the other riders in battle, but going with Aaron to the palace was even better. That would put her in close proximity to Davira. Whatever happened in the next several hours, she was going to get at that harpy and figure out exactly what happened to Timothy.

Talas's smirk started to fade when she did not answer right away. She reached back and slipped the sword into its sheath next to the matching one.

"I'm not going to kill her." Well, not unless she had to in order to save someone or prevent their defeat. It wasn't her place to exact judgment, as tempting as it was. She raised a brow at him. "But I am a physician. I know exactly where to inflict a non-fatal wound if necessary."

He snorted and shook his head. "You're scary."

She shrugged. If scary helped her find Timothy and aided in ending this war, then scary she would be.

She sighed, not quite sure what to do with herself now that she'd finished with her swords. Fiddling with a strand of beads and leather woven into her hair, she looked around. No fires burned. They were too close to the city for that. Rayad stood nearby, talking in low tones with Charles and James. Like her, they insisted on coming along, drawn by the desire to find their loved ones. Glynn and Naeth were over by the dragons, ready to join her and Aaron as soon as it was time.

She stood up and put her hands on her hips, tapping her fingers against her belt. Though she'd wanted to go into the city with Aaron when they'd left to find Avery, they'd been too afraid she would stand out in the group. So now she had to wait until they returned. But she needed to get used to waiting tonight. Once they managed to get into the palace courtyard, they would have to wait until the right moment to strike. That, too, would require patience.

A stirring of commotion drew her attention across the temporary camp. It took a moment before she spotted Marcus. Her heart thumped. He was alone, which meant the meeting had either gone well or terribly wrong. She watched him closely as he spoke with some of his men, and a little of her tension drained when none of them seemed to panic.

He finished giving them his orders before working his way over to Rayad and the others. Leetra was just close enough to pick up what he said.

"Jace and Kyrin are alive."

Leetra couldn't hear the sighs, but she did see how their shoulders sagged in relief. At least there was some good news, and she tried not to let it sting that he hadn't said Timothy. After all, it didn't mean he was dead; it just meant they still didn't know where he was.

"The last time Avery saw Holden, he was badly injured, so we don't know about him. But he and Jace are at the arena." Though the trees shadowed Marcus's face, Leetra could see how his lips pressed in a thin line. "Davira has been sending Jace out to fight."

Rayad's posture stiffened, his fists balling at his sides. Leetra didn't know much about Jace's past other than what was common knowledge, but she was very much aware that Rayad had saved him from a life of slavery as a gladiator. Throwing Jace back into that was the height of cruelty, and it showed on Rayad's face. Leetra might not be the only one Talas should worry would stab Davira.

Marcus quickly explained a plan to liberate the captives at the arena, and Rayad, Charles, and James all volunteered to help execute it. He then turned and caught sight of her. Something in the way he looked at her set her heart to beating harder again. Was that almost a smile on his face? He walked toward her, and she braced herself, though she wasn't entirely sure what for.

The almost-smile grew into a real one. "Timothy is alive. He's at the arena too."

Leetra's breath left her lungs in a gust. Her legs turned to water, and only sheer willpower held her upright. He was alive. She'd hardly dared to let herself hope, but it was true.

Talas's hand squeezed her shoulder, and she reached up to grasp it, needing something to hold onto. Moisture pooled in her eyes, stinging her nose. Timothy was alive, and she would see him again. Once they were reunited, she was never going to leave his side.

DANIEL WATCHED THE first hint of light tinge the eastern horizon—the start of a brand new day that could change everything. A day that would hopefully end the war that had been brewing since before he'd even been born. Any time now, Marcus would lead their men into the city, and their attack would begin. In just a couple of hours, this could all be over. He bowed his head and closed his eyes for a moment, opening his heart to Elôm's guidance and praying for direction, wisdom, and protection for everyone. His sense of peace and certainty still told him this was the right decision, and he believed it would finally bring them the victory they'd fought and sacrificed so much for. A new beginning Arcacia desperately needed, and the anticipation thrilled him.

Raising his head, he looked about. It was hard to see without lanterns in this mostly abandoned part of the city, but his men stood at his back, ready and waiting. Aaron, Leetra, Glynn, and Naeth had left about an hour ago to get into position at the palace. Though he had sensed how much Aaron, and especially Leetra, had wished to go to the arena for Timothy, they'd both accepted their roles in this plan without protest. This was one of the riskiest parts they had yet to execute, and he prayed they

343

remained undetected. Though he couldn't see the palace from here, everything seemed quiet across the city so far.

That is until a rooster crowed somewhere in the distance. As if in echo, the deep tone of a bell tolled, rolling across the city. Seconds later, another joined it, and then another.

The city alarm. It was starting.

Something jarred Jace to consciousness. He raised his head, his body painfully protesting yet another night of trying to sleep on cold stone. Swallowing down a groan, he listened. Though muffled by the thick walls of the arena, bells rang deeply somewhere outside. Other prisoners stirred in their cells, and Jace looked over at Timothy as they both sat up.

"Do you hear that?"

Timothy's brows scrunched together as he tipped his head to listen. "It's the city alarm."

"Why would there be an alarm?"

Timothy shook his head. "The only things I can think of would be fire or an attack."

Surely there was no way their army could have reached the city by now. They hadn't even breached the fort yet when Jace had been captured. Perhaps people were uprising? That wouldn't surprise him, considering what he had witnessed in the arena yesterday. Maybe some of the people had finally had enough.

He'd probably never know the cause unless the guards deigned to tell him. With nothing else to do, he shifted to check on Holden. He was still asleep as far as Jace could tell, but his breathing was shallow and wheezing. Jace lightly touched his forehead. Too warm. The wound had seemed a bit too red and inflamed last night. He'd hoped administering the last of the antiseptic would help, but without fresh bandages, it was a losing battle. Holden wouldn't have long now.

Letting him sleep, Jace rested back against the cell wall as the bells continued to toll outside. If it was a fire, it probably wouldn't interrupt anything here at the arena, which meant he only had a couple more hours before his next fight. After yesterday, he didn't have much hope of victory. His strength was spent, and Davira would never match him against another opponent who would let him live. Today Kyrin would have to watch him die. The cold certainty of that flowed icily through his body, dousing any of the heat he would need for a fighting chance.

Eventually, the tolling bells fell silent. Though no outdoor light reached the cells and no guards had come by, Jace sensed morning had dawned. He focused on prayer and struggled not to acknowledge the weakness of his body and the emptiness in his stomach. These twice-a-day feedings of stale bread just weren't enough to keep him fueled for daily fights. At least Jasper had kept him well fed, though never out of kindness.

A muted flurry of shouts erupted from somewhere inside the arena and broke Jace from his prayers. The clash of metal joined it. He exchanged a look with Timothy, and they scrambled to their feet. From the sound of it, there were multiple combatants. Had someone broken free of their cell? Did it have anything to do with the alarm bells?

Jace stepped to the door and pressed his forehead to the bars to peer down the hall but couldn't see far before it turned a corner. The fighting intensified and drew a little closer. Holden stirred. Jace looked over his shoulder at him, but he didn't fully return to consciousness. That was concerning.

Almost as quickly as the fighting had started, everything fell silent. For several heartbeats, no one moved. An inexplicable disappointment descended on Jace. He wasn't even sure what he'd hoped for in that brief time, but anything that might have changed what lay in store for him today would have been welcome.

He hung his head and turned away from the door but then froze. Footsteps approached at a quick pace. He spun back around. Torchlight lit up the corner. A moment later, a group of men rounded it into view. Avery's right-hand man, Tavor, held the torch, but Jace's eyes locked on the second man. He gasped, his legs nearly buckling.

"Rayad!"

"Jace!" Rayad rushed ahead of Tavor, followed immediately by Charles and James.

Jace grabbed the bars, hardly daring to believe his own eyes. How was this even possible?

Was it all a dream? He'd had dreams before that seemed to offer hope only to snatch it away. Rayad shoved a key into the lock, and the door swung open. Jace was afraid to even breathe in case it shattered the dream and he awoke to guards instead. But when Rayad grasped his arms in a firm grip, he knew it had to be real. He released a shaky breath.

"How did you get here?"

Rayad looked him over, hesitating on his injuries before holding his gaze. "We came with Prince Daniel and a small force he brought to infiltrate the city. He's on his way to the palace now to take out Davira. Avery told us you were here, so we came to get you out and gather anyone who can help fight."

Kyrin. The thought struck Jace like lightning. She would be in grave danger once the attack started. He couldn't lose her. Not after all this. She had to be the one to survive.

"I have to get to Kyrin." He moved past Rayad, out into the hall where others were gathering from their open cells. But then he hesitated and looked back. Holden still lay unconscious. What if he died all by himself in this cold cell before help could arrive?

Timothy stepped to Jace's side. "I'll stay with him. You go find Kyrin."

Mira bustled past both of them into the cell. "I'll stay with him as well."

Jace didn't know how to thank either of them, but his attention focused on Tavor, who addressed everyone around him.

"Your rightful king is fighting his way into the palace as we speak. Anyone willing and able to aid him, come with us." He turned to Jace. "Do you know where we can get weapons?"

Jace nodded.

"Good, you lead. We'll release people along the way."

Kyrin jolted awake to the sound of a door grating open. She pushed herself up, apprehension darting through her middle. Was it time for breakfast already? But she was always awake before that. It seemed too early, though it could be midday for all she knew. She was bound to start losing track of time in this dark cell. Her stomach rolled in protest at the rude awakening. She swallowed hard to keep it in place. Trying to eat might not make that possible.

Two guards appeared, and her nausea intensified. Only one guard ever brought her food. Davira sent two when she wanted Kyrin brought from her cell, and breakfast always came before the daily games. Goosebumps rippled across her arms at this sudden change in routine.

The guards drew near. One of them was Collin. At the cell, she met his gaze while the other guard unlocked the door. She wanted to ask him what was happening, but the question froze on her tongue at his taut expression and the slight sheen of sweat on his brow and upper lip. His gaze darted between her and the other guard, his throat convulsing as he swallowed. Her heart gave her ribs a strong thump. He was about to do something.

The cell door swung open. Collin lunged. He wrapped his

arm around the guard's throat from behind and locked it there. The man struggled, but Collin held firm until the guard's movements grew sluggish. Finally, he went limp, crumpling to the floor. Kyrin and Collin both gaped at his still form until Kyrin shook herself from shock. "What is going on?"

Collin blinked hard, snapping back to reality. His voice came out in a breathless rush. "We need to hide. Prince Daniel's men are attacking the city. If they reach the palace, Davira will kill you."

Kyrin's heart leapt. Daniel had somehow already made it to the city. But nausea crashed back in with a vengeance. She had no doubt they would be victorious, but she was stuck here with a madwoman who would sooner burn the city down around her than lose control.

"Where can we go?"

Collin bent to grab one of the guard's arms. "I don't know. I'm just hoping the guards will be too busy trying to defend the palace to search for us."

Kyrin had a feeling Davira would make hunting her down a priority, but trying to hide was better than sitting helplessly in this cell. She hurried out to help Collin drag the unconscious guard inside and lock the door.

Collin grabbed a pair of shackles and turned to her. "This has to look real if I'm going to get you past the guards upstairs."

She drew a breath and then held out her wrists. Collin had already signed his own death warrant by choking out the guard. She had to trust him if either of them hoped to survive this. And survive she must. Her baby's life hung in the balance. She prayed to Elôm for protection as the cold metal clamped around her wrists for what she desperately hoped would be the last time.

Collin took her by the arm to guide her through the dungeon. "I don't suppose you know of any good hiding spots in the palace?"

Kyrin shook her head. If only she knew where to access the secret passages Daniel had mentioned once. Then again, they'd probably be the first places Davira would look. "None Davira doesn't surely already know about."

Collin's lips formed a thin line, and his brows furrowed. "Then we'll just have to try to stay out of sight for however long it takes for someone to get here."

Realistically, that could take hours, perhaps days. Kyrin had no idea what was going on outside or what the plan was. Yet, somehow, she and Collin had to remain unseen in a palace full of servants and guards, who would soon be hunting them. *Elôm, please shield us and hide us from our enemies.*

She scrambled to remember all the places she'd seen in the palace and where might provide the best hiding spot. Somewhere the guards wouldn't think to look, at least not right away.

They reached the stairs leading up into the palace, and Kyrin's pulse quickened. Collin hesitated, but they kept going. The two guards at the top gave them a probing look.

"Where's Hask?" one asked.

"He's checking to make sure the outer door is secure." Thankfully, none of Collin's uncertainty bled into his voice.

He led Kyrin forward without waiting for another question. They rounded a corner out of sight, and he released a breath, but his expression mirrored Kyrin's own tension. What if they ran into more guards? How many excuses could Collin make before someone grew suspicious? It was only a matter of time before Davira grew impatient and someone found the guard in the dungeon.

The faint roar of a dragon filtered in from outside. It really was happening. Not that she'd doubted Collin, but part of her had hardly dared to believe Davira's reign was this close to falling. Now, if she and Collin could just find somewhere to hide, they might live to see it.

They stayed toward the outer edge of the palace, well away from the throne room where Collin said Davira was waiting. Thankfully, they didn't run into any servants who might give them away. Not yet, anyway. Looking both ways, he opened a door, and they slipped into a small sitting room facing one of the gardens. Here, he turned to Kyrin and reached for her shackles to unlock them.

"We can't keep sneaking around. If Davira doesn't know I've helped you yet, she will soon, and she'll have men everywhere."

Kyrin rubbed at the cold sensation around her wrists and looked to the windows. Should they try to hide outside? Or would Davira suspect that? If only the secret gate behind the temple hadn't been blocked. She winced, the beginnings of a headache stabbing at her temples. She was too exhausted to try to outthink Davira.

Collin ran his hand through his hair, his eyes darting here and there. This was Davira's domain. Neither one of them possessed enough knowledge of it to outsmart her. If only they had allies within the palace. There was Mister Foss, but would he be aware of any hiding spots? Where would he even be this time of day? Searching for him would probably be even riskier than finding a hiding place on their own.

Before Kyrin could suggest it, Collin met her gaze, a little of the panic in his expression settling. "I have an idea."

He motioned for her to follow, and they left the room. They crept down the halls as fast as they dared, stopping at every intersection to listen. Kyrin's heart raced so loudly in her ears she was afraid she wouldn't be able to hear if danger was approaching. She dragged in deep breaths to try to calm it, but her ribs pressed into her lungs.

When they reached a tall, carpeted staircase, Collin motioned her upward. Kyrin looked up to the second floor—the royal family wing of the palace. Where would they possibly find a hiding place here? Or maybe he thought Davira wouldn't think to check there. It certainly wasn't the first place Kyrin would think to go.

They'd nearly reached the end of a long hall when he stopped at one of the closed doors. He cast a glance back the way they had come and knocked. Wait, he was actually looking for someone? But who would help them that had access to this area of the palace? Long, tense seconds drew out. Kyrin's heart pounded in her throat now, almost gagging her. Though she'd forgotten her nausea in the escape from the dungeon, it stirred again, squeezing her stomach. She swallowed hard. Finally, the door opened, just a couple of inches at first, but then more fully to reveal Queen Solora on the other side.

Kyrin's heart nearly crashed out of her chest, and she stumbled back. Collin, however, did not even flinch, nor did any hesitation tinge his voice.

"We need your help."

Solora looked from him to Kyrin, holding her gaze for a moment. Uncertainty flashed in the woman's expression. Would she turn them away or, worse, call for the guards? She looked down the hall as if considering it but then stepped back to allow them access to the room. Collin ushered Kyrin into the opulent apartment. Solora closed the door behind them and turned to give Kyrin another long, calculating look before switching her gaze to Collin. It was hard to tell if the way her brows lowered was out of anger or concern.

"What are you doing?"

"Prince Daniel's men are taking the city."

Solora drew a sharp breath, her brows lifting now.

"Once they reach the palace, Davira will kill her." Collin nodded at Kyrin. "She already sent for her. I can't let that happen. Is there anywhere we can hide until Prince Daniel has taken the palace? Please, you're the only one who can help us."

Solora didn't speak for a long moment. Kyrin had never personally interacted with the queen while working at the palace. She'd seemed so aloof and disinterested in Kyrin. But Daniel did have a close relationship with his mother, and she had helped plan his escape. Kyrin prayed this meant she was more reasonable and merciful than Daican and Davira. Collin seemed to think this was the case. Clearly, he and Solora had some previous interaction if he trusted her with their lives.

At last, Solora released a long breath and gave a curt nod. "There is a hidden room in the library."

"Does Davira know about it?"

"I don't think so. Not this one."

"How do we find it?"

Her face pinched, and Kyrin was afraid she might change her mind, but then she said, "I'll have to show you."

Just telling them was one thing, but showing them made her complicit. If they were caught, Davira would know she was helping them. But Solora seemed certain about her decision now. She turned to the door and motioned for them to follow. Out in the hall, they looked both ways before heading back the way Kyrin and Collin had come.

Halfway to the staircase, they skid to a halt. Muffled footsteps thumped rapidly up the steps toward them. Solora spun around to usher them the other way, her face a shade paler than usual. They hurried on as fast as possible without making noise to alert the approaching guards. Just as they turned a corner at the far end of the hall, a second group of men appeared ahead. The one in the lead shouted a warning. Now Kyrin felt the blood leave her face, making her lightheaded. They spun away from these pursuers only to find the others already closing in. *No!* It couldn't end like this. Victory was too close.

Collin yanked out his sword and pushed her behind him. She backed away until her shoulders bumped the wall. How could he even hope to take on Auréa's security force by himself? The clash of swords rang in the hallway, striking at her nerves. The guards behind Collin closed in, and though Solora placed herself between them and Kyrin, the former queen had no weapon to fight.

Kyrin stood frozen, her gaze darting between both groups of guards, and she caught the moment one of the men slashed Collin's shoulder and batted his sword to the ground. Collin grabbed for the wound and stumbled back. That's when Solora raised her hands and shouted for everyone to stop. She swept the guards with a commanding gaze befitting a queen.

"Your rightful king is on his way to take this palace. Davira will not be in power much longer. You will stand down unless you wish to go down with her."

A couple of the guards glanced at each other. Kyrin held her breath and prayed for a miracle. But despite the truth and the power behind Solora's words, they closed in. They seized Collin and Solora first before reaching for Kyrin.

PANIC EXPLODED THROUGH Kyrin. She scrambled away from the guards, lunging for the only small opening between them, but one caught her by the arm. She yanked against him, digging in her feet. A desperate cry clawed up her throat. She had to get away. The guard grabbed her other arm. She tugged and twisted but could not break the crushing grip. Then an icy cold voice robbed her of any remaining strength.

"Betrayed by my own mother."

The guards parted to let Davira through. Her flashing emerald eyes narrowed on Solora. The former queen stood firm, but her voice softened to a gentle plea between mother and daughter. "You don't have to do this, Davira. There has been too much death and bloodshed. I'm sure your brother will be merciful if you stand down."

Davira snorted, her nose scrunching in such vicious disgust Kyrin shivered. "I don't want his mercy. If he is going to take everything from me, then I'll take everything I can from him first."

She reached for a fold of her dress. A warning burst through Kyrin, but it didn't make it to her lips before Davira yanked out a dagger and plunged it into her mother's stomach. Solora gasped, her eyes going wide. Kyrin read the shock in them. As evil as Davira was, her mother hadn't truly believed she'd try to kill her. Not until this moment. Kyrin flicked her gaze over to Davira, but she didn't find a whisper of regret in her twisted expression. She simply yanked the dagger back out, and her mother sank to her knees with a soft groan.

Davira swung the dagger around and pointed the bloody blade at Collin, who stood restrained between two guards. "And *you*. Did you forget what we had together? You owed me your loyalty."

Collin gulped, his face going a bit green like he was about to be sick.

Davira waved the dagger at the guards now, her eyes flashing a warning that they would be next if her orders weren't followed to the letter. "Dispose of him, and then guard this palace with your lives, do you understand me?"

They nodded without a word and led Collin away. Only the one still guarding Kyrin remained. Now Davira's cutting gaze landed on her. Kyrin's mouth turned bone dry, and her knees shook. Was this it? Was this finally the end?

Davira snatched her arm and jerked her away from the guard. Before Kyrin could react, Davira spun her around and pressed the dagger against her throat. She didn't even dare flinch as the sharp edge dug into her flesh. She'd had a blade to her neck before, but death never felt so near.

Davira's free hand crushed Kyrin's arm as she spat orders at the guard. "Go defend the doors. I'll take care of her."

The man hurried away, and Davira shoved Kyrin forward, past her mother, and down the hall. Her hot breath brushed Kyrin's ear, but her words chilled her to the core.

"You and I are going to the front balcony. If my brother does make it through the gate thinking he's won, the first thing they will see is me slitting your throat and throwing you over the edge. They may take my throne, but they won't have everything."

A wave of despair crashed over Kyrin, choking the air from her lungs. She'd survived ryriks, battles, fever, and capture. All of it only to be used by Davira to taint their moment of victory. How would Jace even live knowing she and their baby were dead?

No. It couldn't end like this. Not without a fight.

Adrenaline flushed through the despair, forcing clarity to her mind. She was not helpless. Not against Davira, who may have a knife but had left herself without any backup. A sense of calm settled even as her heart raced. She sucked in a deep breath past the blade, prayed for strength, and grabbed Davira's hand. Davira released something between a shriek and growl as Kyrin yanked the blade away from her throat. She turned her body just enough to give herself the space to drive her elbow into Davira's ribs.

Davira grunted, and Kyrin spun to face her. They both struggled for control of the dagger, fighting to twist it out of the other's grasp. Davira's bared teeth flashed, her eyes wild. Her strength was frightening as she tried to wrench the dagger away, but Kyrin refused to let go. Kyrin's pulse thundered in her head, but the only thought that raced with it was the overwhelming need to protect her baby. Davira did not get to claim that victory.

Blood slicked Kyrin's hands, but Davira's grip faltered first. Kyrin ripped the dagger from her grasp the moment she felt it loosen. With a furious screech, Davira lunged for her face. Kyrin raised one arm to shield herself and jerked the dagger upward, right under Davira's ribs just like she'd practiced in self-defense training with Jace.

Davira stopped short with a gasp, her mouth gaping. At first, her eyes registered only shock but then blazed with a fury unlike anything Kyrin had ever seen. A guttural scream erupted from her chest, and she reached for Kyrin again. Still gripping the dagger, Kyrin scrambled back away from the madwoman.

Davira lunged after her but tripped on her own skirt and fell to her knees. Her loud, gasping breaths filled the hall. The gold brocade of her bodice turned rapidly crimson. Even so, she pushed to her feet only to collapse once again when she tried to take a step.

"No!" Davira's frantic cry echoed around them. She clawed at the carpet to drag herself toward Kyrin, but she only made it a couple of feet. Falling face down on the floor, her body convulsed with two final, rasping breaths before going still.

Kyrin couldn't move. She just stared at the body until her own weak gasps broke her away from the shock. She looked down at the bloodied dagger. The dagger she'd just used to kill Davira, her nemesis for so long. Her hand started to tremble. But she shook her head and gulped in a steadying breath. Now was not the time to fall apart. She still had enemies within the palace.

She glanced down the hall, where the guards had gone. Collin sprang to mind, but what could she do with only a dagger? The fight with Davira had already nearly drained her of strength. In all likelihood, he was already dead. He'd risked his life to save her. If she went to try to find him and got herself killed along with him, it would all be for naught. Besides, she had to think of her baby.

Gathering her remaining strength, she turned away from Davira's body and hurried back the way they had come. Solora was leaning against the wall when Kyrin reached her. She couldn't help Collin, but maybe she could help the former queen. She knelt beside her and laid the dagger to the side. The queen took shallow, shuddering breaths, but there wasn't as much blood as Kyrin had expected. She hoped that was a good thing.

Before she could decide what to do, Solora's gaze shifted to the dagger. "Is she dead?"

Kyrin met her eyes and gave a short nod. Solora didn't respond, her lips set grimly, but acceptance, perhaps even relief, settled in her expression. It was over now, and whether her demise came at Kyrin's hand or another's, Davira never would have surrendered. Kyrin knew beyond a doubt she would have fought until the bitter end. Bloodshed had been the only way.

Kyrin forced herself to focus on Solora's wound and what she could do. She'd never assisted Josef or Leetra with anything this serious, but keeping the bleeding under control was top priority until an actual physician could take over. She looked around the hall. Pushing back to her feet, she hurried to the door directly behind her. It opened into another bedroom, and she quickly grabbed a blanket from a nearby sofa. She brought it back to Solora and pressed it to the wound.

Solora groaned, and Kyrin winced. The former queen wouldn't have been stabbed if not for lending her aid.

"Thank you for trying to help me." It was little consolation for being stabbed, especially if she might be dying, but Kyrin hoped she would understand the depth of her gratitude.

Solora breathed out a careful breath, her voice catching. "Are you friends with Daniel?"

"Yes, good friends." Family, actually, and that made Solora extended family as well. Davira too. What a bizarre thought. But she would let Daniel explain all that once he arrived.

She closed her eyes and prayed Solora would survive. Taking the throne would be hard enough for Daniel without losing his mother on top of it. He would benefit from her experience as a ruler even if he did things differently.

After a few minutes, she carefully peeled the blanket back to check Solora's wound. "The bleeding has slowed."

She glanced up and briefly made eye contact with Solora. The woman's eyes were the same color as Davira's, though they lacked the cunning, snake-like quality. Solora breathed more slowly and evenly now. Still, she must be in pain.

Kyrin searched for something to distract her and was about

to mention how well Daniel had been doing when the distant echo of footsteps cut her off. If the guards found Davira's body, they would no doubt kill Kyrin on sight.

Solora grabbed her wrist. "You must hide."

Where? She'd already tried.

Anywhere. It didn't matter. She just had to stay hidden. Shoving to her feet, she turned to run, but a voice called out. She stilled. Could it really be? Her legs wobbled, almost sending her back to her knees. She turned toward the footsteps that now drew near. A group poured into the hall a moment later. Daniel was in the lead, but Jace pushed past him.

He blurred behind a flood of tears, and, at first, the sheer wave of relief that washed through Kyrin kept her from moving. But then she ran to meet him. The tears poured down her face the moment his arms wrapped around her. She squeezed her own around his neck and couldn't stop the sobs that shook her. She'd all but given up hope of being safe and secure in his arms again. She cried into his shoulder, never wanting to let go.

She wasn't sure how many minutes passed before she managed to calm herself. Jace's breaths shuddered in her ear, and slowly his secure grip loosened. He backed away just enough to reach up and cup her face. She looked up into his eyes. They glowed vivid blue and were wet with tears that had left tracks down his cheeks. His gaze roamed her face, pained in its intensity. "Are you all right?"

She nodded against his hands. Miraculously, yes.

His chest collapsed with a huge breath, and Kyrin pulled herself closer for another clinging embrace before becoming aware of the others around them. She lifted her head from Jace's chest. Daniel and Leetra now knelt next to Solora. She also caught a glimpse of Collin at the back of the group, holding his bloodied shoulder. Daniel and the others must have arrived and found him just in time.

Carefully, Daniel gathered up his mother and carried her back to her room. Leetra followed while everyone else remained in the hall. Kyrin shifted to Jace's side, and he kept his arm protectively around her waist. All eyes seemed to focus on her. Rayad reached out to gently squeeze her shoulder.

"I'm glad you're all right. We weren't sure what we would find when we got here."

They all knew Davira well enough to have surely guessed she'd try to kill Kyrin as soon as they attacked the palace. Had she succeeded, Kyrin could have been lying dead in the court-yard right now. She shuddered. Jace's arm tightened around her, and she leaned into him. To find her like that would have destroyed him.

She forced the horrific thought away. She was safe now. And most importantly, their baby was safe, as long as the strain of the last few days had not harmed it.

"How did you all get here so fast?"

Rayad gestured toward Solora's room. "It was Daniel's plan to sneak in with only the Militia. We hope, if he can establish control here, we can avoid a bigger fight."

It was a good plan, and one she prayed worked. So far, it seemed successful.

Daniel returned a couple of minutes later. The way he looked at Kyrin, specifically how he glanced toward her middle, said he knew about the baby. No doubt Elanor had shared with him after the attack. Kyrin couldn't blame her. She knew the burden of carrying such a secret by herself.

"You two stay here." He motioned her and Jace toward his mother's room. "Rayad, you, Charles, and James stay with them to guard the room until we've secured the palace."

Jace ushered Kyrin toward the doorway. As they passed him, she caught Daniel giving Collin a speculative look before motioning to him as well. "You can stay too."

Inside the royal suite, Leetra was working on Solora in the bedroom. Daniel cast them a worried glance from the doorway before closing the door. Rayad, Charles, and James stood near to guard it, but Kyrin's attention focused fully on Jace.

"How is Holden?"

"Alive when I left him, but unconscious. Infection is setting in."

At least he was still alive. That gave Leetra a chance to save him.

Jace's hands cupped her shoulders, drawing her gaze to his eyes. "Are you hurt?"

"I don't think so." Now that the adrenaline was wearing off, she took stock of herself. A sharp sting and throbbing ache drew her attention to her left hand. Fresh blood oozed from a cut along her palm that she hadn't noticed before. She winced. "This must have happened when I fought Davira for the dagger."

Jace grabbed a towel from a nearby washstand and pressed it gently to her hand. He cradled it between them and said nothing for a moment but then spoke in a quiet tone.

"You killed her?"

His eyes searched hers, probing deeply for answers she wasn't sure she even possessed yet.

"Yes."

Kaden dove to avoid a firedrake, skimming just over the tops of the buildings near the palace. About three dozen of the beasts had engaged them at the beginning of the fight, but they were down to about half that now. The drakes lacked the agility to get as close to the buildings as the dragons, which gave Kaden and the others the advantage they needed to maintain their numbers and protect their ground forces. It appeared Daniel had made it inside the palace, but the skirmish at the gate was still ongoing. The soldiers didn't seem to realize yet that the whole thing was a ruse to keep them distracted.

Kaden looked toward the palace, but gold and black flags still waved from the towers. The plan was for someone to replace them with Arcacia's old blue and gold flag once Davira was neutralized and they had control. For the first time, he wished he was part of the ground assault—part of the group inside the palace. The pull to be down there and look for Kyrin tore at him. What if she was dead already? He'd have no idea until this was over. He shook his head. He couldn't think like that right now. He needed to focus, not only for his own survival but for his men.

As he searched for the nearest drake, movement at the palace caught his eye. A dragon soared over the wall as if it had taken off from the back courtyard. None of his riders would have had any reason to be back there. He swung Rhune around in that direction to get a better look. The dragon headed north, toward the mountains, and away from the fight. Definitely not one of Kaden's men. He directed Rhune to pursue it. Drawing closer, he recognized the female dragon's markings. He'd seen that same dragon when he'd been held captive just outside Samara—a dragon that no doubt belonged to Richard.

Leaning over Rhune's neck, Kaden urged him for more speed. Rhune responded with swift, powerful flaps of his wings. It didn't take long to start catching up to the fleeing dragon. The rider looked back, and though Kaden couldn't make out specific facial features, he was sure it was Richard attempting to make his escape. That could only mean Daniel had successfully taken the palace even though the flag was not yet raised.

Rhune quickly shrank the distance between them. A little closer and they'd be within range of his fire. Before Kaden could give the command, Richard's dragon dove into a steep descent toward the forested slopes outside the city. Rhune folded his wings to follow without even a prompting from Kaden.

Kaden held on as the ground raced up to meet them, sending his stomach up into his throat. That horrible moment of plummeting to the ground with Exsis flashed into his mind. He shoved it away.

Just before it would have been too late, Rhune opened his wings and beat them hard, sending pine needles and pebbles spraying across the rocky ground. They landed with a thud several yards from where Richard had made his landing. He waited there, sword drawn, standing close to his dragon like it was his attack dog. Of course, he would want to settle this on the ground. He was no dragon rider.

His eyes narrowed, his expression sharp and taut. "*You.*"

Kaden took immense pleasure in the fury that practically rolled off Richard upon seeing him alive. He let a grim smile twist his lips. "Surprise."

Richard strangled his sword in both hands. "I should have taken your eye and slit your throat when I had the chance."

"You should have. I tried to warn you about Altair and Veshiron blood."

"Well, it's certainly not a mistake I will make again."

"You won't be getting another chance." He pointed his sword at Richard. "I suggest you surrender. You have nowhere and no one to run to."

"Or what?" Richard sneered. "You'll sic your dragon on me like a coward?"

He did step a little closer to his own dragon, showing no qualms about using it as a shield. Who was the coward now?

Kaden shifted his attention to the creature.

"*Sora,*" he commanded, using the crete word for fly.

The dragon tipped its head as if confused or uncertain.

Richard's gaze darted between the two of them. "What are you doing?"

Kaden maintained eye contact with the dragon. In his most commanding tone, he ordered, "*Sora!*"

This time Rhune added a menacing growl. Richard's dragon ducked its head submissively before spreading its wings and launching into the sky.

"What are you doing?" Richard shouted at the creature. "Get back here!"

Kaden couldn't help but smirk as the dragon soared over the trees and disappeared from sight. "I take it Falcor never told you dragons are trained to follow crete commands. Or you never bothered to learn them."

Richard bared his teeth and raised his sword in what would be a feeble defense against a dragon. Kaden opened his mouth to demand surrender, but Richard spun around and plunged into the forest undergrowth. Kaden bit back a curse. Richard could *not* get away again. Making a split-second decision, he jumped off Rhune and charged after him. It would be too easy to lose him in the trees from the air.

Rhune grumbled loudly behind him, and gusts of air beat the ground again as he took off. But Kaden did not look back. He focused straight ahead on the swaying branches. Brush snapped and crackled, though it was hard to hear over his own crashing through the trees. He realized a second too late when it stopped and only just managed to duck as he broke into a small clearing. Richard's sword whirred over his head. Kaden stumbled and regained his footing just as Richard lunged for him again, their swords crashing together. The impact reverberated up Kaden's arms.

Richard sneered in his face. "This time, I'm not going to try to take your eye. I'm just going to take your whole head."

He swung again in a fury. Kaden blocked, and then twisted his sword away to attempt an attack of his own. Richard met it easily. They traded their blows back and forth, circling the clearing. The long days of travel, battle, and lingering weakness weighed on Kaden's limbs. He could almost hear Kyrin telling him she told him so as sweat beaded and rolled down his face and neck. He just prayed both of them would live for her to be able to actually tell him.

A wide attack from Richard missed Kaden's neck by a breath, and he stumbled back. If he wasn't careful, Richard really would take his head. He pushed himself to focus past the fatigue and attempt an answering attack. Richard blocked with contemptuous ease, batting Kaden's sword to the side and then swinging low for Kaden's legs. Kaden gave ground. This would be going very differently if he were well-rested.

Richard did not let up, taking full advantage of his weakness. Several savage attacks later, hot pain tore across Kaden's left arm. He backpedaled again. This time, his foot snagged on something, and his back hit the rocky ground. The air gusted from his lungs, another flash of pain shooting through his arm. Richard was right on top of him, about to drive his blade home. He scrambled to find his feet.

The trees exploded. A deafening roar blasted overhead, along with a wave of heat. Kaden fell back and covered his head as the roar mingled with a scream. A moment later, everything fell silent. Kaden lifted his head. Rhune stood protectively over him. Several feet away, Richard lay in a charred, smoking heap. Rhune snorted out two streams of smoke before curling his head down to peer at Kaden. Kaden blew out a long breath and wearily reached up to pat his dragon's cheek.

"Thanks." He sat up slowly as Rhune backed off. He checked his arm. Blood stained his sleeve, but the wound wouldn't kill him. He then pushed to his feet, though his legs wobbled a bit. That had been entirely too close. He took a couple of steps toward Richard and cringed at the gruesome sight. No one could survive such a concentrated blast of dragon fire.

Breathing deeply to slow his racing heart, Kaden turned to Rhune and pulled a blanket from his saddle. He brought it back to Richard's scorched body and wrapped him up. He deserved to be left to rot, forgotten on the mountain, but Kaden just couldn't do that. Once he'd secured the body to his dragon, he dragged himself back into the saddle.

He and Rhune took to the air again. Once they'd cleared the trees, he spotted Richard's dragon circling nearby. He called for it to follow, and they flew back down toward the city. When they drew near the palace, the black and gold flags were gone, replaced by one big, glorious blue and gold one.

DANIEL STARED AT the throne from the base of the dais. A throne his father and sister had occupied and used to spread such terror the last couple of years. As long as he lived, he would do everything in his power to ensure that never happened again, but he did not climb the steps to claim it yet. There was still too much to do before it would seem right.

He turned away from it and scanned the vast throne room. Members of the Militia, acting as his guard, stood at each entrance and in a protective circle around him. Once they'd successfully infiltrated the palace and located Kyrin, everyone had not so subtly insisted Daniel remain in a secure location under guard. As much as he hated sitting around and waiting, he understood their success now rested entirely on his survival. So he'd let Aric and Trev handle security while he oversaw their operations from the safety of this room.

Footsteps echoed in the outer hall. The guards went on full alert, and even Daniel's heart gave a nervous thump, but they relaxed when Aric and Trev entered the room.

"Good news," Aric announced as he drew near. "The firedrake riders fled once they noticed our flag, which led to the soldiers' surrender at the gate. I was also informed Kaden just brought in Richard's body. Apparently, he tried to flee the palace on his dragon."

Daniel gave a grim nod. While he hadn't hoped for Davira and Richard's deaths, the outcome was no shock. They'd brought such fates upon themselves. At least Richard wouldn't be around to make trouble or seek vengeance now that Davira was dead. "And how secure is the palace?"

"We've contained what we believe are all the guards and staff. I still have to speak with Foss and see if he can tell me whether anyone is missing. It's about as secure as we can make it right now. We thoroughly searched and cleared the guest wing as you requested and have guards at both entrances."

"Good. Send Aaron for Holden and the others and take them there. Also, get word to Marcus. I want the commanding officers held at the fort, but send the rest of the soldiers to their homes until things are settled with the army. I know they won't show up immediately, but close all the smaller gates and guard the main ones. If Kaden hasn't sent a message back to our armies yet, have one sent right away to let them know of our victory. They need to watch carefully in case someone decides to send the firedrake force here."

A whole army of the beasts could burn and topple the palace down on top of them if left unchallenged.

"I will go to him now and see that the rest is done."

"Thanks, Aric."

He inclined his head and half-turned to go before pausing. "One more thing. What do you want us to tell people? The city will want to know what's going on."

Daniel considered it a moment. It was a lot to juggle—making sure their position here was secure while also taking the whole city into account. "Tell them I've returned to make things right."

For now, it would have to do.

Aric nodded again and walked out.

Now that the most important issues had been addressed, Daniel's mind shifted to more personal matters he'd had to set aside in the midst of securing the palace. He turned to Trev. "I'm going to go check on my mother."

He'd had to leave so fast he had no idea how she was doing or if she was even still alive. Leetra hadn't had enough time to give him an assessment of the severity of the wound. The placement worried him. Subconsciously, he'd been counting on his mother to help him navigate the beginning of his rise to power. Whether or not they saw eye to eye on everything, she understood the ins and outs of ruling a country and could help him avoid any major political blunders.

Trev and several of the men followed him out of the throne room and back upstairs to the family wing. Just down the hall from the stairs, he stopped at Davira's body. He'd barely paused when he'd seen her before, too concerned for his mother and Kyrin, but he did now. Trev and the others hung back as he knelt beside her for a moment. Was it wrong that he didn't feel much but the lingering anger over the pain she had caused? They'd never been close. Not even as children. He'd felt something when his father died but couldn't seem to summon the same regret after everything Davira had done.

Slowly, he rolled her over. Even dead, her gaunt face looked angry, and he shook his head. He looked down at the slit in her dress near her ribs that was almost black with blood. He hadn't asked and probably wouldn't, but it seemed clear Kyrin was the one who had killed her. According to Collin, she was the only one around besides his mother, who had already been wounded. He hated that she was the one to carry the burden, but it seemed grimly fitting that she and Kaden were the ones who had ended this—first with Davira and then with Richard. So much of this struggle had started with them.

With a sigh, Daniel pushed back to his feet and looked at Trev. "Whenever there is time, have the body taken away and prepared for burial. I'll let you know when I decide how it should be done."

What his sister deserved was an unmarked grave in some desolate place, but he'd probably have her buried with their father and the rest of the family as one last kindness. His mother would probably want that if she survived.

They moved on again. Just before they reached the royal suite, Trev spoke up. "What do you want us to do with Collin?"

Daniel paused. Collin had warned them about Davira and appeared to have been injured opposing her men. He could probably be trusted, but Daniel also knew about his dealings with Davira. It was a complicated mess he didn't have time to unravel just yet. Like the rest of the staff, he would need to determine Collin's loyalty at some point once things were more settled.

"Put him with the rest of the palace guard, but keep an eye on him. Make sure he is well treated and not harassed by the others. I want to trust him, but we have more pressing matters to contend with right now."

Daniel took a slight detour and entered his own bedroom. Surprisingly, it looked just like it had the day Davira had thrown him into the dungeon. He opened his wardrobe and found all of his clothing still there, neatly pressed. He'd expected Davira to burn his belongings just out of spite, but she must have been too focused on hunting him down. He grabbed a blue shirt from the pile and left the room again.

Upon entering his mother's room, his gaze went straight to her bed. She lay there, eyes closed, and he prayed she was only resting. He'd already watched his father die in that bed. He didn't want the same memory of his mother.

Movement to his right grabbed his attention. Leetra appeared to have just finished bandaging Jace's arm. Kyrin had a bandage around her hand, and Collin's arm was in a sling. Daniel walked over to them, a little scared to ask Leetra, "How is she?"

"Alive." She glanced back toward his mother. "Since I can't see internal damage, only time will tell. But… I'm hopeful."

It was the best Daniel could hope for, considering. He shifted his focus to Kyrin. "Are you all right?"

He had noticed the blood on her hands, but it had been hard to tell whether it was hers, his mother's, or Davira's. Probably all three.

Kyrin's fingers brushed over the bandage. "Yes, just a cut. Leetra doesn't think it needs stitches."

Still, weariness dragged on her expression, creating shadows under her eyes, and he could only imagine how she and Jace had suffered the last several days. Both of them needed rest, but Kyrin especially. He wanted to ask about the baby, but too many others were present. Did Jace even know yet? If Davira had separated them right away, Kyrin might not have had the chance to tell him.

Daniel shifted to motion them toward the door. "I've had the guest wing of the palace secured and guarded. You can rest and recover there. I've already sent for Holden."

This seemed to distract Jace from how he hovered around Kyrin, not that Daniel blamed him. "He'll need treatment right away."

Leetra started gathering her supplies, and Daniel handed Jace the shirt he'd brought from his room. Jace nodded in thanks and slipped it on, covering up the dark bruises across his chest. If he didn't have any broken ribs, it was a miracle. Daniel wasn't sure he even wanted to know what had caused them.

"I'll see that more fresh clothing is brought to you." After several days as captives, especially in the dungeon, they probably wanted to burn what they were wearing. "Food as well."

Kyrin's face pinched into a queasy frown, and she rubbed her hand over her stomach. "None for me right now, but thank you."

Her lack of appetite was understandable between her pregnancy and everything that had just happened with Davira. That, however, didn't stop Jace from looking at her like he was expecting something to go wrong at any minute. He probably had a million questions he wanted to ask her in private. Best to give them a chance to do so.

He instructed Trev to take them to the guest wing and see to their needs. Once they had left with Rayad, Charles, and James, he turned to Collin, who wouldn't meet his gaze. "For now, you will stay with the rest of the palace guard until I have a chance to sort out loyalties."

Collin dipped his chin even lower. "Of course, Your Highness."

Daniel motioned for one of the guards to lead him out, and then his attention focused solely on his mother. He crossed the room to her bedside. Though he thought she was asleep, her eyes opened as he carefully sat down on the edge of the bed. It felt like so long since he'd seen her. He hadn't even been able to say goodbye when he and Aric had fled the city. Only now did he realize just how much he had missed her.

He reached to take her hand. "How do you feel?"

"I'll be fine."

That didn't exactly answer his question, but he prayed it was true. His mother was a very proud, and sometimes stubborn, woman. She would fight to survive this.

Daniel smiled and squeezed her hand between both of his. "You better be. You need to be here to meet my wife when she arrives."

His mother's eyes rounded, her dark brows rising. He almost laughed. It was just how she'd always looked at him when he'd said something outrageous as a child.

"Your wife?"

This wasn't how he'd intended to tell her, but it was good to give her something more to fight for. And if she did take a turn for the worse, he wanted her to know.

"Yes. I got married in Samara. Only three weeks ago, actually. And the crazy thing is, aside from the fact she's a believer, I think Father would have approved of the marriage."

She gave him a prompting look when he paused. "Well, who is she?"

"Elanor Cantan. Sir Rothas Cantan's daughter."

Now Mother released what may have been a light, breathless laugh. "Yes, I think you're right. Your father would have approved."

"I'm sorry you weren't there for the wedding."

Her expression softened, a content smile bringing a little warmth to her pale face. "I'm just glad you're happy. I'm sure it was a much nicer wedding than you ever hoped for here."

"It was small and intimate." Daniel laughed. "And very rushed, but perfect in every way."

Her eyes closed for a moment, and she released a sigh as if this were the fulfillment of everything she had always wanted for him. "It will be good for the people to know you are married. It will prove you're not the reckless prince they remember."

Daniel hadn't thought of that aspect, but his mother was probably right. Anything that would help with this transition was welcome.

"I can't wait for you to meet her. I know you'll like her." Who wouldn't love Elanor?

"I'm sure I will."

Jace kept his arm around Kyrin's waist and held her close as they followed Trev through the palace. His gaze darted to each hall and door they passed in case of danger. In a place this big, enemies could be hiding anywhere. It did help to have Rayad, Charles, and James at his back.

When he wasn't looking for danger, he was watching Kyrin. She seemed calm and unharmed other than the cut on her hand and a bruise on her cheek that hadn't been there when they'd been separated, but he couldn't stop worrying about her. Outward appearances were deceiving. What might she be battling on the inside? Though she had killed a ryrik before, it hadn't been in such an up close and personal way as using a knife. Even if she had killed Davira in self-defense, he was still afraid of how it might impact her. If only they had been able to reach her sooner, he could have done it instead.

Clear on the other side of the palace, they finally arrived at the entrance to a long hall. Two militiamen guarded it, and two more stood at the far end.

"All of the rooms have been thoroughly searched inside and out." Trev gestured to the rows of doors. "You are welcome to any of them. We believe the palace is secure, but we'll keep guards here at all times until we know for certain."

After the incident in Amberin, Jace welcomed the precautions, though it would take time before he was convinced the palace was safe.

Rayad came up behind him and rested his hand on Jace's shoulder. "You and Kyrin should rest. There's nothing more you need to do right now."

Though it was still early morning, Jace's strength was nearly spent. His body seemed to realize he did not have to fight anymore. All he wanted was to be with Kyrin and give in to his body's craving for true rest. Like Kyrin, he wasn't even hungry at this point. But, before he could do that, he had one last thing to see to first.

"Let me know as soon as Holden arrives."

"We will."

With that promise, Jace guided Kyrin toward the nearest room. He opened the door and stepped in first, scanning every inch of the space, even if it had been cleared. Once satisfied, he ushered her inside and closed the door behind them. Kyrin just stood in the center of the room with her back to him. Her silence left dread settling in his stomach. What was she thinking? Reliving? Was there something she hadn't told him? He took a step closer, and she turned, throwing her arms around him and burying her face in his chest. Her grip was tight and desperate, and though his ribs protested, he wrapped her up in an equally strong embrace.

They stood that way for a long moment as if letting go would tear them apart forever. Then Kyrin shifted enough to tip her head up, and Jace bent to meet her lips, kissing her like it could erase all the pain and fear of the last several days.

When he finally pulled away so they could both catch a breath, he found that a few tears had leaked down her face. He reached up to wipe them, dread still knotting his insides.

"Are you sure you're all right?" He let his hand fall to rest against her belly, almost choking on his own voice. "The baby?"

"I think so. Nothing seems to be wrong that I can tell, but I will talk to Leetra when she is not busy." She rested her hand over his. Though no more tears fell, the deep emotion pooling in her eyes made his heart ache. Her voice trembled. "I really thought I was going to have to watch you die."

He pulled her into his arms again. "It's over now," he whispered in her ear.

She nodded against him, and they stood in silence for another moment or two until someone tapped on the door. They parted slowly, and Jace brushed his fingers over Kyrin's damp face once more. He hated the dark circles around her eyes. As soon as he saw that Holden was safe, he would devote every waking moment to making sure Kyrin was healthy and comfortable. He tore himself away from her and turned to the door. Rayad stood on the other side.

"Holden is here."

Jace glanced back as Kyrin joined him, and they both stepped out of the room. In the hall, Kaden waited just beyond Rayad. His taut expression lifted the moment he spotted Kyrin. She gasped his name and hurried past Jace. Kaden caught her up in his arms, and Jace had a feeling he'd probably been pacing in the hall waiting for them. He appreciated that he'd let them have time and privacy, as hard as that had probably been. It must have been torture for Kyrin's brothers to know she was Davira's captive. In that moment, he was thankful they did not yet know about the baby. He wasn't sure how they would have endured it.

When they parted, Kaden held her at arm's length to look her over, his brows drawn together. He'd probably notice every scratch and bruise just like Jace did. She assured him she was all right but grew distracted by his bloodied sleeve. "What about you?"

Kaden shrugged, though his nonchalance seemed a little forced. "I'm fine. Richard just made the mistake of thinking this would finally be the time he killed me. Rhune foiled those plans."

Jace picked up the unspoken information behind those words. At least they wouldn't have to worry about Richard ever again. With both him and Davira gone, maybe they could finally find peace.

Kyrin just looked at him for a long moment, probably picking up a lot more than Jace could before she breathed out a long sigh. "And Marcus? He's all right?"

Kaden gave a firm nod. "Yes, I checked in with him before I came here. He wanted to come with me but has a lot to over-see right now. I promised him I'd go back and let him know as soon as I saw for myself that you were okay."

"You better go do that then. And make sure you get your arm taken care of."

Kaden smirked, a spark of mischief in his eyes that Jace had not seen since before the attack in Samara. "Yes, Mother."

He squeezed her shoulders and then looked past her, trading a nod with Jace. They still had a lot to recover from, but they would be all right.

When Kaden left to return to Marcus, Rayad led them into one of the other rooms. Aaron and Timothy were there, along with Mira, who was helping Leetra remove the bandages from Holden's chest. Holden was still unconscious, which was probably a mercy right now. Jace wished he could help, but it was best to let Leetra work. So he stayed back and put his arm around Kyrin, praying Holden would be all right.

They all watched quietly as Leetra cleaned, stitched, and re-bandaged the wounds, and Timothy stood with his head bowed in prayer. Once Holden was resting under the covers, Jace worked up the courage to ask, "Will he be all right?"

She turned to him. While he expected a cool, matter-of-fact answer, her voice and expression held a much softer and more understanding quality than usual. "If I can successfully treat the infection, he should recover. He's fortunate the wounds weren't any deeper or lower. A drake could easily gut a man. I'll keep a close eye on him and keep treating the infection. It's good we got here when we did."

Some of Jace's tension eased, and he dared to hope that maybe the worst was past. Kyrin leaned into him, some of the tension leaving her body as well. He rubbed her arm. Though he would have liked to stay with Holden, she was his priority. Keeping her close, he turned toward the door and met Rayad's understanding gaze. "Let me know if anything changes."

He patted Jace on the shoulder. "We will. You two just rest."

They returned to their room. Water had been brought up for them to wash, and fresh clothing, including nightclothes, lay in two neat piles on the bed. First, they helped each other clean away the dirt and grime of their captivity, and then they sank into bed, where Jace put his arm around Kyrin. He released a long sigh with the way the soft mattress cradled them instead of cold, hard stone digging into his sore muscles.

For a minute or two, silence settled around them. Then Kyrin started to shake beneath his arm, and he realized she was crying again. He lifted his head, fear punching his stomach. She'd said she was all right but was something actually wrong?

Before he could ask, she grasped his hand more firmly in her own, hugging it tightly to her chest. "I'm all right. I just need you to hold me."

And so he did until they both fell asleep.

LEETRA FINISHED CLEANING up her equipment before checking on Holden once more. His forehead was a bit too warm to the touch, but at least it was a low fever. The herbal mixture she'd managed to get him to drink should help soon.

Now that her most pressing cases were tended to, she could switch her focus to the one person constantly lingering in her mind. She looked across the room where Timothy stood quietly, just watching her work. Everyone else had left the room to see to one thing or another, but he had remained.

Her gaze was drawn to dark bruising along his jaw and around one eye as well as the dried blood flaking on his chin and neck. The way he kept holding his chest told her his shirt hid even more damage. It set a blazing fire in her chest.

She picked up her bag and walked over to a dressing table at the edge of the room, where someone had left a fresh pitcher of clean water. She motioned to Timothy. "Come over here so I can check your injuries."

"They're not that bad." But he walked over and sat on the edge of the dressing table, failing to hide a slight wince as he did so.

She raised a brow at him. "Take your shirt off."

Only after the words left her mouth did she realize how inappropriate they sounded under different circumstances. The way his lips twitched in a near-smile only made it worse. Heat flushed through her cheeks. She looked to her left, glad the door to the room stood wide open, or this would have been even more uncomfortable. She scolded herself for letting her feelings distract her from her duties as a physician.

The sight that greeted her when he pulled his shirt over his head promptly doused the burn in her cheeks. Beyond more bruising, he bore numerous burns and forming scars like the one on his jaw. His ribs poked out noticeably. Anger blazed back to life, making her throat thick.

"Who did this to you?"

"Most recently? A couple of guards at the arena." Timothy glanced past her. "I was caught trying to smuggle medical supplies for Holden. I only managed to get him a roll of bandages and antiseptic."

Leetra breathed shallowly, her lungs heavy with both the anger and a love she once would have fought to deny. "You probably saved his life. The infection would've spread much faster if not for that." She forced herself to focus once more on the task at hand, eyeing his protruding ribs. Normally, she'd feel for fractures, but that didn't seem to be the best idea in this instance. "Is anything broken?"

"Just bruised, I think."

"Well, let me know if you need your ribs wrapped. I can give you something for the pain." She reached to pour the water into the basin and wet a clean cloth.

"I'm sure I'll be fine with some rest."

"And food."

"Yes, that too."

His smile was enough to make her heart melt into a warm puddle. This made things all the more difficult when she had to lean in close to carefully clean the blood from his face. They didn't say much while she worked, and she had the feeling he was probably just as aware of their close proximity as she was.

Once she finished and had applied a healing salve to a couple of the fresher wounds, he slipped his shirt back on, which helped a bit. He didn't move from his spot, however.

"I missed you."

His low murmur stole her breath. She paused from putting her supplies away to meet his gaze. "Missed" was a pretty weak word for what she saw in his eyes—what she felt in her own heart. The pain she'd experienced, thinking he might be dead, was something she never wanted to have to endure again. Despite all the effort she had once put into fighting it, she had developed such a deep love for him she couldn't imagine her life without him there. "Promise me we'll never be apart again."

"What?"

"Promise we'll never be apart again." While neither one of them could control the future, she needed to hear him say it.

He held her gaze for a long moment before a slow smile broke out. "That sounds a bit like a proposal."

Maybe it was. "Is that a bad thing?"

His smile grew, and he shook his head. But, instead of giving her his promise, he reached for her hands and drew her closer. "Leetra, will you marry me so we never have to be apart again?"

She hated how close she was to dissolving into tears. Choking them back, she managed, "Yes, I will."

He grinned now. When he reached up and cradled her face in his strong hand, she held her breath. They'd never shared a real kiss before, but the longing beat inside her. His thumb gently caressed her cheek before he drew her to him for a soft kiss. Leetra melted into it, losing all thought but him. The connection was painfully fleeting. If things weren't so chaotic, she might have tracked Daniel down and demanded he marry them right now.

She was done with the distance that had existed between them for so long.

Timothy just smiled as if reading her thoughts, his thumb stroking her cheek again as he looked into her eyes. "You're sure this is the life you want? I have no idea what the future holds; I only know that people all over Ilyon don't know or need to be reminded of Elôm and Elon's sacrifice. He has called me to reach them, and I'm not sure yet what that will even look like. I'm sure it won't be the kind of life you're used to."

Once that would have scared Leetra, but not anymore. "I know. But as long as we're together, I'll follow you anywhere."

Love deepened his dark eyes, and he drew her in for one more agonizingly brief kiss before they realized someone stood in the doorway. They both turned to see Aaron. Leetra ducked her head, her cheeks catching fire again.

Aaron smirked at them. "Sorry if I've interrupted something."

Timothy shifted, taking her hand. The pure joy in his expression washed away her embarrassment. "Just Leetra accepting my marriage proposal."

Now Aaron's face lit in a bright smile of genuine happiness. "Congratulations."

They thanked him, and Timothy's attention returned to her. The way he gazed at her gave her so much anticipation for their future that she couldn't possibly have been any happier at that moment. After Falcor's betrayal and coming to terms with her own failings, this love she had found was more than she ever dreamed possible.

A soft whimper invaded Jace's consciousness and drew him from sleep. He opened his eyes and listened. At first, he thought maybe it was just in his head, but then Kyrin flinched next to him. Another slight sound escaped her, and her breathing grew choppy and rapid. She shook as though crying, and he pushed himself up. Her eyes were shut tightly, hair clinging to her sweaty face. A mumbled cry that sounded a bit like his name broke from her lips.

He gripped her shoulder and shook her gently. "Kyrin, wake up."

She only curled in on herself with another whimper. He tried again more urgently. This time, her eyes flashed open, wide with terror. She gulped in breaths as if she'd been drowning.

"Kyrin, it's all right. I'm right here."

She blinked several times before she truly focused. Tears filled her eyes, and she reached for him. He gathered her up into his arms and held her to his chest. She clung to his shirt, trembling like a scared child. His heart thumped his ribs where her head rested. In all the months they'd been married, he'd never seen her suffer like this from a nightmare. He wasn't even sure what to do. Nightmares were his territory, his burden. She should not be the one battling them now. What if they became a nightly plague the way his had at times? He prayed it wouldn't be so. He couldn't bear to see her suffer like that.

He rubbed his hand up and down her back until her breathing slowed and the tremors stopped. Only then did he speak. "Do you want to talk about it?"

She sighed against him, a heavy, tired sound. "We were in the arena. You died."

Jace gritted his teeth. Even dead, Davira's actions and memory remained to haunt them.

He shifted enough to rearrange the pillows so they could lean against the headboard and settled Kyrin against him. For a long time, they just sat there in silence. Only time dulled the effects of nightmares, and he was prepared to sit with her as long as needed.

After a while, he slid his hand down to rest on her stomach. The reality that a baby was growing there was something too surreal, too breathtaking to fully wrap his mind around. Until just a couple of years ago, he hadn't even entertained the possibility of ever having a child of his own. Just the idea would have sent him running.

Kyrin shifted now and tipped her head up to look at him. The terror had subsided from her eyes. He leaned in to close the inches of space between them and kissed her, assuring her the dream was not real and that he was still here with her. In the midst of it, her stomach gave a loud grumble. A soft giggle broke the kiss, and it was a far better sound than her cries.

"Sorry, I'm starving. For the moment, anyway. My stomach might decide otherwise at the first whiff of food."

Jace's own stomach was an empty cavern. "I'll see if I can get us something to eat. You just keep resting."

He slipped out of bed, rearranging the blankets around her.

She settled back against the pillows. "How long do you think we were asleep?"

He glanced toward the window. It looked like morning still. "Unless it's only been a couple of hours, I'm guessing a full day and night."

He pulled on the clothes that had been left for him. Judging by the fine quality, he guessed they had come from Daniel's own wardrobe. Kyrin must have noticed, too, because she gave him an appreciative little grin. "Look at you, dressed like a prince."

He eyed the fine linen shirt and wrinkled his nose. There was even gold embroidery around the cuffs that he wasn't altogether sure wasn't real gold thread. "I'm afraid I'll spill something on it."

Though she still had faint shadows under her eyes that would only disappear with more rest, the nightmare seemed to have lost its hold. "Well, he is your brother-in-law now. He won't mind."

"I still don't know if I'm ever going to get used to that."

Jace let himself out of the room and looked up and down the hall. The men at each end were different from those who had been guarding it before. He was about to approach the nearest ones to ask where he could get some food when a door opened a little farther down. James walked out, his expression lifting, and Jace waited for his brother to join him. "Has it been a full day?"

James nodded. "No one wanted to disturb you."

Jace appreciated that. Kyrin, especially, needed the rest. He just hoped her sleep had been peaceful up until the nightmare this morning. "How is everything?"

"Good, as far as I know. Aric and Trev finished securing the palace last night. Right now, everyone is just waiting for word from the army. I would assume the Arcacian soldiers have heard of our victory here."

If only Davira's death meant everything was finally over, but the Arcacian army did still pose a threat. A battle might still be coming. One Jace wasn't sure he'd be physically or mentally prepared for. But that was out of his hands. All he could do right now was make sure Kyrin was safe and comfortable.

James gave him a quick look up and down, his brows dipping. "How are you feeling?"

The genuine concern in his question was a stark contrast to the first time they'd ever met. While Jace's first instinct was to tell people he was fine, he wouldn't dismiss his brother like that. Especially since he'd probably looked pretty rough when they'd released him from his cell yesterday.

"Sore." He rubbed his chest. It would be a while before each breath didn't hurt, but he'd dealt with bruised ribs before. "I don't think the wounds are infected anymore, at least. It will take a little time to recover fully, but considering where I was yesterday, it's just a miracle I'm still alive."

James shifted from one foot to the other. He opened his mouth to speak, though it took a second for his voice to actually follow. "It must have been hard being forced to fight again."

Jace's mind went back to the moment Davira had ordered her guards to take him to the arena and the panic that had gripped him. A little of it built up even now as a cold weight on his lungs. He swallowed hard, reminding himself to breathe. "It was."

James cleared his throat. He looked almost as uncertain and uncomfortable as he had during their reunion at Westing Castle. "Well, if you ever want to talk about it…or anything else…"

It occurred to Jace that James had to have seen his scars yesterday. The sight would be shocking for anyone not expecting such a gruesome glimpse into his past.

"Thanks." It meant a lot that James was trying to connect. Not only that, but he was here instead of back at Fort Rhall with the rest of their army. "And thanks for coming to help rescue me."

Jace didn't know what all had gone into Daniel's plan, but coming to Valcré had to have been a great risk. They couldn't have known what they would face when they arrived, and if anything had gone wrong, it would have meant certain death for everyone. Yet James had chosen to come anyway and specifically chosen to go to the arena to rescue him. He'd risked everything, even after how nervous he'd been in Samara.

James just shrugged. "We haven't known each other for very long, but I knew you would do the same for me. I didn't want our family to suffer from losing you again."

Family. When Jace had escaped Ashwood, he hadn't thought he'd ever experience a true family with his mother and siblings. He could only nod, not sure he trusted his voice.

James's gaze strayed past him for a moment to the door of Jace's room before shifting back to him. "I was just about to go see if there's anywhere I can help out. Do you or Kyrin need anything?"

"Yes, we're both hungry. I was going to ask where I could get some food for us."

"I'll go down and see what's available and have it brought up to you."

Once again, Jace thanked him and then returned to the room. He found Kyrin sitting up in bed, her long hair falling down her back and around her face. She stared at her hand and lightly ran her fingers over the bandage. His conversation with James flew his mind, all his thoughts focusing on her. Was she thinking about her confrontation with Davira? Did she regret what she'd done? He sat down next to her.

"You didn't do anything wrong." He took her hand gently. "I wasn't there, but I know it was self-defense."

A sort of sad smile claimed her lips. "I know. And if I think about it too deeply, it does bother me, but…I know I didn't act out of revenge or hatred or anything like that. I didn't even consider how it would help with our victory. All I felt at that moment was a desperate need to protect my baby."

Jace rubbed his thumb over her fingers. If only he had been there to protect both of them. "You did what you had to do."

She nodded, and he prayed she would be able to live in peace with that. He didn't want her to have even an ounce of the same regrets he did.

A few minutes later, he answered a knock at the door, and Trev stepped in with a servant carrying a tray of food. Jace thanked them and set the tray on a table at the foot of the bed. As Trev was about to leave, Jace stopped him at the door.

"How is Holden?"

"I spoke with Leetra earlier this morning. His fever is down, and the infection is responding to her treatments. He hasn't been awake yet, but she expects he be will soon."

Jace silently thanked Elôm for this miracle. He had truly expected to lose his friend back in the arena. "Have someone let me know when he does."

"Will do."

Jace closed the door behind him and joined Kyrin at the table, where they enjoyed an assortment of fruit, bread, and boiled eggs. Thankfully, Kyrin's nausea didn't seem to flare up because she ate much more than Jace thought she would. He'd been afraid he'd have to encourage her to eat.

Once she was full, she got dressed and turned to him, her hand on her stomach. "Have you told anyone about the baby?"

"No."

"You should know I told Holden." She winced a little, and he hoped she didn't think he was upset about that. "It was so hard after you were taken away. I was so scared, and it just felt like a secret too big for me to carry by myself. I'm sorry. I know you would've liked to tell him."

He shook his head. "Don't be sorry. I'm glad of anything that could bring you some comfort."

She sighed and rubbed her arms, a faraway look taking hold as if she were reliving something. He put his hands on her shoulders, drawing her gaze back to him and the present.

"What's wrong?"

"Nothing, it's just…" A shudder passed through her. "Davira figured out I was pregnant."

The words seemed to steal all warmth from the room, and Jace had to remind himself Davira was no longer a threat. Kyrin's shoulders lifted in a deep breath as if she were assuring herself of the same thing.

"She planned to keep me alive and take the baby once it was born. Then, yesterday, once everything fell apart, she wanted to cut my throat and throw me off the balcony for you all to see, even knowing I'm pregnant."

The horror of what could have been closed around Jace, and he pulled Kyrin into his arms, holding her securely. He wasn't even sorry to be glad Davira was dead. Someone so evil was too dangerous to be kept alive, and he was thankful never to have to fear her trying to harm Kyrin or his baby ever again.

As they pulled apart, Kyrin looked up at him with a tired but joyful smile that erased the gloom from before. "You should tell Rayad. He'll be so happy."

Jace smiled, too, thankful to push aside thoughts of Davira and the fear of knowing he had not one but two major vulnerabilities now. "I will when I get the chance."

"I want to tell Kaden and Marcus so bad, but I really should wait until Liam is here, at least. And just so you know, Elanor and Anne know. Cassie too. Actually, Elanor and Anne figured it out before I did. Pregnancy symptoms are something I know frightfully little about."

Jace grinned to think of his sister figuring it out and the joy it must have brought her. He couldn't wait until they could share a moment of celebration.

Kyrin tipped her head with a thoughtful expression. "Judging by how he looked at me yesterday, I think it's safe to assume Daniel knows too. Elanor probably told him after we were captured. It would have been painful to bear alone, especially believing we would probably be killed."

Jace winced now. Surely Elanor had received word they were all alive and well. He would hate for her to have to worry longer than necessary.

A knock at the door drew their attention, and Jace answered it. This time it was Leetra.

"I came to change bandages if you're not busy and to tell you Holden is awake. He asked about you."

Jace stepped back to let her into the room and looked down the hall as he closed the door, anxious to check on his friend.

Kyrin gestured to him when he turned back toward her. "Change Jace's bandages first so he can go see him."

He sent her a grateful look. She always cared so much about how he was feeling.

Once Leetra had cleaned his wounds, which were no longer inflamed and oozing, and applied the fresh ointment and bandages, he walked down to Holden's room. No one else was present for the moment, and Holden looked like he might be asleep again. However, his eyes opened as Jace approached the bed and took a seat in the chair someone had placed next to it.

Though his face was still pale and bruised, Holden smiled. "Leetra said you were well. I'm glad to see it."

"And you."

Holden shifted and winced but then settled comfortably. "Well, a drake was a good try, but it'll take more than that to kill us."

Jace released a short laugh, glad he could do such a thing. Those days in the arena had been so bleak that any happiness now almost felt too good to be true.

Holden took a slow breath, which Jace imagined wasn't pleasant with his injuries. Bruised ribs were bad enough. "I hear both Davira and Richard are dead."

"Yes."

"What's happening now?"

"I'm not sure exactly. Kyrin and I have been asleep since yesterday. I think we're just waiting to see if the Arcacian army surrenders." If not, the city would soon be under siege, and a bloody battle would be waged just beyond the walls. Jace shook that thought away. He should focus on the present and the blessing of still being alive.

Holden nodded against his pillow. His gaze then locked on Jace, a grin growing on his lips. "So you're going to be a father."

Jace flashed a smile. Even now, he could hardly grasp the realness of it. "Yes."

"You'll be a great father." Just as quickly as the grin had sprung up, it faded, and Holden's eyes took on a more serious, questioning look. "Leetra said Kyrin was all right, but is she?"

"I think so. She's with Leetra now, so I'm sure she'll ask questions."

Still, Jace worried now that he was thinking about it. What if the trauma of the last few days had harmed the baby? They could lose their child without ever getting to meet it properly.

Kyrin joined them a few minutes later, and fear darted through Jace's stomach. Would she bring any bad news after talking to Leetra? He watched her closely for any signs of distress, but the soft smile on her face eased some of the apprehension. He got up to let her have his chair and stood beside it. After she greeted and exchanged a few words with Holden, he put his hand on her shoulder.

"How is everything?"

She smiled up at him and clasped his hand. "Everything seems fine. Leetra just said I should rest, eat well, and avoid stress as much as possible going forward."

Whatever it took to make that happen, Jace would do it.

DANIEL KNEW HE needed to rest at some point. He'd barely slept since they'd taken Fort Rhall, but there was just so much to do. Half the time, he wasn't even sure where to begin. How did one just step into the role of a king after such a tumultuous time? Thankfully, there had been no unrest in the city. Instead, Aric reported that dozens of people were showing up at the gate, leaving flowers and waving hastily constructed gold and blue flags. At least a large portion of the population seemed happy with his return. Hopefully, they would find the same to be true for the army.

Taking a break from the logistical nightmare of trying to operate the palace with only the small number of staff members Mister Foss had vouched for, he headed to his mother's room. After all, it didn't matter if the palace essentially ran like a glorified camp right now. Eventually, things would settle and run more smoothly.

His mother was awake this time, unlike when he'd checked on her early this morning. Leetra stood at her bedside, along with Mira. Daniel praised Elôm that she and Ben had not been executed in the arena. Instead of returning to their homes for much-needed rest, the two of them had remained here with everyone. And despite the nightmare they must have lived, Mira had even stepped right in to help, putting herself to work in the kitchen so that everyone had enough to eat this morning. Trust her to see to his mother's welfare, too, even though they'd never even met before. A tray sat on the side table with some fruit and a mostly empty bowl of broth, so she must have brought food up for her.

Daniel stopped at the foot of the bed and gripped the corner post closest to Leetra, who was packing her supplies. "How is she?"

"No worse."

He couldn't detect any concern in her voice and considered the lack of change a good thing.

Slipping her bag over her shoulder, Leetra turned for the door. "I'll check back again later. Let me know if you need anything."

Across the bed, Mira picked up the tray and gave Daniel a probing look. "Did you eat? I sent Trev with a tray for you."

He smiled at her mothering ways. "I did. Thank you. And while I appreciate everything you've done to help, you really should be resting."

Mira propped the tray on her hip and shook her head. "I like to keep busy."

"Even so, you were a captive for weeks. Please, take the time to rest. You and Ben both. I'll go down to the kitchen and make everyone food myself if that's what it takes. I won't have you overtaxing yourself."

Mira waved her hand dismissively, but Daniel sent her what he hoped was an authoritative look. She had always been a very healthy weight with a lovely glow to her olive complexion, but her face was far too thin and pale right now. He wasn't about to have her fall ill on him due to her sacrificial nature.

He must have succeeded because her expression changed, allowing some of her true weariness to break through and line her face. "All right, I'll rest."

"Good."

Once she was gone, hopefully to find Ben and a soft bed, Daniel turned his attention fully to his mother. He took a seat next to her, careful not to jostle her too much. Even so, she grimaced and breathed out slowly. He put his hand on her arm. "Are you in a lot of pain?"

She didn't respond at first but then nodded. She was one of the strongest women Daniel knew, so any reaction spoke volumes.

"Leetra gave me something for it. It just needs to kick in."

He prayed it would work quickly. It was hard to see her in such pain. "Well, she's an excellent physician, so I'm sure it will help."

"I know your father and sister had dealings with some of them, but she's the first crete I've met."

"She can be a bit rough around the edges, which I guess is probably normal for most cretes, but she takes her role seriously. I'm thankful she's here to look after you. I wouldn't want to lose you now that I'm back home."

Her tense features smoothed a bit, and she patted his hand. "You won't lose me. I don't intend to let your sister succeed in her attempt to hurt you."

So stabbing their mother had been Davira's last-ditch effort at causing him pain, not just because she'd helped Kyrin. He ground his teeth together. Part of him was very glad Davira was already dead. He would have had a difficult time making a decision about what to do with her that wasn't guided by his emotions.

The same emotions must have shown on his face because his mother squeezed his hand this time. "I'll be fine. Now, tell me more about Elanor."

With this prompting, the acidic burn that had risen in his chest died, and what must have been a pretty sappy smile took over his face. He was more than happy to talk about his wife to distract his mother from her pain and his thoughts toward Davira.

"As I've said, you'll love her. She has a joy about her that's contagious. It's been a hard year, and even though I've still had to be a prince, getting to know her outside of the palace and royal life was an incredible blessing. I never imagined I'd get to experience a normal relationship like that." He laughed a little. "I even had to work up the courage to ask her rather intimidating older brother for his blessing both in courting her and then to marry her."

Mother laughed quietly with him but then frowned. "I didn't know her brother was part of your resistance. When did he join you?"

"Oh, that's right. You wouldn't know. I'm actually talking about Jace, not James. It's a long story, but he is Elanor and James's older brother."

Now Mother's brows lifted. "The half-blood?"

Daniel hoped she wouldn't find that distasteful—or at least would grow to understand ryriks weren't the monsters they'd once believed they were. "Yes, he's my brother-in-law now, which means he and Kyrin are both family. I'm not sure what Father would have to say to that."

"Oh, he would have something."

They laughed again, but it seemed to cause her pain this time, so they stopped short. In the silence that followed, sadness ghosted across her expression. An ache built in Daniel's chest. His exile had come so quickly after his father's death, and she'd had to deal with it alone.

"I'm sorry you were here all alone through everything. I know how much you must miss him. We rarely agreed on anything, but I never truly hated him. I know he loved you and was a good husband to you. That is one thing I do commend him for, and I'm sorry you lost that."

It was one of the only times he'd ever seen his mother get teary outside of the night his father had died. He couldn't quite imagine the true extent of what she had endured, losing her spouse only to watch one of her children turn on the other and then try to kill her on top of it.

Before he could say more, Trev came to the door. "I'm sorry to interrupt, but our messenger has returned. He's waiting in the throne room."

A messenger meant news about the army. The past twenty-four hours of waiting for word had put Daniel on edge. One way or another, it would be good to know what was coming next.

He bent down to give his mother a quick kiss on the forehead. "Duty calls."

He hurried downstairs to the throne room with Trev. Several others had gathered there, including Jace. He seemed well, considering. If he was here and not glued to Kyrin's side, hopefully, that meant she was too. He'd have to ask, but right now, his attention focused on the Landale Rider standing with Kaden and Marcus.

They all turned when they noticed him coming, and the rider gave a quick bow.

"My lord, the Arcacian forces broke camp early this morning. If they've already started marching, we estimate them to arrive here at the city sometime tomorrow morning. As requested, our army will follow."

This was what they had been waiting for. Whether peaceful or violent, tomorrow's confrontation would determine if he had succeeded in avoiding catastrophic bloodshed.

Kaden jerked his thumb over his shoulder. "I've sent a couple of riders out to monitor their progress. We'll have ample warning before they arrive."

"Good." Daniel turned to Marcus. "Double the guard at the main gates. As soon as the army is near, I want every gate closed and secured until we know how this will go. I also want all of our forces at the wall at that time. If the worst happens, and they decide to besiege the city, we'll need to hold the gates until the rest of our army can aid us."

Though their force was small, Marcus's steady voice carried confidence. "We'll be ready."

"Elôm willing, they'll surrender, and I'll negotiate terms. Most of the army will be dismissed to Fort Rivor until loyalties can be established. I want the generals and highest-ranking commanders to remain here at the fort so I can meet with them. They'll not be held prisoner, but I do want them to surrender their weapons until I have their allegiance."

Though Marcus waited quietly until Daniel finished, he wore a rather determined look. "With all due respect, my lord, you can't leave the palace. Not after everything we've managed to accomplish. I fully support your decisions to get us here, but this is where, as your general, I have to insist you step back. Now is when we have to protect you at all cost. I will oversee the surrender. That is what I am here for."

Daniel's first reaction was to argue—old, rebellious tendencies still more a part of him than he'd realized until this moment. But Marcus was right, of course. Daniel had accomplished what Elôm had led him to do to stop Davira, but now he had to step back and let those around him do their jobs while he did his. Even if that did mean staying out of the action. It wasn't easy after a year of unparalleled freedom, but it was time now to be their king, not their exiled prince.

"You're right. I will leave tomorrow's negotiations in your hands."

The barest smile on Marcus's face hinted at both relief and respect. "I will do whatever I can to ensure it ends peaceably."

Jace waited until Daniel had finished discussing the army with Marcus before approaching him. He hadn't wanted to leave Kyrin, but this was important. If he succeeded, maybe it would help dispel a little of the clinging darkness that had caused her nightmare this morning. Daniel offered a welcoming smile when he noticed him, though weariness seemed to weigh on it. Jace didn't envy all the burdens he carried now. Though he hated that Elanor would have similar burdens, he found himself wishing she were here already to help Daniel. He could probably use her cheerful presence.

"Jace, I hope you were able to rest well. Is there anything you need?"

He didn't want to add yet another burden, but he hoped his request would be simple. "I did, thank you. And there is something I wanted to ask."

"Anything."

The fact that Daniel didn't even hesitate when he already had so much on his mind made Jace realize just how much he appreciated his kindness toward him, even when his own feelings hadn't always been the most charitable. Daniel had never once used his rank to dismiss or diminish him. "I was wondering if I could look through Davira's rooms. She took something from Kyrin when we first arrived. She may have destroyed it, but I need to know for sure."

"Of course. I can take you up there now."

Daniel motioned to him, and they left the throne room. On the way upstairs, he glanced at him. "What is it we're looking for?"

"Kyrin's stone necklace." Jace's mind flashed back to the first time he'd seen it, that painful day on the mountain not far from here. The first time he'd seen Kyrin break. "It was her father's. Davira threatened to destroy it, but I'm hoping she didn't have the time."

Daniel's jaw clenched, a hard frown furrowing his forehead.

Upstairs, they passed the spot where Davira's body had lain. A tarp covered the bloodstained carpet, blocked off by a couple of chairs. Someone would have their work cut out for them, trying to clean it.

Daniel stopped at a door a couple down from the royal suite and opened it. They both stepped inside, pausing. The room was dim, the heavy drapes half drawn across the windows, and a bone-numbing cold seemed to linger as if Davira were still present. Chilly pinpricks crawled along Jace's skin, and he tried to shake it off, reminding himself she was very much dead. Still, the last thing he wanted was to rifle through her belongings. He felt like he might be defiled just touching something. But he had to try to find that necklace.

He glanced at Daniel. The way his face scrunched and he leaned toward the door like he wanted to back out said he was just as uneasy and repulsed by the space.

"I haven't set foot in this room since I was a small child. I valued my life far too highly for such a risk."

Jace didn't blame him, especially when Davira had still been alive.

Pushing past the discomfort, they spread out to either side of the room. Jace started by scanning the top of one of the dressers, only touching things if he absolutely had to. It was cluttered with jewelry and other odd trinkets. Kyrin's necklace could easily get lost in the mess. A cloying scent of perfume wafted up around him. He choked, his stomach rolling. While he hadn't noticed it at the time, Davira had been wearing that same scent when she'd had him taken to the arena. He fought to calm the way his heart started to race.

"I tried to help him escape."

Jace's attention snapped to Daniel. He was staring off toward one of the windows as if lost in thought. Shoulders drooping, he looked at Jace.

"Kyrin's father. I was going to try to get him out through the hidden gate behind the temple, but the guards had orders not to allow anyone in the dungeon, not even me. My father caught me and confined me to my room before I could figure out another way." He hung his head and shook it. "I wish he was here now. He and Marcus would have made an excellent team."

That they would have. The quiet sadness in his voice ached inside Jace. If only Daniel had succeeded. It felt so wrong that Jace's family was finally coming together when Kyrin's would never be complete. But he had to remind himself that if William hadn't died for his faith, Marcus might still be part of the army marching toward them.

He cleared his throat, forcing his voice past the clog lodged there. "I never got to know him nearly as well as I wish I had."

Daniel raised his head again. This time, a faint smile broke through the sorrow. "He and Kyrin are a lot alike. He was one of the only people I knew back then who treated me as more than just the prince. He treated me as a person."

Jace had to swallow hard again to speak. "Me too."

Blinking back the sting in his eyes, he refocused on the search. Several silent minutes passed as they dug through Davira's things. Jace was starting to lose hope when Daniel spoke up again. "Is this it?"

Jace spun around. Daniel stood at Davira's dressing table, a simple, blue stone pendant hanging from his fingers. Jace hurried over to him and reached for it, letting out a huge breath once it rested in his hand.

"Yes. Thank you." He wound up the leather cord and wrapped his fingers securely around the necklace, his heart whispering a prayer of thanks. "Kyrin will be overjoyed."

Daniel was smiling, though it started to fade after a moment. "How is she this morning?"

Maybe it was from being around Kyrin so much, but Jace picked up something deeper and more probing about his tone that went beyond that simple question. He recalled his conversation with Kyrin just a bit ago. At least this was one burden Jace could remove from Daniel's mind.

"As far as Leetra can tell, the baby is fine. We're just praying now that it remains that way."

A breath whooshed from Daniel's chest, his shoulders sagging as if Jace had indeed lifted a weight from them. "I didn't want to ask, but I was worried. When Elanor told me after you were captured…" He grimaced and shook his head, likely shaking away thoughts of what could have been. "I've lost multiple nieces or nephews to Davira's depravity over the last few years. I did not want this to be another. If there is *anything* Kyrin needs, just let me know. I will see that she gets it."

KYRIN RELAXED IN a comfortable chair next to the window and looked down into the back courtyard of the palace. The garden appeared to be in full bloom, splashes of vivid color accenting the green foliage. Maybe, when Jace returned from checking in with the others, they could go for a walk. She could use some fresh air. It would help distract her from her churning stomach. She was starting to regret eating so much, even if she did need the food. Though she'd kept it down so far, the threat of losing her breakfast was still very real. Leetra needed to hurry with the tea she said would help.

Thankfully, she arrived a couple of minutes later, carrying a tray. Behind her followed a young woman with cinnamon-colored hair tucked neatly into a white cap. Kyrin started in recognition. "Holly."

Her former maid from when she'd worked here at the palace gave her a bright and gentle smile, though it wasn't quite as shy as Kyrin remembered. "Miss Kyrin, I brought another change of clothes for when you need them. I know the dresses are rather plain, but they are the best I have besides my uniforms."

Kyrin took the clothing from her, her words caught in the shock of seeing such a familiar face from her past. She hadn't considered others she might see here at the palace beyond Collin.

So that's where Daniel had managed to dig up clothing that would fit her when all of her belongings were still back at Fort Rhall. She shook her voice loose and returned Holly's smile.

"Don't worry. I've been living in the forest for three years. Plain is what I'm used to. Thank you for sharing with me."

"My pleasure, my lady. And I'd be happy to take any laundry that needs washing."

Kyrin glanced at the pile of dirty clothes she and Jace had left in the corner. "Well, I must warn you, after several days in the dungeon, it's pretty rank. Some might not even be salvageable."

"Don't worry, I'll take care of it."

Holly scooped up the pile without hesitation. She turned for the door but then paused and faced Kyrin once more. "If I may, I wanted you to know after you defied the emperor, it made me want to learn more about Elôm. Because of your bravery, my whole family and I, as well as a few of the other servants, have become believers since then."

Tears prickled Kyrin's eyes, and a weight pressed on her lungs. That day in the temple had set off a massive chain of events, many painful and difficult to bear. But, as always, Elôm had worked it all together for good, not just in her own life but in others'. "You are the brave ones, having lived and worked here all this time."

Holly ducked her head and shrugged. "Still, thank you for standing up for your beliefs and for fighting to free us all. It helped us have courage here." She backed toward the door. "I will let you rest now. I just wanted to tell you."

She bobbed a quick curtsy and left the room. Jace walked in right after, sending a questioning glance back her way. When his gaze settled on Kyrin, everything about him became both fearful and protective, as he must have seen the lingering tears in her eyes. "What's wrong?"

"Nothing. That was Holly. She was my maid when I lived here. I always had so much regret that I never shared my faith with her, but she just told me that she and her family turned to Elôm after I defied Daican."

His concern melted into a smile, the warmth of it washing over her. "You do inspire people."

Kyrin found herself blushing, which only made Jace's smile grow. Before they could get too carried away, Leetra handed her a cup of the tea. Kyrin accepted it gladly, ignoring the raised brow Leetra shot at both her and Jace. She'd been distracted from her nausea while talking to Holly, but it returned now with a vengeance. She took a small sip, praying it would stay down and she wouldn't have to scramble for the chamber pot she'd been eyeing by the bed. The tea tasted distinctly of peppermint, laced with notes of other herbs and honey to sweeten it.

Leetra pointed to the teapot on the tray. "There's more if you need it."

Kyrin thanked her, and then she left rather quickly, probably to give them privacy before they got all sappy again. Jace closed the door behind her, and Kyrin sank back down in her chair with a sigh. She hadn't been up for very long, but weariness had already crept in again. She took another sip of tea and watched Jace. There was something about his demeanor, like he was holding something in or trying to hide something. At first, fear that something was wrong stirred up the nausea, but he seemed too calm for that, and she forced herself to relax.

"What's going on?"

Now a satisfied little smile crept to his lips. "I was going to wait until you were feeling a little better…"

Kyrin shrugged. "Well, I'm not actively losing the contents of my stomach, and a distraction might help."

His smile grew, and she realized he held something in his closed fist. She momentarily set her cup aside as he stepped closer and knelt in front of her. When he opened his hand, her gaze locked on the familiar blue stone and leather cord lying in his palm. Tears gushed into her eyes again, and she reached for it, hardly daring to breathe. "You found it!"

"Daniel helped."

Her hand trembled as she picked it up, a cascade of memories so quick to rush in. A couple of tears dribbled down her cheeks. The necklace could never bring her father back, but it had become such a precious symbol of his love. Her heart had ached to think she'd never see it again.

"Thank you."

Jace nodded and then took it from her to help her bind it around her neck where it belonged. She clutched it to her chest and let a few final memories filter through her mind before Jace bent down and obliterated them with a kiss.

Jace breathed in deeply the salty evening air. He still couldn't decide if he liked it or not. It certainly couldn't beat the refreshing earthiness of a forest. Still, any sort of fresh air was a welcome reprieve from being inside. Though he and Kyrin had taken a walk around the gardens earlier, it wasn't enough to satisfy the restlessness that always nagged at him when stuck indoors. Though the palace was big enough for one to get lost in it, it still felt claustrophobic inside.

So, he made his way through the garden again, wandering amongst the fountains and carefully cultivated greenery. He would have much preferred the forest to the cobblestoned courtyard, but at least he had the wide open sky overhead and could listen to the nighttime insects begin their chirping. He longed to get back to simpler life and prayed that, after tomorrow, it would finally be within reach.

He hadn't been wandering around for long before familiar footsteps approached. He stopped and turned to let Rayad catch up to him. Jace had barely seen him since they'd taken the palace. Everyone had been so busy helping Daniel, and Jace hadn't wanted to leave Kyrin's side. Even now, the itch to make sure she was safe almost drove him back inside, but he told himself to trust Elôm and the men standing guard.

Rayad smiled at him, and the depth of it revealed just how thankful he was that Jace was safe. "Kyrin told me you were out here."

"She insisted she would be fine by herself and sent me out to get some air."

Rayad's low chuckle was a soothing sound. "She does tend to know you better than you know yourself at times."

Jace couldn't argue with that. It had been true since the moment they'd met.

Silence settled between them. Rayad just studied him, searching his eyes like he was trying to determine something before finally speaking in a somber tone. "How are you doing? I know you had to fight again."

Jace took a moment to consider the weighty question. He couldn't just shrug it off. Rayad was the one who had rescued him from slavery as a gladiator—witnessed what it had made him—and understood how much he had feared ever being thrown into that world again. But, in truth, he was nothing like the broken, scared boy he'd been back then. This time he hadn't had to face his fears alone.

"Better than I would've expected." It felt good to say that. To see clearly how he had changed and how his faith and those around him had given him a strength he hadn't possessed in his past life. "When Davira first told me I was going to fight, I panicked. I still feel it when I think of that day. I was so uncertain and was prepared to die rather than fight again, but in the arena, I felt Elôm tell me to defend myself. I hate that I had to fight, but I don't carry the guilt I used to."

Rayad reached up to grip his shoulder. "Good. You shouldn't."

Jace drew another deep breath to keep the emotions and the horrors of the arena from weighing too heavily. "I lost the last fight." It was the only fight he had ever lost. "The gladiator who defeated me was the same man I fought the day you rescued me. I couldn't believe it when I recognized him. Because I let him live that day, he came to know Elôm, and he, in turn, defied Davira to let me live. She had him killed for it."

If Jace carried any guilt over the days in the arena, it was for that. But he also knew it was out of his control. If Elôm hadn't placed that man there at that moment, Jace would be dead, and Kyrin would have been left to bear and raise their child without him. For that reason, he would be forever thankful to the man for sparing his life at the cost of his own.

"I'm sorry," Rayad murmured.

Jace would always regret what had happened, but at least the man's eternal future had been secure. If only Jace had known his name so he could be properly honored and remembered. Perhaps he could still find out, though that would mean asking around in the gladiator community. With that came the risk of running into an old nemesis once more.

"I also saw Jasper."

Rayad's eyes turned flinty, his tone carrying a sharp edge. "He's here in Valcré?"

"Yes. I had to fight two of his men. He came to my cell beforehand to gloat, I guess." It hadn't been pleasant, but he knew he'd come out the victor. "Thanks to you—your faith in me, your persistence, guiding me to Elôm—I was able to face him and not falter."

Rayad's smile returned, softening some of the lines Jace was sure had come from caring for him the last few years. "I'm glad,

Jace. I'm so proud of the man you've become. I give all the praise to Elôm."

"You still responded to His will. You could've just ridden away when you saw Jasper beating me, and you could've let me run off so many times, but you never gave up on me."

Rayad's eyes turned a little watery, and so did Jace's, but he pressed on because of the news he had to share. "Your persistence enabled me to become someone I never thought I could be. To become the kind of man who, though still terrified, is prepared to soon be a father."

Rayad's eyes widened on the last word, his mouth opening, but no response came for a long moment. At last, he managed, "Kyrin is…"

Jace swallowed hard to loosen his throat and nodded. "We're going to have a baby."

The tears filled Rayad's eyes, making Jace's water all the more. Apparently incapable of words, Rayad dragged him into his arms, and Jace returned the embrace. Now the tears did fall, the relief, the joy, the thankfulness all overwhelming him at once. From the arenas of his past to this moment was a miracle of love he couldn't begin to adequately thank Elôm for.

In all the years he'd known him, Jace had only seen Rayad cry actual tears a couple of times, but he was wiping them from his face as they parted.

Jace smiled, wiping his own face. "This makes you a grandfather, and I don't know anyone who will do a better job of it."

Rayad's eyes twinkled, still misty. "I look forward to every moment of it."

THE CRISPNESS OF the early morning almost crackled with a current of anticipation running through every single person gathered at the main gate. It coursed through Marcus's taut muscles. He knew as soon as he stepped foot outside the city, he would see the army approaching in the distance. Would they even stop to negotiate, or would they attack the moment they reached the city? It was up to him to find out.

He turned to the horse one of his men had brought to him and checked the saddle. While he was sure it was already secure, it gave him something to do in these final moments of preparation. Footsteps tapped the cobblestone behind him. He looked over his shoulder to find Kaden suited up for battle if that's what it came to. Marcus shifted to face him, and Kaden eyed his uniform before meeting his gaze.

"Ready?"

Marcus tamped down the apprehension that quaked somewhere deep inside him and threatened to elevate his heart rate. His duty was to push aside his emotions and be the leader his men and his king expected him to be. "Yes."

Kaden studied him again as if he could sense what Marcus hid beneath his soldier exterior. After all, Kaden would always see him as his brother, not as a general. If he was thinking of questioning Marcus, he must have thought better of it. A smirk claimed his face.

"Well, Rhune and I will be watching. You know, just in case they don't play fair."

Marcus laughed, and a little of the tension inside of him released. Kaden had said almost the same thing their first time in Samara. In fact, with the Militia lined up along Valcré's walls, it did remind him of when he'd ridden out with King Balen and others to parley with the General. He had no doubt the General would again head up negotiations today. Whether that would be a help or a hindrance, he had yet to determine. His grandfather seemed to have softened while in their captivity, but that could very well have changed in the last few weeks now that he was back amongst his allies.

Marcus clapped Kaden's uninjured shoulder. "Thanks for watching my back."

"Always."

With that, they parted, and Marcus led his horse to where the rest of their leaders gathered at the gate. Captain Darq, General Mason, Prince Haedrin, General Torva, and Saul had all flown in just before dawn while they still had the cover of darkness. They truly would present a united Ilyon to the Arcacian army, provided they chose to parley. And every one of them was looking to him to lead.

He drew a steadying breath and swept his gaze over them. "Let's ride out."

As one, they mounted their horses. Parker walked up to him and handed him the parley flag. Marcus grasped the sturdy pole and nodded his thanks before touching his heels to his horse's sides and moving to the head of the group. Some of the militia-men opened the gate before him, and he led the way out of the city. There, he looked to the north, where thousands of Arcacian soldiers stretched into the horizon. It wouldn't be long now before they would either attack or send their own delegation to parley.

He urged his horse on about a hundred yards and stopped on neutral ground between the city and the army. The others fanned out on either side of him. He lifted the parley flag high and let it unfurl, bracing the end of the pole on his stirrup. The flag caught the breeze and rippled lazily.

To his right, General Mason leaned on the pommel of his saddle. "So what's the plan if they just keep marching toward us and don't send anyone to talk?"

Marcus glanced at the wall where the Landale Dragon Riders perched. "Then you will all fall back to the city. I'll hold out as long as possible, and Kaden and his men can cover my retreat."

He wanted to be absolutely sure there was no possible chance of negotiation before he gave up on peace.

On the opposite side of Marcus, Captain Darq shifted in his saddle like he wished he was on his dragon instead and gave the army long consideration. "It is promising that they don't have any drakes in the air. If they intended to fight, you'd think the beasts would be circling."

Marcus prayed he was right, but his tension began to build again as the minutes dragged by. The army drew steadily closer, the rumble of marching feet carrying toward them and rising in volume. He was just beginning to calculate how long he would wait before he gave the others the order to retreat when the army finally stopped about half a mile off. A little too close for his liking. His hands were getting tacky around the flag pole and his reins.

Another few minutes of tense silence stretched out until, at long last, he spied a black and white parley flag emerge from the opposing army. Only two riders approached. Even at a distance, Marcus recognized the General's tall figure. He handed the parley flag to General Mason and nudged his horse a couple of paces beyond the others.

The riders quickly closed the gap between them. The General sat straight and imposing upon his horse, much more reminiscent of the man Marcus had always known as opposed to the captive he'd guarded through the winter. And yet, Marcus struggled to detect the usual arrogance his grandfather had once exuded. In this, he found a glimmer of hope.

For a moment, only the creak of the saddles and a couple of the horses chomping their bits broke the waiting silence. Gathering his fortitude, Marcus let his voice ring out.

"I speak on behalf of King Daniel, rightful heir of the Arcacian throne. Davira is dead and can no longer terrorize those around her or take vengeance on those who have no true desire to uphold her will. We hold the city and wish to avoid any further bloodshed. This fight has gone on long enough."

The General's gaze swept past Marcus, over the other leaders, and then to the walls of the city. Finally, it slid back to Marcus, and his grandfather dipped his chin in the smallest hint of a nod. "And what terms do you offer for surrender?"

"Arcacia's army, along with its captains and lieutenants, is to march peacefully from here to Fort Rivor as King Daniel's authority is established. All generals and other commanders are to remain here at the fort so King Daniel may meet with them at an appointed time to determine loyalty and establish allegiance. You will not be prisoners, but we do require you to surrender your weapons. We only wish now for a peaceful transition."

An echoing silence followed Marcus's words, and the General just stared at him. If only Marcus could figure out what thoughts or calculations might be brewing behind the General's stony eyes. Was he trying to intimidate him? Or was he deciding how best to take the city? Kyrin's abilities would have come in handy at that moment, but he was glad she was safe at the palace. For now, anyway.

Then Marcus caught a slight softening in his grandfather's expression just before he spoke.

"I accept your terms." Was that a note of relief in the General's voice?

Or perhaps Marcus was only projecting his own relief, though he maintained a cool and composed front. Inside, his heart was racing against his chainmail and breastplate.

The General shifted, glancing back at the vast amount of men he commanded. "I will gather the commanding officers and send the rest of the army to Fort Rivor. They will pose no trouble."

Marcus nodded, careful to maintain a professional tone despite feeling a little breathless. "As soon as the army is on its way, the officers will be escorted into the city to the fort, where provisions and lodging will be provided until King Daniel can meet with them."

"As you command…General."

So word of his promotion had reached the Arcacian army. Hearing such words from his grandfather's mouth, spoken without derision or spite, stole the rest of the air from Marcus's lungs. They rang in his mind as his grandfather turned his horse and rode back toward the army. An army that would soon march away peacefully. No fighting. No slaughter.

Tears burned the back of his throat and up into his eyes. His composure slipped, a choked laugh breaking from his chest. He turned to face the others and found them grinning at each other with a joy so great and so pure it was as if the sun had just burst through the clouds after a raging storm. The struggles, and the suffering, and the pain that had drawn them all together over the last three years had finally ended.

They had won.

The unbridled air of celebration that permeated the palace was something Daniel had never experienced in all the years he'd lived there. The moment he, Aric, and the others who'd remained safely at Auréa had received word of the army's peaceful surrender, cheers and laughter erupted, and even some tears were shed. Elôm had brought them victory. Now the army had left for Fort Rivor, the officers were secure at the fort, and their allies were setting up camp outside the city, further ensuring the peace. Daniel had found himself doubting their success more than he cared to admit, but it was done.

Of course, it brought a whole slew of new challenges on his part, but he welcomed it if it meant an end to the bloodshed and terror. And today was a day to revel in the victory. He just needed one thing now to fully celebrate—his bride. He'd been just a tad jealous of how Jace had swept Kyrin into his arms and kissed her in the joy of the moment. He wanted to share the same joy with Elanor. Even just the four days they'd been apart felt like an eternity. Perhaps that was a bit dramatic, but he was still a newlywed after all.

Therefore, he didn't feel the least bit embarrassed as he paced in front of the palace doors, impatiently waiting for her to arrive with the other leaders. The palace would be their home from now on, so he wanted to be there the moment she arrived to show her inside. Each minute dragged by torturously, and he caught Aric giving him a little smirk. Daniel was going to remember that when Lydia Altair showed up. He hadn't failed to notice how reluctant the two of them had been to say goodbye when they'd left Landale over two months ago.

At long last, approaching footsteps came from outside the gate, and Daniel felt a little like a child again, anticipating a grand event. A few moments later, the guards allowed a large group to enter, escorted by soldiers from each of their armies. Daniel hurried down the steps to meet them. He'd been waiting for this moment since they had taken the palace. The soldiers parted, allowing their leaders through. Daniel couldn't hold back the grin that sprang to his lips when he spotted Elanor in the crowd. Her searching gaze caught his, and the same joy and excitement radiated from her smile.

All he wanted was to shove through everyone to reach her, but a romantic reunion would have to wait. Everyone seemed to surge forward at once to offer congratulations and share in the spirit of victory. For some, like Balen and Prince Haedrin, that meant hearty back-slapping and laughter. Others, like General Torva, were more composed yet no less pleased.

While Daniel tried to engage with everyone, his gaze constantly darted to Elanor, following her progress until she finally worked her way to his side. He had to fight the overwhelming urge to gather her into his arms and kiss her. As much as he envied Jace's freedom, the time had come for him to be the responsible king they'd all fought so hard to see him become. Though he was sure no one would blame him for being distracted by his wife, this was a once-in-a-lifetime moment. He wanted to do it right.

As the flutter of celebration quieted a bit, he ushered Elanor along with him and climbed a couple of steps. Here, he turned to face the gathering, and everyone fell silent, all eyes on him.

"I can't tell you what it means to me to see all of you here as friends and allies. Never in my lifetime, or my father's, or even my grandfather's, has Ilyon ever been this united. This victory would not have been possible without you, and I will do everything in my power to see that what we've accomplished here lasts for generations. For too long, the rulers of Arcacia turned old allies into enemies, but now, as its new ruler, I just want to say, welcome to Auréa."

An exuberant cheer burst forth, swelling inside Daniel's chest. It was at that moment victory truly sank in, and with it, an overwhelming peace. He was exactly where he belonged and where Elôm wanted him.

Reveling in this certainty, Daniel finally turned his undivided attention to Elanor.

"And you"—he offered her his arm—"welcome home."

She wrapped her hand around his arm with a wondrous smile, and he drew her close as he led her and the others up the steps and into the palace. He watched the look of awe claim her expression as she slowly took in the massive foyer, her eyes drawn upward to the towering ceiling before settling on the winding central staircase. She may have come from a wealthy home, but nothing could compare to the magnificence of Auréa.

He leaned in to murmur in her ear. "I'm sure it's over-whelming, but just think of all the children we could have running around in all this space."

A smile jumped back to her lips, and her cheeks turned pink. Nothing would make him happier than having a large family with her. He prayed that they and however many children Elôm blessed them with would fill this palace with a kind of love and faith it probably hadn't seen in many generations. The kind of love that could erase the pain and fear that had taken residence here for too long.

A bit of chaos followed as Daniel worked with Aric to arrange rooms for everyone. They still didn't have a full working staff to handle such matters, but they had it sorted out before too long. At least with the armies here, they had extra soldiers to rotate on guard duty and patrols so the Militia could take a well-deserved rest.

The moment things seemed settled and no one was looking, Daniel grabbed Elanor's hand and tugged her with him as he ducked out of the hall of the guest wing. She didn't ask questions, just giggled as he whisked her toward the family wing of the palace like they were a pair of love-struck teenagers. When they arrived, he checked that the coast was clear and pulled her into his room. There he finally kissed her like he'd been dying to for the past half an hour.

When they did eventually break the kiss, he stared down at her, running his fingers over her face. If he had it his way, they'd never be apart again.

Her eyes crinkled mischievously. "So, is this our life now? Having to sneak off for time alone?"

"Unfortunately, probably. At least until things are more settled." He matched her little grin with a playful look of his own. "Good thing I know many secret areas to sneak off to."

Her cheeks flushed again, and he had every intention of kissing her some more, but her attention shifted to the area around them. "Is this your room?"

"Yes, it is." He glanced around with a critical eye, realizing he hadn't kept it particularly tidy over the last couple of days. Oh well. "Our room, for the time being, though I'm sure my mother will have us moved into the royal suite as soon as she can. Thank Elôm Davira never moved into it. Her room will have to be scrubbed from top to bottom just to get rid of her presence."

Elanor's nose wrinkled. "I hope your mother won't mind being displaced. Where is she?"

"Well, she's resting. Davira stabbed her when we were just about to take the palace."

Elanor sucked in a breath, her expression morphing into one of true concern. "Oh, I'm sorry. Is she all right?"

"I think she will be, despite Davira's efforts to the contrary. She hasn't taken any turn for the worse, so Leetra is hopeful." Daniel took her hands. "I know this is all a lot, but do you want to go meet her? I'd like you two to get to know each other…just in case."

"Of course, I'll meet her." She shrugged, and it was the first time he picked up a trace of uncertainty since she'd arrived. "I just hope she isn't too upset about our rushed wedding."

Daniel shook his head and squeezed her hands. "Not at all. I told her all about it, and she's very happy for us. In fact, she thinks it's a good thing I married before taking the throne."

Keeping hold of one of her hands, he led her out of his room and down the hall to the royal suite. He opened the door quietly in case his mother was asleep but saw her lady's maid sitting with her. Mother was propped up in bed for the first time since she'd been stabbed and looked a little less pale than the last couple of days, a very encouraging sign.

The maid rose and curtsied as they approached before turning briefly to his mother. "I will return in a little while."

She then slipped out of the room to allow them privacy.

Daniel studied his mother. "You're looking better."

Her smile held more strength than in previous days. "I feel better. I don't think you have cause to worry anymore."

Daniel breathed out a sigh. "Thank Elôm."

Mother did not make any attempt to contradict him. She almost seemed to nod in agreement. It gave him a fresh burst of hope that, given time, she would come to share his faith. Her attention then shifted to Elanor, and he wrapped his arm around her, drawing her near.

"Mother, this is Elanor, my wife."

Elanor dipped her head respectfully, displaying all the poise and grace that would serve her so well as the next queen. "I am very pleased to meet you, my lady."

A kind smile claimed his mother's face, and he silently thanked Elôm once again. Things would have been challenging had his mother not accepted the marriage.

"And I am so pleased to meet you. I look forward to getting to know you over the coming days."

Daniel rubbed his hand along Elanor's arm, relishing the moment. Only he and his mother remained of his immediate family, but he'd gained so much in marrying Elanor. He couldn't wait to see how his family would continue to grow from here.

AFTER FOUR DAYS, life was starting to take on something of a routine for Daniel. He still faced a never-ending list of things needing to be done, but having Elanor and his friends around helped keep him from becoming overwhelmed as he sorted through what most needed his attention. However, one situation, in particular, loomed over him. Unsure of the best way to proceed, he'd put it off, but the time had come to deal with it. After discussing it with Elanor, Aric, and Sam this morning, he prayed the decision he'd come to was the right one. While it hopefully wouldn't topple everything he'd just started building, it could have potential consequences.

Absently, he thumbed through the mountain of documents still needing his attention from his seat at his desk as he waited. His mind drifted back to the day Davira had barged into this office to have him arrested. He'd been foolish then not to take more precautions against her. Now he made sure to always have loyal guards outside the door even though she was gone.

Finally, the door opened. Aric stepped in first, followed by Alex. Though Alex was one of the most self-assured people Daniel knew, he only met Daniel's gaze briefly, and his bland expression seemed a little too forced.

Daniel nodded to Aric. "Thank you. You can leave us."

Aric hesitated for a brief second but said nothing and stepped back out. Perhaps it wasn't the wisest move, but if Alex had wanted to kill Daniel, he'd had ample opportunity over the past week.

Daniel gestured to the chair in front of his desk as the door closed. "Please, sit."

Alex took the seat, his comfortable, lounging posture belying the keen understanding and resignation in his eyes.

Daniel folded his hands and leaned forward on the desk. "I have to say I'm surprised you're still here. I had half expected you to slip away to parts unknown in all this chaos."

Alex fiddled with one of his rings and gave the roguish smile Daniel always remembered. "I admit, the thought did cross my mind. Self-preservation and all that. And more than one of my men pushed for it…" He paused then, straightening in his chair, and his smile faded to one of the more severe expressions Daniel had ever witnessed on his face. "But I don't want to live as a fugitive for the rest of my life. Not when you're the king. So I stayed to face the consequences of my actions."

Daniel appreciated and respected that he was taking responsibility for what he had done. It proved how much he had grown in the past years, but it didn't make the situation any easier. "You assassinated the emperor. Just about anyone not well acquainted with the situation would recommend or even demand execution."

He caught the way Alex's throat moved in a hard swallow. Nevertheless, his tone remained even and calm, carrying not even a hint of pleading. "I know. And I deserve no less."

Daniel sighed heavily and rubbed his brow. Being the king was going to be exhausting. "The truth is, I've been wrestling with this decision for days. I don't know the right answer; I only know there has been entirely too much death for too long. You are also my friend and have played an instrumental part in where we are today. I know some will question my decision, but…I will not have you executed."

A breath whooshed from Alex's chest, and he sagged a little in the chair. Execution wasn't pleasant any way you looked at it. "Thank you."

Daniel nodded slowly. "I know I will face many difficult decisions as king and will have to live with the choices I make. Executing you was not one I wanted to live with. Besides, I'd rather not alienate your men. I think they're more loyal to you than they are to me."

Alex grew serious again and shook his head. "They are good men. As long as you're fair and honest, they will follow you, regardless of what happens to me. I've made sure of it."

That was good to know. They'd been a great help the last few days in patrolling the city for trouble and spreading support and excitement for the change in leadership. They could just as easily have turned the city against Daniel.

"I'm glad I have their support. There do still have to be consequences for your actions, though."

"I understand." Alex drew himself back up again to accept whatever sentence Daniel pronounced.

It would have made it all the harder to punish him if Daniel didn't truly believe his plans would work out well for both of them. "I see no choice but to strip you of your rank and title and possessions in Keaton, which brings me to the where-abouts of your uncle. I assume you still have him held captive somewhere."

The first hint of resistance crept into Alex's expression, and he answered slowly, drawing out the answer. "Yes."

"Unfortunately, you'll have to release him as he technically has not broken any laws."

Alex forced out a hard breath, and Daniel wondered for a moment if he would refuse. Who knew where his uncle was being held prisoner? If Alex chose to remain stubbornly silent as to where they'd kept him, his men surely would too. But then he dipped a nod in surrender, though his distaste was evident.

"I'll have Tavor let him go."

Relief washed through Daniel. The more cooperative Alex was, the better things would be for both of them. "Thank you. And don't worry about Keaton. Your uncle won't have any holdings there either. I intend to appoint a new baron in the area."

Alex perked up a bit at this. He may be losing his home, but at least his conniving uncle would be outed.

Now that the situation was settled, Daniel shifted the conversation back toward Alex's fate. "As for you, I don't want to have to imprison you." A muscle in Alex's jaw twitched at the mere suggestion of that. Someone like him would go insane locked up and would probably rather be executed given a choice. "So, after discussing it with various others, I have decided to appoint you as head sheriff here in Valcré instead."

Alex's brows shot upward, his jaw falling slack. For once, he seemed without a smooth or snappy comeback. It was almost comical, and Daniel had to smother a smile in order to maintain some semblance of kingly composure as he laid out his plan.

"As you well know, murder and other crimes were rampant during my sister's reign. Innocent people will be seeking justice. I'm tasking you with providing it for them. You've already proven your resourcefulness and have the connections and knowledge to gather the information you need to find the perpetrators. I have a couple of others in mind who may be interested in joining you. And if any of your men would like to work with you as well, they are welcome."

Alex's mouth still hung open, and it took a moment for words to form. "This is a very generous offer of clemency."

Daniel shrugged. Now that he'd put forth his plans, he had

no doubt he'd made the right choice. "Some might call me weak for it, but I prefer to see it as extending the same mercy Elôm has extended me. And it will serve Arcacia much better than having you dead or behind bars."

"I'm more than happy to do the job." There was that roguish glint back in his eye. The position would suit him much better than baron anyway.

Daniel reached for a paper where he'd been collecting his thoughts on how this would all work out. "We will set up a system of communication and a headquarters for you. I'm afraid, after today, I have to bar you from the palace, considering your past actions. My mother is recovering well and will be up and about in a day or two, and I can't have you near her."

"I understand but know that I never had anything against her. I would never—"

"It's more for your safety than hers." Daniel rested back in his chair. While he didn't think his mother would go so far as to personally try to kill Alex, it was best to avoid the possibility altogether. That and protect her from the distress Alex's presence would cause. "I'm at a place where I can forgive you, but she is not and may never be. She knows you've helped us but isn't aware you've been here at the palace. For everyone's sake, it's best your paths never cross."

"Understood."

After a casual lunch in the dining room, Jace found himself on his own as Kyrin went off with the women to one sitting room or another. She had been spending a lot of time with Elanor, Anne, Cassie, and Leetra, apparently talking all about babies and Leetra's upcoming wedding. Though Leetra and Timothy had yet to set a date, Kyrin did say they both wished to get married in Landale. Jace was happy to see her enjoying herself and resting, though it had been hard not to constantly watch over her when they were outside their room.

Since she was occupied with her friends, Jace joined Rayad, Holden, Charles, and James in finding their own place to sit and relax. Holden was doing much better after a few days of rest. Leetra had relented in letting him get out of bed a couple of days ago, though he still had to take it easy with the pain of his healing wounds.

They had been sitting for about an hour and were discussing Daniel's plans for Avery and how Holden was thinking about joining him when Trev stepped into the room. "Aaron just got back from Landale. Looks like he brought several others from camp with him."

They all pushed up from their seats, Holden moving slowly and pressing his hand to his chest as he did so. Jace stayed close in case he needed a hand and caught the grimace that crossed Holden's face. Holden, however, just waved him off. "I'm fine."

He was as stubborn as Jace was when it came to injuries.

Shrugging, Jace turned his thoughts back to Aaron's arrival. He had left the morning after the army surrendered to bring news of the victory back to camp and collect Lacy and the rest of her family. Jace was curious who else had joined them. He hoped Kyrin's mother and Ronny had made the trip. He knew how much she had missed them in the last couple of months.

They all followed Trev toward the throne room, pausing along the way at the sitting room the women liked to occupy. Kyrin was there, as expected, along with Elanor and Anne. The three joined them, and merry voices drew them into the throne room. As hoped, Jace spotted Kyrin's mother and Ronny first. Kaden, Marcus, and Liam already stood with them, talking animatedly. Kyrin rushed to join them. Aric was there too, and though he hung back a little to let Lydia reunite with her children, his smile betrayed how happy he was to see her. Jace had a feeling Kyrin's mother would be making a move to Valcré in the near future. While Aric could never replace William, it would be good for her not to be alone and for Ronny to have a father figure around. He was still young and would need that guidance as he grew into a man.

Nearby, a couple of young women and an older woman Jace didn't know caught his attention, but he did recognize Lacy. A dark-haired baby rested in her arms, giving Aaron a wide, toothless smile. No one would have been able to tell just by looking at him that he wasn't Aaron's child. Hopefully, Aaron could make up for the time he'd lost with them.

Just to their right, Jace saw Charles and James standing with their backs to him, speaking to someone else. He couldn't see exactly who until he'd walked a little farther into the room.

Recognition swelled in his chest. "Mother."

He wasn't sure if she actually heard him or not, but at that same moment, her gaze shifted and met his. Her expression lit up as she stepped away from Charles and hurried forward to meet him. Pressure clogged the back of Jace's throat. During all the turmoil of the past two years, he hadn't known if he'd ever actually see her again. He'd spent all of three days with her after first learning she was his mother. Being forced to leave her had been an agony he'd struggled with for a long time. But, as she wrapped him in her embrace now, any of the lingering pain from that time was healed with the knowledge that this was only the beginning of the time they could now spend together.

"It is so good to see you," she breathed into his shoulder.

Nearly robbed of his voice, he cleared his throat. "You too. I didn't know you would be coming here."

She squeezed him a bit tighter before taking a step back to study his face. Tears had welled in her eyes. "When I heard Davira was defeated, I had to come and see if everyone was all right. I met the others on the road. Aaron recognized me and invited me to travel the rest of the way with them."

Then she noticed something beyond him. Jace looked over his shoulder and stepped aside to let Elanor join them. Witnessing their reunion brought him just as much joy as his own. After all, Elanor had left right after he had. Neither of them had seen their mother in two long years and were very different people now.

After they'd embraced, his mother reached for him again and held both of them in front of her. "I've missed you both so much. You're looking so well."

Jace traded a grin with his sister. "A lot has changed since we were last together."

Mother's smile deepened. "I can see it in your eyes. There's peace."

"Yes." To be able to say that without any uncertainty brought him immense joy. He'd been so broken when he'd had to say goodbye to her—the beginning of a downward spiral that had led to his darkest time. But Elon had met him in the deep darkness and given him that peace.

Out of the corner of his eye, Jace caught Kyrin lingering nearby, her expression soft and loving as she observed them. He motioned her near, and Mother immediately wrapped her in her arms. Jace couldn't be more thankful for how much his mother clearly liked Kyrin despite barely knowing her. It made it all the sweeter when he put his arm around Kyrin to make an announcement.

"We're married now. Five months."

Teary delight shone in Mother's eyes. "Oh, that is such wonderful news. I'm so happy for you."

Jace looked down, sharing a loving gaze with Kyrin, and admitted, "It took me far longer than it should have and nearly losing her to overcome my fear and ask her to be my wife."

"Well, I knew you belonged together, and I'm so glad Elôm worked it out, and now I have such a wonderful daughter-in-law."

She and Kyrin hugged again, and Jace glanced at Elanor. He wasn't the only one who'd gotten married recently. She looked hesitant, and he gave her a nod to let her know she wouldn't overshadow his announcement with her own. But maybe she was more nervous about sharing the news than reluctant to take the spotlight. At least their mother had known Kyrin prior and had already seen something between her and Jace. Elanor's marriage would certainly come as a surprise.

After Mother and Kyrin parted, Elanor rather timidly stepped in. "Jace isn't the only one with relationship news."

She looked past them, and that's when Jace spotted Daniel. He hadn't even noticed him, but no doubt Daniel had been watching the whole time, waiting for this moment. She beckoned him closer, and he strode toward them. Though his steady gait suggested confidence, Jace was pretty sure his brother-in-law was sweating a bit.

Elanor took him by the hand. "Mother, have you met the king yet?"

"I did, briefly." Mother's brows lifted, and she seemed unsure how to respond properly as she looked back and forth between them.

Daniel flashed a winning smile, no doubt trying to charm Mother. Jace hoped, for Elanor's sake, it was working.

"Well, the thing is…" Jace had never seen Elanor so nervous. Usually, he was the one who struggled with things like this. She glanced up at Daniel before finally coming out with it. "Daniel and I were married a few weeks ago in Samara."

Mother's deep blue eyes rounded. "Married?"

Elanor rushed to explain. "See, we'd been courting for a few months, and when he proposed, we didn't want to wait. With the future so uncertain and our march into Arcacia, we didn't want to risk losing each other before we could be married. I'm sorry you couldn't be there. I hope you are not too disappointed or upset."

The shock in Mother's expression melted into a warm smile. "No, not upset at all, simply surprised. I've prayed diligently you would find a good husband, I just did not think to anticipate you would be, well, queen, and that my son-in-law would be the king."

"I know. I'm sure it's overwhelming. But I can assure you I gave the decision much thought and prayer. Jace went through all of your same emotions before giving his blessing to the relationship." Elanor cast him a grin.

Mother looked at him too, and he shrugged. Nearly all of his misgivings had faded since they'd been married, especially in the last few days. "I admit, I was hesitant in the beginning, but Daniel is a good man, and they do work well together."

"I can attest to that," Charles joined in. "I haven't known our new king for very long, but I couldn't be happier to know the future will now be guided by both him and Elanor."

Daniel gave both Jace and Charles a nod. "Thank you. I'm honored to have such support, not only as king but as family."

That night after dinner, Kyrin sat tucked in next to Jace in one of the drawing rooms with their two families. It was a wonderful thing to see them all blended together as one. She loved how her mother and Rachel talked like friends, and she was shocked that her brothers were speaking to James. She'd expected the hostile feelings to linger, but it seemed their victory put everyone in a forgiving mood. Granted, it was mostly Marcus doing the talking. Liam didn't say much, as usual, and Kaden just kind of stood there looking more intimidating than necessary, but at least he wasn't glaring.

Rayad and Elian were there too, of course. They were just as much family as anyone. Kyrin had seen Rachel and Elian speak briefly when they'd first walked in, but neither seemed exactly sure how to respond to the other. It had to be strange figuring out how to interact with Rothas now dead, especially after being apart for so long. Kyrin would love to see them together, but she was sure things were complicated.

Absorbing all the happy chatter and laughter, Kyrin leaned into Jace. "Just look at the family we have."

The content smile on his face warmed her heart. He had grown up without a family. Not even a single person to show him love, until he met Rayad. Now, between the two of them, their family numbered over a dozen people. And that number would only grow. She rubbed her hand over her belly. She couldn't wait until she was far enough along to feel the baby moving. It had been hard the last few days not to know for sure the baby was all right, but so far, Leetra assured her everything seemed normal.

She looked around the room again. Only Elanor, Daniel, and Rayad knew about the pregnancy, but that was the reason she and Jace had suggested the family get together tonight. Now that they'd given Jace's mother a few hours for the news of the marriages to sink in, it was time for the next big reveal, and Kyrin could barely contain herself. She couldn't wait to see how her mother and brothers would react.

Jace must have noticed her giddy wiggling because he nudged her and gave her a nod. They both stood up to face everyone, and the talking quieted. Kyrin took a deep breath, jittery with the anticipation.

"I know there were a lot of surprises today, but Jace and I have one more to share." She cast a quick grin up at him before facing everyone again. "We're going to have a baby."

The room burst into a mix of cheers, laughter, and congratulations. Kyrin's mother rushed forward, joyful tears already flowing down her cheeks as she wrapped Kyrin in a hug. Kyrin's own tears leaked out. She never used to cry so easily, but according to the other women, that was part of pregnancy. Over her mother's shoulder, she saw Rachel hugging Jace and crying as well. Though his face remained dry, Kyrin did spot the tears in Jace's eyes, and her heart swelled to near bursting as she thought of how scared he used to be of this moment. Now there was only joy.

Everyone surrounded them, sharing one embrace after another. Kyrin's brothers were all grins as they jostled for a turn to hug her. For once, Liam's hug didn't nearly squeeze the breath from her lungs. It was as if he were taking extra care not to crush the baby growing inside her. She made up for it with her own tight embrace.

When it was Ronny's turn, he looked at her, his eyes wide with wonder. "Does this mean I'm going to be an uncle?"

Kaden gave him a slap to the back. "We're all going to be uncles."

"Awesome!"

Everyone laughed, and Kyrin couldn't help thinking of her father. He would have loved nothing more than to see his family together, celebrating such a joyous moment. Tears burned her eyes anew, but there was too much joy to let the sadness take hold. She reached up and squeezed her stone necklace, rejoicing that they would all get to celebrate together again someday.

DANIEL SIGNED HIS name and then folded and sealed the parchment in blue wax before handing the document to Sam. "That should be the last one."

Sam added it to an impressive pile in the basket they had set on the desk. "Soon, all of Arcacia will know you are king and that believers are safe to worship Elôm in peace."

Daniel gave a satisfied nod. The announcements would go out across the country in the hands of their dragon riders to inform all major lords and barracks commanders of the change in leadership. They also bore Daniel's command that any believers who had been arrested and were being held captive were to be released immediately, their homes and possessions restored. Anyone who failed to comply with this command would be arrested for treason. He prayed there wouldn't be too much resistance.

"Thanks for your help, Sam." He'd been invaluable to Daniel the last few days. While Mister Foss helped explain the day-to-day political ramifications and weed through paperwork, Sam had been right there to counsel him in matters of restoring faith in Elôm to a country that desperately needed it.

"It is my honor. I am here to help in any way I can."

And Daniel was truly grateful for that. Sam was one of his oldest and truest friends, even if Daniel hadn't realized it in the beginning. As his mind wandered briefly back to past years, he laughed, and Sam sent him a questioning look.

"I was just thinking about that night I let you escape with the Scrolls. Thank Elôm, I had just enough sense to keep my mouth shut, or I don't know where we'd be."

Sam smiled fondly. "That night gave me hope of the king you would become."

"I will try not to disappoint."

"I'm sure you won't."

Having people like Sam alongside him would make all the difference. Providing Sam stayed in Valcré. Daniel hadn't even thought to ask before now. For all he knew, Sam might return to Arda with the rest of the talcrin army. "So, what do you plan to do once things are settled? I've never heard you talk about the future."

Sam crossed his arms and leaned on the desk. "Well, I'm waiting to see if it is where Elôm guides me, but it has been a dream of mine to set up a university and invite other talcrin scholars from Arda to come and teach. I would like to see our countries working together closely again, especially in areas of learning and faith."

Daniel sighed quietly. He'd been a little worried that Sam might leave, but this was exactly the opening he'd been hoping for. "I am pleased to hear you say that because I have a proposition for you. Tarvin Hall. Obviously, it can't continue to run as it has. I won't be following my father's example of taking children from their families to essentially raise them as my own personal army. But it was a university at one time, was it not?"

"Yes, that's how it started."

Daniel caught the tone of interest, lifting Sam's voice. "Then make it a university again. I give you full control and will provide whatever you need to start it. Turn it into the place of education you've been dreaming of."

Sam's gold eyes gleamed. "My lord, nothing would make me happier."

"Excellent. I'll have Mister Foss draft an order right away, making you the head of Tarvin Hall. If you could see that the students currently enrolled are returned to their families, I would very much appreciate it. Any, who wish to return as students of your university, are welcome once you're ready. As for those without families, we'll have to figure out how to proceed. Unfortunately, I know my father and sister created many orphans."

"I will see to it."

The moment Mister Foss returned from an errand, Daniel had him write out the transfer of power over Tarvin Hall. Once it was signed and sealed, he gave it to Sam, glad his friend would be close by and available should Daniel wish to seek his counsel.

Sometime later, after Sam had left and Daniel was going over more tedious matters with Mister Foss, Daniel's mother entered the room. She'd been up a few times yesterday and looked even stronger today. Daniel welcomed the distraction and rose from his chair. "Mother, please, come sit."

She took a seat in one of the padded chairs across from him, and Mister Foss excused himself. Daniel set aside a stack of parchments before focusing on his mother. "The paperwork is never ending."

She smirked, her green eyes twinkling. "Your father hated it too."

Daniel laughed a little. He could just imagine his father rolling his eyes as Mister Foss set another giant stack of papers in front of him. Perhaps they did have more similarities than he'd realized. However, the mirth faded as his thoughts shifted. "It feels strange, though, doing all this when there hasn't even been a coronation. I'm not officially the king, yet I've walked in here acting like I am. I don't want to come across as a usurper like Davira."

This was the first he'd spoken of the fear that had been needling him the last few days. Sure, he was the rightful heir, but he hadn't followed the proper protocol of succession.

His mother gave him a thoughtful look and then got up. She walked over to an ornate box sitting on a stand in the corner and opened it. She lifted his father's crown from inside the plush velvet interior—shimmering gold studded with blue sapphires that glittered as they caught the light. It was the first time he realized they were Arcacia's original colors. Somehow, in all of his predecessors' scheming and quest to eradicate faith in Elôm, the crown had remained true to Arcacia's beginnings.

His mother cradled it gently in her hands and just looked at it for a long moment before turning to Daniel. "Come with me."

He rose and followed her out of the office and into the throne room. It was empty right now, and their footsteps echoed on the smooth tile. The room always seemed cavernous when there weren't many people. Today especially. The sheer size seemed to contain all of the responsibilities and pressures that came with his position, robbing a little of his breath.

They stopped at the dais, and Mother nodded to the throne. "Sit."

Daniel gave it a long look. He had not yet sat in that seat since they had taken the palace. Like signing documents and giving orders, it just didn't feel right without something more official than Davira's death to make him king. But that one word from his mother held something of a command to it, and he obeyed.

Slowly, he climbed the steps and took a seat on the throne his father had once occupied, looking out over the empty room. One day soon, the space would no doubt be filled with his subjects, who would look to him for answers and guidance. It was a daunting prospect, but one he knew Elôm would give him the wisdom and strength to fulfill.

His mother stepped up beside him and, without a word, nestled the crown on his head. It was heavy—a lot heavier than he'd imagined—signifying the weight of his kingdom and all those in it.

"There, now it's official."

Daniel cast her a skeptical look. After all, it was just the two of them. No witnesses. No ceremony. Nothing but his mother's declaration.

However, her voice held power and authority. "Davira was the usurper. I was the queen, and you are the rightful heir. It's official if I say it is. Besides, the people already see you as king. A coronation won't change the minds of those who are opposed. Right now, Arcacia just needs you to lead and fix what your sister destroyed."

Daniel nodded slowly. She was right, and he accepted that responsibility.

A smile then grew on her face. "The crown suits you. I will search your sister's room for mine. For Elanor."

Rain had fallen during the night, making the gardens even more lush and fresh as Jace joined his mother, Elanor, and James for a walk. To spend time with the three of them was something he had never even dreamed possible not too long ago.

Being in the garden reminded him of when he and his mother had spoken together at Ashwood. At that point, they'd had to do it in secret with Elian standing watch. Jace still remembered that day quite vividly, how his mother had tried so hard to get him to accept that Elôm loved him. Thankfully, her efforts had not been in vain. And this time, they were in no danger of Rothas storming up and threatening him. That day seemed like a lifetime ago.

Jace shook off those thoughts and looked over at James. Their mother and Elanor were several paces ahead, discussing Elanor's position as queen and what they hoped the future held for all of them. So far, James had not yet said a word. In fact, now that Jace thought about it, he said very little in general to anyone. While Jace wasn't much of a conversationalist himself most of the time, James seemed more withdrawn than quiet, almost as if he tried not to be noticed. Of course, his faith had changed him, but it seemed a little extreme for someone who had once been so self-assured and outgoing. Jace had thought it was only because he was nervous about fighting, but it remained, even now, after their victory.

"Are you all right?"

James's gaze snapped to him. His brows bunched, and then he looked away, but not before Jace caught a flash of something pained in his eyes. "I'm fine."

Jace almost snorted. He'd gotten a lot better at sharing his feelings over the past year, but now he knew how Kyrin and Rayad had felt so much of the time. What a strange twist of roles that he would now be the one trying to draw someone out of their depressive shell.

"Well, it just seems like you avoid engaging with others as much as possible. I used to do the same thing."

James's long exhale and sagging posture confirmed it even before he nodded slowly. "I guess I have found it difficult. Everyone knows what I've done, and I guess I just…" He grimaced and swallowed hard, not meeting Jace's gaze. "I'm afraid they will see me as I still see myself. As a…"

His words trailed off, but Jace's mind filled in the blank with the cold, accusing voice that had tormented him throughout so much of his life and robbed him of so many years of peace. Just thinking the word brought back some of the pain he used to suffer. "A monster?"

James's gaze darted to him briefly before he hung his head and nodded again. What a sad thing to see his own struggles mirrored so clearly in his brother. Jace drew a deep breath. Though he had mostly healed and put his past behind him, speaking of one of his darkest moments was still difficult. But James needed to hear it. If nothing else, perhaps he wouldn't feel so alone in his struggle.

"I murdered a fellow slave when I was fifteen."

They had stopped now, and James turned to face him, his eyes widening though lacking condemnation. Now it was Jace who found it difficult to maintain eye contact, the sting of guilt quick to resurface. He took a moment to let it pass before forging on.

"Kyrin might try to tell you it was mostly self-defense, but I know what was in my heart when I did it. I antagonized him into a fight and did it with every intention of killing him. That day proved to everyone around me that I was just as dangerous as they believed I was and that I was a monster. That's what led to me being a gladiator. It's the one thing in my life I would go back and change if I could. I still have nightmares about it."

Understanding lurked in James's grim expression. Maybe he had his own nightmares. Even if he didn't, memories were torment enough. They always came at the most unwelcome times.

Jace reached out to put his hand on his brother's shoulder, holding his gaze, this time without wavering. "There are no excuses for what either of us did, and part of the consequence is having to live with it. There will always be people who look at us and see only our pasts, but that's when we have to focus on who we are now, thanks to Elon's sacrifice. Holden once told me our pasts can make it hard to differentiate between who we are now and who we were then, but we can't get trapped into thinking we're the same men we used to be. Elon gave everything for our forgiveness, and if we remain stuck in our own sense of guilt, then we're wasting the gift He's given us."

At last, a bit of light seemed to return to James's eyes, and his demeanor changed. "You're right. Thank you. I'll try not to forget it." He looked to where Mother and Elanor had gotten quite a ways ahead of them. "I haven't told her yet, but I don't think I will return home with Mother. At least not right away. I don't want her to be alone, but facing those I've hurt every day... It's not helping them or me. Knowing how much damage Davira did, I want to find somewhere I can help people rebuild their lives. I know nothing I do can erase or outweigh the terrible things I've done, but I need time to find out what Elôm wants me to do with my life going forward. I might as well be helping people while I figure that out."

It would probably be hard for their mother, but Jace understood his need. "It sounds like a good plan; just don't avoid your family and the people who care about you. That doesn't solve anything. Believe me, I would know."

James offered a small smile. "I won't."

Satisfied his brother was in a better place than before they'd talked, Jace turned so they could catch up to Mother and Elanor, who were now waiting for them near one of the fountains. When they reached them, Mother gave them a searching look as if she sensed the heaviness of the conversation that had just taken place, but she asked no questions.

Elanor gestured to the bench and decorative iron chairs facing the fountain. "Why don't we sit and talk here for a bit?"

Jace had no complaints about relaxing here in the garden, and they all took seats—Elanor and Mother on the bench while he and James each claimed a chair on either side. The bubbling of the fountain filled the brief silence between them before Elanor turned slightly toward their mother. Jace had a feeling from her tone that this was a topic she had specifically waited to bring up until all four of them were present.

"I haven't seen you and Elian spending much time together."

Jace studied Mother's reaction to this. She just sort of shrugged, but he had made the same observation. Maybe he was wrong, but it was almost as if they were avoiding each other.

She only responded verbally when Elanor fixed her with a prompting look. "I've mostly been with you three."

It was clearly a deflection, and Elanor glanced over at Jace, but he wasn't quite sure what to add. Delving into the past and feelings of guilt with James was one thing, but relationships were a little trickier.

Elanor sent him something of an exasperated look before focusing back on their mother. "You two should talk...about the future."

Again, Mother didn't answer immediately, and Jace caught her twisting the wedding ring on her finger. The one signifying her marriage to Rothas. "The future is...complicated."

Elanor must have noticed the action as well. "Because of Father?"

This time she didn't answer. Elanor traded looks with both Jace and James, but their mother's uncertainty didn't dissuade her. "He's gone. We all know you love Elian."

Mother straightened, putting on a brave face, and spoke as though the matter were already settled. "He hasn't been gone that long. I can't take advantage of what happened."

Some part of her probably felt guilty even considering a life with Elian, and Jace didn't want that. There was already more than enough guilt in this family between him and James. "His death is not your fault. You played no part in it."

In Jace's mind, Rothas's demise was just recompense for all the pain he'd caused, but he wouldn't say it in front of Elanor and James. The man was their father, vile as he had been. "There's no reason you can't live your life and live it happily."

"Jace is right," Elanor jumped back in eagerly. "You were faithful to Father despite how despicably he treated you. But now that he's gone, there's no reason you can't be with Elian and finally enjoy a life of love and peace. We want you to be happy. I don't think the three of us would have any objections if that's what you're worried about."

Mother looked at each of them. Jace gave a firm nod to Elanor's words, and so did James.

"You and Elian are still young." Elanor gave their mother a nudge, her eyes twinkling with a little grin. "You two could even have a baby."

"Oh, goodness." Mother's cheeks flushed bright pink.

Jace coughed to cover a laugh. He hadn't even considered the possibility of Elanor's suggestion before, but now that he thought about it, he rather liked the idea of a baby brother or sister. The two of them certainly deserved to be able to raise a child together. While he wasn't sure his mother would appreciate his input on this subject, he had to agree with Elanor. "You could."

"Now, let's not get ahead of ourselves." Mother tried to give them each a serious look, but Jace had a feeling the way all three of them were grinning at her only flustered her more. She smoothed her skirt in an obvious attempt to compose herself, but even her ears had turned red.

Jace could tell Elanor was biting back laughter, but she quickly schooled her features to a more tempered smile. "If nothing else, you could have a long, happy life together. I know it may be a bit awkward figuring out how to go about things, but if one of you doesn't say something, then I just know Elian will remain here as my bodyguard, and you will go back to Ashwood alone."

Elanor was absolutely right. She and Jace both knew him too well. "It's true. He will do what he thinks is the honorable thing and stay away if he believes you're uncomfortable with moving forward."

This look at reality seemed to give their mother pause. Very slowly, her mood shifted as if she were only now allowing herself to consider a future with Elian. When she finally spoke, the tenderness and buried love Jace had been waiting for bled into her voice. "Yes, he will." A soft smile claimed her face as she looked at each of them. "I will talk to him."

It was getting close to supper time as Kyrin wandered through the palace looking for Jace. She hadn't seen him since lunch. No doubt, he had spent much of his time with his mother. She was so happy to see them reunited and able to fully get to know one another without the threat of discovery or danger.

When she came across him in one of the halls, he was talking to Rayad, Charles, and Holden. They looked like they were all on their way toward the dining room, and Jace hung back to wait for her. She hurried to catch up. It may have only been a few hours, but she did find herself missing him when they were apart after coming so close to losing him. "Have you enjoyed your afternoon?"

He gave her a ready smile, and the peace resting so comfortably in his once-tortured eyes was something she would never take for granted. "Yes. And you?"

"Same. Talking with my mother has helped me feel far more prepared for our baby than I was. I'm glad I'm not so clueless anymore." It was utterly terrifying to think of having to figure things out on her own. She was so thankful her once-broken relationship with her mother had been restored.

"Good."

She took his hand, and the two of them followed after the men toward the dining room. They had nearly reached it when Daniel walked into the hall. They greeted each other, and he focused on Kyrin.

"Could I talk to you and Jace for a moment before we go in for supper?"

"Sure."

He seemed just a little hesitant, but Kyrin had watched how well he had stepped into his role and fully taken on the mantle of king over the last few days. It was quite magnificent to see, especially having known him before the Resistance.

He cleared his throat, his gaze darting to Jace before settling resolutely on Kyrin. "Tomorrow, we will bring in all the army leaders for them to swear allegiance. I was wondering if…perhaps, you might agree to sit in and observe."

Kyrin practically felt the way Jace bristled beside her. She glanced at him and found him giving Daniel a rather icy look. He knew how much she'd hated having to sit and observe Daican's dealings with the people and report to him. He hadn't been happy about it in Samara either, but there was a new ferocity behind his protectiveness now that she was carrying their child. She touched his arm to try to calm him.

Daniel, obviously reading Jace's tense body language, held up his hands in a defusing manner. "You're entirely free to say no. I only ask because I would truly value your input, but you're under no obligation to do so. The last thing I would ever do is try to use you as my father did."

Jace's low voice cut in before Kyrin could say anything or even really consider a reply. "Leetra said you needed to avoid stress."

That was true, but at the same time, she desired to help Daniel, and working with him was not nearly as stressful as working for his father. It was imperative he make the right choices regarding who to trust when it came to their military leaders, not just for himself but for all of Arcacia. If she could help, she did feel an obligation to do so. Elôm had given her a gift. It seemed a waste not to use it when it truly mattered.

She squeezed Jace's arm. "I think I can manage without getting too stressed."

He didn't look convinced.

Though Daniel appeared to be questioning whether he should even risk speaking again, he assured her, "You can quit at any time you feel you're not up to it. And, Jace, you're more than welcome to be there with her. Marcus will also be there, along with Aric and Trev, and plenty of security."

And that would make all the difference. She would be surrounded by friends and allies, whereas when she'd worked for Daican, she'd felt like she was drowning in a sea of strangers and hostile forces. "I will be there."

Jace sighed, but she caught his gaze and offered a calming smile. "I'll be fine. I promise I'll stop if it's too much…or if you think it's too much for me."

He nodded slowly in acceptance, a little of his tension dissipating. Hopefully, by tomorrow morning, she would be able to convince him she truly would be fine.

BUTTERFLIES STIRRED THE inside of Kyrin's stomach, though thankfully, nausea did not join them. Breakfast had initially caused some queasiness, but so far, Leetra's tea had helped settle it. She rubbed away the remaining tickle and drew a deep breath. Jace must have noticed because she caught him watching her in the mirror of the dressing table where she'd just finished arranging her hair. She turned in her seat to meet his rather dour look.

"I'm fine. I'm not even that nervous about this morning. I was just thinking about the first day I worked with Daican. I never thought I'd be in this position again, but it's completely different this time. Back then, I had no one here with me who I could trust."

He didn't look entirely convinced, so she got up and walked over to him, draping her arms loosely around his neck. "You know how important this is. We can't risk a traitor in our midst. It could jeopardize everything. My input can help avoid that."

At first, Jace's expression remained stubbornly resistant, not quite hiding the true fear behind it, but slowly it melted away. "I know."

Kyrin smiled and leaned in to give him a soft kiss that erased any lingering traces of reluctance on his face. "I'll be fine, especially since you'll be there with me."

She then stepped back and looked him over. He'd borrowed another outfit from Daniel—a deep blue shirt and tailored black jerkin that accentuated his strong shoulders. While she liked his more rugged, everyday clothing, it wouldn't stop her from appreciating him in a more formal outfit. His lips twitched with a smile at her perusal, and she grinned before turning back to the mirror to check her own appearance once more.

Mira had found her a beautiful blue linen dress that was nearly a match to the color of their flag. The pleated bodice and full skirt were much better suited for an official meeting than her usual, more practical dresses that didn't have such an excess of fabric. "I guess I'm ready."

She took Jace's hand, and they left the room. As they walked the palace halls, her mind once again drifted back to when she'd been here before. Three years was not a lot of time, yet so much had happened and changed. She'd been a terrified girl back then and had felt so alone. She wasn't much older now, but she had grown considerably. They had all gone through and survived too much not to. And now she had more family and friends surrounding her than she ever could have dreamed possible.

Upon entering the throne room, Kyrin had to pause for a moment in awe of the sight of Daniel and Elanor. It was the first time she had seen either of them look so regal. Their gold crowns caught the light and shone brilliantly against their dark hair. Elanor, too, wore a blue dress, though hers was made of satin instead of linen and was far more elaborate than Kyrin's.

She leaned into Jace. "Your sister is a beautiful queen."

A proud smile claimed his face. At least it provided a momentary distraction from worrying about her.

Solora was also present. She wore a black and gold dress, an understated gold circlet resting on her brow. It seemed fitting— a symbol of the old supporting the new. Kyrin was thankful the former queen had survived Davira's attack. Her presence seemed to have helped Daniel slip more easily into his role as king.

Daniel hastened from his place near the dais to greet them since they'd had a private breakfast in their room and hadn't yet spoken this morning. "Thank you so much for being here. I wouldn't have blamed you if you'd changed your mind overnight."

Jace had given trying to talk her out of it one more shot before they'd gone to bed last night, but Kyrin was committed to it. She could easily imagine the pressure Daniel was under to make the right decisions about who he trusted and how costly a mistake could be. That was why she could never have said no to him. Yes, her well-being was important, but the new Arcacia they were trying to build was still fragile. She would do all she could to ensure peace would thrive so she and Jace could raise their family without fear.

"I'm happy to do it."

She greeted Elanor next and then Marcus. Like Jace, he questioned her to make sure she was up for this. She was half surprised Kaden and Liam weren't there to hover around her too. Assuring him that all was well, she followed Daniel toward the dais.

"We brought a chair for you." Daniel gestured to the padded seat a little to the side and behind his throne. He then glanced at Jace. "I wasn't sure if you would want one."

Jace shook his head. "No, I'll stand."

No doubt, he felt more alert and prepared for trouble while standing.

Daniel led them up the marble steps to the top of the dais, pausing next to the thrones to face Kyrin. "We've mostly sorted out staffing, but there are a few members left who wish to remain in employment that I'd like your input on just to be sure. After that, we'll go through palace security and then on to the military commanders. Trev will be standing by to take notes. If you have any suspicions about anyone, just let him know, and I will confer with you once we're finished or sometime later today if you'd like to rest first. You're welcome to leave at any time you wish."

Kyrin glanced at the thrones that had once been so intimidating to her, but they were just chairs. What mattered was who was sitting on them. "I'm sure I'll be fine. At least I know what to expect. When I first started working for your father, I was just sort of thrown into it and expected to know what I was doing. I was terrified of making a mistake."

Daniel grimaced as if fault somehow rested on him. "Well, I hope you aren't worried about that now. After all, the future is ultimately up to Elôm, so don't feel like it's all on you."

"I won't."

Now that everyone was present, they moved to their places, and Jace followed Kyrin to her waiting chair. It was much softer than the one Daican had offered, with a winged back and padded armrests. It also sat much closer to the throne. Before, they had tucked her back where she could observe and not be noticed or take any attention away from the emperor. But here, it was clear she was present to assist Daniel.

She settled in and smiled at Trev, who stood just to her right. Jace took up a position to her left. Between the two, she couldn't have felt more secure.

She looked over at Daniel and Elanor seated on their thrones. The last time she had been in this position, it had been Daican and Davira sitting there. She could never have imagined the path her life would take—who she would become, the people she would meet. Overcome with gratitude, she closed her eyes for a moment in thanks to Elôm and then reached for Jace's hand to gaze up at him adoringly. He raised a brow in question, but she just laughed quietly to herself. She would have to explain later.

With everyone in position, Daniel motioned to Aric, who left through the door at the far end of the room. He re-entered a moment later with a group of guards leading several people along with them. They all wore palace uniforms. Most were men, but one of the two women jumped out to Kyrin immediately—Lady Videlle, former headmistress of Auréa. Kyrin hadn't thought of her in a very long time and hadn't had any idea she was still at the palace. The middle-aged woman was just as poised and graceful as ever, but while she'd clearly tried to look her best, her uniform was just a bit wrinkled, and her cosmetics didn't quite hide the fine lines in her face. Kyrin almost felt bad for her. She could just imagine the woman lamenting her appearance before this meeting.

Videlle was the first to be ushered forward to swear her allegiance to Daniel. With a low, sweeping curtsy, she did so without hesitation. Though it was a bit on the dramatic side, which was typical for Videlle, Kyrin didn't detect any dishonesty in her manner or words. Daniel thanked her, and she curtsied again before glancing at Kyrin. Recognition crossed her face, along with a flash of something Kyrin interpreted as desperation for approval. It was an incredibly strange shift in roles.

The rest of the morning passed smoothly. At first, Kyrin was hyper-alert and a bit nervous she might miss something. But, eventually, she relaxed, little details and mannerisms popping out more easily to her as time went on. Most who came in to swear their allegiance truly did desire to serve Daniel. Some were a little more hesitant but willing. She was actually surprised by how few she had Trev take note of but glad to see it, especially amongst their military leaders.

When the final group left, Kyrin breathed a sigh. She wasn't too taxed, but the hint of a headache squeezed the back of her neck, and it would be nice to get up and move about. Her stomach had also started to growl, signaling lunchtime. Maybe she and Jace could eat it outside. The fresh air would help clear her head and hopefully halt the headache.

However, before they could be dismissed, Daniel got up and faced her. His drawn expression showed reluctance, just like when he'd asked for her help yesterday. "We do have one more person to bring in. Your grandfather."

Kyrin had been too focused on her duties to think about the fact her grandfather had never been present. Just the thought of him dumped more anxiety into the pit of her stomach than she'd experienced all morning.

"I wanted to warn you before he was brought in, so you can leave if you wish." Daniel motioned to the side door— Kyrin's escape if she wanted to take it.

She pulled in a deep breath. It had been incredibly difficult to face her grandfather back in Samara. It would probably be just as hard now, but she had truly desired to forgive him. She looked up at Jace, expecting him to shake his head or do something to get her to leave, but he only held her gaze, waiting for her to decide. In the end, she was here to help Daniel, regardless of her history with her grandfather.

She straightened her shoulders. "I'll stay."

Daniel nodded, though his expression remained rather cautious. "You should also know, Marcus and I have discussed his future at length. Being he is such a well-known and celebrated figure to all of Arcacia, my decision is not as simple as it will be for the other military commanders. I know the pain he has caused, but if he pledges his allegiance and is sincere, I have decided to let him retain his position."

This did come as a bit of a surprise to Kyrin, and the scarred part of her heart, which had been wounded deeply, cried out in protest. However, she bit back the reaction to let Daniel continue.

"He is highly respected in the military. I believe, in working closely with Marcus, he can help stabilize the transition to a peaceful Arcacia. If I have his support, then I believe there would be much less potential for dissension amongst the other commanders."

Kyrin looked over at Marcus, who was watching her, his expression one of understanding even as he agreed with Daniel. "I, too, believe stripping the General of his rank or bringing any other legal actions against him could incite ill will."

Kyrin breathed out heavily. They were right. The ramifications of the decision went far beyond the feelings or hurts of one family. "I agree too."

Jace's hand closed over her shoulder, squeezing it assuringly. She cast him a thankful glance, rubbing her hand over his. Repairing a broken country was no easy task.

"Good." Daniel seemed relieved. Maybe he'd feared his decision would cause a rift in his newly established family. "I would like to let him know of the decision before he is dismissed because I think it will help settle some of the tension I'm sure the others are feeling. Would it be alright if I consult you for your opinion during the exchange?"

It would be uncomfortable either way. "Yes, do whatever you need to do."

Daniel turned to go back to his seat, but Kyrin stopped him. "May I stand while we do this?"

Though the dais placed her above anyone who came to the throne, sitting in the General's presence brought Kyrin's mind back to Fort Rivor when he'd had her and Kaden chained to chairs. That had been right after he'd had Jace whipped, and she did not want to relive the awful, helpless feelings of that time.

"Of course." Daniel gestured to the throne. "Come stand closer to me. That way, we can talk if we need to."

Kyrin stepped toward the throne, taking her place to Daniel's left. Jace stood behind her, his strong presence lending her comfort.

With a word from Daniel, the General was brought in, and Kyrin had to swallow down a sudden wave of nausea. Memories of Fort Rivor and Michael rose up with it, but she forced them far back into her mind behind a stony wall to deal with later.

Her grandfather strode straight and tall toward the throne, but now that she'd dealt with her initial reaction, she realized his frighteningly commanding presence was gone. In place of it, she witnessed a broken man held together only by years of training and self-discipline. She hadn't believed it when she'd seen him in Samara, but she did now. The war had changed him just as it had her and those around them. Only time would tell if it was for the better.

At the throne, he dropped to one knee and bowed his head unbidden. "Your Majesty, I swear my allegiance to you and your queen. I know my actions have not supported you in the past, and I have brought pain to many, including my own family. I deserve your wrath for my crimes and will accept your judgment."

The conviction with which he spoke echoed through Kyrin, rattling her long-held perceptions of the man. His voice carried a sharp note of self-loathing that suggested he actually wished for Daniel's judgment. A memory flashed to mind of the moment he'd come upon Michael lying dead at camp and the shock that had filled his eyes. She hadn't wanted to accept that something had changed in him that day, but what she saw now convinced her it had. The convoluted emotions that rose within her, seeing him kneeling there, put a weight on her chest and made her throat ache. Why was it so much easier to hate him for what he'd done than believe the regret so clearly displayed in his posture?

She prayed for a change of heart and nearly missed Daniel looking at her. In fact, almost everyone was looking, waiting for an answer. Her grandfather's fate was in her hands. Daniel would base his decision on what she told him—whether or not her grandfather was telling the truth and could be trusted. Her words would determine if he retained a position of honor or was dismissed and perhaps even imprisoned if Daniel believed him untrustworthy. But, of course, she must tell the truth. Elôm would take care of the rest.

"He is sincere."

The brief flash of a comforting smile told her Daniel understood just how difficult her position was. He turned his attention back to the General. "You may rise."

The General did so, but instead of looking at Daniel, his gaze rested on Kyrin. Her heart choked a little before racing on. No doubt he'd heard her assessment since it hadn't occurred to her to murmur or whisper it. Something like both confusion and gratitude swirled in his expression before his focus shifted back to Daniel. Kyrin's heart continued its thunderous beat, unsure of what to feel. Taking a deep breath, she focused on Daniel's voice instead of her racing thoughts.

"General Veshiron, I accept your oath of allegiance. While I don't follow my father's beliefs nor condone his actions, I know you faithfully served him and our country. You're highly respected and regarded as a hero amongst the military and the citizens of Arcacia. I am willing to overlook your service to my sister if you will now serve me with the same faithfulness you did my father."

Surprise flickered in the General's eyes, but a little strength had returned to his posture. "I will, Your Majesty."

"Then you will retain your rank as general, though from now on, you will answer to General Altair in all matters." Daniel gestured to Marcus, who stood tall and proud, undaunted by the challenges ahead. Kyrin's heart swelled to see his steadfast courage. It couldn't be easy for him to face the reality of going back to dealing with the General regularly after all that had transpired since Marcus had left that life. And yet she found no hesitation in his expression.

Neither did she find it in the General's as he nodded in acceptance.

Daniel's voice changed slightly then from the one he used as king to the one she knew was simply Daniel.

"We have much damage to repair. Arcacia has been hurting for too long. People want peace and to feel secure. That can't happen if there is any dissension in our military. I'm charging you and General Altair with making sure there is order and unity, and I expect you to work side by side to see that it is accomplished."

The General once again bowed his head. "It will be, Your Majesty."

"Good. It is my hope and prayer that what we've accomplished will bring peace and prosperity to Arcacia and our allies for generations to come. I know many wrongs will need to be made right and that the pain that has been suffered will take time to heal. It is my personal hope that you will seek to make amends with your family. I know it won't be easy"—Daniel glanced at Kyrin—"but with so many families torn apart, I would like to see any that can come back together."

Now the pressure in Kyrin's throat burned with welling tears.

Her grandfather looked between her and Marcus, something tentatively hopeful in his usually cold eyes. "I will do whatever I can to make that happen."

The promise rang true of genuine intention. While Kyrin wasn't sure if she would ever be able to trust him completely, she knew she had to be willing to take steps toward it. If men like James, Holden, and even Jace could change, so could her grandfather.

A QUIET LUNCH with Jace was just what Kyrin needed to relax and process the emotions of seeing her grandfather. It restored enough of her energy that she was ready to go over notes about the morning with Daniel as soon as they finished their meal. This time, she and Jace met him in his office. It was the first time she'd been in the room since they'd taken the palace, and a wave of memories washed over her. Any time she'd been summoned here by Daican had been fraught with fear. This was where he had gathered condemning information from her about Avery's father and where he'd questioned her loyalty before dragging her to the temple.

She took a shallow breath, a cold sensation filling her chest, but the sight of Daniel sitting behind the desk soothed it. He'd laid his crown aside and must have run his hand through his hair because it was no longer lying neatly. It reminded her of the first time she'd seen him, bursting into the dining room all disheveled from a day of riding in the forest. She laughed quietly to herself, her lungs freeing up.

The sound must have caught his attention. He stood up as they walked farther into the room and gestured to the two empty chairs across from him. "Please, sit."

They did so, and he focused on Kyrin. "Thank you for your willingness to get this over with right away. Are you feeling all right?"

"Yes, better now that I've eaten." Thankfully, fresh air had indeed eased her headache.

"Well, let me know if you need a break or want to finish some other time."

He took a seat again and picked up the notes Trev had made. Solora was there as well, sitting a little off to the side. She offered her advice on dealing with some of the more problematic people on the list, and it didn't take nearly as long as Kyrin anticipated to work through everyone. She was a little queasy at one point, but Daniel sent for tea, which helped.

When they finished, he set aside the notes and seemed almost as relieved as Kyrin. "Now I can finally focus on getting things running smoothly here at the palace and get the military in order. We'll be that much closer to functioning normally as a country again."

Peace and normality were exactly what Kyrin was hoping for. "I'm glad I've been able to help."

"You've more than just helped. You've given me a sense of security in my decisions, which will certainly grant a peace of mind moving forward."

Kyrin smiled. It was so different using her abilities to aid Daniel than it had been with his father. So much fear had been involved with Daican, but this was much more fulfilling, even if she wasn't keen on ever having to do it again.

"Before we go, I wanted to mention one person from the army. He wasn't here today because he's not a commander, but I think you should be aware of him. His name is Scerle. He is the one who led the surprise attack at Fort Rhall, took us captive, and ordered the killing of the other prisoners. He used to work under Marcus and has a reputation as a cruel interrogator."

Kyrin grimaced. He had also been the one threatening to cut her throat when she, Jace, and Kaden had been captured and taken to Fort Rivor. "I don't think he's going to be one to take this transition well."

Daniel scribbled the name on a piece of paper. "I'll bring it up with Marcus and the General. If he hasn't disappeared and remains with the army, I'll make sure he's watched and kept on a short leash."

If anyone deserved to face charges for his conduct over the past couple of years, it was Scerle, but Kyrin understood how tricky matters were for Daniel where the military was concerned. At least steps would be taken to make sure Scerle's cruelty didn't continue.

Now that they had finished, Daniel started to rise, but Solora spoke.

"Have you decided what you will do about Collin? I know he desires to remain employed as a guard here at the palace."

Daniel sank back down, his brows furrowing. "I guess I hadn't given it thought yet. I figured I would discuss security personnel with Aric." He cast Kyrin a questioning look. "You don't have any doubts about his loyalty?"

"No. He risked everything to help me. He was a prisoner of Davira's whims, and I can't imagine how he suffered for it. And continues to suffer. He needs to heal, and I think remaining in employment here is the best way to do that. Especially since he will be exposed to your faith and Aric's and others around him. Only Elôm can completely heal him."

She prayed for this outcome. Her heart still hurt to remember the hopelessness she'd seen in his eyes at the arena. While she'd never exactly considered them friends, they did have a long history.

Daniel turned back to his mother. "I guess I see no reason not to keep him on as palace security."

"Good." Solora seemed oddly pleased as she gracefully rose from her chair. "Send for him. I have something to show you."

She left the room without explanation. Daniel traded a look with Kyrin and Jace, one brow raised, and then shrugged before getting up to send Aric to get Collin. Kyrin wasn't sure whether she or Jace had any part of this, but curiosity kept her in her seat. Collin had been part of her everyday life for a good number of years. Part of her was invested now to see where he ended up.

A few minutes later, Aric brought him into the office. Collin bowed to Daniel before darting a glance at Kyrin. His rigid posture radiated uncertainty, and he kept his gaze downcast as he addressed Daniel. "You sent for me, Your Majesty?"

"Yes. Well, actually, my mother did. I'm not quite sure where she went, but she should return shortly."

Collin's forehead crinkled a little, proving he had no more knowledge of what this was about than they did.

An awkward silence followed. Kyrin was about to break it and assure Collin he wasn't in trouble because his breaths were far too measured, but the click of Solora's heels did so instead. She entered the office, a soft pink blanket bundled in her arms. An angelic face with wispy blonde hair and two tiny little hands peeked out. The baby couldn't have been more than a couple of months old. Kyrin shared a confused look with Jace. No one had mentioned anything about a baby in the palace.

Daniel was just as bewildered, judging by the frown on his face as he eyed the infant from across the desk. "Whose baby is that?"

"Your sister's."

Kyrin's jaw dropped open. Davira? A mother? She couldn't wrap her mind around such a twisted individual, even going through the process of carrying a child. Why had she?

A choked sound came from Daniel's throat as he gaped at his mother. "Davira had a baby?"

"Yes. She wanted a son to raise as emperor, but she had a daughter instead." Solora adjusted the blanket, and the baby, eyes closed in sleep, shifted a little and smacked her lips. Kyrin had never seen such a soft and loving look on the queen's face. "She wanted her killed, but I insisted on taking her."

Daniel just blinked, still gaping, though whether it was simply due to the baby or that Davira was so evil as to want to murder her own child was hard to say. The thought of it sent a chill creeping down Kyrin's back, and she rested her hand over her stomach. Thank Elôm that Davira was no longer a threat to anyone's life.

Daniel's mouth worked before finally finding his voice again. "Who's the father?"

Solora turned slightly to the one person everyone had momentarily forgotten in the room. "He is."

Everyone's gaze swerved to Collin.

Now it was his turn to gape, his voice raw and breathless. "What? But…she said I wasn't."

"Only because she didn't want you to have any claim to her heir if it was a boy."

Collin's too-wide eyes shifted between her and the baby. He hardly seemed to breathe at first, but then each breath came too rapidly, and Kyrin read every sign of growing panic. Solora approached him and held out the baby. He stood frozen, the fear becoming more evident. Fear and self-loathing. It was clear in the way he seemed to shrink away from her and into himself. For a moment, Kyrin thought he would turn away, but then he took a gulping breath and reached out slowly for his daughter.

The baby gave a mournful whine at being disturbed and stuck her lip out as her face scrunched. Her tiny fists waved before she pulled them toward her face, where her thumb plopped into her mouth and her expression smoothed peacefully. It wasn't even her baby, but Kyrin's heart melted. How could Davira reject something so precious? The same emotions must have ignited inside Collin because the tension released from his shoulders, and his breathing slowed. His expression shifted to one of wonder, a hint of a smile growing on his lips.

Solora took a step back. "We've been calling her Elodie."

Collin repeated the name as if in a dreamlike state.

Solora smiled, though it slowly dimmed, and she crossed her arms over her chest like she mourned the loss, bereft of the baby. "I wasn't sure if I would tell you. I didn't want you to take her away, but…she should know her father. I only ask you, please, do not take her far. She is my first living grandchild."

Collin lifted his gaze from his child, blinking back into reality. "I won't."

Daniel stepped around the desk to approach them, staring at little Elodie. Kyrin was sure his eyes were a bit watery as he brushed his fingers lightly over his niece's wispy hair with a gentle smile. After a moment, he cleared his throat and raised his gaze to Collin. "You may remain here at Auréa and resume your post if that is what you wish. Of course, everything will be provided for Elodie's needs, regardless of whether or not you stay."

Collin dipped his head. "Thank you, Your Majesty. It would be my honor to continue serving you here at the palace."

The three of them went back to gazing at the baby, and Kyrin smiled at the quiet joy surrounding the moment. This was just what Collin needed. With Elodie in his life, it gave him both family and a purpose. A reason to put the darkness behind him and seek a brighter future.

Not wanting to interrupt this time of bonding, Kyrin motioned to Jace, and they quietly slipped out of the room. Out in the hall, she released a happy sigh.

"Isn't it amazing how something so precious could come from such evil? It's beautiful how Elôm can do that." She rubbed her hand over her belly. "Just think, several months from now, we'll be holding our own baby."

She caught Jace's brows quirk oddly.

"Will it be that small?"

"It may be even smaller. I'm not sure exactly how old Elodie is, but she's probably grown since she was born."

He didn't say anything, but some trepidation now lurked in his eyes. She smiled and leaned into him.

"Don't worry. It'll be all right. At least we have time to prepare for it."

A cool breeze smelling of salt, pine, and rock gusted down from the mountain peaks overhead. It whipped Leetra's hair around her shoulders and made her eyes water. At least, that's what she wanted to blame the moisture on. It couldn't explain away the heaviness in her lungs, however, as she stood beside the pile of stone she had helped construct in the cold and snow two and a half years ago.

Timothy knelt near the head of Josan's grave, his hand resting on one of the stones. Aaron stood behind him, gripping his shoulder. While neither of them cried, Timothy's eyes looked just as wet as Leetra's, and that choked her all the more. She blinked hard and glanced to her right where Talas and Darq stood, both stoic, as they all remembered Josan. She had been such a stubborn fool back then.

Timothy finally rose and had to clear his throat twice before speaking. "He would be so happy to see how far we've come." He smiled tearfully at Aaron. "He would love Lacy and Isaac."

Then his gaze shifted to Leetra. No doubt he'd been about to say how happy Josan would be for them, but the words didn't come as his expression dipped to one of concern. He walked over to her. "You shouldn't be feeling guilty."

Oh, but she still did. She sucked in a breath, trying to open her lungs and fight the burn in her nose. She couldn't find the strength to look him in the eyes. Falcor's crimes were not hers, but her connection to him still left her feeling tainted. To think of the hurt he had caused so many, especially Timothy, burned inside her because she couldn't help but wonder if she could have stopped it had she not been so blind and arrogant.

Timothy rested his hands on her shoulders, warming the skin through the thin fabric of her sleeves. The warmth seeped down into her chest along with his gentle voice.

"It's time to let go of what happened and focus on the future. *Our* future."

Slowly, she lifted her gaze to his. As always, his deep brown eyes were soft and understanding, soothing the ache in her heart. Two tears slipped from her eyes. Her first instinct was to swipe them away, but she resisted. He had taught her it was okay to be vulnerable. Okay to let those who loved her see her broken pieces. She took another deep breath of the mountain air, letting the freshness wash through her. Yes, she would not let the past ruin their future.

Timothy rubbed her arms and gave her an encouraging smile before looking at Darq. Something unspoken passed between them, and Timothy nodded to a silent question. With this approval, Darq focused on Leetra.

"You should know that Falcor will face justice for his crimes."

Leetra straightened, letting some of her defenses fall back into place. They hadn't seen nor heard any word from Falcor since Samara had fallen. The traitor crete they'd captured in Dorland last summer had been the last one to even mention him. Leetra had accepted the belief he'd simply disappeared as things tipped in their favor, though the idea of him lurking somewhere in the shadows had left her unsettled. But Darq's words suggested that wasn't true.

"What do you mean?"

"From what we've gathered, Davira imprisoned him shortly after Daican's death. He was held at the arena for much of the past several months. Jace fought him."

The thump of Leetra's heart echoed in her ears. "Is he dead then?"

"No, Jace let him live."

Not entirely sure what emotions surged inside of her, Falcor's betrayal still stabbed at her, though not with the ferocity it once had. Relief had overshadowed it. Relief to have discovered his true nature before being bound to him in marriage. Now she simply suffered the anger over how he had hurt others. She wasn't sure she would have been so merciful in Jace's position.

"Where is he now?"

"Still at the arena along with some other prisoners. I've spoken with the king, and the decision has been made that when our riders depart for Arvael, we will take Falcor with us to stand trial there."

He was a traitor to his people and an enemy of Ilyon. Leetra knew what his fate would be.

Darq's voice lowered compassionately. "It won't repair the damage he did, but at least it will bring closure and, I hope, allow you to put it behind you."

He was right. It wouldn't bring back Josan or William Altair. It wouldn't erase the scar Talas bore from Falcor's blade or ease the pain and shame his family had to endure. It wouldn't fully erase the pain of betrayal. But it did mean they could move on. No one else would get hurt.

She dipped her chin in a firm nod and turned back to Timothy. His eyes searched her face, no doubt to determine whether or not she was all right. A couple of years ago, she would have shut him out and blocked herself off behind her walls with anger simmering and pain eating away. That was no way to live.

Leaving it to Elôm, she leaned closer to Timothy, resting her hands on his chest and not caring a bit that everyone was watching. "Let's talk about our future."

The warmth of his smile about made her knees give out. "Well, how about we walk down to the trees and see where Aaron said would be a good spot to build a house or two? We'll need a place once I start teaching at Tarvin Hall with Sam. I don't think the rooms there are set up to accommodate hammocks."

She grinned, and he shifted to wrap his arm around her shoulders. Together, they led the way toward the majestic pines farther down the slope.

DANIEL STOOD IN the shadowed, cavernous interior of the temple, the air cool and still laced with spicy incense. It was empty now, save for a couple of torches he would remove when he left. His shadow wavered against the bare ledge where the gold idols once stood. He'd had them removed and melted down into coins, which would help support the widows and orphans left in Davira's wake. It wouldn't be nearly enough, but it was a start.

A little over a month had passed since they'd defeated Davira, and today marked the official celebration. He'd made sure the whole city was included, hiring local bakers and entertainers to offer free food and amusement in the city square. Though he couldn't see it for himself, others had reported it was a massive success. Much better than the executions that had been held there so frequently.

Here at the palace, nobles from across the country had been arriving since yesterday for the royal celebration planned this evening. Overseeing it all was a chaotic whirlwind, but things were going about as smoothly as one could hope, especially for his first time hosting guests as king. He prayed it wouldn't end as catastrophically as Auréa's last celebration. There would be no accepting drinks or participating in any random toasts for him tonight, or probably ever.

He was glad for a moment away from it all. The temple wasn't the first place he normally would have chosen, but it was quiet and a good spot to reminisce over what had brought him here. Kaden, Talas, Darq, and a few of their other riders waited outside with their dragons for him to leave so they could begin tearing down the structure. What better way to commemorate the day and show his dedication to Elôm and to ending the fear and violence perpetrated by those dedicated to idol worship?

Light footsteps echoed behind him, and another shadow moved into the circle of quivering torchlight. He turned to find Kyrin. Her eyes were lifted, taking in the yawning darkness high above them before dropping to his.

Daniel gestured to the space around them. "This is where it all started for you, isn't it?"

She nodded, a half smile in place. He could tell she was reliving it in vivid detail.

"It was one of the most terrifying moments of my life, but I'll never forget how Elôm gave me the courage to defy your father. I can't explain it—how absolutely clear the choice was and the peace it gave me."

If only Daniel could have seen it. It must have been a sight to behold her standing up to his father like that. "I remember when you were dragged out and then hearing what happened. I applauded you for your bravery."

Her smile grew for a moment before dimming. "When I saw you, I was so disappointed in myself that I had never talked to you about Elôm. Do you remember the day you and your father came bursting into the library arguing and shouting, not realizing I was there?"

It took Daniel a moment, but it all came rushing back, along with some embarrassment. "Ah yes, when I was acting the imma-ture fool and nearly threw a book at your head? Granted, it was by accident." He rubbed his hand over his face. He *really* hoped

Jace didn't know about that.

Kyrin laughed, the sound dispelling a little of the gloom around them. "Yes, that day."

"I probably won't forget it again now that you've reminded me. I made a fool of myself quite often back then, lashing out. I'm sorry you had to witness it, especially now that I'm king, and I know you'll remember every detail of it for the rest of your life."

She laughed again and shook her head. "Don't worry; I won't go telling everyone."

"You have my undying gratitude." He was only half teasing.

Kyrin released a sigh, her brows lowering to erase the remnants of her laughter. "You aren't the only one with regrets. I brought it up because I should've told you about Elôm that day. I wanted to, but I was so afraid, and I just froze. I've always regretted that."

Daniel could hardly blame her, considering her tenuous position at the palace and the danger involved, but he understood the regret of not taking action. "Well, thankfully, Elôm is not dependent on our actions and can still work in our failures. You might not have said anything then, but standing for your faith, even to the point of execution, inspired me. I may not have been open to accepting Elon when He appeared to me had you not shown such dedicated faith."

Though it wasn't his intent, her eyes grew awfully watery-looking in the torchlight as he spoke. "Sorry, I didn't mean to make you emotional."

Her smile returned, and she blinked away the tears. "No, thank you for telling me."

Daniel took one last look around the temple, where he, too, had declared his faith before his father. How many empty prayers had filled this space, his own among them? He raised a prayer now that, through his leadership, his people would come to know Elôm's deep love for them.

Filled with a fresh sense of purpose, he grabbed the nearest torch. "I suppose we should leave before the others get too antsy and start tearing this place down on top of us."

Kyrin's laughter filled the temple once more as they turned toward the entrance. "Probably."

Jace typically didn't like parties, especially on this grand scale, but Kyrin was excited, and it was to celebrate their victory, so he determined to enjoy it. He would undoubtedly be dragged into other such gatherings in the future now that his sister was the queen. It would be best to get used to it. He would feel better once Kyrin joined him, but she was still upstairs getting ready with her mother, Anne, and the other women. He'd wanted to wait up there with her, but she'd gently shooed him away and told him to go find his friends.

So he'd found an out-of-the-way spot to wait with Rayad, Holden, Elian, Saul, and others of their group just outside the ballroom. Most of the guests mingled inside the room, and the longer he could avoid them, the better. Most of those present tonight were strangers to him, being lords and ladies from throughout Arcacia. They made Jace nervous. There was no telling where their loyalties lay, and that made them dangerous. Only Elôm knew what they could be plotting. But, as Kyrin had reminded him, there was always danger in politics and ruling a country. All they could do was be vigilant and pray that most would hold at least some loyalty to Daniel after tonight. That was one of the primary purposes of this celebration.

At least Aric had stationed plenty of security around, remaining watchful at the edges of the gathering. Jace might even find himself benefiting from such protection. He'd already received some sideways glances and suspicious looks from passersby.

However, they weren't nearly as hostile and obvious as the looks Saul received.

Just now, a stuffy, thin-faced noble passed, his lip curled as he shot Saul a scathing look and gave the whole group a wide berth. Jace's insides prickled, and he had to tamp down the urge to leave the situation entirely. Across from him, Holden drew himself up and pinned the noble with a smoldering look of his own. The man tipped his chin up and increased his pace, practically scurrying into the ballroom. Holden snorted and turned to Saul. "You're brave for being here."

The fact that he was the one to stand up for Saul and offer the compliment showed how far he had come in his own prejudice toward ryriks.

Saul shrugged, seeming undaunted by the hostility. "Tonight is about unity. The king wants to continue building a friendship between Arcacia and the ryriks of Dorland. To do that, perceptions have to change, and that can't be accomplished by hiding. I knew exactly what I was getting myself into when I accepted the invitation."

Jace caught a couple of women huddled together, whispering behind their hands and pointing even now, their gazes darting between both him and Saul. Next to his friend, he probably appeared the same as any other full-blooded ryrik. "You are handling the hostility better than I typically have."

Really, his calm acceptance was enviable. Even now, the attention made Jace's skin itch.

"I do not blame them for their suspicion and fear. They haven't yet been given a reason not to fear ryriks."

He did have a point. Even Jace had held the same suspicions and fears before meeting Saul and those from his village. Still, he didn't quite excuse the outright disgust many of the people exhibited. It wasn't like Saul was here uninvited. That should count for something.

Saul gestured toward the ballroom. "Besides, the cretes and Dorlanders are getting their share of gawking looks."

That was true. No one was particularly shy or subtle about gaping at Captain Darq and the other cretes, whose leather clothing and long beaded hair were nothing like the fancy tailored outfits and ball gowns everyone else wore. But it was Prince Haedrin who drew most of the attention. How could he not when he stood a good four feet taller than just about every other person except his fellow giants? Even though Jace was now used to cretes and giants, seeing them in this formal setting beside Arcacians, Samarans, and talcrins was quite a sight.

"I was talking to the king and Lord Trask earlier." Saul's voice pulled Jace's attention back to the conversation. "They told me about your camps in Landale and how they'll likely be empty once everyone returns home. They've extended an invitation to the ryriks of Dorland that if any of us wish to settle in Arcacia, we're welcome to make homes in the camps."

This was the first Jace had heard of the idea. "Really?"

"Yes. Trying to fit in and live alongside Arcacians will not be easy, but Lord Trask thought this would be a good way to begin. The camps are far enough away from more populated areas to allow people to get used to the idea as well as provide some security for our families."

"Would you ever consider moving there?" Jace wasn't sure where he and Kyrin would find themselves—they hadn't yet discussed that particular detail—but wherever they ended up, having Saul in Landale would be much closer than Dorland.

"Of course, I'd have to discuss that with Jayna, but I'm open to the possibility. I know it won't be easy for our people to gain acceptance, and it may take a few generations before that becomes a reality, but I think Landale would be a good start."

Jace agreed. Though he hadn't initially wanted to be there, there was something special about Landale, and it seemed like the perfect place for peaceful ryriks to settle, especially with Trask being lord over the area.

Before anyone could voice further thoughts on the matter, a large, imposing figure approached the group. Jace couldn't help the way his body tensed at the sight of the General. He hadn't seen him since the day he'd sworn his allegiance to Daniel in the throne room. Tonight he was outfitted in what must be a newly constructed general's uniform of blue and gold. To see it on him after everything that had happened over the past three years didn't quite feel right, but Jace understood and even agreed with the decisions that had been made regarding the man. Still, it didn't alleviate the apprehension that darted through his stomach when he realized the General had focused on him.

Pausing at the edge of the group, the General glanced at the others before settling his heavy gaze back on Jace. He seemed much more like his intimidating self than he had as their prisoner, though his voice didn't hold the sharp-edged derision it had when he'd addressed Jace in the past. "Might I have a brief word?"

Jace exchanged looks with Rayad and Holden. Both cast the General mistrustful glances as if he had no business speaking with him, and Holden looked like he might be contemplating telling him off. Jace knew for a fact that the entire group would rally around him if needed. The General must have sensed this as well because a little of his self-assuredness seemed to fade as he shifted uncomfortably.

While Jace had no desire to speak with him, he had to accept that the man was family. Reconciliation might never be possible, but he did wish to see Kyrin's family continue to heal. For that to happen, he, too, would have to put aside past hurts.

With a nod, he stepped away from the group and joined the General in a more secluded corner nearby. His heart gave a nervous thump as they turned to face each other. The last time they'd had any direct interaction was at Fort Rivor when the

General had let his men beat Jace half to death immediately after having him whipped. Jace's breaths grew shallow, phantom pain knifing across his ribs and up his back. But he did not back down. He stood his ground and held the man's gaze.

Despite his own discomfort, he found it was the General who had trouble maintaining eye contact. The man cleared his throat twice and smoothed the front of his surcoat before finally speaking.

"I understand you're the one who told Kyrin she should forgive me before I was traded in Samara."

Jace nodded slowly, unsure how he'd figured that out or how he felt about it. "Yes. I didn't want her living with that bitterness."

Again, the General cleared his throat. Considering how brash and in control he'd always been, his unease was strange to witness. "I thank you for that, even though it was for her benefit, not mine."

Jace shrugged, and now the General's eyes locked with his. The measure of sincerity in their depths was not what he expected.

"I was wondering if I might also be granted your forgiveness for what transpired at Fort Rivor. I now realize that my perceptions and beliefs were inaccurate." The General sent a glance toward Saul. At least someone here was open to seeing ryriks in a better light. "And my actions were cruel. I should not have had you whipped or beaten. I apologize, though I'm sure it's of little consolation."

It must have been particularly difficult for a man of such pride and authority to admit his mistakes. Though it would be hard to forget the pain and cruelty he had inflicted entirely, Jace was in no position to hold the past over him. "I accept your apology, and I do forgive you."

The General slowly released a breath as if the forgiveness had released a burden. Maybe it had. When he spoke again, his words were less stilted but more tentative. "I'm sure nothing will ease the pain I caused for Kyrin, but I hope, perhaps, this conversation may bring her some manner of peace. She clearly loves you deeply. That much was evident even back at Fort Rivor."

Jace couldn't hold back the smile that thought evoked. "And I have always loved her just as much."

The General gave a satisfied grunt that suggested he truly cared about his family underneath all his unraveling, misguided ideals. "Good."

He straightened, becoming the self-assured general of Arcacia's army once again, and gestured toward the group. "I will let you return to your friends before they see fit to remove me from your presence."

Jace looked over at the others, only realizing now how they were all staring the General down. He chuckled to himself, and he and the General parted ways. They may never consider each other friends, but he prayed tonight was a step toward healing for their family.

Everyone eyed Jace when he rejoined them, but it was Holden who asked, "Well?"

"He apologized for Fort Rivor."

Brows lifted. Though the General had clearly been repentant regarding his family, Jace hadn't expected to receive such remorse himself. Judging by their reactions, the others hadn't either, but Rayad did look distinctly pleased by it. Hopefully, Kyrin would be as well.

A few minutes later, movement from the double staircase nearby caught Jace's attention. The women had appeared, though only one captured his gaze. Kyrin descended the stairs gracefully in a shimmering sky-blue gown with gauzy white sleeves nearly as long as the dress. Silver embroidery and crystal beading caught the light across the front of the bodice while her hair curled in rich contrast across her shoulders.

The breath evaporated from his lungs, and someone nudged him forward. He didn't even know who it had been, but he strode to the base of the staircase, still gazing at Kyrin. This time she met his eyes, hers gleaming as a brilliant smile lit up her face. At the last step, he reached for her hand and looked her up and down, taking in every part of her, including the little swell to her belly that had shown up just recently. He found himself looking for it often these days, and he liked how easily he could spot it in the fitted dress.

At the moment, he wasn't sure he could form any words, but as usual, she read him well enough without them.

"You're certainly reacting better than Kaden did the first time he saw me all dressed up."

The breath returned to Jace's chest with a small laugh, and he leaned closer to murmur in her ear. "Well, Kaden is your brother, not your husband."

She laughed, too, a twinkle in her eye, and Jace had to remind himself of the crowd lest he kiss her in front of everyone. Not that he particularly cared at this moment, but he'd rather not draw unnecessary attention to either of them. He offered her his arm, and they stepped aside to allow more room for the others.

Though he hated to tear his eyes away from Kyrin, he did see Trask step past them to reach for Anne. He looked equally as smitten with his wife as Jace was with Kyrin, but it was Elian who caught Jace's full attention. Jace's mother descended the stairs just behind Anne, dressed in a shimmering, deep blue gown, and Elian was right there waiting for her. Jace had seen them talking more in the last few weeks. They took things slowly, but the way Elian gazed at Jace's mother revealed the deep love in his heart. Judging by the softness of her expression and the way she held his gaze, she felt the same. As she reached for Elian's arm, Jace realized this was the first time he'd seen her without her wedding ring. Happiness settled warmly inside him. Perhaps tonight marked a shift in which both his mother and Elian could forget the past and have a future filled with love and joy.

He felt Kyrin hug his arm a little closer, and they shared a smile.

A short time later, everyone was called into the ballroom in preparation for Daniel and Elanor's entrance. Holding Kyrin close, Jace guided her into the room with the rest of the crowd. Conversation buzzed all around, everyone anxious for the arrival of the king and queen to officially commence the celebration.

They joined Kyrin's mother and brothers off to the side. Liam and Ronny were dressed in typical formal attire, but both Marcus and Kaden wore fresh military uniforms. Jace envied them. At least they were wearing something familiar and comfortable. Jace had a feeling Ronny would agree with him based on how he fidgeted and tugged at his collar. But it didn't take away from the wonder on his face as he tried to take everything in, hardly able to stand still amidst the excitement of the evening. His mother put a hand on his shoulder to try to still him, and Jace chuckled to himself.

A couple of minutes later, Aric called for everyone's attention. It took a few moments for all of the talking and murmuring to die down completely, but when it did, it was as if everyone was waiting with bated breath. The silence almost made Jace uncomfortable, but then Aric's strong voice cut through the stillness.

"Presenting Their Majesties, King Daniel and Queen Elanor."

The door at the other end of the ballroom opened, and Daniel and Elanor entered to collective oohs and ahhs that quickly broke into cheers and applause. The two were radiant in their coordinating blue and gold outfits, Elanor especially. Her blue satin and gold brocade gown was certainly fit for a queen. Seeing her in a crown was still strange, but she wore it with all grace and dignity.

The guards cleared a path for them to a small cordoned-off area where it would be easy to greet their guests in an orderly manner. A line quickly formed of nobles who wished to meet the two of them personally. Jace did not envy them one bit, but at least Daniel liked people, and Elanor had always had a bubbly, friendly personality.

Those who didn't immediately get in line continued to mingle. Through the crowd, Jace spotted his mother again. This time she wasn't just with Elian but with two other people Jace recognized. His grandparents. He hadn't realized they were in attendance tonight, though he should have anticipated it. His grandfather was an earl, after all.

As soon as it became apparent his mother was leading them toward him, tension spread across his shoulders. While he was more than happy to see his grandmother again, the last time they'd all been together, his grandfather had been willing to let Rothas hang him.

Kyrin's hand closed comfortingly around his arm. He looked down, her gentle smile soothing him. He drew a deep breath and squared his shoulders. It didn't matter what his grandfather thought of him anyway. If he could handle Kyrin's grandfather, he could certainly handle his own.

The moment his mother and grandparents reached them, his grandmother did not hesitate to draw him into her embrace.

"Jace, it is so good to see you. I'm so glad you're well." They parted, though she kept her hands on his arms for a moment longer. "You've had my prayers daily since you left Ashwood."

"Thank you." Mere words would never adequately express just how much he appreciated those prayers. "I know they've been answered in many different ways."

All eyes now turned to Jace's grandfather. Jace didn't need Kyrin to read the discomfort lining the man's face. He seemed to be looking anywhere but at Jace before finally catching his gaze and nodding. "Jace."

Though his voice was a bit gruff, Jace had the distinct feeling guilt prickled underneath it. He returned the nod. "Grandfather."

While no verbal apology was forthcoming, Jace was willing to accept the unease as a sign his grandfather's heart had changed in the last couple of years. As with Kyrin and her grandfather, a relationship was something they would have to build over time.

Another awkward silence grew between them, but Grandmother hurried to fill it. "I hear you're married now." She cast Kyrin a warm smile.

Jace drew her closer, letting any lingering bitterness toward his grandfather fade. "Yes, this is my wife, Kyrin."

Grandmother took Kyrin's hands in her own. "I am so pleased to meet you, my dear. Now that you can safely visit Ashwood, I want you both to know you're welcome at Brandell." She sent Jace an earnest look. "I so very much want to get to know both of you better."

Jace nodded. He would never stop thanking Elôm for the miracle of now being able to visit his mother and the rest of his family whenever he chose without fear. "Thank you. You can be sure we'll visit."

Kyrin shifted back to his side and leaned into him, her hand rising to rest on her belly. "Yes, we will want you to meet your first great-grandchild."

Grandmother's mouth opened, though words didn't immediately come, and her round eyes filled with moisture. When Jace glanced over at his grandfather, he found that the stubborn look he seemed to wear regularly had softened, and even his eyes grew a little misty.

KYRIN HAD A feeling that, underneath his gruff exterior, Jace's grandfather was more of a softy than he let on. Considering the family history and the devastation he must have felt when Jace's mother was attacked, she wouldn't be surprised if his blustery personality came as a form of protection against the pain he'd no doubt suffered over the years. In many ways, it reminded her of Jace. He had tried many times to hide his pain and protect himself with a cold exterior since they'd first met.

But that was the past, and she looked forward to seeing how his grandfather might open up and soften as Jace had now that the family was reunited and growing. At least the relationship wasn't quite as complicated as the one with her own grandfather.

Charles joined them then, bringing his calm, positive manner with him. It helped his father to relax even more, and they all talked companionably about the future and the opportunities it brought.

A few minutes later, Kyrin caught sight of a woman making her way toward them. She was a bit taller than Kyrin but willowy and graceful. The dark curls gathered up at the base of her neck were surely natural, considering how they wisped out a bit rebelliously around her face. Though she was about ten years

Kyrin's senior, a youthful smattering of light freckles dusted her face. How refreshing that she had not tried to conceal them with cosmetics as vainer noblewomen would have.

Shyness dominated her demeanor as she drew near, but her smile was bright. "Excuse me. I do not wish to intrude." She cast an apologetic look at the group as a whole, though her gaze rested first on Jace before focusing on Kyrin. "I hope this is not too strange of me to ask but are you Kyrin and Jace?"

Kyrin traded a glance with Jace, who looked a little bewildered that a stranger would know his name. "Yes, we are."

The woman's hazel eyes lit with a joy Kyrin couldn't hope to understand until she spoke. "I've heard so much about you these past couple of years—about how you stood for your faith and your time with Elon. It has been such an encouragement to me. I knew I had to meet you and was afraid I would lose my nerve if I didn't do it now. I do apologize for interrupting."

It took Kyrin a moment to find her voice. "No, no, not at all. I'm glad you did." She glanced over at Jace again and nearly laughed at how uncomfortable he looked to be the subject of such admiration. She barely knew what to do with it herself. "I think you'll find us both a bit shocked, though. We're only a very small part of what Elôm has done in the last couple of years."

"Even so, you brought light to darkness, and for that, I am thankful. Now, before I ramble on and completely forget my manners, I'm Lady Emaya. My father is the Earl of Covel. I don't wish to take any more of your time; I only wanted you to know how Elôm used you to touch my life."

She dipped in a small curtsy and half-turned to leave before Charles stepped in.

"Covel? That's quite some distance northeast of here, isn't it?"

Emaya turned back to them, seeming to relax at the mention of her home. "Indeed. It was quite a long trip, but one we were more than happy to make."

"Did you travel with your husband?"

Kyrin had to bite back a smile. Though a casual question, she did not miss the interest in his tone.

Emaya ducked her head, the slightest shade of pink dusting her freckled cheeks. "No, with my parents. I am unmarried." She raised her gaze back to him. "I suppose that is strange for a woman my age, but finding fellow believers has not been easy."

"No, it hasn't." The understanding hum to his voice surely didn't go unnoticed.

Emaya tipped her head slightly, her tone turning her words into a subtle inquiry. "Hopefully, that is changing."

Charles's handsome answering smile was surely enough to melt the heart of any unattached woman, particularly the one standing before him, and Kyrin fought doubly hard to smother a grin. No doubt she would be recounting this story for years to come.

He formally introduced himself then, along with the rest of the family. Emaya greeted them all with such a sweet, genuine quality it only reinforced what a lovely match she made with Charles. At least in Kyrin's mind. He inquired about her parents, and she revealed that her father had been imprisoned for his faith for nearly a year, while she and her mother had been placed under house arrest. Now Kyrin could understand why Emaya would draw encouragement from what she and Jace had been through.

Before long, dinner was announced. Kyrin wasn't the least bit surprised when Charles offered to escort Emaya to the dining room, and the two of them stepped away to locate her parents. Kyrin shared a delighted look with Rachel and then turned to take Jace's arm as everyone moved toward the dining room.

Leaning close to him along the way, she murmured, "I think you just met your new aunt."

One of Jace's brows lifted. "That's rushing it a bit, don't you think?"

"Maybe, but there is definitely a strong connection there, and I think they're positively adorable together. Your mother agrees with me."

He still did not look entirely convinced, but she would absolutely remind him of this moment when the time came.

In the dining room, Daniel and Elanor sat at a raised table, along with their ally leaders, overlooking the rest of the room. Kyrin and Jace sat at a table nearby, quickly joined by their closest friends. Kaden sat to Kyrin's left, Ronny just down from him. The meal before them rivaled even that of Tarvin Hall's celebration feast. Ronny verbally exclaimed his wonderment, and he and Kaden dug in with abandon. Kyrin laughed at both their enthusiasm and their mother's exasperated eye roll as she reminded them they were in a formal setting.

Though Kyrin had noticed not every noble looked particularly pleased to be here tonight, everyone seemed to relax during the meal. As far as she could tell, whenever she looked around, no one seemed to be complaining or quietly scheming amongst themselves other than a few withering looks cast at Saul. She supposed that was to be expected. Only time would change that.

The meal concluded some time later with everyone in high spirits, and they returned to the ballroom where both Arcacian and crete musicians took turns performing, encouraging couples to pair up to dance. Timothy and Leetra were amongst the first, a stark contrast to how Leetra used to avoid him at celebrations.

Before Kyrin could think about joining in with Jace, she spotted Collin standing guard at the perimeter nearby. She had not had a chance to speak with him properly since Davira's demise.

She touched Jace's arm to get his attention. "Excuse me for just a moment."

Leaving him to talk with Holden and James, she wove through the crowd toward Collin. Seeing him standing there reminded her of the first formal dinner she had attended after coming to the palace. Though she didn't miss the way he had so boldly flirted with her back then, it hurt to see his vibrant personality so subdued. However, the smile he gave her as she approached held more peace, and his eyes lacked the tortured quality she'd seen at the arena.

"Kyrin, you're looking well tonight. Jace is a lucky man."

It was a genuine compliment, and Kyrin accepted it with a smile. "Thank you. How are you settling into being a father?"

There was that twinkle in his eyes that she remembered, though now it held a deep and genuine love. "Better than I expected. Elodie smiled at me for the first time the other day. It's hard not to just sit and watch her."

Kyrin grinned and rubbed her belly. She couldn't wait to experience that firsthand. "I'm sure it is. I'm very happy for you." She paused, considering the long history between them. "It's crazy the two of us being here like this again after everything that happened."

"It is. It's hard to believe I'm even here tonight. Thank you for confirming my loyalty to the king."

"It was the least I could do after what you did for me. That's why I came over here. I wanted to properly thank you for trying to protect me from Davira. I would never have survived otherwise. You saved my life…and my baby's."

Collin grinned, fully erasing any lingering darkness. "Congratulations. You'll be a great mother."

"Thanks. I certainly hope so. It's not the kind of thing they taught us at Tarvin Hall."

He laughed and shook his head. "No, it isn't."

Kyrin glanced back, searching to see if Jace was still where she'd left him. "Well, I don't want to distract you from your duties, but I just wanted to make sure you knew the magnitude of what you did and what it means to Jace and me."

Night fell, making the ballroom's chandeliers shine even brighter as couples swayed and spun around the dance floor. Daniel was a bit disappointed he'd only been able to share one dance so far with Elanor, but there were far too many people demanding his attention to indulge in such things. Creating relationships and letting the guests get to know him was the most important part of the night. That was his duty now as king.

Still, it didn't stop his eyes from searching Elanor out when she was not at his side. She made an absolutely stunning image, and he couldn't help but look forward to the end of the night when they finally had some time alone. He'd barely seen her since they'd shared breakfast early this morning. He imagined that was how much of their life would be now. But he didn't regret it as much as he once thought he would. It was, after all, the path Elôm had laid before them, and His ways were always best.

As it grew late, a servant informed him that the final planned event of the evening was ready. He made his way over to the tall glass doors that led out onto the adjoining patio and called for everyone's attention. Once the talking had quieted and all eyes turned to him, he spoke.

"Ladies and gentlemen, thank you all for joining the queen and me tonight to celebrate a new beginning for our country. As part of the celebration, our crete allies have put together a display with their dragons. Any who wish may view it from the patio."

Dragon fire would be particularly spectacular at night, and if it reinforced how powerful his allies were in the minds of those who might be plotting against him, well, that would be an added bonus.

Talking resumed, and the majority of the guests wound their way outside. Daniel waited at the central door for Elanor to join him and traded smiles with Ben and Mira as they passed by. He was so glad to see both of them looking healthy once more. Though he hadn't seen much of them just lately, he'd heard they'd opened both their home and Ben's warehouses to provide shelter and help get the prisoners from the arena back on their feet. He couldn't have been more in awe of their generous spirit, and he was determined to emulate it in any way he could.

A moment later, Elanor emerged from the thinning crowd. Though he was starting to feel the length of the day, her eyes sparkled as bright as ever. He offered his arm, lowering his tone to one he knew would draw a smile. "Care to join me to watch the show?"

Sure enough, she rewarded him with a grin and even a bit of a blush. She wrapped her hand around his arm, hugging it close. "I would be delighted."

He led her out into the starry evening, the crowd parting to let them through. A minute later, a dark shape soared high above the palace with a whoosh, and a stream of fire lit up the sky. Two more came along behind, and soon bursts of fire were criss-crossing in all directions to the amazement and audible delight of the crowd. Daniel shifted to stand behind Elanor, resting his hands on her shoulders as they both tipped their heads back to watch. After a moment, she leaned into his chest, and he wrapped his arms around her, letting his cheek rest against her hair.

"Are you happy?"

He felt her let out a sigh. "Immensely."

Grinning to himself, he planted a covert kiss on her neck below her ear and then looked over the crowd gathered with uplifted faces. Their friends. Their allies. Their people. Tonight had shown him with fresh clarity exactly what it was they were creating—a united Ilyon bound together by faith in Elôm. It was a weighty responsibility but one he accepted with gratitude and excitement for the adventure to come.

Though Kyrin enjoyed the celebration, she was glad when the evening ended, and she and Jace could retire to their room. Most of their friends had moved out of the palace in the days leading up to the celebration to make room for all the guests, but Daniel had insisted she and Jace stay since they were family. He'd even moved them to the family wing, which was much more luxurious than anything either of them had experienced before. Neither of them needed a space with its own sitting room, but they happily accepted it anyway.

When they reached their chambers, Kyrin changed into a comfortable nightgown and crawled into bed, sighing to be off her feet. She got tired so much more quickly now that she was pregnant. Sinking into the soft pillows and mattress felt heavenly. Jace lay beside her, propping himself up on his elbow as he ran his hand gently over her belly. She loved how infatuated he had become with watching it grow. Almost every night, he lay and caressed it as if he were noticing it for the first time.

She rested her hand on his head and brushed her fingers through his hair. "It was good to see your grandparents tonight. Judging by his reaction, I think our baby will have your grandfather wrapped around its little finger the moment they meet for the first time. And I'm very interested to see if Charles and Emaya continue talking."

The two had barely parted all evening.

Jace just hummed his agreement, clearly lost in his own reflections. She was quiet for a long moment, watching his expression shift subtly with one thought or another. "What are you thinking about?"

Now he seemed to hear her fully and looked up. "Just about our future. Everyone will be leaving in the next few days. We haven't decided yet what we are going to do. We've been living as one big group for so long, but now I'll need to make a living to provide for us." He shook his head, a thoughtful frown in place. "It's something I've never had to do before, but I was remembering something Warin said once just after we first met. We were talking about how I had trained Niton. He said training horses like that would be good money if one were to pursue it."

"You'd be good at that." Working with animals instead of people was just the sort of job he needed.

His voice gained surety now as the idea took shape. "I'm thinking about asking Rayad if he wants to get back into breeding horses. We could do it together, and I could handle the training."

Kyrin loved hearing the note of excitement in his words. "That sounds like a wonderful idea."

He fell silent for another moment, fixating on her stomach before bringing up another decision they had yet to make. "We haven't decided where we will go."

It was true. They had never actually spoken of where that would be in all their talk of the future and the life they wanted to create. On her part, it was because she'd been waiting for him to bring it up and tell her what he wanted. Of course, she desired to be near her family, but she knew how important it was for Jace to be somewhere he felt secure. For that reason, she was willing to follow him anywhere.

"Where do you want to go?"

He slowly let out a sigh. "Home."

Kyrin turned a little now, looking him in the eyes. There had only ever been one place she had heard him call home. "The farm?"

To her surprise, Jace gave a slight shake of his head. He reached up to brush back a strand of her hair, his fingers trailing along her cheek. "Landale."

A grin parted Kyrin's lips. "Really? I thought all this time you wanted to return to the farm."

"I did. Ever since Rayad and I had to leave, the thought of going back has always pulled at me, but…" He reached for her hand and twined his fingers with hers. "Something changed in the last few weeks. Now that I finally have the chance to go back, I've realized it isn't what I actually want. The farm is where I first found a family, and it will always be a special place to me, but Landale is where we've built a life."

A quiet but indescribable joy wrapped warmly around Kyrin's heart. She cuddled up closer to him, resting her head on his chest. "Then let's go home."

WITHIN THREE DAYS of the celebration, the armies, which had camped outside of Valcré for a month, were gone. While it had been sad for Kyrin to say goodbye to Balen, Josef, and others, it was also a moment to celebrate—the ultimate end to the struggle. So many were able to return to their homes and families. She was especially happy for Balen. He'd been away from his people for so long and could now return to truly being their king. She hoped, someday, she and Jace and however many children they had at that point could revisit Samara and see how it would surely thrive under Balen's reign.

Once the armies were gone, all that remained were those from Landale and the Landale Dragon Riders. According to Kaden, the riders would remain at Valcré for the time being as a precaution since they were still deciding what to do about the remaining firedrakes. The goal was to train the drakes and their riders better to work alongside the dragons. Daniel did, however, completely shut down the drake breeding program so there would be no more firedrakes in the future.

After a full morning of saying goodbye, which had resulted in more than a few tears, Kyrin was thankful for a relaxing afternoon. The weather had turned hot and sticky, so she was more than happy to accept Elanor's invitation for all the women to join her in taking advantage of Auréa's shaded outdoor pool. The cool water was a delight, and even Leetra joined them. So did Aaron's wife, Lacy, who Kyrin enjoyed getting to know. She brought little Isaac along with her, and everyone nearly scrambled for a turn to hold him.

As they all lounged in the water or at the pool's edge, Kyrin took advantage of a lull in the conversation to ask Leetra, "So when is the wedding?"

Leetra fiddled with one of her braids, securing a couple of the purple beads that must have come loose. "Soon. We haven't set a date yet. We want to let everyone settle, but then we'll come to Landale to have the wedding."

The water swished as Anne shifted to look at her. "I bet Timothy is anxious."

The entirely smitten and almost shy smile that blossomed on Leetra's face was an expression Kyrin had never witnessed on her before. "Yes." She cleared her throat, apparently trying to tamp it down. "We've been talking about building our house. He and Aaron found a perfect spot up in the mountains north of here near where Josan is buried. We may even be able to find some trees large enough for a treehouse."

Anne turned to Lacy now, drawing her into the conversation. "How do you feel about living in the mountains?"

"Well, I've only ever lived in the city, but the short time I was in Landale showed me how much I would enjoy living in the quietness of the country, especially when raising a family." She shifted her grip on little Isaac, who was back in her arms, fast asleep. "I'm not so sure about a treehouse, though, especially with children. Isn't that dangerous?"

"That's what ropes are for," Leetra said matter-of-factly.

Kyrin couldn't hold in a giggle at the surprised and mildly horrified expression on Lacy's face. She looked like she couldn't decide if Leetra was serious or not. "It's actually true. Cretes do tie safety harnesses on their young children."

Leetra must have noticed Lacy's discomfort over the whole idea because she cast her an apologetic look. "I don't think Aaron was talking about a treehouse. Just Timothy and me."

It was sweet how quickly she reassured her. They were going to be sisters, after all. And despite them being two very different people, Leetra was clearly making an effort to form a relationship, something that probably didn't come all that easily to her. This would be especially important if they were planning to live so close together. Kyrin had to wonder, though, if Leetra was as accepting of her new home as she was of Lacy. Family was of utmost importance to the cretes, and Leetra would be far away from hers.

"Do you mind staying near Valcré?"

Leetra shrugged, back to her stoic self. "As long as I don't have to live in the city, I don't mind. Timothy is overjoyed to run Tarvin Hall with Sam. It's always been his dream to teach. And since Aaron will be working with Avery, I'm just glad the two of them can stay together."

It spoke of great character growth on Leetra's part that she was happily willing to leave behind her familiar life in Dorland so that Timothy could live his dream and stay near Aaron. Especially considering how the two of them had started. And as long as Leetra was truly happy, it was the perfect situation. So many new students would benefit from Timothy's teaching, and Aaron was perfect for the job of seeking justice for people in Valcré. He and Avery already worked well together and would make a great team tracking down those who had taken advantage of Davira's depravity to get away with hurting others.

This shifted the topic to Aaron and Avery's mission, and Lacy gave them a firsthand account of what it had been like to live here in Valcré over the years. Even before Davira, many people had suffered injustices, something Elanor promised she and Daniel would fight to change.

But Valcré wasn't the only place that would see changes. Elanor turned to Anne and brought up one of Daniel's most recent actions as king. "How does Trask feel about Daniel making him an earl and expanding Landale's borders?"

Kyrin had been especially thrilled about this news now that she and Jace were making Landale their permanent home. Over the last couple of years, Trask had been far more than a baron. He'd been a leader to everyone, even to Daniel and Balen. He deserved this promotion in rank as well as the expanded influence it would grant him.

"He's excited. More land means more people we can help. He's already talking about ways Landale can continue to offer aid to those who have suffered. He's always had a heart for others, so this just enables him to continue that."

"That's what Daniel and I thought when we were discussing it. Landale has become such a beacon of hope for all of us. We want to do all we can to preserve that legacy."

"We're both very grateful." Anne paused, a secretive sort of smile growing on her face. "I think the whole thing was a bit overshadowed by other news, however. News that Kyrin and Jace's baby won't be the only one born in Landale this winter."

Exclamations of joy echoed off the water and the roof above them, and there went Kyrin's tears again. It was so easy to cry at everything these days. Elanor was closer to Anne and reached her for a hug first, but Kyrin was right behind her.

"I'm so happy for you!" Kyrin cried as she embraced her friend tightly. She'd been so afraid Anne and Trask might never be able to have a child. They would make such wonderful parents.

Anne's whole face was alight with a grin when they parted, and Kyrin should have noticed before now how she was glowing.

Apparently, she'd been too caught up in her own pregnancy to catch the signs in someone else.

"I'm actually only a couple of weeks behind you. I think I was in denial for a while because I've been hopeful and then disappointed before, so I was a little hesitant to believe it at first."

Elanor released a little squeal. "Trask must be beside himself."

Anne laughed. "Believe me, he is. I'm surprised he hasn't shouted the news from the rooftop."

When Trev came to tell Jace that Daniel wanted to see him in his office, he didn't know what to expect. He was still trying to figure out exactly how the dynamic worked, with Daniel being both the king and his brother-in-law. He wasn't exactly nervous as Trev led him to the room, but something uncomfortable prickled inside him nonetheless.

At the office, Trev opened the door to let him inside and then closed it behind him. It helped a little to find he wasn't the only one present. Rayad and Holden both waited there, reclining in the padded chairs. Daniel sat on the edge of his desk, looking more like Jace was used to seeing him over the past year, despite his fine clothing.

"What's going on?" Jace glanced at Rayad, unsuccessfully trying to determine what he was thinking.

Daniel shifted to stand now. "Well, Rayad came to me a few days ago and shared a few details about your past, particularly about your old master."

Jace couldn't help how his stomach knotted at the mention of Jasper. Perhaps he'd never be able to rid himself of the gut reaction.

Daniel paused briefly, probably picking up on more than Jace wanted him to see. Sometimes it was still hard to let people witness his vulnerabilities.

"We both talked to Holden, and he has found that Jasper is still in the city. Apparently, he thinks I will continue hosting daily games at the arena like Davira did and hopes to profit from it."

Jace snorted, a bitter taste in his mouth. "That's Jasper."

He wasn't sure he'd ever met anyone more guided by greed.

"Unfortunately, as much as I'd love to, I really can't have him arrested since nothing he did to you at the time was against the law. But just letting him continue in his ways doesn't sit well with me, either. The last thing I want is for others to suffer at his hand. That's why I wrote this."

Daniel handed Jace a folded document bearing the royal seal in a shimmering blue wax.

"What is it?"

A distinctly pleased smile spread across Daniel's face. "That is a royal decree banning him from all activities related to gladiators, which means he can't own them, train them, or even bet on them."

Jace's breath stalled in his chest. He'd never even hoped for some sort of justice for the torture Jasper had inflicted, but Daniel had just laid that very thing in his hand.

"I thought you might like to deliver it to him personally." Daniel motioned to the others. "I'm sure Rayad will join you, and so will Holden now that he works in an official capacity as sheriff with Alex."

The two of them looked only too happy to do so.

A cool gleam flashed in Holden's eye as he smiled at Jace. "What do you say? Should we go see to it that he can never again do to others what he did to you?"

How could Jace say no to that? Not only would it bring him some justice and peace, but no other gladiator would have to suffer such cruelty to satisfy Jasper's greed and whims. He nodded, and the three of them headed for the door. However, Jace paused, a hundred different memories all racing through his mind before one jumped to the forefront. The memory of a gentle bay horse that had been one of his only comforts during such a dark time.

He turned back to Daniel and hesitated. He wasn't one to ask for favors, but Daniel was family now. "Could I possibly borrow some money? I'll pay you back once I've established an income."

Instead of answering, Daniel reached into a drawer in his desk and pulled out a pouch that clinked with coins. He tossed it to Jace. The weight was much more than he needed, but Daniel stopped him before he could say anything.

"No need to pay me back. I owe you far more than gold could ever cover."

Jace offered his deepest thanks and then led the way out of the office. Outside the palace, they headed toward the arena, where Holden had last seen Jasper. It was eerie to walk this path again so soon, especially knowing he was about to face his old master. Jace couldn't stop the way his pulse picked up or the moisture that built on his skin that had nothing to do with the warm weather, but having Rayad and Holden at his side helped keep the panic at bay.

When they arrived, the arena loomed over them, but Jace focused on Holden, who indicated an area where various entertainers had temporarily set up camp. Apparently, they waited to see what profit might be had in the coming days.

They wandered into the camp, and it did not take Jace long to spot a familiar barred wagon, red paint chipped and peeling from the letters along the side. He wasn't as prepared as he thought for the way the sight of it punched the air from his lungs. How many times had he been locked in that wagon like an animal, bruised, beaten, and transported from one hellish experience to another?

He didn't realize he'd stopped until Rayad's hand clasped his shoulder. Jace met his compassionate gaze, his mind rushing back to their first meeting. The first time anyone had looked at him as more than a monster. The first time anyone had cared. Because Rayad had followed Elôm's guidance that day, Jace no longer had to fear the past or its darkness.

He drew a solid breath, and Rayad offered him a firm nod before they moved forward. Drawing near the wagon, he spotted Jasper under an awning. His arms flailed as he complained about something to Zar, who leaned against the wagon, his expression a grim mask as always.

"Jasper."

He spun around to the sound of Jace's voice. His eyes popped as he froze. Then, as Jace stepped under the awning, he backed away until he'd bumped into a barrel. Not so tough now that Jace wasn't behind bars. Jace didn't check his stride until he stood over Jasper. The man practically laid across the barrel now, throat gulping. Jace shook his head, only now realizing just how pathetic Jasper truly was. A little of the man's audaciousness returned when Jace didn't immediately strike him dead. He straightened slowly, tugging his too-tight jerkin back down over his stomach. His gaze darted to Rayad and Holden before climbing again to meet Jace's.

"What do you want?" His eyes had narrowed in defiance, though he shot a couple of looks toward Zar as if to silently command the man to remove Jace from his presence.

"I have something for you." Jace held out a document Daniel had given him. "It's from the king. My brother-in-law."

Jasper's eyes bugged again. "Your…what?"

"My brother-in-law. He's married to my sister. The Queen."

Jasper blinked several times, his mouth opening and closing like a half-dead fish left in the sun. At last, his jaw snapped shut, and he sniffed as if now trying to act like Jace's connection to the throne was of little importance. He tipped his head imperiously and eyed the parchment.

"What is it?"

Jace shifted to look at Holden, motioning for him to explain.

Holden stepped forward, satisfaction alight in his eyes, though he spoke very calmly. "As an official of His Majesty, it's my pleasure to inform you that this document is a royal decree stating that, from this moment forward, you are forbidden from all gladiatorial activities. You are not allowed to purchase, sell, own, or train gladiators or even bet on them. To do so will be considered a crime against the crown, the penalty for which is life in prison."

Jasper's jaw fell open, floundering again before he started sputtering. Old, familiar rage that Jace had borne the brunt of so many times reddened his face. "But, but—that's my livelihood!"

Holden's voice took on an icy edge that Jace imagined he'd once employed to gather information from Daican's enemies. "Then I suggest finding a new form of employment." He gestured to the wagon, which Jace now saw contained half a dozen gladiators. "These men are free now, as well as any left at your estate. If you would please release them."

Jasper sputtered, nothing intelligible coming out but a few curses. With a huff, he tipped his chin up and crossed his arms in refusal. Jace raised his brows. If Jasper thought Holden was bluffing, he was in for a rude awakening. But before Holden could arrest him, they caught a faint jangle. Jace looked over to where Zar still leaned against the wagon, a ring of keys dangling from his outstretched finger. Jasper made a choking sound, and Holden pinned him with a dark look. "You're lucky."

He took the keys from Zar and proceeded to unlock the wagon, ushering the men out. To each, he offered a handful of coins from a pouch that looked very similar to the one Daniel had given Jace—just enough to get them started in their new lives. Some just gaped at Holden and the coins, while others appeared suspicious. Jace suspected some of them would return to the arena—it was just in their nature—but he hoped the others would seize the chance for a better life.

Jasper puffed and panted through it all like he was about to pass out, his face nearly turning purple as his former gladiators disappeared.

When the last man had gone, Jace faced him once more. "I'm buying Rohir from you."

Jasper looked one furious second away from spitting out a colorful protest before Jace tossed a few coins at him. It was more than generous, considering. Jasper's mouth snapped shut as he scrambled to grab up the coins that had dropped and said not a word as Jace walked to the wagon where the bay gelding stood quietly.

"Hey there, boy." Jace ran his hand down the horse's warm neck, the memories making his throat a bit thick.

Rohir turned to sniff him, his breath whiffling Jace's chin. The horse then dipped its head and nibbled at his shirt as if looking for a treat. All at once, tears bit Jace's eyes. Could the animal possibly remember the bits of bread he'd saved for him? It was impossible to say, but Jace remembered.

He untied the lead rope. As he turned, he caught Zar's eye. The man had never been kind to him—quite the opposite—but Jace had the odd sense that, unlike Jasper, it hadn't been out of maliciousness. It was just the way things had been.

"You don't have to stay with him, you know. You could find far better employment elsewhere." Jace reached into his pouch again and withdrew a handful of coins that he held out to Zar. "You could start a new life with this."

Zar just stared at the coins for a long moment, his face expressionless. Then, at last, he took the money and pocketed it. Turning slightly, he grabbed a bag, slung it over his shoulder, and walked away without a word.

"Zar! What are you doing? Get back here! You can't do this!"

But Zar didn't even glance back at Jasper's voice that rose to a near screech. Once he'd disappeared in the crowd, Jasper just stood gaping. He didn't even seem to realize at first that Holden approached him until he suddenly jerked to face him. Holden leaned close, making Jasper shrink a bit.

"If I hear any word that you have returned to your old ways and are back in the gladiator business, I will hunt you down and see you locked up for the rest of your life. Do you understand?" The same coldness from before laced his voice again. "And beyond the king's decree, should you come within a hundred miles of Jace, you have my personal guarantee a prison cell won't even be necessary."

Jace raised his brows. Holden could be downright terrifying.

And with that, the three of them walked away, Jace leading Rohir behind them.

JACE WASN'T EXPECTING to get summoned by Daniel yet again after yesterday's confrontation with Jasper. This time he'd sent for him and Rayad, and they were to meet him outside the stable. Together, they walked out into the sun. Despite how warm the air was again today, Jace still preferred it to being inside the palace. Though he did not look forward to saying goodbye to Elanor, he was more than ready to return home to Landale. The group had decided at breakfast that they would leave tomorrow morning.

Off to the far side of the palace grounds, opposite where the now-demolished temple had stood, they approached the royal stable. Jace had visited it for the first time yesterday when he'd stabled Rohir. While he'd seen and worked in some fine stables in the past, nothing could compare to the magnificence or size of Auréa's. He'd been happy to wander the aisles and stop at each stall to observe the horses.

Daniel stood just outside the building with a few of the grooms and four horses, including a handsome blue roan stallion Jace had admired yesterday. All four horses gleamed in the sunlight from thorough grooming. The three mares consisted of a white, a coppery sorrel, and a golden palomino. Daniel seemed to be inspecting them before he noticed Jace and Rayad coming.

"So, I heard you're going to start a horse breeding business in Landale."

Jace glanced at Rayad, who nodded in confirmation. "That's the plan."

"Well, since we're family now—and not just because I married Elanor—I would like to help you get started." Daniel motioned to the horses. "These are some of my father's broodmares and one of the young stallions. I'm assured they have the best bloodlines. The mares have also been bred, so they should produce foals next spring. You're welcome to check them over, Rayad, since you're the expert and I'm not. If satisfied, you can take them to Landale with you."

Jace and Rayad both just gaped at him. Breeding stock from the royal bloodlines would make them the envy of every horse breeder across Arcacia. Offering the stallion for stud services alone would bring a tidy profit.

Rayad shook his head, finally finding his voice for both of them. "This is far more than generous. Are you sure you want to give away such fine animals?"

"Of course. They'll benefit you far more than they will me. After everything you've both done and sacrificed, I want to make sure you have everything you need to rebuild your lives." He winked at Jace. "Especially since you have a family to provide for. I'm not about to let any niece or nephew of mine want for anything."

Jace still stood dumbstruck. While he'd been prepared to work as hard as he had to in order to provide a comfortable home and life for Kyrin and the baby, having this kind of security lifted so much of the weight. He cleared his throat, working his voice loose. "Thank you."

Daniel offered an understanding smile. "You're welcome." He patted one of the mares before stepping back. "I'll make sure you have all the documents detailing their bloodlines before you leave tomorrow."

With that, he headed toward the palace and let Jace and Rayad look over their new horses. While Rayad inspected their conformations, Jace took a moment with each one. He let the horses take in his scent as he stroked their faces and necks, getting an idea of their personalities. Though he could work with any horse, calm, reliable animals would be most desirable. The mares were sociable, and even the stallion seemed more even-tempered than Niton had been when Jace had first met him.

"They are magnificent animals," Rayad breathed. He just stared at them for a moment, a faraway look in his eyes, before focusing on Jace. Emotion thickened his voice. "For so many years, I worked with my father, learning everything there is to know about horses. Now I get to continue that work with you. Perhaps, one day, one of your children will even join us as well."

Jace reached out to grip Rayad's shoulder, his throat a bit tight. "I would like that."

Kyrin wandered through the garden, brushing her fingers delicately across some of the flowers. It was the first time she had been out here alone. It was nice to have a moment to herself to contemplate everything that had happened in the past several weeks and what lay ahead.

Tipping her head back, she let her gaze trail over the walls and ornate windows of the palace. It was hard to believe everything that had taken place here—from her first day of being primped and prepped by Lady Videlle to the dark hours of both her stays in the dungeon until, finally, this quiet moment. She couldn't say she would be sad to leave it behind in the morning, but she wouldn't mind visiting and adding more good memories to overshadow the bad.

Voices drew her attention out past the edges of the garden to an area not far from the stable, where a contingent of their dragon riders milled about, always on guard just in case. She recognized Kaden among them and followed the garden path in his direction. He was talking to Talas as she crossed the bit of open courtyard between them.

Talas greeted her with a smile and then excused himself to join a few other riders nearby, leaving her and Kaden amongst the dragons. Kyrin eyed him for a moment, thinking back to Samara. It had taken a long time for him to fully recover from the ordeal.

"So, how are you feeling?"

He flashed a grin. "Great." He flexed the arm that had been injured. "I think I'm finally rid of the last of Richard's attempts to end me."

"Good." Kyrin's attention shifted to the dragon lounging at Kaden's side. Its bright eyes inspected her curiously. "How are you getting on with Rhune?"

A little of Kaden's smile faded now as he turned slightly to put his hand on the dragon's neck. Sadness lingered in his eyes, but there was hope too. "Better than I expected."

"I know he can't replace Exsis, but I hope your bond with him will be just as strong."

"Well, he did save me from Richard, so we're off to a good start. He's quite protective."

He gave the dragon a pat before turning fully back to Kyrin. Silence fell between them as Kyrin's thoughts drifted to tomorrow. As excited as she was to return home, parts of it would be hard, and the emotions already rose up to weigh on her.

Kaden tipped his head down to look her in the eyes. "What is it?"

"I was just thinking about leaving. Here we are, me heading off to Landale and you staying here in Valcré again." She blinked hard to stop tears from forming.

Kaden's lazy smile bolstered her. "At least, this time, it's our choice, and I hope it won't be for too long. Our goal is to set up a garrison here near the city where we can have riders on rotation, but our headquarters will be in Landale. It's where we plan to recruit and train new riders." He nodded to her stomach, his smile growing. "And don't worry; I'll be sure to be there to meet my niece or nephew. It's not far by dragon."

Kyrin's outlook grew brighter, and she rubbed her hand over her belly. Such wonderful times lay ahead of them. "You'll be a terrific uncle."

Kaden drew himself up. "I'm going to be the favorite uncle."

Kyrin laughed now, shaking her head. Of course, he would say that. "You might have to fight Marcus, Liam, and Ronny for that distinction, and that's only on our side. On Jace's side, you've got Daniel and James to contend with."

He shrugged as if that were of little consequence. "I'm the only one who's an official dragon rider for the King…well, until Ronny gets older."

"What about me? Do I get to be in the running? Because, if so, *I* am the only crete."

Kyrin hadn't noticed that Talas had worked his way back to them. She met his sparkling grin with one of her own. "Of course, you'll be an uncle too. The rest you'll have to take up with each other."

It was time to go home.

Jace checked over the horses, making sure Kyrin's saddle, especially, was secure. He'd chosen the palomino for her to ride, deeming the mare the calmest and most surefooted of the group. He attached some of their belongings, such as food, to the saddles. The rest he packed onto Gem and Ivoris, who would follow from the air. Now that he was satisfied, the only thing left was to say goodbye.

He turned to the large group gathered in the palace courtyard—half remaining and half heading out for Landale. Elanor was saying goodbye to Anne and Trask as Jace made his way over to Kyrin, who stood with her mother and brothers. Though Liam and Cassie were joining them in Landale, the rest would remain behind, including Kyrin's mother. Just as Jace had expected, Aric had asked her if she would stay in Valcré and continue their relationship with the intent to marry soon. Jace was happy for them, especially after all the loss the Altairs had suffered, and he knew Kyrin was happy about it, too, even if it meant saying goodbye today.

After saying his own farewells to them, Jace left Kyrin to conclude hers and made his way over to Holden. It was strange parting ways for now. Holden had been around from the very first moment Jace had arrived at camp. "Landale won't quite be the same without you."

Holden nodded, his reluctance to say goodbye evident. "As much as I'll miss it, this is where I need to be, for now anyway." He glanced past Jace, out towards the city, before meeting his eyes again. "There are so many wrongs that need to be righted, and I can already see the difference Aaron, Alex, and I are making. At least this way, I can take parts of my past and use them to help people instead of hurt them."

Jace understood how he felt and was glad he'd found such purpose. They clasped arms, and Holden put his other hand on Jace's shoulder. "Despite where we started, you're like a brother to me, Jace. I won't ever forget that."

Jace had to swallow to loosen the knot in his throat. He'd thought he could do this without getting emotional, but that was easier said than done. Holden had been at his side during some of his darkest times. "Neither will I."

They embraced then, and Jace thanked Elôm for their friendship and for healing Holden after the arena. Even though Elôm had guided Jace to his real family, He had provided a family for him well before that in the men and women like Holden.

As they parted, Holden smirked. "Say hello to that demon-possessed wolf of yours for me when you get back to camp."

Jace laughed. They really had come a long way. "I will."

Finally, after many more goodbyes, it was suddenly time to go. And though Jace's heart was a little torn at leaving so many behind, the pull toward Landale was only getting stronger. With everyone else looking on, the Landale group mounted their horses. They called and waved their final farewells as Trask and Anne led the way to the gate and out onto the street.

On their way through the city, they passed a few former members of the Militia who had been officially promoted to city guard. They all waved and called farewell to the procession until, at last, they arrived at the edge of the city and passed through the main gate. Here, Jace glanced back only once before setting his gaze on the forest road leading them home.

LANDALE.

The familiar, rolling miles of farmland stretched out before them, green and lush with crops. Jace's heart welled at the sight of it, the word *home* whispering through his consciousness. It was so different from when he'd arrived three years ago, broken, grieving, and hopeless. He'd failed to see the beauty and opportunity then, but he drank it all in eagerly now. This was where he and Kyrin would continue to build their life together.

Word of their arrival must have somehow preceded them because as they neared Landale Village, they found the path lined with people. Cheers erupted when the villagers spotted the group with Trask and Anne in the lead. Men and women waved their hats and scarves in the air while their children jumped and danced and laughed merrily. It was the most beautiful welcome home anyone could ever ask for, and Jace grinned at the look of pure joy radiating from Trask's face as he greeted his people.

The villagers followed them in a long procession all the way to Landale Castle. When they entered the courtyard, they found the reception there just as meaningful. The servants waited outside, along with Anne's parents, Warin, Lenae, and Meredith, with broad smiles on every face. Everyone dismounted, and Warin stepped forward, meeting Trask with a great bear hug.

"Welcome home, my lord."

If there was ever a time Jace thought he'd see Trask cry, it was now. Tears did waver in his eyes and choked his voice as he smiled and clasped arms with Warin when they parted. "Thank you."

It had taken much struggle, loss, and pain to get here, but Trask was finally able to return to the home he'd grown up in and lead his people as he'd always wanted to.

As everyone started greeting each other, a black shape dashed through the crowd straight toward Jace. Tyra practically lunged at him, her tail wagging frantically. He dropped to his knees and wrapped his arms around her neck, scrubbing his fingers into her thick fur. But she wouldn't hold still, and he laughed when she knocked him back in her enthusiasm. He hadn't seen her this excited since she was a pup.

"I know, I know. It's been a long time." Longer than he'd ever wanted to have to leave her, and he didn't intend to do it again.

She nuzzled his clothes and face and gave him a few sloppy, wet kisses for good measure. He laughed again, and then they both became aware of Kyrin. Tyra turned her attention to her, though she instinctively seemed to know to be a bit more gentle. Her tail continued to whip, but she stood still for Kyrin to rub her chin and ears and tell her how much they'd missed her.

While she was distracted, Jace pushed back to his feet, using his sleeve to wipe his face. He gave Tyra a loving pat on the side before their attention was drawn to Lenae.

She motioned to the castle. "We've prepared dinner for everyone."

Trask stepped forward to lead the way but paused and turned to Anne, a twinkle in his eyes. "We have to do this properly. After all, I'm bringing my bride home for the first time."

Before she even had a chance to say anything, he swept her up in his arms and carried her across the threshold to the cheers of everyone.

Jace took Kyrin's hand and gave her a loving smile as they followed the others inside.

They all gathered around the dining table, filling the room with chatter as they told Warin and the others all that had taken place in the last couple of months. The news of Kyrin and Anne's pregnancies was celebrated with great joy. Jace often found himself just watching Kyrin, enjoying the contentment on her face. Tyra had squeezed in between their chairs, and he rested his hand on her head, rubbing her ears as he listened to the conversations around him. Three years ago, he could never have imagined himself welcome in such a tight-knit group. Now he could envision many gatherings like this at Trask's table.

And that was what made Landale home. Not just because this was where he'd met Kyrin or found peace but because of the friends and neighbors who surrounded them. People who had fought and risked their lives beside him and for him. That was something he'd never had and never would have found back at the farm in Kinnim. He'd once believed no good could possibly come of what happened to Kalli and Aldor, but he could see now that nothing would have dragged him away from the farm as long as they were there. Rayad may have left, but he would have stayed there, hiding from the world for the rest of his life. He would never have met Kyrin. He would never have been a father. And he would never have had this sense of community. While the past still hurt, the present and future were infinitely better for it, and he thanked Elôm for creating such beauty from ashes.

After dinner, the group was on their way again toward camp, this time with Warin and Lenae taking the lead while Trask, Anne, and her parents remained at the castle. The sun hung low in the sky now, and Jace looked forward to a restful, quiet evening back at the cabin with Kyrin. He thanked Elôm they had somewhere to call home until they could decide where to build permanently. With the baby on the way and foals likely to be born this spring, he hoped to have a place for them before winter.

But for tonight, he savored what they already had and the peace that surrounded them. He particularly felt it when they turned off the road into the forest and didn't have to worry about covering their tracks. No longer would they have to fear soldiers showing up and attacking.

The sight of camp, nestled amongst the trees, had Jace breathing a deep sigh. Those still here welcomed them with as much enthusiasm as the villagers had. No doubt they were just as anxious to hear about everything that had happened in Valcré, but Jace was ready for some quiet. He excused himself and Kyrin from the group, and they rode to the stable. Rayad joined them to help Jace unsaddle and tend the horses and dragons. Once they had carried all the supplies to the cabin, they bid each other good night, and Jace closed the door.

By this time, Kyrin had the cabin lit up with candles, and Tyra had already found a place on her favorite rug. Kyrin stood in the center of the room, looking around, and then ran her fingers over the table.

"This place is certainly in need of a good dusting."

Jace came up behind her and wrapped his arms around her, placing a kiss at the base of her neck. "That can wait until morning."

She turned to face him, putting her arms around his neck. She gazed up at him, her eyes deepening with love, and he bent to kiss her.

Bird songs echoed in the trees outside. Kyrin hadn't even realized how much she'd missed it until this moment, lying in bed next to Jace. His arm draped over her, and she could tell by his breathing he was still asleep. She let the comforting, peaceful sound and the birds lull her back into semi-consciousness for a while.

Sometime later, Jace stirred, and Kyrin shifted to look at him. He usually woke before she did, so she didn't get to watch him wake up often. When she did, she always thought he was so cute coming out of sleep. He rubbed his face and blinked before finding her watching him. He quirked his brow, a still-sleepy little smile on his lips.

She cuddled closer to him. "Good morning."

He echoed her, rubbing his hand along her back. "Did you sleep well?"

"I did. And birds are much more pleasant to listen to in the morning than sounds of a city."

"I agree." He propped himself up, leaning over to place a kiss on her lips and then her belly before getting out of bed.

She could tell he was anxious to get the day started. Right before they'd fallen asleep last night, he'd talked about looking for a place to build their home as soon as possible. Tyra got up to meet him, giving a big stretch first, her tail wagging lazily. Kyrin pushed herself up next, sitting on the edge of the bed and combing her fingers through her tangled hair. After getting her ears rubbed by Jace, Tyra came over to Kyrin. Immediately, she nosed Kyrin's stomach and then laid her head in Kyrin's lap, staring up at her with soulful crystal eyes. Kyrin stroked her smooth, black head with a smile.

"I think she knows I'm pregnant."

Jace looked over at them from where he was getting dressed. "I think so too."

"She's going to be as protective of our baby as we are." Kyrin gave the wolf a quick kiss on her head and then got up to dress as well. As she laced up her overdress, she peered around the cabin. In daylight, she could see it was even more in need of a cleaning, and the shelf in the corner was bare except for their dishes and a sack of flour. "I don't think we have much in the way of food supplies here in the cabin."

Jace stepped to the window and looked out at camp. "I don't think we'll need any this morning. Lenae is down by the fire with a big coffee pot and fry pans."

Kyrin joined him at the window, leaning against his shoulder. "Of course, she would do that."

They both left the cabin and walked down to the central campfire as they had so many times in the last couple of years. So much had happened here. Kyrin had seen Jace for the very first time sitting at this fire. She so clearly remembered his tortured eyes that night. Often she thanked Elôm for how He had transformed Jace into the man who was now her husband and the father to their unborn child. She would never have been able to imagine such an outcome back then.

Rayad joined them a moment later. If only Kaden were there too. This morning reminded her of his first morning in camp. Despite what had lain ahead, everything had felt so right at that moment. But change was part of life, even the good parts, and often it brought about the very best parts.

After breakfast, Jace headed to the stable to saddle the horses, this time Niton and Kyrin's horse Maera. Though Niton wasn't nearly as excitable as Tyra, Jace could tell the stallion did recognize him and was maybe even glad to see him. He liked to think so, anyway.

He led them out of the corral, and Rayad followed with Aros. They could have taken the day to rest and relax, but Jace couldn't fight the urge to go out and find a spot to build a home. Gathering materials and building a cabin and stable would take time, and it was best to get started on it as soon as possible. Of course, he and Kyrin could stay here at camp as long as they needed, but deep down, he wanted his child born in a home of their own.

Though he'd told Kyrin she could stay at camp and rest while he and Rayad scouted the area, she insisted on coming along. And, in the end, he did need her input when they chose where to settle. He wanted it to be perfect for her.

So the three of them rode out of camp together. It was a leisurely ride, and Jace didn't think he'd ever been so at peace. They followed the road until they reached the edge of the forest. There they turned off and followed the tree line to the east. Trask had assured him that this area of the forest was far enough from the village that he could build anywhere along its edge without worrying about being too close to another farmer's land.

They rode along, stopping every so often to discuss an area. Many spots would be suitable for building and pastureland, but none, in particular, spoke to Jace. Maybe he was comparing them too much to the farm. But this would be their home for the rest of their lives. It had to be right.

As the afternoon waned, they came upon a small rise that overlooked the rolling hills of Landale. Just within the trees, a clearing opened up with enough room to hold a cabin or two. Ancient maples and oak trees stood around the perimeter, offering cool shade from the summer sun, and a short distance away, a small stream babbled. Jace stopped at the edge of it. Could this possibly be the same stream where he'd spent so many miserable, sleepless nights? It seemed to be in the right location to have flowed from that area of the forest. He shook his head to himself. That stream he'd suffered by would be a valuable asset for a farm.

He dismounted, and Kyrin and Rayad joined him. They stood in silence for a long moment as Jace looked around and imagined where a stable would go, where the foals and mares would graze on sweet spring grass, where his child would play and grow. It was surprisingly clear in his mind and felt so…*right*.

His heart beat harder as he turned to Kyrin, hoping she would feel the same. "What do you think?"

She, too, looked around, taking it all in, breathing deeply. "I think it's beautiful."

"Would you like to live here?" This time he held his breath.

She stepped closer to him and reached up, resting her hand on his cheek as she looked him in the eyes. "I want to live where you're happy. From the moment we met back at camp, it has been my deepest desire to see you at peace. And now I can see it in your eyes. You love it here. So yes, I would very much like to live here."

Jace couldn't hold back the smile that sprang to his lips, and he drew her close for a kiss before taking her hand and looking over the land again. This was it.

They were home.

EPILOGUE

KYRIN PULLED THE last of the dry laundry from the line and carried the basket up to the front porch. Sunlight streamed through the trees, highlighting the pure white trilliums and vivid violets surrounding the cabin. She never grew tired of seeing them, nor did Jace grow tired of bringing in fresh bouquets for her every few days.

Inside, she set the basket on the table in the spacious dining and kitchen area and looked around in contentment. She still couldn't believe this was their cabin, though they had lived there for several months now. She'd expected something smaller and would have been perfectly fine with it, but Jace had insisted on giving her the best. She had also thought it would take a lot longer. But with no end to the friends they had who wanted to help, they'd had the cabin up and ready to live in before the first snow of winter—as well as the stable and a second, smaller cabin just for Rayad. Though she and Jace had invited him to live with them, he'd insisted they should have their home to themselves and was more than happy with his own. Thanks to everyone's unfailing generosity, they'd quickly built a true home here in Landale.

It was nearly lunchtime, so Kyrin gathered ingredients to make sandwiches with the fresh bread she'd baked earlier. She'd just laid it all on the table when a soft coo caught her attention. She wiped her hands and walked over to the cradle near the sofa, her heart melting as it always did to be greeted by the most angelic little face she had ever seen.

"Well, hello, sweetheart. Did you have a good nap?"

Little Grace reacted with the happiest toothless grin, kicking her legs and waving her chubby arms in excitement. Kyrin didn't know how she could feel more and more in love with her child every time she saw her. She took a long moment to study her as she often did. Though it was a little thinner now than when she was born, Kyrin was glad Grace had retained her wispy dark hair. It wasn't quite as black as Jace's but was much darker than Kyrin's. She did have Jace's eyes. Not the typical dark blue all babies had that eventually changed to their true color. No, Grace's were bright and vivid and dazzling, just like Jace's. And while her ears were not pointed, they were subtly peaked. It overjoyed Kyrin to see parts of the man she loved so dearly passed on to their child. It didn't matter to her in the slightest that these traits came from Jace's ryrik blood, and they would both make sure it didn't matter to Grace either.

Just like that, Grace's happy cooing morphed into fussing. Kyrin reached for her, lifting her out of the cradle. "All right, sweetie, you get lunch first. Then we'll see how your daddy is doing with the horses."

Carrying her into the bedroom, she sat down in the rocking chair Trask and Anne had gifted them and hummed softly while Grace nursed. When the infant was full and happy once again, Kyrin tucked her into one arm and carried her outside. A well-worn path led them away from the cabin toward the stable. They didn't have to go far to see Jace in one of the small pens, working on halter training the gorgeous cream-colored filly that had been born to the palomino mare Daniel had given them. Kyrin knew she was one of Jace's favorites. He said he could tell she had a sweet temperament like her mother.

Rayad leaned on the fence, observing and discussing their progress as Jace walked the filly around next to the mare. Jace noticed them coming first, and then Rayad turned to look. His face lit up. Kyrin had appreciated having him around over the past few months. He'd done so much around their farm and the cabin while she and Jace had figured out their routine as new parents.

He grinned at Grace. "How is our girl doing today?"

Kyrin shifted her in her arms as she squirmed, her gaze fixed on Jace. "Very well. She just woke up from a nap and is in a very good mood. We came to let you know I prepared sandwiches for lunch."

They thanked her, and Jace turned to remove the halter from the filly and open the gate to the main pasture. Grace watched, kicking her chubby legs wildly. She let out a squeal when the mare passed close to the fence. She'd been getting more and more interested in the horses over the last couple of weeks.

Kyrin laughed, sending Jace a look. "She's going to be just like you. I just know she'll have a thing for animals, considering how much she already loves Tyra. I have a feeling we're going to have to watch her closely once she starts walking because she's going to be drawn to the stable."

Jace just grinned as he left the pen. He reached out to lightly tickle Grace, earning a gurgling laugh. He then took her from Kyrin, holding her up above his head as she squealed in delight again before tucking her into the crook of his arm. As a newborn, she'd been so tiny that both of them had been a little afraid when they'd held her, but watching Jace grow comfortable in his role as a father was something Kyrin treasured. Now she couldn't get enough of seeing the two of them together.

As they walked up toward the cabin, hoofbeats came from the path that led west toward the main road into Landale. They turned to look as Trask waved and then continued on to meet him at the cabin. He'd dismounted by the time they reached the porch, and he greeted them all with a smile. After taking a moment to lean down and baby talk to Grace, which earned him a wide grin, he straightened and pulled a parchment from his jerkin.

"A letter came in from your mother." He handed it over to Jace. "I thought I'd ride out and deliver it and then head out to camp to see how Saul and the others are doing."

Kyrin took Grace back from Jace as he inspected the letter and nodded toward the cabin. "Would you like to have lunch with us? I was just putting together sandwiches."

"Thank you, but I won't impose. Knowing Jayna, she's likely to insist on offering me lunch as well."

Kyrin smiled. It was hard to say no to Jayna's hospitality. Kyrin had enjoyed having them as not-too-distant neighbors since they'd settled at camp a little over a month ago. "Well, let her and Saul know we'd like to have them to supper soon."

"I'll mention it. Anne and I hope to have everyone out to the castle again soon as well. When I was younger, my father used to host all kinds of celebrations and parties for the village. I want to continue that tradition. Especially if it'll help people get used to Saul and the others."

So far, the people of Landale had been leery of the ryriks' arrival, but Kyrin hadn't heard of any hostility so far. It helped that the villagers held such a deep trust and respect for Trask.

"That sounds wonderful." A celebration at the castle would be like celebrating at camp again. Kyrin loved how easy it was to visit the village and especially quick if they took the dragons.

Spring, however, was a busy time, so she hadn't had a chance to visit Trask and Anne recently. "How is Axen doing?"

Trask's eyes shone at the mention of his son. "Growing like a weed. Seriously, I don't think I realized just how fast babies grow."

"Tell me about it. Before we know it, they'll be walking and getting into all kinds of trouble."

Trask laughed. "Anne is already afraid of that. She says he's entirely too much like me for his own good."

Kyrin shared in the laughter. She could totally see little Axen following in his father's mischievous footsteps. But if he also inherited his father's generosity and compassion, she knew Anne would never complain.

Task asked about the horses then, and the men discussed farming for a few minutes until he backed toward his horse. "Well, I won't keep you from your lunch."

He remounted, and they bade him farewell before Kyrin led the way into the cabin. Jace and Rayad took seats at the table, and Kyrin secured Grace in her highchair with a toy. As they ate, Jace opened and read over his mother's letter. At the end, he chuckled to himself, a happy smile on his face.

Kyrin leaned toward him. "What did she say?"

He looked over at her, his eyes twinkling. "She and Elian are going to have a baby."

Kyrin gasped. "Really?" While she knew Jace, Elanor, and James had all encouraged it, she wasn't sure it would happen. "That's wonderful! They must be so excited."

Jace just continued to smile as Rayad expressed his happiness over the news. The thought of Jace having a baby brother or sister was adorable. He'd never had the chance to grow up with siblings, but at least he would see this one grow.

Between Grace, Axen, Elanor and Daniel's newborn son Elan, and now Rachel expecting a child, they were already creating quite a new generation. With Liam and Cassie newly married, they could also have an announcement before too long. Who knew? Maybe Kaden would return from his and Talas's trip to Dorland with a wife of his own, and the family would grow even bigger. After all, Talas had been teasing Kaden about setting him up with Trenna before they'd left.

Whatever happened, Kyrin was simply thankful for how abundantly Elôm had already blessed them in their new lives.

Jace glanced at the letter again. "James is back home, for now at least. Mother says he seems to be doing better."

"That's good. Hopefully, having Elian around and a new baby brother or sister before too long will help him settle." While the memories she carried were still difficult at times, she did have compassion for the guilt James felt. She couldn't imagine how awful it must be to have done such terrible things before coming to know Elôm and then having to live with them.

Jace handed her the letter, and she set it aside to read after lunch, but she did have one particular question about what it contained. "Did she mention anything about Charles and Emaya?"

Jace nodded. "Emaya and her parents will be visiting in a few weeks. Mother thought maybe we could visit then too. Then we'll be there to celebrate if Charles and Emaya make any announcements. Clearly, she expects one."

Kyrin sent him a semi-smug smile. "I told you Emaya would be your aunt."

Jace chuckled again. "You did."

"You three should go." Rayad settled back in his chair across the table. "I can keep an eye on things here. Kal could even come and help me with the chores. If nothing else, it will get him out of Saul and Jayna's hair for a few days."

Saul and Jayna's young son had become obsessed with horses after their first visit to the farm. Now he asked about a thousand questions of both Jace and Rayad whenever they saw each other.

Kyrin was sure he'd jump at the chance to help out, though she did wonder with some amusement if Rayad would be so keen on the idea after a few days of non-stop chatter.

By now, they'd finished their sandwiches, and Rayad pushed back his chair. "We should probably get that last field planted."

Jace agreed.

Kyrin slid back her own chair and gathered up their plates, carrying them over to the washbasin, where she brushed the crumbs into a pail. She heard and felt Jace come up behind her. He rested his hands on the counter on either side of her and pressed a kiss to the side of her neck. Grinning, she turned to face him, still encircled by his arms. His smile was light and content and meant more to her than she could ever put into words.

"I love you," she whispered.

His smile deepened, and he rested his forehead against hers. "I love you too."

And then he kissed her properly.

CHARACTERS AND INFORMATION

CHARACTERS

Aaron—A half-crete and former miner from Dunlow. Timothy's older brother.

Aertus (AYR - tuhs)—Arcacia's male moon god.

Aldor (AL - dohr)— An old friend of Rayad and Jace, who was killed by Dagren's men. Kalli's husband.

Alex Avery—An old friend of Daniel's who assassinated Emperor Daican. Currently a smuggler and champion of the people in Valcré.

Altair (AL - tayr)—Kyrin's family name.

Anne—Trask's wife. Daughter of Sir John and Lady Catherine.

Aric (AHR - ick)—Daniel's head of security.

Aros (AHR - rohs)—Rayad's white horse.

Balen (BAY - len)—Exiled king of Samara.

Baron Thomas—The Baron of Westing. One of Balen's oldest friends.

Ben—A wealthy merchant and leader of the believers in Valcré.

Cassie—One of the Resistance's physicians, and Liam's girlfriend.

Charles Ilvaran—The Viscount Ilvaran, and Jace's uncle.

Collin—A security guard at Auréa Palace, who formerly attended Tarvin Hall with Kyrin.

Dagren (DAY - gren)—A former Arcacian captain with a vendetta against Rayad and Warin. Died of fever after being captured by the Resistance.

Dane—A fellow slave Jace fought and killed in his past.

Daniel—Rightful king of Arcacia, and Davira's older brother.

Daican (DYE - can)—The former emperor of Arcacia. Poisoned by Alex Avery.

Darq (DARK)—A crete captain from Dorland. Leader of the crete dragon riders.

Davira (Duh - VEER - uh)—Acting queen of Arcacia, and Daniel's younger sister.

Elanor—Jace's younger sister.

Elian (EL - ee - an)—Elanor's bodyguard.

Elôm (EE - lohm)—The one true God of Ilyon.

Elon (EE – lon)—Elôm's son, the Savior of Ilyon.

Emaya (Eh - MY - uh)—The daughter of the Earl of Covel.

Falcor Tarn—A crete traitor, and Leetra's former betrothed.

Glynn (GLIN)—Captain Darq's lieutenant and closest friend.

Haedrin (HAY - drin) —Prince of the Dorland giants.

Halvar (HAL - vahr)—Jorvik's younger brother.

Henry Foss—The secretary at Auréa Palace.

Holden (HOHL - den)—A former informant for Emperor Daican. One of Jace's best friends.

Holly—Kyrin's former maid at Auréa Palace.

Jace—A half-ryrik former slave and gladiator.

James—Jace's younger brother.

Jasper—A gladiator owner and Jace's former master.

Jayna—Saul's wife.

Jorvik (JOHR - vick)—One of the giants the Resistance members helped defend Dorland's border from Daican.

Josan (JOH - san)—Aaron and Timothy's uncle, who was murdered by Falcor.

Josef—A physician from Samara and close friend of Balen.

Kaden (KAY - den)—Kyrin's twin brother. Captain of the Landale Dragon Riders.

Kal—Saul's son.

Kalli (KA - lee)—Aldor's wife. An old friend of Rayad and Jace, who was killed by Dagren's men.

Kyrin (KYE - rin)—A young Arcacian woman with the ability to remember everything. Formerly employed by Daican.

Lacy—A former barmaid from Valcré and Aaron's wife.

Leetra (LEE - truh)—A crete physician and dragon rider. Talas's cousin.

Lenae (LEH - nay)—Warin's wife and adoptive mother of Meredith.

Levi—Jorvik's youngest brother.

Liam—Kyrin's older brother and training physician.

Lydia—Kyrin's mother.

Maera (MAYR - uh)—Kyrin's dappled buckskin horse.

Marcus—Kyrin's eldest brother and captain of the Landale Militia.

Mason—Samaran general and close friend to Balen.

Meredith—Lenae and Warin's adoptive daughter. Formerly attended Tarvin Hall with Kyrin.

Michael—Kyrin's younger brother. Died during the winter attack on the Resistance camp.

Naeth Tarn (NAYTH)—Falcor's older brother.

Mira (MEER - uh)—Ben's wife.

Niton (NYE - tuhn)—Jace's black horse.

Parker—Marcus's former lieutenant in the Arcacian army.

Rachel—Jace, James, and Elanor's mother.

Rayad (RAY - ad)—Jace's father figure and mentor, who saved him from slavery.

Richard Blaine—Davira's right hand man and closest ally.

Ronny—Kyrin's youngest brother.

Rothas (ROTH - uhs)—A former war strategist for Emperor Daican. Father of James and Elanor.

Sam—A talcrin man and former scholar at Tarvin Hall. One of Kyrin's oldest friends.

Saul—A friendly ryrik from Dorland and leader of the ryrik army aiding the Resistance.

Scerle (SCERL)—A cruel Arcacian soldier and interrogator.

Solora (Soh - LOHR - uh)—Daniel and Davira's mother and former queen of Arcacia.

Talas (TAL - as)—A crete dragon rider from Dorland. Leetra's cousin, and Kaden's lieutenant.

Tavor (TA - vohr)—Alex Avery's right hand man.

The General—Kyrin's grandfather, and a renowned Arcacian general.

Timothy—The Resistance's spiritual leader, and Aaron's younger brother.

Torva (TOHR - vuh)—General of the talcrin army.

Trask—Resistance leader and rightful baron of Landale.

Trenna—Talas's younger sister.

Trev—A member of Daniel's security force, and formerly Kyrin's bodyguard.

Tyra (TY - ruh)—Jace's black wolf.

Vallan (VA - lan)—Lord of the cretes.

Videlle (VI – dell)—The head mistress of Auréa Palace.

Vilai (VI - lye)—Arcacia's female moon god.

Warin (WOHR - in)—One of Trask's right hand men and husband of Lenae. Lifelong friend of Rayad.

Zar—Jasper's hired muscle and gladiator trainer.

DRAGONS

Exsis (EX - sis)—Kaden's dragon.

Gem—Jace's dragon.

Ivoris "Ivy" (EYE - vohr - is)—Kyrin's dragon.

Rhune (ROON)—One of the dragons Elon healed after the first battle of Samara.

Soka (SOH - kuh)—Leetra's dragon.

Storm—Talas's dragon.

LOCATIONS

Arda—Island country of the talcrins.

Arvael (Ahr - VALE)—The crete's capital city.

Amberin—Samara's capital city.

Arcacia (Ahr - CAY - shee - uh)—The largest country of the Ilyon mainland. Ruled by Davira.

Ashwood—Home of Jace's mother, Rachel.

Auréa (Awr - RAY - uh)—The royal palace in Valcré.

Darham (DAHR - um)—The royal palace in Amberin.

Dorland—Ilyon's easternmost country. Inhabited by cretes, giants, and ryriks.

Fort Rhall (RAUL)—A military fortress northeast of Valcré.

Fort Rivor (RYE - vohr)—Arcacia's largest military fort located southeast of Valcré.

Ilyon (IL - yahn)—The known world.

Landale—A prosperous province in Arcacia, and home of the Resistance.

Samara (Sa - MAHR - uh)—A small country north of Arcacia.

Stonehelm—Samara's greatest stronghold along its southern border.

Valcré (VAL - cray)—Arcacia's capital city.

Westing Castle—Home of Baron Thomas located just west of Stonehelm.

RACE PROFILES

RYRIKS

HOMELAND: Wildmor and Dorland

PHYSICAL APPEARANCE: Ryriks tend to be large-bodied, muscular, and very athletic. They average between six to six and a half feet tall. They have thick black hair that is usually worn long. All have aqua-blue colored eyes that appear almost luminescent, especially during intense or emotional situations. Their ears are pointed, which makes them very distinct from the other races. They have strong, striking features, though they can pass as humans by letting their hair hide their ears and avoiding eye contact. Ryriks typically dress in rough, sturdy clothing—whatever they find by stealing.

PHYSICAL CHARACTERISTICS: Ryriks are a very hardy race and incredibly resistant to physical abuse, making them seem nearly invincible. They are resilient to sickness; however, they have one great weakness. Their lungs are highly sensitive to harsh air conditions, pollutants, and respiratory illness. Under these conditions, their lungs bleed. Short exposure causes great discomfort, but is not life threatening. More severe, prolonged exposure, however, could cause their lungs to fill with blood and suffocate them. It is said to be a curse from choosing to follow the path of evil. Ryriks' eyes are very sensitive, able to pick out the slightest movement, and they can see well in the dark. Both their sense of hearing and smell are very keen—much higher than that of humans. In times of great distress or anger, ryriks can react with devastating bursts of speed and strength.

RACE CHARACTERISTICS: Ryriks are the center of fireside tales all across Ilyon. They are seen as a savage people, very fierce and cunning. To other races, they seem to have almost animal-like instincts; therefore, it is commonly believed they don't have souls. They are a hot-blooded people and quick to action, especially when roused. They have quick tempers and are easily driven to blind rage. They prefer decisive action over conversation. Many have a barbaric thirst for bloodshed and inflicting pain. They view fear and pain as weaknesses and like to see it in others. They are typically forest dwellers and feel most comfortable in cover they can use to their advantage.

SKILLS: Ryriks are highly skilled in the woods and living off the land. They are excellent hunters and especially proficient in setting ambushes. They're experts in taming and raising almost any type of animal. They make the fiercest of any warriors. A ryrik's favorite weapons are a heavy broadsword and a large dagger. Wildmor ryriks aren't masters of any type of craft or art. Most of their possessions come from stealing. What they can't gain by thieving, they make for themselves, but not anything of quality. They think art, music, or any such thing to be frivolous. Most can't read or write and have no desire to. Dorland ryriks are very practical but more civilized and educated in their ways.

SOCIAL: Wildmor ryriks are not a very social. Their settlements are scattered and usually small. They have no major cities. Families often live on small farms in the forest and consist of no more than four to six people. Children are typically on their own by the time they are sixteen or seventeen. Even younger for some males. Outside of Dorland, ryriks have a poor view of women. They see them as a necessity and more of a possession than a partner. Once claimed, a ryrik woman almost never leaves her home. She is required to care for the farm while the men are away. Most ryrik men group together in raiding parties, pillaging and destroying unprotected villages and preying on unsuspecting travelers. Ryriks have an intense hatred of other races, particularly humans.

In Dorland, ryriks live in small but close-knit communities alongside the giants. They are family oriented and desire to live in peace with their neighbors.

GOVERNMENT: Ryriks have no acting government. Raiding parties and settlements are dictated by the strongest or fiercest ryrik so the position can be challenged by anyone and changes often. Dorland communities are governed by a chosen leader, though they give deference to Dorland's king.

OCCUPATIONS: The vast majority of ryriks are thieves or farmers. A few hold positions as blacksmiths and other necessary professions.

FAITH: Ryriks were the first to rebel against King Elôm and lead others to do so as well. Most disdain religion of any kind, but the majority of those who dwell in Dorland follow faith in Elôm.

TALCRINS

HOMELAND: Arda

PHYSICAL APPEARANCE: Talcrins are a tall, powerful people. Talcrin men are seldom less than six feet tall. They have rich, dark skin and black hair of various lengths and styles. Their most unique feature besides their dark skin is their metallic-looking eyes. They have a very regal, graceful appearance. Men often dress in long, expertly crafted jerkins, while women wear simple but elegant flowing gowns of rich colors, particularly deep purple.

RACE CHARACTERISTICS: Talcrins are considered the wisest of all Ilyon's peoples. Some of their greatest pleasures are learning and teaching. Reading is one of their favorite pastimes. They have excellent memories and intellects. Talcrins are a calm people, adept at hiding and controlling strong emotion. They are peace-loving and prefer to solve problems with diplomacy, but if all else fails, they can fight fiercely. They have a deep sense of morality, justice, loyalty, and above all, honesty. They are an astute people and don't miss much, particularly when it comes to others. Besides learning, they are also fond of art and music. Most talcrins are city dwellers, preferring large cities where libraries and universities can be found. Of all the races, they live the longest and reach ages of one hundred fifty, though many live even longer. Because of this, they age slower than the other races. Talcrin names are known to be very long, though they use shortened versions outside of Arda.

SKILLS: Talcrins excel in everything pertaining to books, languages, legal matters, and history, and are excellent at passing on their wisdom. They are often sought as advisors for their ability to easily think through situations and assess different outcomes. They are master storytellers and delight in entertaining people in this way. Though they strive for peace, most talcrin men train as warriors when they are young. They make incredible fighters who are highly skilled with long swords, high-power longbows, and spears. When not reading, many talcrin women enjoy painting and weaving. Their tapestries are among the most sought after. Both men and women enjoy music and dancing. They are expert harpists. Beautiful two-person dances are very popular in talcrin culture and are considered an art form. Metal-working is another skill in which talcrins are considered experts. Their gold and silver jewelry and armor are some of the finest in Ilyon.

SOCIAL: Talcrins are a family-oriented people and fiercely loyal to both family and friends alike. Families are average in size, with between three to seven children. Men are very protective of their families and believe their well-being is of utmost importance. Their island country of Arda is almost exclusively populated with talcrins. Scholars from the Ilyon mainland often come to visit their famous libraries, but other races rarely settle there. Many talcrins inhabit the mainland as well, but are widely scattered. The highest population is found in Valcré, the capital of Arcacia. They get along well with all races, except for ryriks. Though generally kindhearted, they can hold themselves at a distance and consider others ignorant.

GOVERNMENT: The governing lord in Arda is voted into authority by the talcrin people and serves for a period of two years at a time, but may be elected an unlimited number of times. His word is seen as final, but he is surrounded by a large number of advisors, who are also chosen by the people, and is expected to include them in all decisions. Those living on the mainland are under the authority of the king or lord of whichever country they inhabit.

PREFERRED OCCUPATIONS: Scholars, lawyers, and positions in government are the talcrins' choice occupations, as well as positions in artistry.

FAITH: Talcrins are the most faithful of all races in following King Elôm. The majority of those living in Arda are firm believers, but this has become less so among those living on the mainland.

CRETES

HOMELAND: Arcacia and Dorland

PHYSICAL APPEARANCE: Cretes are a slim people, yet very agile and strong. They are the shortest of Ilyon's races, and stand between five foot and five foot ten inches tall. It is rare for one to reach six feet. They are brown-skinned and have straight, dark hair. Black is most common. It is never lighter than dark brown unless they are of mixed blood. Both men and women let it grow long. They like to decorate their hair with braids, beads, leather, and feathers. Crete men do not grow facial hair. A crete's eyes are a bit larger than a human's, and very bright and colorful. A full-blood crete will never have brown eyes. They dress in earthy colors and lots of leather. All cretes have intricate brown tattoos depicting family symbols and genealogy.

PHYSICAL CHARACTERISTICS: The crete's body is far more resilient to the elements and sickness than other races. They are very tolerant of the cold and other harsh conditions. Their larger eyes give them excellent vision and enable them to see well in the dark. They don't need as much sleep as other races and sleep only for a couple of hours before dawn. Their bodies heal and recuperate quickly.

RACE CHARACTERISTICS: Cretes are tree dwellers and never build on the ground except when absolutely necessary. They love heights and flying and have a superb sense of balance. They are very daring and enjoy a thrilling adventure. They mature a bit more quickly than other races. A crete is considered nearly an adult by fifteen or sixteen and a mature adult by eighteen. They are a high-energy race and prone to taking quick action. Cretes are straightforward and blunt, coming across as rather abrupt at times. They are not the most patient, nor understanding, and they have high expectations for themselves and others. They are a stubborn, proud, and independent people, and don't like to conform to the laws and standards of other races.

SKILLS: Cretes are excellent climbers, even from a very young age, able to race up trees effortlessly and scale the most impassible cliffs and obstacles. Because of this fearlessness and love for heights, they are renowned dragon trainers. They are masters at blending in with their surroundings and moving silently, which makes them excellent hunters. All crete males, as well as many females, are trained as skilled warriors. Their choice weapons are bows and throwing knives, though they can be equally skilled with lightweight swords. Cretes are also a musical race, their favorite instruments being small flutes and hand drums.

SOCIAL: Cretes live in close communities and often have very large families, maintaining close connections with extended family. They are very proud of their family line and make sure each generation is well-educated in their particular traditions and histories. They consider it a tragedy when a family line is broken. Still, all children are cherished, both sons and daughters. Every crete is part of one of twelve clans named after various animals. Men are always part of whichever clan they are born into. When a woman marries, she becomes part of her husband's clan. Though cretes are proud of their clans, they show no discrimination, and their cities always have a mixed-clan population. Cretes are hospitable to their own people and well-known acquaintances, but suspicious and aloof when it comes to strangers. It takes time to earn one's trust, and even longer to earn their respect.

GOVERNMENT: The highest governing official is the crete lord. He is essentially a king, but directly below him are twelve men who serve as representatives of each of the twelve clans. The lord is unable to make any drastic decisions without the cooperation of the majority of the twelve clan leaders. Each crete city has a governing official who answers to the twelve representatives. Directly below him is a council of men consisting of the elders of each major family in the city. In the past, the cretes ultimately fell under the authority of the king of Arcacia, but with the deterioration of the Arcacian government, they've pulled away from its rule.

PREFERRED OCCUPATIONS: Hunters, dragon trainers, and warriors are the favored occupations of the cretes. But leather-working is another desirable occupation. This is typically done by the women of a household.

FAITH: Most cretes have remained faithful to King Elôm, or at least are aware of Him.

GIANTS
(Also known as **Dorlanders**)

HOMELAND: Dorland

PHYSICAL APPEARANCE: Giants are the largest race in Ilyon. Standing between seven to nine feet tall, they tower above most other peoples. They are heavily built and powerful, but can be surprisingly quick and agile when the occasion calls for it. They are fair-skinned, and their hair and eye color varies greatly like humans. They dress simply and practically in sturdy, homespun clothing.

RACE CHARACTERISTICS: Despite their great size and power, giants are a very quiet and gentle people. They dislike confrontation and will avoid it at all cost. They are naturally good-natured and honest, and enjoy simple lives and hard work. To those who don't take the time to get to know them, they can seem slow and ignorant, but they are very methodical thinkers, thinking things over carefully and thoroughly. While not quick-witted, they are very knowledgeable in their fields of interest. They are generally a humble race and easy to get along with. They tend to see the best in everyone. Their biggest failing is that, in their methodical manner, it often takes too long for them to decide to take action when it is needed.

SKILLS: Giants are very skilled in anything to do with the land. Much of the gold, silver, and jewels in Ilyon come from the giants' mines in the mountains of northern Dorland. They are also excellent builders. While lacking in style or decoration, the architecture of their structures is strong and durable, built to last for centuries. They have often been hired to build fortifications and strongholds. Unlike other races, it is not common for giants to train as warriors. Only the king's men are required to be able to fight. While not a musical or artistic race, giants do love a good story, and they've been said to have, beautiful, powerful singing voices.

SOCIAL: Giants typically live in tight farming or mining communities. Family and friends are important. Families usually consist of two to three children who remain in the household for as long as they wish. Many children remain on their parents' farm after they are married, and the farm expands. Giants are known throughout Ilyon for their hospitality. They'll invite almost anyone into their homes. Some people even find them too hospitable and generous. They are very averse to cruelty, dishonesty, and seeing their own hurt. Despite moving slowly in most other areas, justice is swift and decisive.

GOVERNMENT: Giants are ruled over by a king who comes to power through succession. However, most communities more or less govern themselves. The only time the king's rule is evident is when large numbers of giants are required to gather for a certain purpose.

PREFERRED OCCUPATIONS: The majority of giants are farmers, miners, or builders.

FAITH: Almost all giants agree King Elôm is real, but in their simplistic and practical mindset, fewer giants have actually come to a true trusting faith.

Acknowledgements

I want to give a huge thank you to everyone who has followed me on this incredible journey. I am so happy to have finally shared the ending with you. It was a long time coming, and I am so thankful to everyone for sticking with me to the end. The support and the love you have all shown me and this series mean so much.

Massive thanks goes to three of the best friends a writer could possibly have. Tricia, Morgan, Addy—I'm not sure where I'd be without you and our nearly daily texts. If not for the Evil Author Retreat of 2022, the beginning of this book would not have been nearly as exciting. Thank you so much for always cheering me on and celebrating all the steps it took to complete this book.

Special thanks to my mom for always being there for me and pouring so much work into helping me make this book the best it could be. You're my best friend.

And, finally, thank you Krystal, Gabriella, Joshua, Cynthia, and Carolyn for backing the creation of the *Resistance* audiobook all that time ago. I have not forgotten it. Thanks for helping that project become a reality.

About the Author

Jaye L. Knight is an award-winning author and shameless tea addict with a passion for Christian fantasy. Armed with an active imagination and love for adventure, Jaye weaves stories of truth, faith, and courage with the message that, even in the deepest darkness, God's love shines as a light to offer hope. When not writing fantasy, she dabbles in contemporary romance under the name Jaye Elliot.

To learn more about Jaye and her work, visit:
www.jayelknight.com

www.ingramcontent.com/pod-product-compliance
Lightning Source LLC
Chambersburg PA
CBHW032108110726
47902CB00003B/514